"A solid fantasy with an entirely engaging Everyman of a character who comes with an equally engaging cat. . . . A fun opening to a new series."
—Fantasy Literature

BOOKS BY BENEDICT JACKA

THE INHERITANCE OF MAGIC SERIES

An Inheritance of Magic
An Instruction in Shadow

THE ALEX VERUS SERIES

Fated

Cursed

Taken

Chosen

Hidden

Veiled

Burned

Bound

Marked

Fallen

Forged

Risen

AN INSTRUCTION IN SHADOW

Book 2 in
the Inheritance of Magic series

BENEDICT JACKA

ACE
New York

ACE
Published by Berkley
An imprint of Penguin Random House LLC
penguinrandomhouse.com

Copyright © 2024 by Benedict Jacka

Library of Congress Cataloging-in-Publication Data

Names: Jacka, Benedict, author.
Title: An instruction in shadow / Benedict Jacka.
Description: First edition. | New York: Ace, 2024. |
Series: Inheritance of magic series; book #2
Identifiers: LCCN 2024002752 (print) | LCCN 2024002753 (ebook) |
ISBN 9780593549865 (trade paperback) | ISBN 9780593549872 (ebook)
Subjects: LCSH: Magic—Fiction. | LCGFT: Fantasy fiction. | Novels.
Classification: LCC PR6110.A22 I57 2024 (print) |
LCC PR6110.A22 (ebook) | DDC 823/.92—dc23/eng/20240119
LC record available at https://lccn.loc.gov/2024002752
LC ebook record available at https://lccn.loc.gov/2024002753

First Edition: October 2024

Printed in the United States of America
1st Printing

In memory of Siranus Ojeni Dermen

1942–2023

A glossary of terms can be found at the end of this book.

AN
INSTRUCTION
IN SHADOW

CHAPTER 1

IT WAS WET, it was cold, and I was worried.

Misty rain was falling, too heavy for drizzle and too light to be a downpour. Where the yellow-white lights of the Olympic Park shone, you could see the raindrops slanting down against the darkness of the overcast sky. I was sheltering under a tree, and the wind was blowing gusts of rain in under the branches, sending cold droplets flying into my face.

It was a Saturday night in East London, and I was in Stratford, on a grassy bank above a road called Marshgate Lane. A small grove of trees grew next to a chain-link fence, and had there been any passersby, they might have wondered what was so special about this particular grove that I was choosing to spend my Saturday night here in the cold and rain. The answer was simple: beneath one of these trees was a Well.

Wells are gathering points for essentia, the raw energy used in drucraft. I'd become pretty good at judging their strength over the past six months, and I estimated this one as on the low end of

D+. Which meant that Linford's, the corporation I worked for, would pay me £700 for it. But they'd only pay me that £700 if it was still there, and when I found this Well there'd been someone loitering, a boy in a thick hooded anorak. He'd retreated at my approach, but he'd lingered just a little too long afterwards before disappearing. Which was why I was out here, getting rained on, making sure that when the corp extraction team arrived, there'd be a Well here to get paid for.

The wind shifted, sending another gust of rain into my eyes. I shivered and edged around the tree, though there wasn't much point—my fleece and trousers were thoroughly damp by now. I checked the time to see that it was seventy minutes since I'd made the call. There's no telling how long it'll take a drucraft corp to respond to a Well alert; it can take hours, or days, and they won't tell you which.

I wished I could just go home. That's what I normally do when I call in a Well; corps don't pay you to stick around; they pay you to send them the coordinates and then get lost. But something about that boy had set off alarm bells. In theory, once you've claimed a Well and logged the data with the Registry, it's the property of whichever House or corporation you work for. But a certain significant fraction of Well hunters don't care about the Registry, or other people's property rights in general, and that was the reason I was lingering out here in the cold rain.

Still, it had been more than an hour, so maybe I *was* worrying over nothing. The Well was only a D+ . . . hardly enough to get a raider gang excited, especially not in this kind of horrible weather. None of the Ashfords would even get out of bed for something like this.

Thinking about the Ashfords was a mistake. It sent my thoughts back to what had happened this afternoon.

FIVE HOURS EARLIER.

I spotted her as soon as she came into view. She was wearing a dark purple blazer over a slim dress and was towing a small suitcase, the heels of her shoes clicking on the polished floor. There was a huge billboard behind her, and for a moment, as she walked by, her shape was silhouetted against the stylised dragon on the ad, purple against gold.

I followed her past the end of the railing. She turned towards the terminal exit, still towing her carry-on, and caught a glimpse of me out of the corner of her eye. She turned with a slight frown.

"Hi, Mum," I said.

My mother opened her mouth, still frowning, then recognition flashed in her eyes. She froze.

We stood there on the terminal concourse. People milled around us, greeting and embracing and chattering, then, once the talking was done, joining together in groups to flow out of the airport and go home. Only the two of us were still.

"What are you doing here?" my mother said at last. She looked shocked.

"I was waiting for you."

My mother looked around. Somewhat confused, I did the same; the terminal floor was crowded, but no one was paying us any attention. "You can't do this," my mother said. "You *can't* be here. If my father finds out—"

"He only told me to stay away from the house and not to try and murder Calhoun," I said. "He didn't say anything about seeing you."

". . . What?"

"He called me in for a talk after the raid," I explained.

My mother stared.

I'd never seen my mother in person, at least not that I could remember. All I'd had to go on for finding her had been some old pictures, and when I'd first seen her walking down the Arrivals corridor, I'd felt no flash of recognition; she'd just looked like a pretty forty-year-old woman in a skirt suit. The longer I talked to her, though, the more something started to stir. The small movements she made, the way she turned her head . . . there was a strange echo there, of the glimpses I'd catch of myself in a mirror out of the corner of my eye.

"I could tell you what happened," I offered when she still didn't speak.

"Not here," my mother said, seeming to come to a decision. She pulled out a card from an inside pocket, then hesitated, shook her head, took out a pen, and scribbled on the card. "Don't talk to anyone else until we've met. Okay?"

". . . Okay."

"I have to go," my mother said. Without waiting for an answer, she grabbed the handle of her suitcase and strode away, heels clicking. After fifty feet or so she looked back. I waved; she gazed at me for a second, then disappeared into the crowd.

The wind shifted, sending another gust of cold rain into my face and pulling me back to the present. I shook myself awake, huddling back under the tree and taking another glance around. The Olympic Park was just as empty as before.

Maybe it wasn't just the Well I was worried about. I'd walked out of Heathrow this afternoon feeling—well, not *happy*, but as though I'd accomplished something. And when I'd decided to spend the evening hunting for Wells, I'd thought of it as a victory lap.

But as the rush had faded, and the hours had passed by, I'd started to feel . . . what? Bothered? Uneasy?

Dissatisfied. It had left me dissatisfied.

When you spend a really long time looking forward to meeting someone, you build it up. You rehearse it in your mind, spin out fantasies of how it's going to play out. But when it actually happens, it never seems to go the way you've planned. Because of course, you've thought of all the things *you're* going to say, but not the things that the *other* person's going to say. And so it always goes in some direction you didn't expect.

I hadn't expected my mother to run at me and give me a hug. Still, I'd been hoping for something . . . well, more. I'd been replaying the conversation in my head, and the more I did, the more I couldn't help noticing that there hadn't really been any point at which my mother had seemed especially happy to see me. Or be around me at all.

The fact that she hadn't remembered that it was my birthday hadn't helped.

The more I thought about it, the more it bothered me. You'd have thought the weather would have been a distraction—waiting around in freezing rain might be a crappy way to spend an evening, but if there's one good thing you can say about it, it at least keeps you focused on the present—but it wasn't doing as much as I'd hoped. I was starting to get the vague, unsettling feeling that by meeting my mother I'd disturbed something that might have been better left alone.

I shook my head and tried to push the whole thing out of my mind. One hour and twenty minutes since I'd registered the Well.

Maybe I should just go home. It wasn't as though there was any trace of . . .

. . . wait.

Between me and the stadium was a car park. Yellow-white lights reflected off the wet tarmac, and in their glow I could make out shadowy figures heading my way.

Instantly I was on full alert. I flexed my fingers, checking my sigl rings and reminding myself of what was on each finger. Slam and light sigls on my left hand, flash and haywire on my right. My strength sigl was tucked away under my T-shirt, hanging from a cord around my neck, and I sent a flow of essentia into it. Energy came flooding out, pouring into my chest and spreading through my muscles. Now that I'd channelled through it, it would keep drawing essentia without further concentration.

I took another look at the approaching figures.

There were four of them, all wearing hoodies. I couldn't make out their faces, but from the combination of speed and swagger, I pegged them as late teens or early twenties, like me. Given that the only other things in this stretch of the Olympic Park were a construction site and a running track, I could think of exactly one reason why these four would be converging on this spot.

I focused on the four shapes ahead of me, opening my senses.

Ever since this April, I'd been able to see essentia. All dru-crafters can sense it, but I can *see* it, currents and eddies appearing in my vision as swirls of colour. The reddish brown glow of the Well behind dominated my vision, spilling out past my feet and down the hill. Even a weak Well like this had vastly more essentia than any human or sigl, but I was still able to look through it, focus on the shapes of the four boys and see . . . nothing. No active sigls of any kind.

Which was both good and bad. Good, because it meant these guys were probably small-time. Bad, because it meant my haywire sigl was useless. I'd designed it to sabotage enemy strength sigls, and in the battles last week it had been my trump card. But it did nothing against an enemy with no sigls of their own . . . and my ability to see essentia wasn't going to do me much good, either.

The four boys crossed the road and came to a stop at the bottom of the grassy bank, not quite close enough to be threatening. They stared up at me. I stared back at them.

"Howzigoan?" one of the boys called out.

"Aright," I said guardedly.

"Yawrigh?"

I made a noncommittal sort of noise.

There was a pause. Rain sheeted down.

"Gotturligh?" the boy asked.

"What?" I said. Living around my part of London, you get pretty used to weird pronunciation, but this guy had such a thick MLE accent that even I couldn't make it out.

"Gotta light?"

I shook my head. The boy made a disappointed sound.

None of the other three had moved. Their whole manner was weirdly friendly. They weren't acting as though they were here to—

Wait. Suspicion flashed through me. *Why* were they acting friendly?

I glanced over my shoulder.

The guy behind me had already started his rush and I jumped aside just in time. His outstretched arms clutched at my fleece, tugging me off balance before his momentum sent him sprawling down the slope. I whirled back to see that the guy who'd been keeping me talking had closed the distance; I extended my left arm and sent essentia leaping down through my muscles and into the sigl on my forefinger. The sigl erupted in a cone of brilliant blue-white light, and for a fraction of a second night became day.

The boy and the one next to him yelled, clutching at their eyes. I triggered my slam sigl and sent two concussive blasts of air at his head; blinded and off balance, he went head over heels.

I felt a flare of satisfaction as I saw him go rolling down the bank, but as I looked around it faded quickly. There were more of these guys than I'd realised. Five, six—

Shadows closed in. I made a quick rush and hit one with my slam sigl; he staggered away, shielding his head, but before I could press my advantage I had to whirl to face a guy who'd been coming up behind me. He backpedalled but now I was surrounded. I backed up to the tree, trying to make it a little harder for them to get behind me. The circle had closed; blinking my eyes against the rain, I finally managed to get a count on them. Seven.

I stood with my back against the tree, rain still misting down. The guys surrounding me crowded in, confident enough to take the fight, wary enough to not want to be the first one in. A gust of cold wind cut through my clothes. Fear and adrenaline pumped through me, heightening my senses. Things had gone bad and they had the potential to get much, much worse. Deep down, a disbelieving part of me was thinking: *All this for £700?*

One of the boys called out to me, followed by another. I blocked out their words, not wanting to let them see how scared I was. Instead I narrowed my focus, not letting myself think about anything except the next few seconds. All my attention was on the question of who would move first. Would they come from the left or from the right?

The one on the left shouted an insult. I turned slightly towards him but kept an eye on the second guy to my right. There's always one in a gang who's a little meaner and more aggressive than the rest, and I watched him out of the corner of my eye, pretending I couldn't see—

He rushed me.

I triggered my flash sigl. Blinding light caught him and two more, sending them stumbling back. A guy came in from the other side; I put a slam into his face and knocked him to the wet grass. Looking around, I felt a spark of hope—all were backing away. Wait, I could only see six; hadn't there been—?

Arms grabbed me from behind.

I struggled frantically, but the boy behind was bigger than me and he heaved me off the ground, leaving my legs flailing in the air. The others rushed in; I kicked out and hit one, then they were on me. Fists slammed into my shoulders, my chest, my sides; one glanced off my head, sending a jolt of pain through my neck.

I twisted and thrashed. A blow hit my stomach, making me gasp; the guy behind me pulled me down and a flash of terror went through me as I realised he was trying to wrestle me to the ground. My feet touched the grass, giving me an instant of leverage.

With the strength of panic I wrenched an arm free and drove my elbow into the guy's side; I heard a snap and a gasp and his grip loosened. Punches rained down; I managed to get my arms up enough to take most of the blows on my forearms and wrists, then I squeezed my eyes shut, triggering my flash sigl again and again.

Shouts and curses sounded and for an instant the punches stopped. I opened my eyes, saw a gap in the crowd, and lunged.

Hands clutched at me and then I was away, racing up the grassy bank at a dead run. I could hear yells but couldn't tell if anyone was following. I dashed up and away from the Well until my feet hit the concrete path of the Greenway, then kept running. Only after I'd gone thirty or forty yards did I risk a glance back.

No one was chasing. As I slowed to a jog, I saw two or three shapes emerge out onto the Greenway, but they weren't moving fast enough to catch up. One pointed in my direction and called to the others.

I gave the Well one last frustrated glance, then kept running.

I SLOWED TO a jog around Pudding Mill Lane, then to a walk as I reached the A11. Cars streamed up and down the road, their passage whipping the rain into spirals. I headed towards Stratford with the occasional glance over my shoulder, but the pavement behind was empty and when the turnoff disappeared behind a rise, I knew I was safe.

As I walked, the adrenaline from the fight began to fade, leaving me tired, in pain, and unhappy. I've had heavier beatings, but getting knocked around is one thing; getting knocked around and losing feels a lot worse.

What really smarted was that they hadn't even been *good* raiders. Over the last six months I'd had a series of run-ins with some of the heavyweights of the drucraft world, from House security all the way up to corporate soldiers . . . not quite the drucraft equivalent of the Premier League, but close. And, okay, most of those encounters I hadn't exactly *won*, but I'd held my own. With all that I'd been through, I'd been starting to feel pretty tough.

I should have known better. Getting cocky in a street fight is always a mistake. For all my sigls and training, I didn't have much answer for a gang of thugs just rushing in and beating the crap out of me.

I ducked into the shelter of the doorway of one of the Stratford skyscrapers and called in the attack, but I knew it was a waste of time. The app that I use to register Wells doesn't have a button for "attacked by raiders." All I could do was call the Linford's locator line, and, as usual, I got an automated response telling me to leave a message. I don't know if anyone even listens to these things; in theory I'm supposed to have a supervisor, but I've never met them. Most likely, Linford's would ignore my message, show up at the Well in a day or two, and find it drained, at which point I'd be blamed for calling them out for a Well that didn't exist.

With a sigh I stepped out into the rain and turned my feet towards home. It was turning out to be a really crappy birthday.

BY THE TIME I turned onto my road, the rain had lessened to a drizzle. Out of habit I scanned the street. No suspicious-looking cars, no groups of men, no one outside my door—

There was someone outside my door.

Instantly I was on guard, but as I took a second look I relaxed. The figure was on the short side and was sheltering under a white-and-blue golf umbrella almost as big as he was. I kind of recognised the silhouette and I definitely recognised the umbrella. "What are you doing here?" I called over.

"Waiting for you, what do you think?" the figure from under the umbrella shouted back.

I gave an inward sigh. I knew what he was here for.

Colin is a few months younger than me, with looks that are a mix of his Chinese father and English mother. We don't see each other quite so often now that he's at uni, but he's still my closest friend, and when I'd run into trouble earlier in the year it had been him I'd turned to for help. Colin had come through in a big way, but I'd had to promise him that when it was over, I'd tell him the truth about what was going on. At the time it had felt like a pretty safe promise, since I'd done that several times already and he hadn't believed me, but that had been *before* last Sunday night, when a corp assault team had raided an Ashford Well. Colin and

I had been caught in the middle of the whole thing, and I'd used my invisibility sigl to disappear right before Colin's eyes.

It wasn't a surprise that he wanted some answers.

"Look, I've had a really long day," I tried. "Can we do this tomorrow or—?"

"No," Colin said, glaring at me from beneath his umbrella. "You've been putting me off all week. You promised you'd tell me the truth and you're going to do it or so help me I'm going to kick your arse until you do."

"All right, all right. Just let me clean up, okay?"

I opened the door and we went in. My house on Foxden Road is small and cramped, and I share it with a bunch of Lithuanians. The TV was blaring from the ground-floor bedroom—like most of these houses, the living room has been turned into an extra bedroom in order to squeeze in the maximum number of renters. My room is on the first floor; I sent Colin in to wait, then grabbed some clothes and headed for the bathroom.

It was occupied. I knocked on the door, heard a man's voice call back, then leant against the banister and waited. The door opened a couple of minutes later to reveal Ignas, wearing a sleeveless vest and with a towel around his neck. He saw me and paused.

Ignas is the oldest of the Lithuanians, a tough, heavily-built man with a few days' growth of stubble and salt-and-pepper hair. I'd known him since I moved into Foxden Road, and he'd been very friendly until last week, when a couple of Ashford armsmen abducted me and held the rest of the Lithuanians at gunpoint to make sure they didn't interfere.

The other two Lithuanian men, Matis and Vlad, had taken it pretty well, all things considered. They were younger than Ignas and had been more inclined to see the whole thing as an adventure, at least after I'd managed to convince them that I *wasn't* involved in drug dealing or human trafficking or anything like that. Ignas, though, had stayed quiet during the conversation, and ever since then he'd been giving me looks. I knew he had more to say.

Ignas squeezed past, then turned. "Last week," he told me. "Those men. There going to be more trouble?"

"No," I said again, shaking my head. "No more trouble."

"Good," Ignas said, and paused again.

We stood awkwardly for a moment.

"My wife, she's out working," Ignas said suddenly.

"I thought she worked during the day," I said. I was slightly surprised; Ignas didn't usually talk about his wife.

"She has two jobs," Ignas said. "I tell her, not worth it, she should stay home, but . . ." He shrugged. "We want to have a child this year."

"Oh," I said. "Uh . . . congratulations."

"Thank you," Ignas said, then paused. "We do this . . . the house has to be safe."

Oh, I thought, my heart sinking.

Ignas looked at me. "You understand?"

I nodded.

"No more men with guns," Ignas said. "Okay?"

I wanted to say that I hadn't been the one who'd done that, but I knew that Ignas was right. Those two armsmen had been there because of me. I hadn't wanted them there, but if someone had pulled a trigger, that wouldn't have mattered. "Okay," I told him.

Ignas nodded and walked away. I went into the bathroom.

I'd wanted a hot shower but got a lukewarm one instead—the heating in this house has been on the blink since last winter and the landlord's too cheap to get it fixed. As I shampooed my hair, though, my thoughts were less on the cold and more on Ignas.

I'm used to my mistakes getting me in trouble. But having them get *other* people in trouble was a new feeling, and one I didn't like very much. The worst part was that I couldn't see any easy way to stop it. I'd settled things with the Ashfords—more or less—but the simple fact was that at any time they or anyone else could send their goons back for a production of "Kidnap III: The Revenge," and even if I could get away, that wouldn't stop them from catching someone else in the cross fire by accident . . . or on purpose.

It all seemed really unfair. In movies the heroes get into fights and just walk away. They don't have to stick around afterwards cleaning up the mess. Right now things were quiet, but if that changed, what could I do? Move out? I didn't have the money to keep doing that, and it wouldn't really solve anything, either . . .

I finished my shower, shivering as I towelled myself off, and pulled on my clothes with a wince. I could see the red marks from the punches I'd taken and knew that they were going to really hurt once they stiffened up. I wished my mending sigl could heal bruises. It's designed to treat internal bleeding, which you'd *think* would apply to bruises, but apparently not. Then I towelled my hair some more until it was completely dry, at which point I'd run out of excuses to stall with.

I went back into my room.

Colin was sitting on the only chair with an expectant look. My room's small even for me; with Colin in here as well, there wasn't much space. Colin had already drawn the curtains. Outside, the sounds of the London night drifted over the rooftops, but in here it was just us.

"All right," I said. I locked the door, then tossed my wet clothes into the laundry basket. "How do you want to do this?"

"Start at the beginning," Colin told me.

I sat down on my bed and began.

CHAPTER 2

"WHAT YOU SAW last Sunday is called drucraft," I told Colin. "It uses a resource called essentia to do . . . well, what you'd probably call magic spells."

"Spells," Colin said.

"Yeah."

"But you didn't say any magic words."

"No."

"So . . . they're like what? Psionics from D&D?"

"Something like that."

Colin sat there looking at me. "Why does it work?" he said at last.

"Essentia."

"What's essentia?"

"It's . . . hmm." Colin's studying natural science at Imperial College London; back at school, his favourite subjects had been chemistry and physics. I thought about how to explain it in terms he'd understand. "Think of it like a sort of invisible, undetectable gas. One you can't touch and which can go through solid objects."

"How?"

"Essentia doesn't really interact with matter very much. For the most part it flows right through it."

"So does it have mass?"

"Not really, no."

"Well, then it can't be a gas."

"I said it was *like* a gas."

"So where is it?"

"Here," I said, pointing to the air in front of us. "And here, and here." I could make out the currents that I was pointing to, grey-white swirls in the air that brightened as they flowed. "It's all around you, and inside you, right now."

"So what *is* it? Is it made up out of particles?"

"I . . . don't really know."

"Does it move faster than the speed of light?"

"I don't think so?"

"Can you propagate waves through it?"

"Will you stop?" I said in annoyance. "I'm trying to give you the 'Complete Idiot's Guide to Drucraft' here, and we're only on page one. At this rate we're going to be here all night."

Reluctantly, Colin shut up.

"Drucraft spells are powered by essentia, but for the most part they don't work on their own," I said. I took out one of my sigl rings and held it out to Colin. "You see the little thing in the ring that looks like a gemstone?"

Colin squinted at the ring. It was steel, with what looked like a very small gem on the top. Unlike most of my sigl rings, the sigl was set onto the ring, instead of recessed into it. "Yeah."

"That little sphere's called a sigl." I told him. "Human beings can't use free essentia on their own. We're constantly surrounded by this energy source, but we can't access it. Same way that you can't access the chemical energy in a lump of matter."

"You can set it on fire."

"That doesn't always work."

"That just means you're not using enough fire."

I resisted the urge to hit Colin. "So what sigls do is draw in the free essentia around them and turn it into a spell effect," I said. "Like this." I sent a flow of essentia down through my arm and into the sigl on the ring.

Blue-white light flooded the room. The sigl resting in my hand was the second one I'd ever made, a simple one that converted essentia into pale blue light. It's about the most basic sigl you can get, but it's still useful.

Colin had been about to ask another, probably equally annoying question, but the sight of the active sigl wiped all that away. He leant in to stare, and I lowered the brightness a little so that he wouldn't be dazzled.

"You aren't wearing it," Colin said at last.

"Don't need to. It just needs to be close enough."

Colin kept staring. I kept the sigl going for a while, then when he still didn't say anything I let the flow of essentia cut off. The light vanished and Colin blinked, looking at the sigl as if coming out of a trance.

I lowered the ring. "Believe me now?"

Colin didn't take his eyes off it. "Yeah," he said at last.

It was sort of funny how big an impression my weak little light sigl had made. Apparently no amount of talk is half as convincing as a simple demonstration. "How did you do that?" Colin asked.

"When essentia passes into you, it attunes to you and becomes personal essentia. And personal essentia responds to your will. With enough training, you can channel it into a sigl."

"Can anyone learn to do that?"

"Eventually. You have to learn to sense it first."

Colin frowned. "Wait. All that stuff you used to do with your dad, when you were just sitting around . . . ?"

"Sensing and channelling exercises."

"I thought that was just woo-woo spiritual stuff," Colin complained. "Why didn't you tell me it was for a *reason*?"

"I did. You just never believed me."

"Damn it," Colin said. He thought for a second. "All right, so what's the deal with your new job?"

"To make a sigl, you need a very high concentration of essentia," I told Colin. "Those places are called Wells, and they're the bottleneck for sigl creation. Wells in this country are mostly controlled either by Noble Houses—magical aristocracy, basically—or by drucraft corporations. One of those corporations is called Linford's, and they employ me as a locator. I find Wells, call them in on an app, and they pay me a finder's fee."

"And then they do . . . what? Use the Wells to make sigls?" I nodded and Colin pointed at the ring in my palm. "Is that how you got yours?"

"No, I made it myself."

"Can anyone learn to do *that*?"

"Yes, but in practice most people don't think it's worth it and they just buy them instead. The fact that I could manifest a sigl was why I got into all that trouble back in the spring."

"Wait," Colin said. "This rich family that you were having trouble with, the Ashfords . . . are *they* one of your noble families?"

"They're a Lesser House, and I'm related to them, yeah," I said. "Not that it's done me any good." I slipped the ring back onto my finger, grimacing slightly; my muscles had stiffened up while I'd been talking. It said something about how distracted Colin was that he hadn't noticed I was hurt.

Colin kept questioning me about House Ashford and drucraft

organisations in general, which led into the topic of Well locating, which led into me telling him the story of what had happened in the Olympic Park.

"Man," Colin said once I'd finished. "When you said there was competition for Wells, I didn't think it was that extreme."

"It doesn't even make any *sense*," I complained. "That Well had a finder's fee of seven hundred pounds. With the size of that raider gang, that's a hundred quid per guy! How the hell is that worth it?"

"I mean, you're assuming they're in it for the money," Colin pointed out. "If they're like those guys that hang out around Stratford Park, you wouldn't need to *pay* them to kick the crap out of some pretty-boy white kid. They'd do it for free."

"Yeah, screw you too."

"So what are you going to do now?"

I leant back against the wall, grimacing slightly as pain shot through my shoulder. "For most of this year my big goals were to get stronger at drucraft, find my father, and deal with the Ashfords. That raid you saw on Sunday was the climax of 'deal with the Ashfords.' It's not over, but it's on hold."

"Wait. Today's fight wasn't because of the Ashfords?"

"No, that was just normal risks of the job."

"*That's* normal? I don't think they pay you enough." Colin frowned. "What was that you said about finding your dad?"

"I've been piecing things together over the last six months and I've started to find some leads," I told Colin. "Now that I've got a steady job and the Ashfords are off my back, I can chase them."

The conversation went on for a while longer, with Colin continuing to ask me questions about the mechanics of drucraft. I did my best to answer, even if some of the questions made me want to throw up my hands—how the hell was I supposed to know whether drucraft had a conservation law?—until around two a.m., when I told him that I was officially throwing him out, and that if he wanted to keep quizzing me he could do it in the pub another day, where it was warm and there was something to drink.

"Oh, yeah," Colin said as he grabbed his stuff. "Almost forgot." He handed me an envelope.

I opened it to see a card. On the front was a picture of a twenty-sided die turned to the 20 face, and underneath was the message "LEVEL UP! +1 TO WISDOM!"

"Happy birthday," Colin said.

I laughed and opened the card to see that all of our friend group had signed it. Felix had written a message saying that now I only had another five or ten years to go before I could buy a beer without getting carded, Kiran had told me that I'd better not make a habit of borrowing his car, Colin had written that you knew you were old when you needed more than one d20 to roll your age, and Gabriel had said he'd drawn a picture of me for the occasion, attached to a fairly realistic sketch of a penis.

"Thanks," I told Colin with a smile.

"Just pick up next time I call, all right?"

"I will."

Colin left, and I propped the card up on my bedside table. Looking at it gave me a warm feeling that lasted while I brushed my teeth and got into bed, then turned the lights off to settle down to sleep.

Lying there in the dark, I thought about what I was going to do next. In a lot of ways that talk with Colin had been the last loose end of the Ashford business. Now that it was tied up, I was finally free to move on to something else.

And what I wanted to move on to was finding my dad. It was something that had been growing on me for a long, long time, but which—until recently—I hadn't had the opportunity to do much about. I'd been too caught up in the day-to-day grind of earning a living, and even if I'd had the time to go searching, I hadn't had the means.

But that wasn't quite so true anymore. While being a locator wasn't easy, it gave me a lot more free time than my last few jobs, and it was better paid enough that I'd been able to save up a little. More importantly, I'd started to build up a sigl collection. Strength, invisibility, mending, flash, slam . . . I still had a long way to go, but if I ran into some sort of trouble, I was a lot better equipped to deal with it.

The biggest change, though, had happened during Sunday's raid. On the rooftops of Chancery Lane, I'd met a man calling himself Byron who'd told me that he knew what had happened to my father. He'd left me a card with his number and told me to get in touch if I wanted to know more. That same card was sitting in the drawer of my bedside table right now.

The problem was, what little I'd seen of Byron made me think that he was really bad news. To me, that card hadn't felt like an offer. It had felt like bait.

But it was also my first solid lead in more than three years . . .

I tossed and turned for more than an hour, torn between hope and caution. At last I came to a decision. Off the top of my head, I could think of maybe three or four other approaches to finding my dad that had any chance of working. I'd try them all, and I wouldn't stop until each and every one of them had failed. Only then would I call the number on that card.

Having a plan made me calmer. I settled down into my pillow and went to sleep.

I WOKE UP the next morning to the sound of loud meows.

"Oh, come on," I muttered as I cracked an eye open. Sunrise in

September in London is about six thirty. A glance at the greyish light coming through my window put the time somewhere around "way too early."

Shivering, I pulled myself out of bed and levered open the window. A gust of freezing air rolled in, followed by a largish cat, and I slammed the window shut as quickly as I could. "Do you have any idea what time it is?"

"Mraow," Hobbes announced.

Hobbes is a grey-and-black tabby with yellow-green eyes. I've had him since a year or so before my dad disappeared, and he's helped get me through some pretty bad times, even if he *does* like to wake me up at the crack of dawn. "You could have come in last night," I told him. "What were you even doing out, anyway?"

Hobbes gave another meow and head-butted my leg hard enough to make me stagger. To my eyes, the green glow of Life essentia wreathed him, emanating from the sigl hidden in his collar and flowing out into his muscles. I'm not the only guy in London who knows how to make strength sigls, but I might be the only one who's made one for his cat.

I poured cat food into Hobbes's bowl, making him immediately lose interest in me, and while he was chomping away I went downstairs and made myself a stack of toast. You can get decent-quality bread pretty cheap in London as long as you go for the supermarket own-brand stuff—even once you add in the cost of jam or spread, you still end up with a good-sized meal for less than 50p. I'm not quite as broke these days as I used to be, but when you've been poor enough for long enough, you get careful about these things. On working days my usual breakfast is this, a carrot or an apple, and a big glass of water, and that'll keep me going until afternoon.

Today, though, I had other plans. I went back upstairs, set my plate down on my bedside table, and lay down on my bed with my notebook. Hobbes hopped up next to me, sniffed at the food until I batted him away, then curled up behind my knees.

I turned to a new page in my notebook and began to list all the leads I had for finding my father.

First and most obvious was the private detective route. I'd tried that earlier in the year with some success, but that "success" had led to a short, vicious fight in Hampstead with a sigl-wielding boy who'd been one of the nastier opponents I'd gone up against. I had the feeling he was connected to Byron in some way, which was part of the reason I was so reluctant to call the number on that card.

A much safer approach was my mother. I still hadn't heard back from her, but it felt as though if anyone could tell me something useful, she could. (At which point I put down my pen and checked my phone to see if she'd messaged me. She hadn't.)

A slightly less obvious approach was my employer. Linford's was a drucraft company, not a detective agency, but from what I'd been learning, drucraft companies tended to have their finger in a lot of pies, and in the case of Linford's, I'd heard persistent rumours that they were supposed to have ties to government intelligence agencies. If they really wanted to find something out, they could probably do it. The problem would be making them care. I wasn't optimistic that I could get them to help, but I should probably at least give it a try.

Going further down the list—and I was really scraping the bottom of the barrel at this point—was my aunt. She was my dad's sister, and she and her husband had taken me in for a while after my dad disappeared. The relationship had got pretty strained towards the end, but apart from me, she was my dad's closest living relative. There was a chance she might know something.

And finally, at the very bottom, was Byron. Unlike the others, I was sure that Byron knew something about my dad's disappearance. Problem was, I was also pretty sure he'd been *involved* in it. Approaching him felt almost as dangerous as going back to that boy I'd met in Hampstead.

But no matter how I looked at it, approaching Byron also felt like the plan that was most likely to work.

I closed my notebook, stretched, and got to my feet. It was time to go and see Maria.

MARIA NORONHA LIVES about fifteen minutes' walk away, in a nice extended house in Upton Park. Her job for Linford's is "essentia analyst," which seems to be a cross between sales and middle management, and she'd been one of my early teachers when it came to the drucraft world. I'd started my career in drucraft lacking a whole lot of basic knowledge that drucraft professionals took for granted, and Maria had been happy to help. For a price.

Unfortunately, the further I'd gone from "clueless newbie" and the closer I'd come to "aspiring professional," the less helpful Maria had become. While Maria had a lot of insider knowledge, most of that was related to the sales and management side of things. Also, while she'd been happy to set me up as a locator, her reactions when I'd tried to push beyond that had been . . . less than encouraging.

As was happening now.

"I'm afraid I'm just not sure what I can do to help," Maria said.

"Like I said, I'm trying to find someone," I said. "And I was wondering if Linford's might be able to do something."

"How do you mean?"

It's always a bad sign when someone won't give you a straight answer. "I mean, your company knows people who know how to find things," I said. "Right?"

"Do they?" Maria asked vaguely.

"Doesn't Linford's have ties to information services?"

"Who told you that?"

"Some people on the Internet."

"Oh, they say all kinds of things. I wouldn't pay too much attention if I were you."

I was silent, but inwardly I was doubtful. Reliable information about drucraft corps is hard to find, but I'd heard a *lot* of references to Linford's having intelligence connections. Maria should at least have recognised the rumours.

And I couldn't help but notice that she hadn't really answered my question.

"Anyway," Maria said cheerfully. "How's the locating?"

"Fine, I guess. Although . . ."

Maria gave me an inquiring look.

"Has there been an uptick in raiding lately?" I asked. "Like people going after Wells they wouldn't usually bother with?"

"Oh." Maria sat upright, suddenly looking much more interested. "So you've heard about that?"

"Not 'heard' so much as . . . so I'm not imagining it?"

"We actually had a meeting about it on Friday," Maria said. "With all the shortages and supply-chain issues, it's getting very challenging for people in our industry, and it seems as though some people are taking advantage of that. Apparently there was a really major raid just last week in Chancery Lane. So the criminal gangs who do this sort of thing are definitely getting bolder!"

I kept my face carefully neutral. "Criminal gangs?"

"That's what I've heard. But you might be in luck. They were just saying that there's a company-wide initiative to ramp up supply. I could put your name forward, if you like."

"Ramp up supply how?"

"Well, demand for essentia's gone up and they're trying to meet it."

"Okay," I said slowly. "But . . . I already call in the Wells I find."
Okay, not *all* of them, but Maria didn't need to know that part.

"I don't actually know the details," Maria admitted. "But it'd be a good opportunity for you. Shall I ask them?"

I couldn't help but feel a bit dubious, but it wasn't as though I had anything to lose. "Sure, I guess."

"Great," Maria said. "Oh, on that subject, have you got a finder's stone?"

"No."

"Why not?"

Finder's stones are Light sigls that glow in the presence of Wells. They're extremely short range—the ones I'd seen could only reliably detect a Well within maybe ten paces, and even then, they tell you nothing about it. "Because they're crap."

"They're the most cost-efficient way to find Wells."

"My sensing is better than a finder's stone in literally every way," I told Maria. "It was better when I started this job, and that was *before* I spent half a year as a locator."

"I understand that it's frustrating," Maria said sympathetically. "But sometimes it's important to do these things to show that you're a team player."

"I'm supposed to pay two thousand pounds to prove I'm a team player?"

"I think it's twenty-four hundred, actually."

"Since when?"

"It was probably back in July . . ." Maria turned to her computer and typed something in. "Oh, yes. Our cheapest model used to be two thousand pounds, but that was only if you ordered before the end of the summer."

I gave Maria a look.

"Supply issues," Maria explained. "Costs have gone up."

"Sounds like you're just giving me more reason not to get one."

"Well, with the increase in raids, there's been a push to crack down on unregulated drucrafters," Maria said. "And since locators without finder's stones aren't regulated in the same way . . ."

"You said Linford's offered no-finder's-stone contracts."

"I think the location department is under pressure to stop issuing those," Maria admitted. "You can probably get away with it for now since you signed on back in the spring, but I don't know how long that'll last."

"I don't *want* one of those things."

"Sometimes you have to buy things even if you don't really want them."

I LEFT MARIA'S house in a bad mood. Linford's was starting to remind me of insurance companies. Even when you don't want what they're selling, they'll still try to pressure you into buying it.

My phone rang, and instantly I forgot all about Maria. Pulling my phone out, I saw that an unknown number was calling. A spark of hope lit up in my chest. My mother?

I hit the "Answer" button. "Hello?"

It wasn't my mother, but as soon as I heard the woman's upper-class accent I knew it was the Ashfords. "Hello? May I speak to Stephen Oakwood, please?"

"That's me."

"Oh, hello, this is Clarissa. I'm calling on behalf of the Ashford family. Is now a good time to chat?"

"Are you calling on behalf of one *particular* member of the family?"

"Yes, how did you know?"

My spirits rose. "Just a guess."

"So, the suggestion was to set up a private meeting," Clarissa said. "What sort of times would you be available?"

"As soon as possible."

"Perfect. I'll get back to him and confirm a time."

"That sounds gr—wait, what do you mean, 'him'?"

"Well . . . Calhoun Ashford. Sorry, I should have mentioned his name. It was just that the way you were talking, I thought you already knew . . ."

I stared at the phone, my good mood evaporating.

"Hello?"

"Yeah," I said. "Sorry, changed my mind."

"Um . . . sorry, I didn't quite catch that. When did you say would be a good time?"

"Never," I told her. "Bye."

I hung up, shoved the phone into my pocket, and turned towards home. A small part of me wondered why the hell the heir to House Ashford would want to talk to me in the first place, but mostly I was just annoyed. As far as I was concerned, the only member of House Ashford I wanted to talk to was my mother; the rest of them could go to hell.

But day after day went past, and my mother didn't call.

CHAPTER 3

"Okay, so how do sigls get made?" Colin asked.

"Shaping," I explained. "You find somewhere with enough essentia—which means a Well—and condense and shape it into a sigl. Though you have to be very good."

"Can anyone learn to do it?"

"Yes, but you have to get really good at sensing and channelling first."

We were in the Admiral Nelson, our local pub. The clink of glasses and the chatter of conversation filled the room; the air carried a pleasant smell of beer and old wood. The two of us were settled into a booth in the corner, and we'd come early; Felix, Kiran, and Gabriel were supposed to be coming later, but for now it was just us.

"So it sounds like sensing is really useful," Colin said. "It's how you find Wells, it lets you shape sigls, and it works like 'detect magic' when you run into another drucrafter. Right?"

"You'd think, but everyone I run into seems to think it's the least important."

"Why?"

"The Ashfords don't care about finding Wells because if they want sigls, they just buy them, and Maria says that learning to sense is a waste of time because you can just use a finder's stone instead," I said. "But to be honest I don't understand it, either. Maybe it's like footwork in martial arts? It's the bit everyone wants to skip to get to the exciting stuff."

"Just makes it sound more important to me," Colin said, and paused. "Could I learn to do it?"

I'd been wondering for a while if that was where he was going. "Maybe."

"Maybe?"

"I mean, the short answer is yes. But what you're really asking is whether you could learn to be a drucrafter, right?"

". . . Yeah."

"Anyone can, in theory," I said. "But it takes a lot of time and work, and in practice most people aren't going to get there."

"Hmm," Colin said thoughtfully, then took a drink and looked at me. "All right. You've been telling me all about what this stuff is and how it works. What are you planning to do with it?"

"Get stronger," I said immediately.

"Which means . . . ?"

"Better sigls. Stronger abilities and a wider variety of them. Right now things are quiet, but they won't stay that way."

"Why not?"

"Reasons," I said. I didn't really want to get into Byron and my worries about my father. "I've got an answer for other drucrafters with strength sigls, but that didn't help me much against that gang on Saturday. Or those soldiers the week before."

"Wait, you're expecting to run into *more* people like that?"

"No." *I think.*

"Bloody well better not. All right, what are you thinking of going for?"

"Matter," I told Colin. "According to Maria, my affinities are Light, Matter, and Dimension. Light'll probably always be my best, but I've already spent a while picking the low-hanging fruit from there. Dimension's supposed to be powerful but hard to use, and besides, Britain doesn't have many Dimension Wells. But it does have a lot of Matter ones." I looked at Colin. "Want to help?"

"How?"

I reached into my bag and pulled out a thick leather-bound catalogue, scuffed at the corners. "This is a reference catalogue of sigls you can buy in London. I've been using it to come up with sigl ideas, but there's a hell of a lot of material. More than I can research on my own."

Colin hefted the catalogue in his hands. "So this is . . . what? A shopping list for superpowers?"

"I mean, you're obviously interested in this stuff," I told him. "So how about you see if you can spot anything that looks helpful? You get to learn a bit about it, and maybe you'll come up with something I missed."

Colin was giving the catalogue an extremely interested look. I didn't need to ask him if he was going to do it; I think I'd have had to fight him to take the thing away. My phone buzzed and I pulled it out instantly, wondering if it was my mother. It wasn't, but the number looked annoyingly familiar. "Have to take this," I told Colin.

Colin nodded absently, still staring at the catalogue.

I walked out of the pub and into the cold September night. "Hello?" I said into the phone.

"Hello, may I speak to Stephen Oakwood, please?"

"Not you again."

"I'm calling on behalf of Mr. Calhoun Ashford to arrange a meeting," the voice said frostily. "You do know who he is?"

"Yes, he's the new heir of House Ashford. Why should I care?"

"Well, then I would have thought you'd understand why it's important. Honestly, you ought to be flattered that he's even interested in you."

Okay, now I was pissed off. "Are you one of the Ashfords?"

"I work for Ashford Holdings," the voice said coldly.

"So you're one of their servants."

"Excuse me?" The voice rose in pitch slightly. "I have a BA from the LSE, thank you very much!"

I didn't know what that meant and didn't care. "Look, uh, Claire—"

"Clarissa."

"Whatever. You obviously don't know anything, so I'm hanging up now, all right?"

"Wait!" Clarissa said. She was finally starting to sound agitated. "Why are you making this so difficult? All Mr. Ashford wants is to talk to you. I can't see why you wouldn't want to meet him!"

"You can't see—okay, let me paint you a frigging picture. The first time someone from your House Ashford showed up at my door, they tried to kidnap me. The second time, they got me involved in one of their family knife fights and tried to kill my cat."

"Well, I'm sure—"

"The *third* time," I said, speaking over her, "they sent a couple of their armsmen who marched me out of the house at gunpoint. And after *that*, your boss threatened to have me thrown in a cell if I didn't do as I was told. Is Calhoun going to do the same thing?"

"No!"

"Is he going to pay me?"

"Um . . ."

"Then the answer's no, and if Calhoun Ashford has a problem with that, he can stick it up his arse. Okay?"

Clarissa seemed at a loss for words. I hung up and went back into the pub.

The rest of our group had just arrived. Felix, tall and lanky, was sprawled over one of the benches, while Kiran and Gabriel were sitting opposite, talking to Colin. Gabriel was the first one to notice me returning, and as he saw me his eyes lit up. "Hey, it's Harry Potter!" he called over to me. "Let's see you use the Force!"

I paused. *What?*

"Just ignore him," Felix said with a roll of his eyes. "Happy birthday, by the way."

"Thanks," I said, sitting down. "Hey, Kiran. Thanks for letting us use your car."

"It's fine," Kiran said with a wave of his hand. Kiran's squat and heavyset, with dark Sri Lankan skin, and probably the most generous guy I know. "Hey, did you—?"

"And next time if he can't get your car, he can fly on his broomstick," Gabriel interrupted.

"Gabe, give it a rest, all right?" Colin said.

"Hey, use your invisibility cloak," Gabriel told me.

"I don't have an invisibility cloak," I said curtly.

"That's not what he said."

I stared at Gabriel, then, slowly, turned to stare at where Gabriel's finger was pointing.

Colin was looking *very* uncomfortable.

"*Seriously?*" I asked him.

"Um," Colin said.

"Are you supposed to talk about this stuff?" Kiran asked doubtfully.

"No," Felix told him. "You're not."

"Oh, what's wrong?" Gabriel said with a grin. "The Men in Black are going to come get you?"

"Can you stop making everything into a film reference?" I told Gabriel. "This is serious."

"Ooh, he's *serious*," Gabriel said, his grin getting bigger. "Watch out, guys!"

"Look, I don't know what Colin told you, but you've got the wrong idea. I work for—"

"Bor-ring," Gabriel said with an eye roll, and raised his voice to shout out to the pub. "Hey, everyone! We've got someone who can do magic here!" He pointed at me, looking around. "Come and see!"

I cringed, trying to sink through the floorboards. Luckily we were in a pub, where random drunk people shouting nonsense is pretty much par for the course, so I didn't get many looks—but it was still more than I would have liked.

"Jesus, Gabe," Felix said. "Read the room."

"What?"

"He means shut up," Colin added.

"But you were the one—" Gabriel began.

"*Shut up*," I told him.

"God," Gabriel said with a disappointed look. "It's just a joke."

The conversation turned to safer channels, but it quickly became obvious that Gabriel wasn't planning on letting things drop. He kept trying to make "jokes" about me being a drucrafter, no matter how many times I shut him down. I had to nearly shout at him to get him to finally stop, at which point he finally seemed to realise that I meant it and fell into a sulky silence. At last, after a final complaint about "taking things so seriously," he went home. Kiran went with him.

As soon as the two of them were gone, I rounded on Colin. "What did you tell him?"

Colin was looking extremely embarrassed. "Well . . ."

"*Gabriel*, of all people? Really?"

"Look, you weren't telling me shit," Colin protested. "You can't just drop something like this on me and stop answering your phone."

I sighed. Yeah, I *really* should have talked to Colin sooner. "Okay, whatever you told him, can you . . . un-tell him? Convince him you were kidding or something?"

"Won't work," Felix cut in.

"Why not?" I asked.

"Because he's a moron."

"That's a bit harsh," Colin objected.

"Doesn't make him less of a moron," Felix said unapologetically. "You're going to have to cut the guy off sooner or later. He's too much of a screwup."

"You haven't asked what really happened," I told Felix.

"Yeah, there's a reason for that. And if you're smart you'll stop talking about it. Especially to Gabriel."

We talked a bit longer before going home, but the whole conversation left me with an uneasy feeling. Gabriel's been one of our friends for years, but he can't keep a secret to save his life. The idea of him telling everyone who'd listen that I was a drucrafter was pretty worrying.

I got home to more bad news. There was an automated message from Linford's telling me that, in regard to the registration request I'd made on the seventeenth of September, they'd failed to discover any sign of the Well in question. The email finished by informing me that a note had been placed on my permanent record and warning me that further incidents might lead to my Well Registry access being suspended.

It was a crappy end to what had been a generally crappy day.

But the next morning something happened that put it all out

of my mind. When I woke up, there was a message from my mother.

THE BRIDGE WAS deep in the middle of Hampstead Heath, a wide span of earth and pebbles with waist-high iron railings and a still pond beneath. If you peered over the edge, you could see the redbrick arches of the viaduct, thick pillars going down into murky water.

I leant on the railing as the afternoon light dimmed into dusk. The trees of the Heath blocked my view of the sunset, but I could make out the yellow-grey of the western sky, fading to pale blue above and deep blue directly overhead. An aircraft, high to the west, traced a small contrail; as I watched, it gleamed briefly red as the setting sun reflected off its underside. Far to the south, distant clouds formed a barely visible line above the treetops. The sounds of the London traffic were muffled by the branches, and all was quiet.

If you'd asked me six months ago how I felt about my mother, I'd have probably shrugged. The fact that she'd left when I was age one had been something that had bothered me as a teenager, but my father's disappearance three years back and the cascade of problems that had followed it had mostly driven it out of my mind. You just don't have *time* to agonise about stuff like that when you're worrying about paying rent, or keeping your job, or dealing with all the other tiny emergencies that you get when you're living without a safety net. If someone pressed me for an answer, I might have told them something to make them go away, something about how it didn't really bother me. And I might even have made it sound convincing.

But it wouldn't have been true. It *did* bother me. Little things, glimpses that you see from day to day. Mothers picking up their children from school, scenes on TV with boys and their parents. I didn't talk about it—what would be the point?—but the absence was always there, a small quiet backdrop to the rest of my life.

And then, five months and three weeks ago, I'd met Charles Ashford. My grandfather, though I hadn't known it at the time. He'd told me that my mother had stayed away on purpose and that I should take the hint and do the same.

I'd told my mother I wanted to talk to her, and that was true. And I'd told myself that I wanted to ask her if she could help me find my father, and that was true as well. But underneath it all, what I really wanted was for her to tell me that what my grandfather had said had been a lie.

The first stars were glimmering in the sky when I heard the scuff of shoes on pebbles. I looked up to see a figure appear out of the shadows at the bridge's far side. My mother walked out into the fading light, crossing the bridge to stop a little distance away, studying me.

For a few seconds the two of us looked at each other in silence. My mother was wearing a long belted coat that the last traces of the sunset illuminated in purple and gold. Long, light brown hair, carefully brushed, flowed down her back, and blue eyes looked at me with growing self-consciousness.

"You don't need to stare like that," my mother said at last with an embarrassed laugh. "You'd think you'd never seen me before."

"I kind of haven't," I told her.

I saw a flash of what might have been guilt in her eyes, there and gone in an instant. "Well," she said, taking a deep breath. "Why don't you walk with me?"

I fell into step beside my mother and we began to slowly walk together, following the path that forked off the bridge and ran down along the edge of the pond. Now that we were side by side, I realised that my mother was actually shorter than I was. I don't know why that came as a surprise, but it did.

"All right, first things first," my mother said. "What you did on Saturday? Never do that again."

I looked at her, surprised and hurt.

"We can still talk," my mother clarified. "Just not in public."

"Why not?"

"It's dangerous."

"Dangerous *why*?" I couldn't keep an edge from my voice. *This was the first thing she had to say?*

My mother started to answer, then stopped. "You're angry with me, aren't you?"

I didn't answer.

My mother sighed. All of a sudden she seemed older and more tired. "I'm sorry," she said. "I planned this conversation out so many times. I didn't want . . ." She trailed off.

"Didn't want what?" I asked when my mother didn't continue.

"You don't know the whole story," my mother said. "There are reasons why we can't just go and sit down in a coffee shop. And for why I've had to keep some distance between us."

That caught my attention. It was so close to what I'd been hoping to hear. "Then *tell* me the whole story," I said. "Tell me the *reasons*. Instead of just . . ." *leaving and never coming back.*

"There's a lot of background you need to know," my mother said. "And you're going to find it difficult. But it's very important and a lot of things in your life are going to hinge on what I'm about to tell you here. So you have to promise me to be patient. All right?"

I would have promised her pretty much anything at that point. "All right."

My mother turned and we began walking again, moving slowly

along the path. We'd come down to the edge of the pond; water lilies floated on the murky surface, while behind, the red arches of the bridge rose into a darkening sky. My mother stayed silent for a minute more, then began.

"Our House—your family—is old, but for most of its history it hasn't been important," my mother said. "House Ashford has its roots in Kent. That's where the family lands are, on the edge of the North Downs, and for a long time that was where we stayed. Just pottering around in the old family estate, living off the income from the one B-class Light Well we've had since the time of Charles the Second.

"It was my grandfather Walter Ashford who changed all that. He fought in the Second World War, then stayed on in West Germany for the reconstruction. A lot of men made their fortunes there, and Granddad was one of them. When he came back to England in the fifties, it was with a German wife and the titles to a small empire of Wells. And over the next forty years, he used that to turn House Ashford into a Noble House with a seat on the Board.

"In a way, that was where the problems started. The UK has lots of little old Houses that no one cares about. But once you're a Noble House, people start paying attention. There were probing expeditions, attacks. Most of them we were able to fight off." My mother fell silent for a moment. "Most of them."

I looked at my mother questioningly.

"Anyway, that's all in the past," my mother said. "We're seen as an established House now. But for the past few years, there's been trouble brewing, the same thing that usually brings down Houses. The succession problem."

"Succession?"

"The question of who'll become the next Head of House," my mother explained. "For a House to survive, someone has to take control of its Board seat and its Wells, which means all the other members have to step aside. When they don't, you get a succession crisis, and it's the single most common way that Houses fall. From minor ones barely worth the name to Great Houses with dozens of Wells."

If someone had tried to give me this kind of history lesson six months ago, it would have gone right over my head. But now that I'd met my mother's family—and had those two conversations in Charles's study—it suddenly seemed a lot more relevant. "Is that what Charles is worrying about all the time? How to stop House Ashford having a civil war?"

"It's not his only worry, but it's the biggest," my mother said. "He's sixty-nine. He has to choose the right heir, and he has to make sure everyone else will accept them."

"But he's already picked Calhoun."

"It's not as simple as that."

I frowned. "Why not?"

"Do you know what 'primogeniture' means?"

I shook my head.

"It means that the firstborn child is the one to inherit," my mother explained. "It's not the law, not anymore, but it *is* the custom. When the head of a House is choosing their heir, there's an expectation that, all else being equal, they'll pick their oldest child, especially if that child is a son. Now, they don't have to. They can pick a second or third child, or a niece or nephew, or even someone who isn't a blood relation at all. But like I said, most Houses that fall, fall because of succession fights, and an awful lot of those fights began when an old Head of House chose to skip over an eldest child." She looked at me. "Or grandchild."

That caught me by surprise. Now that I thought about it, I *was* Charles's oldest grandchild. "But I wasn't brought up in the family."

"To someone looking at the family tree, you'd be the one with the strongest claim."

"Yeah, well, your dad made it pretty clear that didn't matter."

"It doesn't matter what he tells you in private," my mother said. "Just by existing, you weaken the claim of any other candidate. Now, *maybe* that wouldn't be a problem if he'd chosen someone else, but now that Calhoun's been named, things are . . . complicated."

I looked sideways at my mother. She was frowning to herself, looking down at the dirt path as she picked her way along it in her velvet shoes.

"Look, I'm really not interested in becoming heir," I said. All of this was filling in quite a few holes—it explained a lot about how Tobias and Lucella had acted, back in the spring—but it still felt very far away from my actual life. Maybe if I'd been told this story six months ago I might have been drawn into the fantasy of becoming some sort of wealthy noble, but at this point I'd learned my lesson. Getting involved with the Ashfords never made anything better.

"It doesn't matter," my mother said. "Just by being alive, you're a challenge to every other candidate. More importantly, you're a point of attack. For anyone who wants to weaken or subvert House Ashford, the simplest way to do it is to go through you. Your father and I—"

I looked up sharply.

"—agreed that we'd keep your links to House Ashford hidden. If you were raised outside the family, without the Ashford surname, there'd be no reason for anyone to make the connection. It . . . wasn't an easy choice to make. We knew we'd be denying you a lot of opportunities. But it was the right thing to do." My mother looked at me. "Do you understand?"

"I . . . guess?" I said slowly.

"If your family history had become known, people would have come looking for you," my mother explained. "You wouldn't have understood what they were doing, not at first. They would have acted as though they just wanted to be your friend. They'd have offered you things, given you advice, a sympathetic ear. The price would have come later."

"That kind of happened anyway."

"Yes," my mother said with a twist of her mouth. "Don't worry, Tobias and I have had a long talk."

"And that was why you haven't been in touch all this time?"

"I know it can't have been easy, but as far as I can tell it seems to have worked. For now at least, no one outside the family seems to have connected you with House Ashford. Now, that may change eventually, but as long as you keep your distance, there shouldn't be any reason for anyone to start looking too closely. And your age will help. A twenty-year-old isn't as appealing a target as a teenager, and that'll only become more true as you get older. But for now, be very cautious of any strangers who seem unusually interested in you. Okay?"

I'm twenty-one, not twenty, I didn't say.

"Honestly, this would have been so much easier if you were a little less eye-catching," my mother said, giving me a rueful look. "If you'd turned out to be some clod with no talent for drucraft, Lucella would never have given you a second look. But you really do take after your father." My mother laughed suddenly. "Edward won't stop going on about his prodigy of a son becoming a manifester at sixteen. But Calhoun's had private tutors drilling him practically since he could walk. You might only have done it at twenty, but you did it all on your own."

"I made my first sigl at eighteen," I couldn't resist saying.

"Oh? That's even more impressive." The words gave me a warm glow, but almost immediately my mother's expression sobered.

"But what you just did there? Don't do that. No matter how stupid it is, every House in the United Kingdom still clings to this idea that strength in drucraft marks you out somehow. As though it's more important than brains, or business sense, or . . ." My mother tailed off and shook her head. "Anyway. Boasting like that draws attention, and I think Lucella already showed you why that can be a bad thing."

Okay, enough of this. I was tired of beating about the bush. "Where's Dad?"

"I don't know," my mother said.

I looked at her suspiciously.

"You don't need to look at me like that. I've been checking up on it ever since I got back. I haven't been able to find any trace of him, and he isn't answering any messages through any of the old channels we used to use."

"When did you last hear from him?"

"Five years ago. What about you?"

"Three and a bit," I said slowly.

My mother stopped and turned to face me from across the dirt path. "And he hasn't contacted you in any way since?"

I shook my head.

My mother frowned. "What is he thinking?" she said to herself. It was hard to make out her face in the gathering dusk, but she seemed genuinely troubled.

"You don't have any way to find him?" I asked.

"He was always pretty good at disappearing when he needed to," my mother said. "Maybe if I'd known earlier . . ." She shook her head, still frowning. "Something's going on, and I don't like it."

"Him disappearing," I said. "Was that anything to do with your father?"

"Nothing like that," my mother said absently. "Daddy agreed

to let the whole thing drop, that was part of the . . ." She seemed to realise what she was saying and stopped. "I'm going to have to keep looking into this. Maybe I can turn something up."

I nodded.

My mother began walking again, more slowly this time. I matched her pace. "I wish he'd told me," my mother said to herself, then looked me up and down quickly. "Have you been doing all right?"

"I've been managing," I said. *Not like I had much choice.*

We'd come all the way back around to the bridge. Up above, the sky was the colour of blue velvet, fading away eastwards to dusky black. "I should go," my mother said.

"Wait. Aren't you going to tell me what happened?"

My mother paused. "With . . . ?"

"With you and Dad," I said, an edge creeping into my voice. "Why your father hates me so much. Why I never heard anything from you. You said you'd tell me the truth, but you've hardly told me anything!"

"He doesn't hate you," my mother said. "It's just . . . you look a lot like your father, and I think he gets reminded of that every time he sees you."

I couldn't keep the frustration off my face. Of all my questions, why had she chosen to focus on that one?

My mother saw my expression and changed tack. "I don't want to give you too much to deal with at once. And there are some things I need to clear up first. I promise I'll tell you the whole story eventually. Just . . . please be patient a little longer. All right?"

I stood silently.

"All right?"

I didn't want to say yes, but I was afraid that if I didn't, she'd disappear again. ". . . All right."

My mother looked me up and down again with a slight smile. "You really have grown to be handsome." She started to reach for my cheek, then hesitated and let her hand fall, her smile fading. "I know it must have been difficult, but . . . keeping you away from the family, keeping everything so secret . . . it was for your own good. Please believe that."

I was silent.

"All right," my mother said. "We'll talk again. Okay?" She walked away across the bridge. I watched her until she disappeared into the darkness, then stood there for a while longer as evening faded into night.

I WASN'T HAPPY on the train home.

I'd wanted a talk with my mother, and I'd got it. And it had filled in some gaps. Some of the strange little details about how the Ashfords had treated me made a lot more sense now.

On the other hand, all the questions I'd *really* cared about, she hadn't answered. In fact, the more I thought about it, the more I started to feel as though my mother had been doing what her family always seemed to do: tell the truth, but leave out crucial bits. Why couldn't she just tell me the whole story? Was it really because she had things to clean up first?

Or was it because there were parts she didn't want me to hear?

I wondered whether that last thing she'd said, about it being for my own good, had been her trying to convince me, or herself.

I sighed and leant my head back against the side of the carriage. The train was carrying me eastwards through London, passing gradually through richer boroughs towards poorer ones. Everyone else in the carriage was staring at their phones, for which I was glad. Right now I wanted to be on my own.

Well, one thing I was pretty sure of: my mother didn't have

any more idea of where my dad was than I did. She'd said she was going to look into it, but she hadn't exactly sounded hopeful. I didn't have much faith that she was going to find him for me.

I was running out of leads to follow. Just one left.

"No, I HAVEN'T heard from him," my aunt said over the phone.

"No letters or emails?" I said. "He hasn't tried to get in touch with you at all?"

"Stephen, I already *told* you that I haven't heard from him," my aunt said. "This is the problem with you, you never listen."

I held back a sigh. It was pretty much what I'd expected.

"I hope you're not still working at that bar," my aunt said.

"I haven't been working there since last autumn," I told her. "I got a job in the Civil Service."

"So have you thought any more about going to university?"

"A bit," I said evasively. "I'd better go. Give my love to Paul."

"Stay in touch, all right?"

I hung up and looked at my phone screen. Well, that was that.

I went back into the house—I'd gone out into the back garden to make the call—then climbed the stairs to my room. Hobbes greeted me with a meow, rubbing himself against my legs. I scratched him behind the ears, then dropped onto the bed and propped myself against the wall. I fished a small card out of my wallet and held it up to the light.

The card had no name or address. There was just a picture of five stylised, slightly curving black wings, their tips pointed outwards to make a sort of five-pointed star. Underneath was a phone number. I stared at the card for a long time, stroking Hobbes as he lay curled up against me, then took out my phone, entered the number, and wrote I want to know more. My thumb hovered over the "Send" button, then stabbed down. The message disappeared into the ether.

Five minutes passed.

My phone vibrated. I looked up from Hobbes and read the reply.

Of course. Just name the time and the place.

CHAPTER 4

THE NEXT DAY, everything went wrong.

I'd stayed up late deciding where to hold the meeting, trying to figure out where I could go that would be safe. Even after I'd finally made my choice, I'd had trouble sleeping and had tossed and turned for hours before falling into a fitful sleep. I'd scheduled the meeting for Sunday, and I found myself wondering if I should go see Father Hawke first.

But when I woke up, it was to a message from Maria. She wanted me to see her at her office on Fenchurch Street.

Right now.

The tone of the email wasn't friendly. I took the District Line to Tower Hill.

THE LINFORD'S OFFICES are in a giant, weirdly shaped steel-and-glass tower near Aldgate whose real name I don't know but which everyone calls the Walkie-Talkie (if you see it, you'll know why). That part of London has lots of these skyscrapers, huge, towering things that look down on you from far above. For me, they're part of the landscape, notches in the skyline that you see when you look out your bedroom window at night. My dad didn't like them—he used to tell me that the people who worked in those things were the enemy. Today was the first time I'd been inside one.

I waited in the big echoing lobby to be given a visitor's badge, then took the lift up to floor twenty-something and walked out into white-painted, navy-carpeted halls. Looking around, it struck me how clean the whole place was. The offices that I'd worked at had always been messy; this place looked as though someone had just been through with a vacuum cleaner. Occasionally I'd get a glimpse through the windows out over the London skyline and the buildings far below.

I found Maria's office, knocked, and went in.

It was on the small side, with windows that would have given an impressive view if they'd been a bit larger. Apparently she was important enough to rate a private office, just not a big one. Maria was sitting behind a desk; as I entered she looked up with a frown.

"What have you been telling people about this company?" Maria asked.

"Uh . . ."

"I just had a call this morning from our legal department," Maria said. "Apparently they've been fielding questions from the Metropolitan Police anti-terror unit. Questions about you."

That brought me up short. "What?"

"The first person they went to was your supervisor, but she claims you've never checked in with her, so now they're going after me, since I was the one who gave you a reference." Maria's mouth was set in a hard line. "Do you realise how serious this is?"

"Wait, wait, wait," I said. "Asking questions about me? Why?"

"Apparently you've been sharing extremist views."

"Wait, *what*? What views?"

"The police officers were called in to Sports Direct to investigate one of their employees," Maria said. "Your name came up. What have you been telling them?"

"Nothing!" I protested. Sports Direct sounded vaguely familiar, but I was very sure I hadn't done anything like that.

"Then how did this person get your name?"

"Which person?"

Maria glanced at her computer screen. "The name the Metropolitan Police gave us was Gabriel Cullens."

I stared at Maria for a few seconds, then closed my eyes. *Oh, God damn it.*

"Well?" Maria asked.

I was going to *kill* Gabriel. "Okay, look," I said. "I know this guy. He has no clue what he's talking about. He doesn't have any links to . . . anything like that."

"I don't *care* what he has links to!" Maria was glaring at me. "Why did you give him this company's name?"

"I didn't know I wasn't supposed to . . ." I said, tailing off. I didn't understand what was going on.

Maria put her hands to her temples and closed her eyes. "What did you tell him?"

"Nothing!" I protested again. "I mean, I told him that I worked for Linford's, but I didn't say anything about what I actually *did*. Just that it was gig work."

"Then why is this acquaintance of yours going around talking about drucraft and invisibility magic?"

Damn it, Colin. "I didn't say anything about that."

"That doesn't matter! What matters is that the police and our legal department have been brought into it! That means this is all going to go on the official record, and since I was the one who referred you, it's going on my record too!"

We stared at each other in mutual incomprehension. Then Maria sighed and the anger seemed to go out of her. "I don't know what I was expecting," she said to herself, and looked up at me. "Look, Stephen. You aren't supposed to talk about drucraft where it'll draw attention. All right?"

"But why?"

"That's just the way things are."

"But . . . this is a drucraft company. Everything you do here is about drucraft."

"That doesn't mean you should go talking about it *outside* the company."

"But—"

"Stephen," Maria interrupted. "Take a hint."

I stopped.

Maria looked at me for a few seconds longer, then her eyes seemed to unfocus and she looked past me. "We'll sort things out," she told me.

"How?"

"I'll talk with the departments and work out something. Just . . . go home. Someone will be in touch."

"Okay," I said slowly. "Should I talk to someone, or . . . ?"

"No," Maria said. She still wasn't looking directly at me. "Don't talk to anyone, don't do anything. Just wait. That's all."

". . . Okay."

"You'd better go."

I left. Maria had started typing at her computer and didn't take her eyes off the screen.

I went downstairs, left the building, and went home. I had an uncomfortable feeling, as though I'd missed something that I didn't understand. I wondered what was going to happen next.

It wasn't long before I found out.

ACCOUNT NOTICE

We take the safety and well-being of all Linford's clients very seriously. It has recently come to our attention that you are currently under investigation for potentially dangerous and/or criminal activity. As such, in accordance with Linford's Community Guidelines, your account has been temporarily suspended until the investigation has been resolved. Please note that this investigation can only be marked as completed by a member of our Incident Response Team and cannot be completed by our Client Support Team.

While your account is suspended, any pending payments due to you will be put on hold. We know that many of our clients are experiencing a steep rise in the cost of living at the moment, so if you're in need of help, check out our online advice for ways to save money. Linford's is committed to our values of fairness, equality, inclusivity, sustainability, and diversity. If you'd like to know more, check out our mission statement on our website. We welcome your feedback and if you have any further questions or concerns, please contact a member of our Client Support Team.

This email was sent from a notification-only address that does not accept incoming email. Please do not reply to this message.

I read the email through twice, a hollow feeling developing in my stomach. My account with Linford's was how I got paid for finding Wells. It was my only source of income.

I tried calling the number for the Client Support Team and got a recorded message telling me to use their online feedback form. I tried calling the Aldgate office and asking for Maria and was told she was in a meeting.

I kept calling throughout the day. At one o'clock I was told Maria was at lunch, at two o'clock I was told she was at lunch, at three o'clock I was told that they'd have to check whether she was in the building and they'd call me back, at four o'clock I was told she was in a meeting, and at five o'clock I was told she'd left for the day. At which point I remembered what Maria had told me earlier about taking a hint.

I tried to figure out what to do. My account was "temporarily suspended," but for how long? Two weeks was no problem. Two months would mean some budgeting, but I could survive. A year, though . . .

I shook my head and forced myself to focus. What was the worst that could happen?

If this was just a temporary suspension, then what I did right now didn't matter. But if this was permanent, then what I did right now was going to matter *very much*. If I tried to wait it out and ran out of money, it would be a disaster. So I should assume the worst.

I was going to have to find a new drucraft company.

I SPENT THE next day job hunting. The results were . . . not good.

First I tried Ivy, a locator I'd met back in the spring who worked for a company called Mitsukuri. I couldn't find out much about Mitsukuri online, but according to Ivy they paid better than Linford's did, so I sent her a text message asking if they had any openings.

Ivy's response was prompt, but not encouraging. Apparently

Mitsukuri only recruited locators who were vouched for by another Mitsukuri member. I asked if Ivy would be willing to vouch for me; she didn't reply.

Other drucraft companies were less picky—they were willing to recruit unknowns, or at least that was what their webpages claimed if you dug deep enough. However, they also wanted references and background checks. I filled in some forms and sent some emails, but I had a nasty feeling that I might be wasting my time.

By Saturday evening I was stressed, tired, and frustrated. As the sun set I closed my laptop and headed for the Admiral Nelson. I had a few things to say to a certain "friend."

I ENTERED THE Nelson to find Gabriel right in the middle of telling Colin, Kiran, and Felix the story.

". . . so then the cop tells me he wants to see my social media to see who I've been talking to," Gabriel was saying. "And when I ask why he tells me 'we take this kind of thing very seriously.' Except he doesn't know how the app works! So all he can figure out to do is open up my DMs and start looking at them one at a time. Meanwhile, the other guy's just standing there looking like he's wishing he was somewhere else."

"All this was happening because you were telling everyone at your job that you were friends with a wizard?" Kiran asked.

"Yeah."

"Why were you even *doing* that?"

"'Cause it was funny," Gabriel said with a grin.

Kiran rolled his eyes.

"Anyway, so he keeps reading them one by one for *hours*," Gabriel went on. "Until the other guy gets bored and gets on my case again and keeps saying 'we take this kind of thing very seriously,' except they can't actually say what the thing is, so when I ask them they have to pretend like they know what they're doing—"

"Didn't you still get fired?" Felix interrupted.

"Eh, who cares?"

I'd had as much of this as I could take. "I care," I said loudly.

"Hey, you made it!" Gabriel called to me. "Where've you been?"

"Job hunting," I told him. "Since you got *me* suspended too."

Colin was sitting on the other side of the table, looking very uncomfortable; he could obviously tell how pissed off I was. Gabriel couldn't. "No kidding?" Gabriel asked with a grin. "Yeah!" He held up his pint of beer, shoving it at me. "Fired together!"

I stared at Gabriel's glass and thought about smacking it out of his hand hard enough to spray the contents all over his stupid face.

The silence dragged out. Gabriel's grin faded. "Uh," he said. "You okay?"

"What did you tell the guys at your job?" I asked Gabriel.

Gabriel looked awkward. "Ah . . ."

"What did you tell them?"

"I mean, I wasn't going to bring it up," Gabriel began. "It was just, I was really high, and everyone was really bored, so . . ."

"Are you *serious*? I'm dealing with this shit because you got *bored*?"

"What's the big deal?" Gabriel protested. "You're always saying how all your jobs are shit."

"It doesn't *matter* whether they're shit! I *have* to do them because it's how I pay my rent!"

"I don't get why you're taking this so seriously. I mean, I've been fired so many times I can't even count—"

"You live with your mother!" I shouted. "None of this matters to you, *but it does to me!"*

"Okay, okay," Colin said. Some people from nearby tables were starting to glance over at us and Colin was looking visibly uneasy. "Let's calm down, all right?"

"Why are you being such a jobsworth?" Gabriel complained. "Work's all bullshit anyway, it's not like any of this really matters."

I drew in a deep breath, about to explode.

"All right, all right," Felix interrupted. He took Gabriel by the shoulder and started pushing him gently but firmly towards the door. "Let's go outside and get some fresh air."

Gabriel resisted briefly but allowed himself to be led away. I heard one last snatch of complaint: ". . . why he has to be so *serious* about this . . ." Then he was gone.

I dropped into one of the chairs and buried my face in my hands.

"Um," Colin said. "You okay, dude?"

"What do you think?" I said, my voice muffled.

"Are you going to be okay for money?"

"I don't know."

"Look, if you're that desperate, I could lend you—" Kiran began.

"No," I said. It was tempting, but Kiran's almost as poor as I am, partly because he's always lending money to people who aren't likely to pay it back. "I mean, thanks, but that's not going to solve anything."

"Can you find another locator job?" Colin asked.

"I don't know."

The conversation petered out from there. Colin kept apologising, which made things worse. I went home early so that I wouldn't be there when Gabriel came back.

I WENT HOME feeling glum. Blowing up at Gabriel hadn't made me feel better and hadn't solved any of my problems.

The one thing I had going for me was that I'd been here before. This wasn't the first time I'd been jobless and facing possible eviction . . . actually, it wasn't even the first time this year. And while it's crap, the one good thing about going through it is that it leaves you better prepared if it happens again.

And now I'd calmed down a little, I could recognise that I was a lot better off this time around. Back in the spring, I'd had two weak light sigls, less than £3,000 in the bank, and almost no knowledge of the drucraft world. This time, I had £6,800 in the bank, a lot more sigls, and a lot more experience. It wasn't much, but it was something.

I shook off my gloom and began to walk more briskly. Done was done and there was no point worrying about it. I'd go home and take another look at those other companies to see if there was something I'd missed.

But as I turned onto my street, I stopped. Standing outside my front door was Calhoun Ashford.

THE HEIR TO House Ashford was a young man in his mid-twenties. He was tall, strongly muscled without being bulky, and ridiculously handsome, with the kind of looks that make girls write fan fiction and make guys get annoyed. Just in case that didn't make him distinctive enough, he had snow-white hair, was wearing an outfit that probably cost more than the entire contents of my room, and had a glove on one hand.

Right now he was standing with arms folded, looking in my direction, and waiting. It wasn't hard to figure out who he was waiting for.

I walked up along the pavement and stopped a little distance away from Calhoun. The two of us looked at each other.

"You're hard to get a hold of," Calhoun said. He had an upper-class accent a lot like my mother's. For some reason it was more noticeable on him than it had been on her.

"Apparently not hard enough," I told him. While I spoke, I was scanning the street. I couldn't see any other people or any of those House Ashford security vans, though that didn't reassure me much. From what I'd seen of Calhoun, he probably didn't need them.

"Clarissa was quite upset," Calhoun said.

"Clarissa can suck it up," I told Calhoun shortly.

Distaste flitted across Calhoun's face. "Perhaps I'm approaching the wrong person."

"You want to go somewhere else, that's fine by me."

We stared at each other for a few seconds.

The silence was broken by a meow. Hobbes came strolling out of the darkness and up onto the pavement. He looked between me and Calhoun with a *So is anyone going to feed me?* expression.

Calhoun looked at Hobbes with a slight frown, then sank to a crouch and held out his hand to the cat. "I believe you may be able to assist me with a problem," he told me, still studying Hobbes.

Hobbes gave Calhoun an appraising look, then ambled over and let Calhoun scratch his head. "I don't exactly have good experiences with members of your family showing up at my door," I told Calhoun. I was watching him very closely; if he tried anything with Hobbes, I was ready to pounce.

"I am aware of your history. That's why I'm willing to overlook your . . . questionable manners."

That pissed me off a bit. He had his underling call me in like a boy being sent to the teacher's office, and *I* was the one with bad manners?

Also, now that Hobbes was right next to Calhoun, it was obvious to me that Calhoun didn't have any active sigls; essentia was flowing into Hobbes, but not into him. That made me feel a little safer, but not much—he might not have any active sigls, but I was pretty sure he was carrying inactive ones. "What's in it for me?" I asked.

"You will be provided with fair compensation for your time and effort."

Okay, that got my attention.

Calhoun gave Hobbes a last stroke, then straightened up. Hobbes looked up at him for a few seconds, then when he saw that no further attention was coming he flicked his tail and walked towards my door. "So?" Calhoun asked me.

I looked back at Calhoun and tried to decide what to do.

I SHUT THE door to my room and turned around. "All right," I told Calhoun. "Let's hear it."

I still had the feeling that this was a bad idea. I did not want to get involved in yet more shady Ashford family politics, and what my mother had told me two nights ago was still fresh in my mind. But given my current financial situation, I couldn't afford to be picky. I just hoped that whatever Calhoun wanted wouldn't end up making things worse.

Calhoun, for his part, was looking around my tiny room. He didn't seem to have heard me. "*Hey*," I said, more loudly.

Calhoun seemed to wake up. "I'm sorry?"

"If this isn't high-class enough for you," I said testily, "we can go somewhere else." I could still remember how Lucella had re-acted upon seeing this place.

"This is fine." Calhoun gestured at my chair, covered in dirty clothes. "May I?"

"Be my guest," I told him grumpily.

Calhoun began neatly folding up my clothes and stacking them on the floor, while I sat on the bed and studied him. Al-though Calhoun was my cousin, this was the first time I'd ever had a close look at him. My mother might believe that I had a stronger claim to the House Ashford inheritance than he did, but it didn't feel that way to me. I was a total outsider, while Calhoun looked exactly how you'd expect an heir to a Noble House to look.

"You're only wearing one glove," I told Calhoun.

"Yes."

The glove on Calhoun's left hand was reinforced with solid material that made it look less like a glove and more like a light gauntlet. During the raid I'd watched Calhoun create cones of freezing air and throw armoured men around like tennis balls, and I was pretty sure that glove was where his sigls were mounted. "You wore two in Chancery Lane."

"I was expecting tonight to be a little quieter," Calhoun said. He sat down on the chair, and Hobbes, who'd followed us in, sauntered over and rubbed his head against Calhoun's leg. I gave Hobbes a dirty look. *Traitor.*

"He's very handsome," Calhoun said. "What breed is he?"

"Moggy," I said shortly. "And you still haven't told me what you want."

Calhoun scratched Hobbes's head. "The matter is sensitive. Can I count on your discretion?"

"I don't even really want to talk about this with *you*, much less anyone else."

"Not exactly the 'yes' I was hoping for, but I suppose I'll take it," Calhoun said. "As I believe you know, my uncle has designated me heir apparent to the position of head of House Ashford. As part of this, I am to be engaged to Lady Johanna Meusel, the second child of House Meusel of Thuringia."

I gestured for him to hurry up.

"I would like for you to help with security."

I blinked. "Really?"

"She is currently studying at her academy, but she has plans to travel to London this winter," Calhoun said. "I will be spending some time with her during this period. I would like for you to oversee these meetings."

"Oversee . . . ?"

"Keep watch for anyone or anything suspicious."

"So you want a bodyguard?"

"I want an extra pair of eyes," Calhoun said. "I believe you've done security work before?"

"I mean, yeah," I said. It had been my dad's job, and it had been what I'd first turned to when he'd disappeared . . . though I did wonder how *Calhoun* knew that. "But . . . not to talk myself down, but you could probably find someone more experienced."

"There are certain reasons why I would prefer to approach you."

"What reasons?"

"For one thing, Lady Meusel seems positively disposed towards you," Calhoun said. "This will be relevant since you'll be liaising with her and her own security personnel. For another, security personnel are typically trained to prevent violence. As far as violence goes, I can take care of myself."

Having seen Calhoun fight, I couldn't argue with that. "Then what *are* you concerned about?"

"We'll discuss that nearer to the time. If you take the job." Calhoun looked at me.

I tried to figure out what to do. I'd been expecting Calhoun to want help with some bit of political intrigue or other and had been ready to turn him down. This, though . . . well, it was actually the kind of job I was fairly familiar with. And I could definitely use the money.

To be honest, if Calhoun had been some random stranger, I would already have said yes. It was the fact that his last name was Ashford that was giving me pause. Everything involving my mother's family seemed to end up making my life more complicated, and I remembered what she'd said about people wanting to use me. Was Calhoun doing something like that? Given that he was heir, it was hard to see why he'd need to. Tobias had claimed back in the spring that Calhoun's position wasn't as secure as he pretended, but a lot of Tobias's claims, historically speaking, had been full of shit.

In the end what swung my decision was the number in my bank account. I might not be desperate yet, but I wasn't that far off it. "How much does it pay?"

"You can charge your usual rate, so long as it's reasonable," Calhoun said. "Clarissa will handle that kind of thing. So?"

I didn't *have* a "usual rate." "All right."

"Good," Calhoun said with a nod. "I'll be in touch."

Calhoun left. I listened to him descending the stairs, then went over to my window. A minute later, I saw him leave by the front gate and walk away down the street.

Well, that was weird. I wondered how much bodyguards made. I'd have to look it up online and see what I could get away with. The Ashfords would probably be willing to pay a lot more than a security agency.

In any case, if Johanna wasn't coming until the winter, it wasn't something I had to worry about right now. Still, as I got ready for bed, the thought from two days ago kept floating through my head. *Getting involved with the Ashfords never made anything better.*

CHAPTER 5

I STOOD ON the busy pavement the next morning, looking at the building opposite and deciding whether I wanted to go in.

It was eleven a.m. on Sunday, and I was on the Dalston main road in between Dalston Kingsland and Dalston Junction. Dalston's in what I think of as the "near" East End, still poor compared to places like Hampstead and Islington, but way more expensive than Stratford and Plaistow. The streets were packed with people flowing in and out of the big market on Ridley Road and looking into the shops, which were a mixture of small, cramped, grubby-looking ones covered in graffiti, and big, spacious chain stores that were clean but sterile. The building I was looking at right now was the second type, a McDonald's with dark green facing and a glass-fronted upper level. Inside, Byron—or one of his underlings—would be waiting.

Now that I was here, I was tempted to call this whole thing off. Agreeing to meet with Byron back when my slate was clean had been one thing; doing it now was another. But at the end of the day, none of the reasons that had made me agree to this had changed. Byron was still the best lead I had on finding my father.

The question was what he'd want for it.

I sighed, huddled down a little into my fleece—we were less than a week from October and the weather was getting colder every day—and crossed the road.

Byron was by the windows on the restaurant's first floor, sitting on a bench and gazing through the glass and up at the sky. There was a small terrace outside, with a metal railing running around its edge that was currently playing host to a mixed flock of seagulls and pigeons. Their calls were muffled by the glass, as were the sounds of the crowds and cars sweeping up and down the street.

I stood at the top of the stairs and studied Byron. From this angle I had a good view of him, his face visible in profile against a background of glass, birds, and sky. In the light of day he looked a little older than I'd initially guessed, maybe in his midforties, dressed in a black suit that looked worn but expensive. He had long blond hair tied back in a braid, sharp features that made me think of a bird of prey, and a downward turn to his brows and mouth that gave him a faintly mocking look, as though he was amused at some joke nobody else could see.

Watching Byron gave me an uneasy feeling, a little spark of disquiet deep down in my gut. Most people would probably have thought he looked either suave or poncy. To me, he didn't come across as either. I didn't have a good read on who this man was or what he was capable of, but my instincts told me he was dangerous.

I stood there for a little longer, then walked across the restaurant's upper level and sat down.

Byron turned from the window to me, lips curving in a smile. "I was wondering if you'd show up."

"So was I," I told him.

Byron gestured in the direction of the stairs. "Would you like some food? The cuisine here isn't exactly my style, but . . ."

"No thanks."

"Then why did you pick it? Not exactly the most high-class establishment."

I couldn't care less whether this place was "high-class." "Because it's public enough to make it hard for you to try anything."

"So suspicious," Byron said with a sigh. "You know, you really should try being a little more open to new experiences."

I gave Byron a stony look.

"Tough crowd," Byron said. "Well, let's talk about the elephant in the room. Why are you so anxious?"

"Because you're Lucella's boss."

Byron gave me a quizzical look. "Where did you get that idea?"

"Uh," I said. "You were giving her orders?" I hadn't eavesdropped on Byron and Lucella for long, but it had been pretty clear who'd been in charge.

"I wouldn't call them orders."

"Then what's the deal with you two?"

"You can think of me as Lucella's mentor," Byron said. "For the most part, I let her go her own way, but from time to time, when she needs it, she comes to me for help."

"Help like putting her in touch with the corporation who sent that raid?"

"I've picked up a few contacts over the years," Byron said agreeably. "One person needs one thing, another person needs something else. You put them together, and . . ." He brought his fingers together.

I looked sceptically at Byron. "And what do you get out of it?"

Byron just smiled.

A waitress came over to our table. "Anything I can get for you?"

"A coffee for me," Byron said, turning his smile on the waitress. "Stephen, are you sure you wouldn't like anything?"

I shook my head. The waitress dimpled at Byron and withdrew. The instant she was no longer looking at him, Byron turned away. I wondered why she'd come over at all; this place wasn't supposed to have table service.

"The last time we met, you kept talking about 'we' and 'us,'" I told Byron. "Who's the 'we'?"

"Ah," Byron said. "*Now* you're asking the interesting questions. I am an agent."

"An agent for what?"

Byron settled back in his seat. "The Winged," he said, and waited.

I looked back at him.

"Perhaps you've heard of us?" Byron suggested when I didn't speak.

Well, I guess that explains the picture on that card. "Not ringing any bells, sorry."

Byron looked amused. "You really are new to this, aren't you?"

"Who are the Winged?"

Byron paused for a few moments, tapping his fingers on the table. "Do you ever think about how unfair life is?"

I frowned at him.

"I mean, it must have occurred to you," Byron said. "Especially since you've started dealing with the Ashfords. They have everything they could ever need—money, access to the best schools and teachers, a family to act as a safety net whenever they're in trouble. Meanwhile, from what Lucella says, you're struggling just to keep a roof over your head."

I didn't like being reminded of that. "So?"

"So why should it be that way?"

"Things *are* that way."

"But what if they didn't have to be?" Byron said. He leant forward slightly, his eyes suddenly intent. "What if you could live your life exactly as you wanted? What if you had everything the Ashfords had and could use it to develop to your full potential?"

Even though I hadn't meant to, I found myself thinking about it. What if I *did* have all that? Enough money that I didn't have to work, teachers so that I didn't have to figure everything out myself, being able to do what I wanted instead of being constantly forced to keep an eye on my bank account all the time . . .

No. I shook the feeling off. "You didn't answer my question."

"The Winged are those who believe things *don't* have to be that way," Byron told me. "Who search for something more."

"So who *are* they?"

"Anyone," Byron said. "Everyone. We're open to any who seek freedom from limits and restrictions, no matter their background. The upper-class heir who lives in comfort and luxury but who's stifled by social codes. The boy who's discriminated against for his desires and his refusal to conform. The creator who wants to go beyond the accepted boundaries and make something more but who's held back by taboos. Anyone who yearns to do more, to be more . . . they're working in support of our cause." His lip rose slightly. "Even if they don't realise it."

"Okay, so you're . . . what?" I said. "Trying to change the world?" I couldn't keep the scepticism out of my voice.

Byron laughed.

"What's so funny?" I asked.

"Stephen, we did that quite a while ago," Byron said with a smile. He gestured to the tables around him, to the shops outside the window. "This world you're living in? It's mostly our work."

"All of it?"

"Oh, well, not *all* of it. But the fact that you're sitting there on that bench right now—that you could wake up when you wanted this morning, talk to me on your phone, and ride whatever taxi or train you took to get here—that's mostly thanks to us. All due to slow, patient work over the centuries."

I just looked at him.

"Don't believe me?" Byron asked.

"Not really."

"Oh, well," Byron said with a shrug. "You'll learn."

"If you guys built this world," I said, "how come you were just talking about how unfair it is?"

"Well, we can't be everywhere," Byron said. "But we've advanced a long way. People like the Ashfords may still be around, but they don't have the status that they did in the past. Once upon a time, your station in life was what you were born with."

It seemed to me as though that was mostly true nowadays as well, but I didn't want to get sidetracked. "So you and the Houses are enemies?"

"Many of our number still come from their ranks," Byron said. "But at the end of the day, the House system is not really compatible with a truly free society. No one's opportunities should be limited by the family they happen to be born into."

All right, I decided. *Let's make him get to the point.* "And what do *you* do?"

"I'm glad you asked!" Byron said with a smile. "I am what you might call a recruiter."

"For the Winged?"

"I seek out promising young people who show talent and potential."

"Like Lucella?"

"Lucella is . . . not *un*talented, but her abilities are limited. You have the potential to be far more."

I happened to glance at Byron just then and caught a flash of something in his eyes, something hungry. It was there and gone in an instant, but it sent a chill through me.

The sound of footsteps announced the return of the waitress, and I looked away, grateful for the distraction as she handed Byron his coffee. All of a sudden the McDonald's seemed very cold. Outside, on the railing, the birds looked in through the glass with opaque black eyes.

"So," Byron said once the waitress had gone. "Interested?"

I was, but I was very uneasy about saying so. "I'm going to be honest," I said. "This isn't really what I'm here for."

"Yes, your father," Byron said. "Very understandable. But have you really not made the connection yet?"

"What connection?"

"Think about it, Stephen," Byron said. "How do you think I came to know your father in the first place?"

I frowned. I didn't see what that had to do with . . .

. . . *wait.* I looked sharply at Byron.

"I recruited your father into the Winged about . . . oh, it would have been twelve years by now. How time does fly." Byron smiled at me. "Interested in following in his footsteps?"

THE UPPER FLOOR of the McDonald's was quiet but for the sound of background chatter and the rustle of traffic on the road outside. Anyone looking at me and Byron would just have seen two people sitting at a table. It would have all looked very normal.

But inwardly, my thoughts were racing. My father had worked for these people? *How?*

"Would you like to know more?" Byron asked.

Slowly, I nodded.

"When I first met your father, he would have been about eight years older than you are now," Byron told me. "Just another

London security guard working doors. You might hire him when you wanted a bouncer who was a little better-looking than the usual, but beyond that, you wouldn't give him a second thought. But at the risk of sounding conceited, I've always had something of an eye for talent. I took a look into his background, and what I found was quite interesting. Apparently he'd been a House arms-man when he was younger, and quite a favoured one. Then all of a sudden things had gone wrong and he'd left under a cloud. By a funny coincidence, he seemed to have acquired a son shortly afterwards." Byron raised his eyebrows. "Sound familiar?"

I was silent.

"Anyway, at the time I met William, he was having rather a rough time of it," Byron continued. "Hard to raise a child on a security guard's salary. His old employer didn't want anything to do with him, and his wife—ex-wife—apparently wasn't being particularly helpful. It was rather a sore spot with him. He had very little good to say about his old House, or the rest of their class." Byron gave me a slight smile. "How did you describe the Ashfords, when we last met? 'Rich bastards,' wasn't it? Anyway, when I suggested that we might be able to help one another, he was . . . receptive. And so, he began to work for the Winged."

I looked dubiously at Byron. *Is he telling the truth?* I thought back, trying to figure out whether it matched with my memories.

It . . . fit. It did fit. At the time Byron was talking about, I would have been . . . what, nine or ten? And back then we *had* been struggling. My dad had been working long hours, leaving me alone most evenings to eat dinner alone in our small flat. A couple of times I'd come in to find him worrying over bills, and I remembered a talk about what we'd do if they turned off the gas or the electricity.

But then at some point all of that had stopped. The red bills had stopped coming through the letterbox, and the fridge and freezer had stopped looking so bare. With hindsight, I should have paid more attention, but when you're a kid you just sort of take this stuff for granted. First there was no money, then there was. I'd never really wondered why things had changed.

But obviously something *had* changed. In fact, it had been only a year or two later that we'd moved into our house, a little two-bedroom place that had felt like a palace compared to our flat. Had that been because of Byron?

I really wished my father hadn't been so secretive about all this. He'd always been vague about his work—even when one of his jobs took him away for a week or more, he'd never tell me where he'd been.

Although, now that I thought about it, if he'd been working for Byron, that might explain *why* he'd been so secretive . . .

Byron had been waiting for me to respond; when I didn't, he went on. "I got to know your father quite well, over the years. I ended up helping him with quite a few things. Drucraft, for one. Your father had a natural talent for it—it was one of the things that caused him to be so favoured by the House he worked for. But once he was thrown out, well, that was the end of that. He'd been trying to study the subject on his own—he was always quite the autodidact—but he lacked resources. But once he had the support, he took off very fast." Byron paused. "He didn't mention to you that he was receiving drucraft instruction?"

I shook my head.

"I did actually offer at the time to find a tutor for his son," Byron said. "It's one of the most common services we offer. People who might not want anything for themselves will go to quite some lengths to secure an education for their children. But your father turned me down. I suppose he was more interested in self-development."

He did find me a tutor, I thought. *Him.*

"Still, it doesn't seem to have harmed your own potential very much," Byron went on. "In fact, you seem to have even more talent than he did. Lucella tells me you're a manifester?"

I wished I'd never told Lucella that, but no point denying it now. "Yes."

"Quite an accomplishment at your age."

I shrugged.

"You don't agree?"

"It's a lot less useful if you don't have money to burn on Wells."

"But you showed quite the variety of abilities in that fight at Chancery Lane."

I didn't answer.

"I've been meaning to ask," Byron said. "How *did* you manage to acquire quite so many sigls? You certainly didn't buy them. Your sensing must be very good to be a manifester, so I suppose you *could* have found that many Wells on your own. But that doesn't explain how you were able to do the shaping."

I didn't like where these questions were going. Being a manifester doesn't let you make any sigl you want—even if you can find the right Well, you still need to know how to use it. The kids from Noble Houses learn shaping from expensive private tutors, and Byron was probably guessing that I had someone doing the same for me. But the real reason I could do all that was my essentia sight, and that was something I was absolutely *not* going to share. "I guess I'm just that good," I told him.

Byron studied me.

"How did—?" I began.

"Ah, ah, ah," Byron said, wagging his finger. "Remember our deal?"

"What deal?"

"I told you when we first met," Byron said. "Work with us, and

I'll tell you about your father. I think I've been quite generous so far. Now it's your turn."

"I didn't come here because I wanted to hear about my dad's life history," I said. In truth I absolutely did, but I wasn't going to admit it.

"Then why did you come?"

I was silent for a moment. "I'm trying to find him," I said at last. It wasn't that much of a secret—Byron might know it already, if he'd questioned Lucella carefully enough—but I was still wary about admitting it.

"Ah," Byron said.

"Can you help with *that*?"

"I can do considerably more," Byron said. "I can tell you exactly what your father was doing with us, and why he felt the need to disappear. And I can show you how to find him again."

I looked at Byron.

"You don't believe me?"

"Maybe."

"Honestly, Stephen," Byron said with a sigh. "Doesn't it get tiring, being so suspicious all the time?"

"You can thank Lucella for that."

"Yes, I'm clearly going to have to have a word with her. So?"

"What do you mean, 'work with you'?"

"You become a member of our association," Byron said. "You agree to support the values we advance, as well as not to work against our other members in any way. Which would mean, amongst other things, that you wouldn't be able to do anything to harm Lucella, and she wouldn't be able to do anything to you. Quite a good deal, from your point of view. And there'd be other benefits."

"Such as?"

"The same ones your father took advantage of. Help with housing and living costs. Access to education, such as drucraft tutoring. And general aid and favours from other members of the Winged."

"And what would I have to do in exchange?"

"Very little! In the long term you'd be expected to take on work for us, but no one would expect anything very significant for a new associate, certainly not for the first six months or so. Oh, and you'd have to make some gestures of commitment, to show that you were actually serious. Attending ethics classes, moving into association-owned housing, that sort of thing."

I glanced up sharply at that last one. Byron's voice was normal, but all of a sudden, I had the feeling that he was watching me very closely. "Why are you offering me all this?" I asked.

"As I said, I think you show potential."

And Tobias didn't? I thought. I remembered the conversation I'd overheard between Tobias and Byron just a couple of weeks ago, in that parking garage in Chancery Lane. Tobias had practically begged to be let into Byron's club, and Byron had brushed him off like an annoying child. What did I have that Tobias was missing?

I could think of a couple of possible answers to that question, and I didn't like either of them. "Did you say the same thing to Lucella?"

Byron paused. For the first time, he looked slightly taken aback. "I . . . may have done."

"But you offered her the same sort of deal, right? So what happened?"

"Lucella became a junior member, and then in time a full associate of the Winged."

"She didn't seem very happy about you making the same offer to me."

"Lucella's her own person," Byron said. He sounded dismissive, in control once more. "She works towards our goals in her own way. I wouldn't worry too much about her if I were you."

That's funny, because she told me that if I didn't stay away from you, she'd make me wish I'd never been born. So there was something else there that Byron wasn't telling me.

It was the one last push that I needed. Actually, I'd already made up my mind; this just made it easier. This whole deal of Byron's smelled bad in every possible way. "I'm going to say no," I told him.

Byron studied me for a few seconds. "Why?"

I shrugged.

"I mean, it's a little odd," Byron said. "From all I hear, you aren't exactly having an easy time of it. I'm offering you a way out."

"I know."

"It's a very generous offer."

"My dad always told me," I said, "that if a deal seems too good to be true, it usually is."

"Ah, yes, your father," Byron said. "Well, if that's your choice, I certainly won't force you. Tell me one thing, though. Why *are* you so concerned with finding him?"

That caught me off guard. "What?"

"A child trying to find his parents is one thing. You're an adult."

"He's still my father."

"Just because he's your father doesn't mean you have to devote your life to him."

I frowned.

"I mean, it's very noble that you're still looking," Byron said. "But after a certain point, don't you think it might be worth re-evaluating things? As I understand it, both of your parents have left. You don't owe them anything."

"My dad didn't leave," I said by reflex.

"That wasn't an insult," Byron said, shaking his head. "So many children grow up trapped by their parents' expectations, having their world narrowed and their choices limited, year after year. It's only once they separate from them that they look back and see everything they've missed. But you've been able to freely develop, all on your own. I'm sure it must have been difficult, but to be quite honest, I'm rather envious of you. I wish I'd had the same opportunity."

I looked at Byron in surprise. He had a distant look on his face and stared off into space for a moment longer before seeming to come back to reality. "So it's still a no?" he asked me.

I hesitated, then nodded.

"Ah, well," Byron said. He didn't seem upset. "If at first you don't succeed, and all that. And I have to admit, this way is far more interesting. Nowadays I have more applicants than I know what to do with. It's a nice change having to work for it again." He smiled to himself, as if at some private joke. "Humans need a challenge to test themselves against, wouldn't you say?"

"Um," I said. "I guess?"

"Well, I've enjoyed our talk," Byron said. He rose to his feet. "If you'd like to know more about your father, do feel free to get in touch. And if you change your mind, the offer is still on the table. But it won't stay that way forever." He gave me a pleasant nod. "Until then."

Byron walked away. I watched him disappear down the stairs, then once he was gone I stood up and took a couple of steps to the window.

A flash of movement caught my eye. A woman—a girl?—turned and ran down the pavement, stuffing something into her pocket. I stared after her, watching her zigzag through the crowd until she vanished from sight.

I'd only caught a glimpse of her face, and it took me a few seconds to put it together with her movements. *Lucella*. It had been Lucella.

I frowned, wondering if I should pursue, but she'd already disappeared and I knew I'd never catch up. What had Lucella been doing here?

I replayed that glimpse in my memory. I hadn't had a good look, but the more I thought about it, the more it felt as though that thing she'd been stuffing into her pocket had been a mobile phone. From that spot on the pavement, she would have just been able to see me and Byron through the window.

Down below, on the nearside pavement, Byron emerged into the midday sunshine. He turned the opposite way to the direction Lucella had taken and began strolling up the road. I looked after him, frowning, until he'd disappeared as well. Only when it was clear that everyone else had gone did I leave the restaurant and go home, checking behind me all the way.

CHAPTER 6

I GOT HOME, dropped onto my bed, and stared at my notebook for a while. I was supposed to be looking into some Matter sigls that Colin and I had talked about, but the meeting with Byron had left me off balance and I couldn't seem to focus.

It wasn't Byron's offer—I had no second thoughts about *that*. I was still worried that he'd try to strong-arm me somehow, but from what I'd seen, Byron seemed to be the type who liked to talk people into things. I didn't feel as though I was directly in danger from him, at least not yet.

No, it was what he'd said at the end, about why I was trying to find my father. Or, more specifically, the fact that I hadn't had a good answer.

I sighed and leant back on my bed against the wall. Hobbes, curled up on the duvet, gave a sleepy "mraow," and I reached over to scratch him between the ears, watching as he drowsily rubbed his head against my hand.

Why *did* I want to find my father so badly? It had been something I'd wanted for so long that I'd never really thought about it—it was just a backdrop to everything I did from day to day. But as Byron had pointed out, it wasn't something I *needed*. My employment situation might be looking a bit shaky at the moment, but I'd lived through rough patches before and I could do it again.

For that matter, it wasn't as though my father had even asked me to look for him. If anything, he'd sort of implied that I shouldn't—he'd just said that he'd be back *"as soon as I can."*

"As soon as I can." That had been more than three years ago. If he'd really wanted to come back badly enough, surely he could have done it by now. My mother *definitely* could have . . .

I remembered what Byron had said about both of my parents having left me. It had been delivered quite casually, as a statement of fact, which actually made it worse.

My dad didn't just leave. He did it for a good reason.

A quiet little voice in the back of my head reminded me that I'd told myself the same thing about my mother.

I squashed the thought. With my father, at least, I had something to go on: the first paragraph of his letter. *"Something's happened and I'm going to have to disappear. I can't tell you the details but understand that I'm doing this for your protection, not because I want to."* Two short sentences, but they'd been a lifeline that I'd held on to for years.

What if the story with my dad *was* the same as with my mother?

With a flash of anger, I squashed that thought too. I went back to my notebook and my sigl designs, then tried to do some research into locator corporations, but couldn't concentrate on either. Byron's words kept drifting back into my thoughts, making them wander back down the same path.

By the time the sun set that evening I'd done nothing useful all day, and I finally decided to go out hunting for Wells. Hobbes had woken up and meowed; I fed him, then headed downstairs.

———

I SHUT MY front door behind me and walked out into the London evening. Hobbes bounded away across the street, disappearing behind the cars of Foxden Road.

Hunting for Wells is both simple and difficult. Simple, because all you have to do is wander around until you find somewhere with a lot of essentia; difficult, because to detect a Well's essentia, you have to get close. The finder's stones that most locators use have to get within twenty feet or so to reliably pick up a Well (more than that for the really powerful ones, but if you find a really powerful one in London, it's probably taken already). Which means quartering the city in painstaking detail.

It's a pretty crude method when you think about it—you'd have thought that with all the centuries drucrafters have had to work on the problem, they'd have come up with a better way. Colin had asked me if there was some way to sense Wells at longer ranges, something like radar or sonar, but I hadn't been able to think of one. Radar and sonar work by sending out waves that hit something and bounce back, but light and sound pass right *through* essentia, just like everything else. As far as I know, the only things that can pick up essentia are living creatures. Which means that if you want to find Wells, you have to send out guys to tromp up and down the streets.

Then again, maybe there *are* sophisticated ways to find Wells, but the corporations don't use them because hiring guys for subminimum wage is cheaper.

Anyway, I've got some things going for me that make sensing a better prospect than usual. For one thing, I can sense, and a drucrafter with good sensing skills can pick up a Well from further away than any finder's stone. For another, I've got my essentia sight. It doesn't boost my range, but it helps a lot for interpreting. Put those things together, and I can sweep an area ten times as fast as a normal locator.

Of course, sweeping an area doesn't mean you'll find anything. Most concentrations of essentia turn out to be just random currents; and even when you do find a Well, it's often too weak to be useful. On other occasions you'll find a strong Well, only to discover that someone else has found it first. Finding a Well that's both full *and* unclaimed is rare, not to mention really unpredictable. I've had days where I've worked morning till night with nothing to show for it but aching feet, and then I've had the same thing happen the day after that, and then again the day after *that*. And sometimes it goes on to the point where I start to wonder if my sensing's stopped working, or if every Well in the city's dried up. And then all of a sudden I'll find three Wells in a row. I never know whether another hour spent searching will be wasted, or the most rewarding one of the whole month.

It's frustrating, but it can get kind of addictive too. I've had days when I've hated my job, and yet I've kept going anyway, trying and trying in the hope of hitting that jackpot, like a gambler feeding money into a fruit machine, or tapping away at a gacha game. The unpredictability keeps you coming back.

Today I was heading up to Forest Gate, an area north of my home surrounded by parks and split by the big Crossrail Line running east-west through its centre. I'd combed it pretty thoroughly back in the spring, but it had been long enough since then that I figured there was a decent chance something new might have sprung up. I skirted West Ham Park, then took a small, hard-to-notice path heading north.

The sounds of traffic faded away as I left the main road behind. The lane I was on was so tiny it didn't even have a name, just a little winding passage squeezed in between buildings and yards filled with broken-down vans and rusting machinery. A big rubbish bin was stuffed to overflowing, black bags and decaying cardboard boxes piled around it; apparently even the bin men didn't come here. A sign loomed up to my left, white on red in the darkness: "CLAPTON FOOTBALL CLUB."

I walked north along the path, my footsteps echoing in the quiet. The sky above was clear on one side and clouded on the other, the ragged dividing line passing right over my head from horizon to horizon, like a vast grey blanket that had been torn in half. At one point a sound from behind made me stop and turn, wondering if it was Hobbes. He likes going with me on these Well hunts, so long as I don't go too far, and we were still close enough to his home territory that he might be following. But the passageway behind me was silent and still, and after a moment I went on.

As the passage up ahead opened up into a dead-end road, I saw what I'd been hoping for: trails of pale essentia in the air. To the left was a battered wooden fence with a football ground behind it, and the essentia trails were stronger in that direction. The football ground was fenced in, but the fences had been damaged and only half-heartedly fixed, and I found a gap big enough to squeeze through.

The football ground was dark and quiet. It was surrounded on three sides by houses and back gardens, muffling any sound from the streets nearby. Bedroom and bathroom windows were glowing yellow squares set into the houses around, but the ground itself was close to pitch black. The grass muffled my footsteps as I traced the glowing strands of essentia to the southwest corner, where they met to form a shining beacon of green. A Life Well.

I decided it wasn't going to work as a usable Well. Its strength was a tiny bit too low, just under the cutoff to make a viable sigl. But although it was only a temporary one, it did feel as though it had room to grow. If I came back in a week or a month, there was a good chance that this might turn into a D-class or a D+. Maybe even a C if I was really lucky.

Of course, as of right now, there wasn't actually anything I could *do* with a Life Well. With my Linford's account suspended, I had no way to sell the thing; I couldn't even check the Registry to see if it was claimed. But just because I couldn't sell a Well didn't mean that it was useless. I could make a sigl, or just sit on it in the hope of selling it once this whole thing with Linford's had blown over. True, I didn't have any Life sigl designs that I was working on just now, but maybe I could take a look at the catalogue with Colin and come up with—

A chill wind swept across the football ground. Behind me, a bird cawed, then fell silent.

I snapped my head around, scanning the grounds. At either end of the football pitch, the goals were white outlines in the gloom. The eastern side, where I'd entered, was dark; there was no trace of movement.

But now that I stopped to listen, the grounds had gone very quiet. Hadn't there been more noise before?

Cautiously, I began to retrace my steps back across the grass. I didn't know what it had been, but my instincts were sounding a warning. As I approached the far side, I slowed, scanning the fence. I couldn't see anything in the shadows.

I stopped and focused on my essentia sight. Green wisps trailed past me to the left and right, drifting lazily on invisible currents. Behind was the green fire of the Well. And up ahead . . .

. . . was something else. Grey-white essentia from the surrounding air was being pulled into a small vortex of green light, clearer and more sharply defined than the trails around me, tracing the vague shape of a human body. There was someone there in the shadows, using an enhancement sigl.

I stood quite still.

The green light moved. It stepped out into the dim ambient light from the London sky, and as it did it took the form of a human, shrouded in the gloom.

I held out my right hand and channelled. Light welled up from the ring on my fourth finger, illuminating the football pitch in pale blue.

The man standing in front of me was a few inches taller than me and maybe a few years older. It was hard to tell for sure since he was wearing some kind of visor made of tinted plastic that hid the upper half of his face, but something about the way he was standing sent a spike of adrenaline through me.

"Light again," the man said. "You really like that shit, don't you?"

The voice sounded familiar. Not in a good way. "Have we met?" I asked.

"'Have we met?'" the man—boy—repeated mockingly. "What do you think?"

I frowned, studying him. Thin, but strongly muscled. Short black hair against pale skin. A memory stirred—a garden?

Then I saw the Life sigl hanging from a chain around his neck, pouring strength and power into his muscles, and it clicked. He was the boy from Hampstead. He'd knocked me around when I'd fought him in the summer, and I'd only managed to get away by running into a crowd.

There weren't any crowds around now.

I thought quickly, trying to figure out what I'd need to say to get myself out of this. "Look, I know I climbed into your back garden," I said, "but isn't this going a bit far?"

The boy stared at me, his eyes invisible behind the visor.

"I mean, it was four *months* ago. I get that you're pissed off, but come on."

"You think I'm fucking stupid?" the boy asked.

I hesitated. Something was wrong. The last time this guy had chased me off, he'd acted like I wasn't even worth his time.

Without taking his eyes off me, the boy pulled out a big smartphone. He tapped at the touchscreen, then turned it so that I could see.

I looked at the screen in puzzlement and saw a photo of a street in the daytime. I was standing too far away to make it out clearly and I definitely wasn't stepping in for a closer look, but it looked like it had been taken from pavement level, angled upwards. There was a balcony in front of a set of floor-to-ceiling windows; the quality wasn't great, but through the glass you could just make out two people sitting down at—

A jolt went through me. It was a picture of me and Byron.

"Well, hey," the boy said. "Would you look at that."

"Um," I said, thinking fast. How the hell had—*oh*. "You got that from Lucella?"

"Uh-huh," the boy said. He was facing me, standing quite still.

I couldn't make out his eyes, but I'd picked up enough cues by now to know that this was very, very serious. "You guys . . . know each other?"

"Last chance," the boy told me.

"Whoa, whoa," I said, raising my free hand and talking fast. "Okay, look, I don't know what Lucella told you, but I'm pretty sure I haven't done anything bad enough to you to make you want to track me down and kill me."

"Oh, don't worry, I'm not going to kill you," the boy said, his mouth curving upwards in a mirthless smile. "I'm just going to hurt you really, really badly."

This was not going well. "Can you at least *tell* me why you're so pissed off?"

The boy studied me for a few seconds, his eyes unreadable

behind that visor. "You know what? Sure," he said. "After I kick the shit out of you first." He stepped forward.

I sent a haywire beam from the Primal sigl on my right hand into the boy's chest.

All the time we'd been talking, I'd been getting ready. The strength sigl the boy was wearing looked to be the same kind that the Ashford armsmen used, and I knew from our last encounter that it was strong enough that he absolutely *could* kick the shit out of me. Which was why I wasn't letting him get close enough to try.

Essentia surged and the strands flowing through the boy's sigl and into his muscles twisted and writhed, lashing like a nest of tangled snakes. He made it two steps, lost his balance, and tripped over his own feet. Then he tried to catch himself, and after *that* he tried to spring back up off the grass to reach me.

It didn't work very well.

"Finished?" I asked once he'd stopped moving.

The boy was sprawled on the grass, panting. From personal experience, I know that it's *really hard* to move properly when your muscles are all different strengths from what they're supposed to be. I still had the haywire sigl focused on him, the invisible beam causing his strength sigl to go out of control. He'd probably pulled about twenty different muscles by now.

"What the f—" the boy began, and cut off with a gasp of pain.

"Hate to break this to you," I told him, "but you aren't the first guy who's thought that a strength sigl means he gets to push me around."

The boy stared up at me. The last time I'd run into this guy I'd blinded him and fled. From the visor, he'd probably expected me to do the same thing again.

"Okay, let's try this again," I said. I kept the haywire beam trained on his chest, while keeping a small trickle of essentia flowing through my light sigl as well. Using two triggered sigls on the same hand at the same time takes skill—it's fiddly to keep the essentia flows going through separate fingers—but I'd had enough practice by now that I could do it without much thought. "So how about you tell me exactly what it was about that picture that's got you so—"

The boy made a short, sudden movement.

Some instinct made me jump to the side. Essentia flared in the darkness; I heard a low, deadly hiss and felt a flutter of air. I reacted instantly, yanking essentia away from my haywire and light sigls and pouring it into my diffraction sigl instead.

The world went pitch black. I backpedalled, stumbling in the darkness. I couldn't see but I could still sense the Well, and I used that to orient myself; once I was far enough away I stopped and dug in my pocket for my vision sigl, fumbling blindly until my fingers closed around the headband and I was able to get it around my forehead and channel a flow of essentia into the sigl mounted into it.

Dim blue light returned to the world. Invisibility is tricky; anything that stops people from seeing you generally stops *you* from seeing *them*. My work-around for that is to have my diffraction sigl let ultraviolet light through and then have another sigl that lets me use ultraviolet to see, but it's a clunky solution and it was causing me problems now. My headband wasn't aligned quite right and the blue tint to my vision wasn't helping.

In the time I'd been blind, my attacker had got to his feet; he wasn't right on top of me but he was uncomfortably close. He was swivelling his head from side to side as if searching for something.

I held very still. As invisibility sigls go, mine isn't great; it causes a sort of goldfish-bowl distortion in the air that gets more obvious the faster I move or the closer someone gets. But it was dark and the guy was wearing a visor. If I just stayed still, he probably wouldn't be able to . . .

The boy kept on scanning left and right. He took one step, then another. He was moving in my direction.

Crap.

Carefully and slowly, I began to edge to the left. The boy's head turned towards me and with a sinking feeling I stopped.

There are all kinds of ways to defeat invisibility. Drucraft companies have dozens of models for vision enhancement, and there's a whole arms race between concealment and detection. But there's a much simpler way, one that takes a lot more skill but doesn't require any special gear. If you're a good enough drucrafter, you can just sense the essentia an active sigl's using.

The boy took a couple of steps straight towards me.

I thought quickly and changed direction, retreating towards the Well.

The boy's head snapped around and he began to follow me, but as I kept backing away he slowed. The trails of essentia from the Well were drifting lazily across the field, swirling between us, and I saw the boy look from side to side, moving more and more slowly until he finally stopped.

Gotcha, I thought with satisfaction. It's not too hard to get good enough at sensing to pick up essentia. But telling the difference between different *kinds* of essentia is another story. As long as I stayed close enough to the Well, I was hidden.

The trouble was, I was also kind of stuck. I could circle around and try to make it back to the gap in the fence, but as soon as I moved out of the Well's radius he'd spot me again. In the absence of any better ideas, I kept still.

"I know you're there!" the boy shouted.

I stayed quiet. My strength sigl kept trying to pull essentia into itself and activate. I stopped it; it was stealth I needed here, not power.

"I'm going to fucking kill you, you piece of shit! I'm going to break every bone in your body, then cut off your dick and shove it down your throat till you choke!"

Oh, yeah, that's really going to make me want to come out and talk.

"What the fuck is wrong with your family?" the boy shouted. "You're all rich already! What, that's not enough for you? You have to get in with Byron as well?"

I frowned. What did he mean, "my family" . . . ? *Oh.* Tobias and Lucella.

I was starting to get a glimmer of what was going on here. Lucella must have told this guy that I was trying the same line as Tobias, and that unlike Tobias, I actually had a shot.

Unfortunately I didn't think that trying to explain that she was lying was going to work very well. There was an unhinged sound to this guy's yells and he didn't seem in the mood to be reasoned with. Carefully I backed away, keeping my movements slow and steady so that he wouldn't be able to catch a shimmer in the air.

"You wouldn't make it, you know," the boy said. All of a sudden his voice was weirdly normal, almost casual. "What, you think you're going to end up like Lucella? Only reason he kept her for so long was because she lucked out. The two after her got used up and thrown away."

I'd reached the edge of the football pitch. The boundary rail was small enough that I could step right over it . . . but the fence behind was ten feet high with barbed wire at the top.

I tried to figure out what to do. If I could make it over the fence and into the back gardens of the houses beyond, I'd be safe. But I didn't like my odds of making that climb while maintaining concentration on my invisibility. If the boy spotted me halfway up, things would get ugly.

The other choice was to fight my way out. The boy's strength sigl was still running; if I hit him with another haywire beam, it should put him down long enough to let me get out of here. The problem was that other sigl. It had happened too fast for me to be sure, but I had a nasty feeling that it had been one of those "missile" ones that threw out projectiles. I'd read about them in the Exchange catalogue, and depending on their power level, they could go from "really hurts" to "lethal." I didn't think I could keep up concentration on my haywire sigl and my invisibility at the same time, meaning the boy would have a clear shot as I decloaked. He'd hurt himself in the process, probably badly enough that he wouldn't get more than one try, but one might be all he'd need.

"Lucella says you're supposed to be good," the boy said. He'd taken a couple of steps forward; his head was scanning from left to right. "I guess you think making your own sigls makes you some kind of prize, right? The guy before me was supposed to be some kind of golden boy too. Wasn't enough. After he failed the third time, Byron dropped him. So he tried the do-it-yourself way. Last I heard, he got sectioned."

I had no idea what this guy was talking about. Not that it mattered; I was pretty sure he was just trying to get me to make noise. But he was getting closer and closer to the Well, and I didn't have much more room to back away. I was going to have to make a decision, fast.

I focused on my sensing, concentrating on the boy. His Life sigl was still active, but I couldn't pick up anything else. But . . . wait, what was that? The glow of a second Life sigl, smaller and further away and close to the ground . . .

Hope sparked within me. Help was on the way.

Now I just had to keep him distracted.

"You know what I've had to do for this?" the boy said. That unhinged tone was starting to creep back into his voice. "I'm not letting you push me out now."

"I'm not trying to push you out," I said.

The boy's head snapped towards me and his right hand twitched; it was only a small motion but I'd been watching for it. "There you are," he said to himself.

"Look, I still don't really know what's going on," I said, "but if it helps, I'm not trying to sign up with Byron."

"Uh-huh."

"Seriously. I'm just trying to get his help with finding someone."

The boy paused. "Finding someone," he repeated after a moment.

"Yeah."

"You want *Byron's* help with *finding* someone."

"Um, yeah."

The boy stared in my direction for a few seconds, then gave a short, barking laugh. "That's the best one I've heard all week."

"Okay," I said slowly. "Point is, I don't think we have to—"

"You really have no idea what you're dealing with, do you?" the boy said. "What they can do?"

"I mean, if you want to tell me . . . ?"

The boy laughed again.

"Oh well, it was worth a try," I said. "But I was serious about not wanting to sign up with Byron. Maybe think about that when you're putting disinfectant on your scratches."

"I'm not going to—" The boy paused. "Wait, what?"

Hobbes pounced on the guy from behind.

There was a flash of essentia, but the boy had been getting ready to take a shot at me, not at something behind him, and it went hissing off into the darkness. Next he tried to round on

Hobbes, at which point he discovered that when cats attack some-one, they don't stand on the ground and scratch, they use them as a climbing frame. After *that* he tried to pull Hobbes off his arm and discovered that trying to use one limb to fight off something that's attacking you with four limbs doesn't work very well. And at that point I hit him with my haywire sigl too.

After ten seconds of yowls, yells, and extreme violence, the boy was on the ground, bleeding all over and trying frantically to fend off Hobbes. I circled quickly around, careful to make sure the haywire beam didn't hit my cat, and called, "Come on!"

Hobbes gave the boy a hiss and a parting slash, then turned and ran, flitting away across the grass. I dropped concentration on my sigl and followed, swerving from side to side to make my-self harder to hit in case the guy took any shots, but none came. Hobbes and I made it through the fence and ran back down the passage.

By the time we got back onto the main road, I slowed to a walk. It's a bad idea to get too cocky about shaking a pursuer, but in this case the guy had just been scratched to ribbons and had pulled more muscles than he probably even knew he had. Right now, he'd have trouble winning a race against a mobility scooter.

Not that that made me feel much better about him tracking me down. "So how did that guy even find me?" I asked Hobbes.

"Mraaaaow," Hobbes said. He'd hopped up onto the wall of the nearest house's front garden and was now trotting along at waist height, matching my speed.

"Lucella," I realised. "She gave him my address. Then he just would have had to find a place where he could watch my front door, wait for me to leave, then follow me."

"Mraow."

"I hope this isn't going to get to be a habit," I told Hobbes. "I mean, it worked out this time, but I don't think I want a rematch."

"Mraaaow."

"Yes, I know it was because you were there."

We walked away down the pavement, Hobbes jumping over the gaps where the front gates were. "Mraow?" Hobbes said.

"I *just* fed you."

"Mraow."

"Fine, I guess you've earned it."

"Mraow?"

"Okay, okay, a treat as well."

We headed home.

CHAPTER 7

"So who the hell is this guy?" Colin asked.

We were in the Admiral Nelson, the warmth and chatter a pleasant contrast to the autumn chill. It was just the two of us today, since I'd made it clear to the others that I wasn't sitting down at the same table as Gabriel until I'd had a *lot* more time to cool off.

"Christ knows," I told Colin. "I first ran into him back in the summer. He's got some kind of connection to the guys who were following my dad." I grimaced. "Just wish I knew whether my dad really was one of them."

"Maybe he decided to leave?" Colin suggested. "I mean, if these guys really are some kind of secret society, they probably don't like it when their members run off."

"But Byron said he could show me how to *find* my dad. How does that work if he's on the run from them?"

Colin shrugged. "I dunno."

The door to the pub swung open, sending a gust of cold air

through the room; men came in, laughing and joking. "You think this boy's going to try and jump you again?" Colin asked.

"I bloody well hope not," I said. "I really don't like fighting this guy. He even brought an anti-glare visor after I hit him with my blinding sigl back in the summer. If he's going to keep bringing counters to whatever I used on him last time, I'm going to run out of tricks." I took a drink, thinking. "On the other hand, it doesn't feel like he's after me *specifically*. I think he just wants me to eff off out of his territory."

"So if you go no-contact with this Byron guy . . . ?"

"Then he might think he's scared me away," I said with a nod.

"So, speaking of new tricks . . ."

We'd had a talk earlier in the week about possible sigls, and Colin had promised he'd have something for me by today. "What have you got?"

"All right," Colin said. He reached down into his bag and pulled out the catalogue, which he dropped onto the table with a thump. "So, your wish list was: you're looking for a sigl that lets you survive getting shot at by armoured soldiers. You're also looking for a sigl that boosts your mobility enough that you can get *away* from armoured soldiers. You'd also like something that lets you fight back, though that's second priority to surviving, and you'd like something that'll let you handle a gang in a fistfight. Does that cover everything?"

"Well, after last night I'd also like something that'll work against high-speed missiles."

"Okay," Colin said. "Next, making these sigls requires you to find the right kind of Well, and you can't expect to find anything above a C-grade, which means you're looking for as few sigls as possible that do as many of those things as possible, each with a carat rating of 1.4 at the most."

"At the *absolute* most. To make a sigl with a carat rating of 1.5 and up needs a C+ Well. Between 0.7 and 1 is a lot more realistic."

"Okay," Colin said again. "So, bad news? You're not getting everything you want."

"That's why I called it a wish list, not a stuff-I-can-afford list."

"Next bit of bad news," Colin said. "That idea you had about using a Matter effect to turn your clothes into armour? It won't work."

"Why not?"

"So the way that would have to work would be by increasing your clothing's shear strength so that it'd flex without tearing. Sort of like Mongolian silk armour."

"Okay . . ."

"But once shear strength is high enough not to break, it doesn't matter if you put it any higher. What matters is shear *modulus*, to diffuse the impact."

"In English, please?"

"If you got shot while wearing that, you'd basically end up getting impaled with a spear made out of your own clothing," Colin explained. "There's a reason people don't wear silk armour anymore."

"So what kind of Matter effect *would* let me turn my clothing into armour?"

"I don't actually think there is one," Colin said. "There's a line of sigls that are meant to protect you against scrapes—it sounds like they're meant for people who do stuff like extreme sports. But they're not going to do much against blunt force. For that you need something rigid, and that's kind of exactly what clothing's *not*."

"Damn it," I said. "Okay, fine. Got any better ideas?"

"Well, maybe stop reinventing the wheel?" Colin said. "Instead of trying to use cotton and nylon as armour, use, you know, *actual* armour. Like those soldiers."

"They were wearing what looked like power armour from *Astartes*," I pointed out. "I can't afford that, and even if I could, I can't exactly go wandering around London looking like I'm cosplaying Master Chief."

"Sounds pretty cool to me," Colin said. "But I was thinking smaller. Here." He opened the catalogue to a page marked with a yellow Post-it note and pointed to one of the sigls in the Matter section.

"'Lightfoot,'" I read, and skimmed the paragraph. "Reduces the wearer's mass?"

"Yeah, though it won't say whether it's *inertial* mass or *gravitational* mass. I tried looking it up in the index, and they act like they're the same thing, which is really annoying because—"

"*Colin*," I said, holding back the urge to sigh. "Does it *really* matter?"

"Well, it would if . . . okay, fine. My advice is, just buy a bulletproof vest, then make yourself one of those sigls."

"Could I afford that?"

"The vest, sure," Colin said. "The sigl, no. But you'd be making that yourself, right?"

"Yeah," I said, looking down at the lightfoot sigl's pricing. It was one of the rare sigls that was sold at every grade from D all the way up to S. The D-rank version cost a few thousand, the A-rank was seven figures, and the S-rank was "price available upon request."

"It'd mean you could wear armour and still be faster than you were before," Colin explained. "That's two of the things you were looking for, right? Plus you could jump further and climb better."

I was actually pretty impressed Colin had managed to put all this together so fast. He's always been good at research. "Yeah."

"You don't seem very enthusiastic."

"I guess I was hoping for something a bit more magical."

"Hey, you're the one who told me to look for a Matter sigl. If you want something more flashy, there are those Motion inertial barriers . . ."

"No, Motion's my worst branch." The last time I'd tried to shape a Motion sigl had been a nightmare, and that had been the simplest kind in the catalogue. I didn't want to think about what trying to make a *complicated* Motion sigl would be like. "I guess I'll give it a try."

"I mean, with your budget, it's the best I can find," Colin said. "Plus armour doesn't need turning on, so it still works even when someone catches you by surprise. That might come in handy someday."

I KEPT A wary eye out for the next few days, but my mystery stalker didn't reappear. In the meantime I kept applying for locator jobs, without much success. None of the companies that were supposed to be any good answered my emails, and the ones that *did* answer were the ones that the anonymous posters on the Back Alley specifically called out as the ones to avoid at all costs.

On Thursday, though, I got an unexpected message: an email giving a number to call if I was interested in locating work. At first I assumed that it was a response to one of my job applications, but when I called the number, I found otherwise.

"Wait," I said. "So I *haven't* sent you an application?"

"No, nothing like that," the voice on the other end of the phone said. It was a man with a faint accent I couldn't place. "Our client is in the market for Wells and is looking for some freelance locators. Your name was passed to us as someone who might be interested."

"I mean . . . yeah, I am. Who's the client?"

"They'd prefer to remain anonymous."

I paused. "Okay."

"Our client's interested in temporary Wells only. Payment per Well, usual terms."

"If they're anonymous, whose name am I supposed to register the Wells under?"

"We don't need the Wells registered."

". . . Okay."

"You don't need to worry about their status; you'll be paid either way."

"Why would your client pay for Wells that are already registered to someone else?"

"Data for their records."

"And you said your name was . . ."

"Mr. Smith. So are you interested?"

". . . Yes."

"Great. I'll send along our rates and contact details. Our client's got some other projects in the pipeline, so if you prove yourself on this, there'll be more work for you. We'll be in touch."

Frowning, I hung up and put down my phone. The promised email arrived shortly afterwards with a table with rates of pay per Well, along with instructions for how to call in a location. Their rates were lower than Linford's.

It all seemed straightforward enough, but some of the details felt off. When I'd signed up with Linford's, I'd had to go through an annoyingly long (and expensive) registration process. I'd learned afterwards that the other drucraft companies did the same thing—it made it harder for you to jump ship later on. So why was this company making it so easy?

And not using the Well Registry was *really* weird. Linford's, like all the other drucraft companies I'd heard of, would only pay for unclaimed Wells. Paying for claimed ones seemed uncharacteristically generous for a drucraft corporation. Was this whole thing just a scam?

I turned it over in my mind for a while but didn't come up with any easy answers. At last I decided that I'd try selling this Mr. Smith the next D-class Well I found to see if he or his mystery clients would pay up. That way, even if it *was* a scam, it wouldn't cost me much.

SEPTEMBER CAME TO an end.

Looking back on it, it had probably been the single craziest month of my entire life. Over the course of three weeks I'd gained the ability to turn invisible, used it to spy on my family, been kidnapped at gunpoint, helped Calhoun fight off a raid, taken down two armsmen, been shot at by soldiers, had a face-off with Byron and Lucella, lost a fight for a Well at the Olympic Stadium, initiated my best friend into drucraft, been fired, met my mother, had someone try to recruit me into some weird secret society, and been ambushed by a crazy guy on a football pitch. Oh, and in the middle of all that, I'd turned twenty-one.

So when first one, then two, then three weeks went by and I *wasn't* either attacked or abducted or fired or recruited or married or divorced, it was quite frankly an enormous relief. After the sheer batshit insanity of the past month, I really needed some time to catch up on sigl research, adjust to my new situation, and most of all just have things be *normal* instead of waking up to a new crisis every third day.

And somewhat to my surprise, I got exactly what I wanted. My mystery attacker didn't come back for another go, and no more family members showed up at my door. I stayed on alert, checking every time I entered or left my house to make sure I wasn't being followed, but as the weeks passed I started to think that maybe my various enemies really had decided to leave me alone for a while. I wasn't stupid enough to think it would stay that way, but, for now, I had a breather.

I made sure to put it to good use. To make that mass-reduction sigl that Colin had suggested, I would need as strong a Matter Well as possible, but that wouldn't do me any good until I'd mastered the sigl design first, and to do *that* I needed to get much better at working with Matter essentia. I was pretty good with Light sigls by now, but my experience with my slam and enhancement sigls had taught me that skill with one branch didn't necessarily translate to the others. For that I'd need practice, which meant finding Matter Wells. Preferably a lot of them.

The good news was that once I did start to find some weak Matter Wells to practice on, I found that Matter essentia was a lot easier to work with than I'd been afraid it might be. Its main problem was that it was *slow*—it took me two or three times longer to shape a Matter construct than a Light one—but once I learned to be patient and be methodical about it, everything fell into place. It made sigl design a time-consuming process, but the good news was that once I did hit on the design, I could do it quite reliably. It was certainly a hell of a lot easier than those quicksilver Motion Wells.

In the course of finding Matter Wells, I unsurprisingly found several times that number of non-Matter ones, and I tried selling some of the cheaper ones to Mr. Smith and his mysterious client. The good news was that they paid up. The bad news was that the income I got from them wasn't quite enough. The cost of living in London had gone up a lot this year, food and energy bills especially, and with the reduced payout for the Wells, I was still in the red. I wasn't *much* in the red—at my current rate I wouldn't be at risk of running out of money for a year or so—but it wasn't a good sign.

In the meantime, though, I had another problem.

I SAW MY mother twice in October. Both times I went there hoping to learn the story of what had happened between her and my father. Both times I didn't get it.

She did tell me some things. Just as Byron had said, my father had worked as a House Ashford armsman, which was how he and my mother had met. Charles hadn't approved of the match and my dad had left House Ashford on bad terms . . . which, now that I thought about it, explained a lot about the way Charles treated me. My mother also made some references to an older sister, who she didn't seem to want to talk about but who I had the feeling might be important.

But while my mother would answer my questions, she never quite seemed to get around to answering the ones I really cared about. I'd ask her something that should have led into it, and she'd reply, and the conversation would get sidetracked, and somehow, without my ever being aware of exactly how, we'd end up talking about something else. In fact, we ended up spending more time with *her* questioning *me*. My mother seemed very interested in what I could do, especially with regard to drucraft. It was nice in a way—my mother's a good listener, and she seemed genuinely impressed with some of the things I'd managed to do. I'd had a pretty lonely life for the past few years, and having someone praise me gave me a warm feeling.

But then I'd leave, and somewhere on the way home I'd realise that she still hadn't really answered my questions, and that good feeling would fade. I started to suspect that she was deliberately avoiding the topic and steering the conversation so that I never got a chance to press her. I tried asking her via text message: the key questions in my messages got ignored. More than once I was on the verge of just getting in her face and refusing to leave until she gave me some answers. But I was afraid that if I did, she might just disappear again.

And out of that, a thread of anger started to grow. The more my mother kept evading, the more I started to feel as though she wasn't doing it because the time was wrong or because it might be dangerous. She wasn't answering my questions because *she didn't want to*. I tried not to let that anger spill over, but as the weeks passed it grew stronger and harder to control.

IT WAS THE evening of Halloween when I went back to see Father Hawke. Small groups of children were trooping around in costumes, holding plastic buckets and being ushered around by parents.

"Stephen," Father Hawke greeted me as I walked into his West Ham church. He's very tall, with shoulder-length black hair, and a lot more strongly built than you'd expect a priest to be. Right now, he was lighting candles. "It's been a while."

"Sorry," I said. "I've had a lot on." I glanced around the church; it blazed with light. "Special occasion?"

"All Hallows' Eve," Father Hawke said, still busy with the candles. "The evening before All Saints' Day, traditionally observed by prayer and fasting. Did you manage to finish that book I gave you?"

"It was pretty difficult," I admitted, leaning on one of the pews. "I still don't really understand what he means by 'technique.'"

"In this context he means the mindset of holding the highest goal to be efficiency," Father Hawke explained. "Which in turn requires organisation through division of labour, setting standards, and so on. The end result is a system that subordinates the natural world, eventually making humanity subservient to technology. It'll make more sense when you read his next book."

"Why is there *always* a next book?"

Father Hawke smiled to himself, lit a final candle, then blew out the taper and set it down in a tray. "Is there anything else bothering you?"

I hesitated for a moment. "Do you know anything about a group calling themselves the Winged?"

"Oh, yes."

I looked sharply at Father Hawke. He was paging through a book and didn't seem to be paying attention. "Is what they say about themselves true?"

"In certain respects."

"The guy I was talking to says they believe in freedom and created the modern world."

"And who would this be?"

"He calls himself Byron."

Father Hawke paused for a second, then went back to turning the pages. "I see."

"So, was he telling the truth?"

"After a fashion," Father Hawke said. He still wasn't looking at me. "Calling them believers in freedom is true, but misleading. The real core of their belief is the rejection of *limits*. If you took someone who only believed in freedom and put them down in the wilderness a thousand miles away from anyone, where they could live out their lives without outside interference, they'd be happy. Do the same with a member of the Winged, and they wouldn't be. You see the difference?"

I frowned, thinking.

"As regards their part in shaping the modern world," Father Hawke continued, "it's not entirely wrong, but it's a bit of an exaggeration. That book you were reading is a better explanation, as far as that goes. Still, even if technique did most of the heavy lifting, the Winged did give things a push. And it's certainly true that they're uniquely suited to the modern age in a way that the others aren't. We live in their shadow, even if most don't realise it."

". . . Others?"

"But I doubt he was giving you that talk just for your education," Father Hawke went on. He set the book down and turned to look at me. "What did he want from you?"

I paused for a moment before answering. "For me to join the Winged."

Father Hawke's eyes rested on me, suddenly as sharp as those of his namesake. "What did you tell him?"

"I said no."

"Why?"

"What do you mean?"

"Why?" Father Hawke repeated. "The Winged might not rule the world, but they're closer to it than anyone else you're likely to meet. They're richer and more powerful than any House or corporation. I'm sure he offered you *something* you wanted."

"Yes," I admitted.

"So why did you turn him down?"

"I didn't trust him."

"Good judgment on your part, but not really an answer. *Why* didn't you trust him?"

I thought about that for a few seconds. Father Hawke was still watching me intently, and something told me this was important. "Because of my father," I said.

Father Hawke blinked and tilted his head. All of a sudden the intensity was gone. "Your father?"

"He's the reason I was there in the first place," I said. "Byron said he could tell me where to find him. But . . . I don't think my dad would want me to find him if it meant doing something like that."

Father Hawke studied me for a few seconds longer, then smiled and turned away. "Interesting."

I watched Father Hawke walk away. "Do you think I was wrong?"

Father Hawke placed the book and the tray with the taper on a side table. "Not at all."

I didn't answer.

Father Hawke turned back towards me, studying me. "You seem troubled."

"Byron asked me why I cared so much about finding my dad," I confessed.

"And?"

"I . . . didn't really have a good answer."

Father Hawke blinked at me. "Why on earth would you think you needed one?"

"Uh . . ."

"'Honour thy father and mother' is one of the most foundational principles of virtually every civilisation in history," Father Hawke said. "If you feel a sense of love and duty towards your parents, then of course you're going to want to find them and help them. I mean, what sort of answer were you expecting? To justify it on some other grounds?"

"I suppose."

"Even if you decided you were searching for your father because of some other reason," Father Hawke pointed out, "you'd still have to explain why you cared about that *other* reason. If you can't justify one, what makes you think you can justify the other? You *should* love and honour your parents. If someone tries to make you question that, it's not because they want to help you."

I KEPT THINKING about Father Hawke's words on my way home. Oddly enough, they did make me feel better. The more I thought about it, the more it felt as though Byron's challenge had been completely unfair from the beginning, in which case I might as well just ignore him.

But that was easier said than done, because right now, no matter how I looked at it, the Winged seemed to be the ones who were holding all the cards. Somewhere in their heads was the information I needed. How could I get it?

Agreeing to Byron's offer still felt like a bad idea. I had the feeling that if I did that, I'd be making the same mistake as my father. There was always the option of pretending to sign up and then leaving once I had what I needed, but something in me instinctively shied away from that plan. I had the feeling that the price could end up being a lot higher than I was willing to pay.

No, getting too close to Byron would be a mistake. The attack in Forest Gate had made that obvious, just in case it hadn't been clear enough already. So for now, I should keep training and settle into wait-watch-listen mode. Sooner or later an opportunity would turn up, and when it did, I'd be ready.

CHAPTER 8

DECEMBER CAME, BRINGING SNOW.

It rarely snows in London. It often dips below zero in the winter, but usually only when the sky's clear and there's nothing to hold in the sun's heat. As soon as it clouds over, the temperature edges back up again, not quite low enough for the rain to turn to snow or ice. So most of our winters are clear days of freezing sunshine, mixed up with cloudy days of not-quite-freezing rain.

But about once a year we get a long cold snap, and this year's was longer and harder than most. The snow started falling one Sunday night, and I woke up the next morning to find my street blanketed in white. It left the house icy cold—the temperature outside was so far below zero that our old boiler couldn't keep up, making evenings in my bedroom chilly and miserable.

But I'd made it through cold winters before. What was really bothering me was my mother, and during the week of that snowstorm I finally snapped.

————

". . . STILL HAVEN'T heard anything back from any of the numbers or addresses we used to use," my mother was saying.

"Okay," I said. We were standing on the same bridge where we'd met the first time, now carpeted in brilliant white. I'd asked last month if we could find somewhere a little less out of the way and had been told that out of the way was the point—my mother didn't want "prying eyes." As usual, she got her way.

"You said you'd been making your own attempts to find him," my mother said. "What have you tried?"

"You haven't really answered my question."

"What do you mean?"

I rested my elbows on the bridge's railings, feeling the cold from the metal cutting through my fleece. I kept my eyes on the sheet ice of the pond below, not meeting my mother's gaze. "I was asking about whether you'd talked to Dad back *then*," I said, trying to keep my voice neutral. "Not now."

"We did, but it . . . didn't go well."

"Can you just tell me what happened?"

"My and your father's marriage was something we both rushed into." My mother seemed to be choosing her words carefully. "The way we met, and how you were born . . . well, it's a long story, and—"

"I already know it."

"You do?"

"You met Dad when he was working as an Ashford family armsman," I said. "You got together, Charles was angry, and you left home to come and live with Dad in East London." I finally turned to look at my mother. "You've dropped enough hints. I'm not stupid."

". . . all right, I suppose it's not such a long story, when you put it like that," my mother said. "Though he was a little more than angry. 'Incandescent' would be closer."

I looked away again.

"It took more than a year for him to calm down enough for us to have a civil conversation. And even then, what finally brought him around was—"

"I don't really care."

"Stephen, he's the head of our House," my mother said, a trace of sharpness creeping into her voice. "I know he hasn't been particularly kind to you, but the two of you are going to have to get along."

"Fine."

"Don't just say 'fine,'" my mother said, and waited for me to answer. When I didn't, I heard the disapproval in her voice. "What are you so angry about?"

"Because you won't tell me what happened."

"I am telling you what happened."

"No you *aren't*." I turned back to my mother, feeling the anger starting to rise. "You're only telling me the bits you want to talk about."

I saw surprise flicker over my mother's face. "What do you mean?"

"You left home and moved in with my dad, and then I was born," I said. "Then at some point you married some guy called Marcus Grasser and moved back into your family mansion and you had two other children. Tobias and my half sister."

"Magnus, not Marcus," my mother said with a slight frown. "That's true, but—"

"So *what happened in between*? How did you go from being married to my dad to married to someone else? Why did you wait until I was one and a half and then disappear and *never come back*?"

A couple of people who'd just passed us on the snowy path

paused and turned back to look. Only then did I realise I'd been shouting. At another time it might have been embarrassing; right now I was too angry to care.

My mother glanced quickly towards the couple, her face a complicated mix of emotions. "There were . . . reasons. Stephen, I understand why you're angry, but . . ."

"Then *tell me*," I said. "Instead of giving me slippery answers, just start at the beginning and *tell me what really happened*."

"All right." My mother took a deep breath, then turned to rest her elbows on the railing in the same position I'd been in. After a moment, I mirrored her. Behind her, the couple watched us a moment longer, then when we did nothing, turned and kept going. My mother waited for them to disappear, then began. "You remember what I told you about my sister?"

"Her name was Victoria and she was two years older than you."

"She was the model heiress," my mother said. "Beautiful, intelligent, graceful, and a talented drucrafter just to top it off. It was obvious from the beginning that she and her future husband were going to be the next rulers of our House. I was the spare."

"What has this got to do with—"

"Everything," my mother said sharply. "*Listen*, Stephen."

I shut up.

"I spent a long time trying to be as good as Victoria," my mother continued. "When I realised I couldn't . . . well, I decided I'd do the opposite. Instead of playing the dutiful daughter, I'd go off on my own, live for myself, and marry whoever I wanted. So that was what I did." She was silent for a moment. "It . . . didn't go well."

I stood quietly, not wanting to risk saying anything.

"Your father and I were just very badly matched," my mother said. "I think I knew it right from the beginning, and if I didn't know it then, I did as soon as I saw that tiny little flat. I should have backed out right then, but . . . I didn't want to go back to my father and admit I was wrong.

"Well, it was a mistake. We fought all the time, about money, housework, family . . . everything. And then you were born and things were even worse. I was all on my own in that flat with nothing to do except take care of you and go more and more crazy. Your father was no help at all; most of the time he wasn't even there. It was the worst year of my life.

"And then I found out that my sister was dead.

"It came out of nowhere. She was engaged by then, to the second son of House Grasser. They'd set the wedding date. Then the next thing we know, there'd been a raid on one of our new Wells. Victoria wasn't even supposed to be there—her flight had been delayed and she'd been called over for some trivial thing that had nothing to do with the attack. The raiders blundered in, found more security than they'd been expecting, and started shooting. They weren't even aiming at her—it was a stray bullet. A stupid random accident."

I looked at my mother, not knowing what to say. She was staring down at the frozen pond. Above us, white cloud shrouded the sky.

"My father called me soon afterwards," my mother said after a minute of silence. "The last time we'd spoken, he'd as good as disowned me. But that was when he had another daughter left." She paused. "We talked around it, for a while. But eventually he just came out and made the offer."

My mother kept on talking. I didn't want to hear it, but I listened.

When she'd finished, I turned and ran away through the snow. I think she called after me, but I didn't look back.

FOR THE NEXT week I threw myself into my work. My goal was a mass-reduction sigl, and I spent the winter days out of the house from morning till night, combing the streets for every Matter

Well I could find. To make the sigl I wanted I needed to be better with Matter essentia, and so I spent every spare hour either searching for Wells or practising with the ones I found. It was hard, slow work, especially in the cold, but I drove myself to keep going. If I focused enough on drucraft that there was no room in my mind for anything else, I could stop remembering that conversation with my mother.

By the time I finally had a blueprint that I thought was good enough, I'd also found a good Matter Well to use it on; a temporary C-rank in an industrial area just downriver from the Thames Barrier. There was the slight problem that it wasn't open to the public, which I dealt with by climbing the fence in the middle of the night. That led to a little bit of excitement with a security guard, but with my invisibility sigl it wasn't too hard to stay hidden until he gave up and went away. Then I dodged guards and cameras until I made it to the Well, at which point I just sat down and shaped the sigl very, very slowly; since Matter essentia didn't seem to require any particular speed, I figured there was no reason I couldn't take my time. It was a long, strange night, kneeling in the dark and cold, watching a tiny bloodred gemstone grow millimetre by millimetre in my hand.

Dawn was breaking when I finally slipped out of the industrial area, shivering but with a new sigl clutched in my hand. I'd made my first ever Matter sigl. Now to test it.

"ALL RIGHT," I told Colin. "Going up to full power. You ready?"

Colin checked his phone. "Good to go!"

The Matter sigl hanging around my neck was pale red with a swirling pattern, set into a temporary ring. I sent essentia flowing into it and my stomach lurched upwards. It felt like the sudden lessening feeling you get in a high-speed lift, except that it didn't stop.

I'd tried out a new design with this one. One of the minor annoyances of my strength sigl was that it kept trying to activate on its own, forcing me to channel away the essentia thread every minute or two. It wasn't a big deal but it was irritating enough that I'd eventually tried mounting it on a small leather patch to put it just far enough from my body that it wouldn't self-activate. That had kind of worked, but it was a pretty kludgy solution and I really didn't want to have to do this with every continuous sigl I made, so after some experimentation I'd come up with the idea of shaping this one with a very thin inert layer that acted as a barrier. The idea was that it'd need you to give it a "push"—that is, actively channel—to get it started, but once started it should be able to pull in enough essentia to stay active on its own. So far, it seemed to be working.

I hopped from side to side, adjusting to my new weight. "Time it," I told Colin.

"Three . . . two . . . one . . ." Colin tapped his phone. "Go."

I took off and nearly went sprawling on the grass. We were out in the dark of Clapton Football Club, in the same spot where I'd been attacked back in September, and the ground was soaking wet where the snow had melted. My feet skidded, but I managed to catch my balance as I ran for the fence.

There were trees growing next to the fence, forming a natural climbing path, and I went scrambling up the gap, pulling myself up by handholds and branches. Once I reached the top I rested a foot on the barbed wire, glancing down into the pitch-black garden beyond, then turned and dropped back down the way I'd come. It was a twelve-foot fall, enough to send a tiny flash of fear through me as I fell, but I touched down lightly. "Time?" I said to Colin as I walked back across the grass.

"Twenty-one seconds."

I made a face. "Go again."

"Three . . . two . . . one . . . go!"

I flew across the grass and up the fence a second time. It was a weird sensation; you spend so much time with your body always weighing the same that there's something wrong about suddenly weighing a third of what you usually do. It wasn't a bad feeling, though; it felt a little bit like being a small child again. If I'd been in a better mood, I probably would have enjoyed it.

I dropped down and walked back a second time. "Time?"

"Seventeen seconds."

"Damn it."

"Dude, what are you upset about?" Colin protested. "You went up that fence like a freaking squirrel."

"That doesn't matter."

"So what does?"

"I'm trying to get fast enough that someone with a gun or a missile sigl *can't* shoot me in the back on my way up."

"So how fast's that?"

"I don't know. Go again."

This time, instead of climbing, I tried to pull myself up in lunges. It took a bit of getting used to—I had to fight against the urge to cling on. One part of my brain knew that I was light enough now to go hand-over-hand, but the rest of it took some convincing.

"Time?" I said after three more tries.

"Ten point five seconds."

I made a frustrated noise.

"Look, if we're running time trials, could we do it somewhere nicer?" Colin asked. "It's dark, it's wet, and it's frigging freezing."

"The next time someone with a bad attitude decides to ambush me, where do you think they're more likely to do it?" I asked. "Somewhere dark and crappy and freezing, or somewhere nice?"

Colin sighed.

"Go again."

I switched to starting with a running jump. The first couple of times didn't help because I was still getting used to my new trajectory. Once I realised just *how* much higher I could jump, I got a lot faster.

But still not faster than someone could pull the trigger on a gun.

"Time?" I asked.

"Four point seven five seconds."

I made a dissatisfied noise. "Go again."

"No."

"Go again."

"You just got *four times* faster at doing the same climb," Colin pointed out. "You're jumping like you're in the Olympics and you're making those parkour guys on YouTube look slow."

"So?"

"So why aren't you *happy* about this?" Colin said. It was hard to tell in the darkness, but he sounded exasperated. "You should be celebrating, not acting like something crawled up your arse and died."

I sighed. "Can we just keep going?"

"You keep going in this mood, you're going to scratch your arm on the barbed wire and get tetanus or something," Colin told me. "We're going to the pub and you're going to tell me what's got you so wound up."

COLIN IS PRETTY persistent when he sets his mind on something. An hour and a couple of drinks later, he finally got the story out of me.

"All right," Colin said. The Admiral Nelson felt warm and cosy after coming out of the freezing evening. The wood stains and mud splatters on my clothing didn't get a second glance from the other pub-goers; it's not a fancy sort of place. "So what did your mother tell you next?"

I traced a finger around the rim of my pint glass. "Back when your mum and dad were having trouble, how long did your mum leave for?"

"Varied," Colin said with a shrug. "Sometimes she'd be there, sometimes she'd be gone. Whenever we'd ask Dad how long it'd be this time, he'd always say he didn't know."

I nodded absently. The wooden table was covered with ring-shaped stains, and I adjusted the glass over one of them, trying to get it exactly centred. "You ever wonder if it was something to do with you?"

"I mean, you kind of have to, don't you?" Colin said. "But my mum and dad both promised us it wasn't. Just said they were 'having trouble' and that it wasn't our fault."

I nodded again.

"So?" Colin prompted when I didn't say anything.

"Turns out in my case it *was* something to do with me."

"Oof. How?"

"So when my granddad got in touch with my mum again, he made her an offer," I said. "'Come home, all is forgiven,' that kind of thing. She'd leave my dad and go back to living in the mansion."

"I mean, you kind of already knew that . . ."

"And she'd take over everything her sister had had," I went on. "Including marrying her sister's fiancé."

Colin blinked. "Wow. That's . . ."

"Cold?" I suggested.

"Messed up," Colin said. "Like getting a replacement goldfish."

"Yeah, well, having met him, I can completely believe it's something he'd do," I said. "But there was a problem. The whole point of these political marriages is to produce heirs. My mother having a child already—an *older* child—didn't fit that picture. So part of the deal was that she had to go no-contact. If she never saw me or talked to me, then everyone could pretend that her only kids were the ones with this Magnus guy."

Colin paused. "Oh."

"You know, all these years, I used to tell myself that my mother had left for a reason." I tilted my glass, rolling its edge around the ring on the table in a circle. "Well, turns out I was right. It's just that the reason was 'being offered loads and loads of money.'" I barked a short laugh. "I suppose I should have guessed. Seems to be all anyone in that world cares about." I paused. "Charles actually warned me, you know that? He told me that my mother wasn't interested and to take a hint. Seems I'm not much good at that."

"What are you going to do now?" Colin asked after a while.

"What am I supposed to do?" I said. "Far as I can see, nothing. Or nothing different. Keep working on my drucraft, keep looking for my dad." I couldn't help letting a little bitterness leak through. "Though maybe I should be having second thoughts about that one after how this turned out."

"You aren't going to talk to her?"

"She's sent me a few messages over the last week," I said. "I've been ignoring them." After how often she'd ignored *my* questions, there was some satisfaction in getting to do the same thing back.

"You want some advice?" Colin asked.

"Not really."

"Don't just ignore this and hope you'll eventually feel better," Colin told me. "Take it from me, it doesn't work."

"So what am I supposed to do?" I demanded. "I went to find out the truth about my family. Well, I found out, and now I'm regretting it. What do you want me to do, keep digging? Because that hasn't worked out great so far."

"You could ask someone else? I mean, there must be *someone* from your family you don't completely hate."

"All the Ashfords seem to care about when it comes to me is finding new and exciting ways to screw me over," I said. "Only one who hasn't yet is Calhoun, and for all I know that's only because he hasn't had the chance. I should probably quit this job of his before he does."

Colin threw up his hands in an *I give up* gesture and dropped the subject. We talked a bit more before calling it a night.

Only when I was on my way home, shivering in the icy wind, did it occur to me that I hadn't exactly been telling Colin the truth. There was *one* other person from House Ashford who hadn't done anything to screw me over. Even though Colin didn't know enough to tell the difference, and probably didn't care, the fact that I'd said that without its being true still bugged me enough that I had trouble going to sleep that night.

At last I decided to take Colin's advice.

IT HAD BEEN a few months since I'd visited the Ashford mansion. White clouds covered the sky, but the wind felt lukewarm after the freezing temperatures of the past week; a warm front had swept in to replace the cold one, and the last patches of snow had already melted into muddy patches on the grass.

The last couple of times I'd had to wait until evening for the person I was looking for. So it was a surprise when, only minutes after I'd arrived, the front door opened and closed and a small figure ran out through the front gate and across the road to confront me.

"Where have you been?" my sister demanded.

The girl standing in front of me was my half sister, younger than me by five years. I hardly knew anything about her—I'd met her for the first time in the spring and didn't find out that she was related to me until long after. In fact, I wouldn't even have known her name except that my mother had made a passing reference to "Tobias and Isadora." In the meantime, since I'd met her on a bridge, I'd decided to nickname her Bridget.

"What do you mean?" I asked.

"You haven't come by in months," Bridget said. She was small and lightly built, like me, with long brown hair and delicate features that were currently creased in a frown. Her long coat was only half-buttoned, as though she'd thrown it on in a hurry.

"The first time I came here your grandfather told me never to show my face again unless he explicitly told me to," I said. "And on that topic, can we move? I don't want to be in view of the windows."

"You could have come anyway," Bridget complained, but she started walking up the avenue. I fell into step beside her.

"Can I ask you something about our family?"

"Sure, I guess."

"I was told your father was originally meant to marry some-one else," I said. "Our aunt, Victoria Ashford. Then when she died, Charles made our mother an offer where she'd leave my dad and me and take over Victoria's place."

"Oh," Bridget said. "That."

"Is it true?"

Bridget thought for a second, then nodded. "Yeah, that's pretty much what happened."

"Did they tell you?"

"Well, they didn't put it exactly like that," Bridget admitted. "But you know how it is. No one ever tells you the truth to begin with. You just sort of get used to putting things together."

I wondered what it was like to grow up in a family where *no one ever tells you the truth to begin with.* My father had avoided some subjects, but as far as I knew he'd never lied to me. "And part of the deal was that my mother would stay away, so I wouldn't be a threat to the line of succession," I said. "Right?"

"They don't say it out loud. But . . . yeah."

Damn it. I looked away. I hadn't really expected it not to be true, but a small part of me had clung to the hope.

"What's wrong?" Bridget asked.

"Nothing."

"Oh," Bridget said. "Is it that you feel like you got traded away? Is that why you're upset?"

"Oh, no, that's completely fine," I said, not meeting Bridget's eyes. "Why would I have a problem with a little thing like that?"

"Um."

We walked a little way in silence.

"It doesn't mean she doesn't care about you," Bridget said.

"I'm pretty sure it *does*."

"You don't understand how it works in Noble Houses," Bridget said. "Inheritance and line of succession is really important. If you have to choose between what you want and what's good for the family, you have to pick the family."

"My mother said she was giving up on all that. That she was going to go off and do whatever she wanted."

"Really?"

"Yes."

Bridget frowned.

We'd come to the more heavily wooded part of the Bishop's Avenue, thickly lined with trees. In the spring and summer this whole area would be covered in green; now the white sky shone through the bare branches. "I mean, if she *really* didn't care about you, she wouldn't have talked to you about that stuff at all," Bridget said as we turned down a side street called Bishop's Grove. "Or at least she wouldn't have told you so much."

"She probably tells everyone that story."

"She didn't tell me."

I turned my head in surprise.

"The way Mummy and Daddy talk, you'd think they always wanted to get married," Bridget said. "At least when other people are around. When they're not . . ." She paused and shrugged. "Let's just say you might have got the better end of the deal."

I gave Bridget a sceptical look, but she was staring down at the pavement and I decided not to press it.

We kept walking in a friendly sort of silence until the street ended in a high hedge and a pair of wrought-iron gates. "All right, I've decided," Bridget said, turning to me. "I'll find out what happened back then, and why Mummy never got in touch. I'm pretty sure I know who to ask. But you have to do something for me."

"Do what?"

"You were there for the raid on our Well in Chancery Lane, right?"

"Yeah . . ."

"The next time you go on one, you have to bring me."

"Wait, what?"

"I got Calhoun to tell me the story," Bridget said. "I always hear about Well raids. I want to see one for real."

"Okay, slow down, slow down," I said. "No. This is a *terrible* idea. Didn't Calhoun tell you what happened during that raid? He nearly got shot."

"I know. It sounds exciting."

"Having men with guns shooting at you is a lot more than exciting! Aren't you scared of getting hurt?"

"I've got an invisibility sigl," Bridget pointed out.

"Okay, even if I was willing to agree—which I'm not—why do you think I'd even be going on a raid? The only reason I got caught up in that one was because things went wrong."

"Well, you *are* a raider."

"Says who?"

"Charles," Bridget said matter-of-factly. "I asked him about you and he said that if you weren't doing that kind of thing already, you would be soon."

Well, screw you too, old man. "Why would you even want something this crazy?"

"Do you know what I do every day?"

"Given that you're about sixteen . . . go to school?"

"King's School for Girls," Bridget said. "It's a drucraft school for the richest and most upper-class girls in the whole country. Do you know what it's like there?"

"Pretty comfortable, I'm guessing."

"*Unbelievably boring,*" Bridget said. "Back when I was a little girl, I couldn't wait to go. I thought it'd be like Hogwarts crossed with Malory Towers. Learning magic, exploring new things, going on adventures . . . I could never figure out why Lucella seemed to hate the place. And then I turned eleven, and I went there and found out. You know what we actually spend most of our time doing at King's? Nothing. And you know why? Because all the girls there are daughters of CEOs, or House heads, or baronesses or dukes or financiers or something. And the single biggest fear of every single teacher is that one of the girls is going to get hurt and their angry parents are going to sue the school for a billion pounds. And so we get supervised every single minute of every single day. There are cameras everywhere and there's always a teacher shepherding you from class to class. After I'd been there for a month, the idea of ever having an adventure in that place was like a joke. You can't even play sports without signing liability waivers and sitting through health-and-safety lectures and only using the official equipment that's all been freshly sterilised with antibacterial wipes. And if any of the girls so much as breaks a nail, everything stops while they're rushed off to the doctor's office where a medical drucrafter scans them. We learn drucraft, but we're never allowed to actually use it unless it's in a specially prepared area with, like, three adults watching. There are rules for everything, and if you ask to do anything different, the teacher will tell you no because they're afraid if something happens they'll get blamed. Most of the girls there are total screen addicts. There's nothing to do, so they spend all their time staring at their phones."

I looked at Bridget with raised eyebrows. She was frowning at the hedges, and her voice had the most emotion I'd ever heard from her. "Uncle Edward says it wasn't always that bad," Bridget continued. "And the boys' school is supposed to be a tiny bit better. But not much."

"If it's so boring, why do they stay?"

"A lot of them don't know any better, because they've grown up super sheltered and that's all they know how to do," Bridget said. "And most of the rest don't care because they're only there to make connections."

I wondered why Bridget was different. Maybe it had something to do with the Ashfords being a "new" family, rather than an established one. "So that's why you're so happy to talk to me," I said. "I'm a distraction from your boring life."

"Hey, don't act as though you haven't been getting anything," Bridget said. "I warned you what was coming back in the spring and I told you about our mother and our family. You owe me."

I made a face.

"So?" Bridget asked.

"I'll think about it," I said reluctantly. It still seemed like a terrible idea, but I had the feeling that I wasn't going to be able to persuade Bridget to change her mind.

"You'd better," Bridget said. "I'll go find out what you wanted, but I'm not telling you until you pay me back."

LATER THAT EVENING after dinner, as I was lying on my bed and stroking a sleeping Hobbes, my thoughts went back to Bridget and my family.

It occurred to me that I could end things with the Ashfords, right here. I'd wanted to find out the truth about my mother, and I'd found out. Charles seemed to have put a lid on the succession issue for the moment, and I hadn't seen Tobias and Lucella in months. The only ones I still had unfinished business with were Bridget and Calhoun, and I could just call them both and tell them that I was cancelling. They wouldn't be happy, but they'd live. Then from that point on, I could just forget that I'd ever had any connection to the Ashfords.

Was that what I really wanted?

Hobbes gave a sleepy meow and stretched against my hand. I scratched his neck, thinking. *Did* I want to cut myself off?

I remembered what Bridget had said about the girls at her school who'd been sent there to "make connections." A lot of times I'd heard people say that it wasn't what you knew, it was who you knew. Sometimes they'd say it angrily, sometimes with a shrug, but the message was the same. Being related to a rich noble family was the sort of thing a lot of people would give an arm and a leg for.

I thought about the advice Father Hawke had given me. "Honour thy father and mother." I didn't feel as though I owed the Ashfords much honour, or anything else for that matter. But they *were* my family, whether I liked it or not.

So far, my family connection to the Ashfords had brought me

nothing but trouble. But maybe that was because I hadn't been taking advantage of it. What if I started going to them instead of waiting for them to come to me?

Hobbes half opened one eye to give me a lazy look, then snuggled down and went to sleep. I gave him a last stroke, then switched out the light and lay in bed, thinking.

CHAPTER 9

THE EMAIL WAS in plain text, without a footer, and was from some provider I didn't recognise.

Hello,
We hear from various sources that you are a dependable locator. We would like to offer you the opportunity for work in the near future. The job will involve working with other locators to secure a Well.

You will be paid £1000 up front, plus an additional £4000 upon delivery of the Well's aurum to our representative.

Due to the sensitive and confidential nature of this operation the location of the Well and the time of the operation will be kept confidential until closer to the time. If you accept you will need to make yourself available to undertake the job at short notice. You will be informed by text message (see below) when the job is due, at which point you will travel to the location provided to meet with

our representative. Our representative will provide you
with the payment of £1000 in CASH and will provide full
details of the Well and make arrangements from there.

Please note that due to the sensitive nature of this job,
no further information can be provided. If you accept
please text the word "Accept" to the number at the
bottom of this email. You will be contacted when the job
is due.

Thank you for your time

The message ended with a phone number. There was no signature.

Frowning, I read it through again. It looked very different
from the emails I was used to seeing from Linford's, or from the
other drucraft companies that had been rejecting my applications. Some of the differences were obvious, like there not being a
footer full of legal disclaimers. Some were subtler, like the repeti-
tion of words, the capital letters for "CASH," and the missing full
stop at the end.

"This feels weird," I told Hobbes.

"Mraow," Hobbes responded. He'd come in this morning
looking rather fat and self-satisfied, with a couple of small downy
feathers sticking to his fur.

"How did they even get my email address?" I asked.

Hobbes was busy licking his paws and didn't answer. "It must
be connected to that Mr. Smith guy," I said with a frown. "Actually,
maybe it's from him . . . but then why wouldn't he sign his name?"

"Mraow?"

"Well, yeah, obviously he's being secretive. But why?"

Hobbes gave the cat equivalent of a shrug and went back to
washing his paws.

I thought about it a little, then phoned Colin. During the

daytime Colin's usually busy with lectures or practicals, but this time I got lucky and caught him. I told him the story.

"Sounds dodgy," Colin said after I'd finished.

"Yeah, I figured out *that* part."

I heard the rustle of papers from the other end. I'd put Colin on speaker and put the phone on my bedside table, while Hobbes watched with lazy curiosity. "Well, I can tell you one thing," Colin said. "Remember when you were asking me why this guy wasn't making you check whether the Wells you found were registered or not?"

"Yeah."

"I think it's because he didn't want to leave a data trail," Colin said. "If you were checking on this Well Registry of yours, then you'd need an account, and that could be traced. Sounds like they're trying to keep the whole thing off the books."

"Because it's a little bit illegal and they don't want to pay tax?" I asked. "Or because it's *really* illegal and they don't want to get arrested?"

"Look, I don't bloody know. Maybe if you'd teach me how to do this stuff . . ."

I sighed. "Go back to work."

"Mraow," Hobbes commented as I hung up.

"Yeah, I know. I can't expect him to know all this."

Hobbes went back to licking his paws, while I stared at the email on my screen, tapping my fingers on the laptop. Colin was right, this *did* sound dodgy. On the other hand, it was also really tempting. Five thousand pounds would stop me from having to worry about money for a long time. And even if the whole thing was a bust and I only got the advance, £1,000 would still help.

But the cautious part of me told me to stop and think. I really needed someone I could go to for advice, but I wasn't sure who. Approaching Maria about something like this was obviously out.

Father Hawke would listen, but this didn't really seem like his area of expertise. It *was* the area of expertise of the anons on the Back Alley, but from what I'd seen of how they reacted to newbies asking questions, most would just point and laugh and a handful would feed me deliberately wrong information because they'd think it was funny.

I needed someone who knew a lot about the business side of the drucraft world, who'd *also* be willing to tell me the truth.

An odd idea struck me. At first it sounded silly, but the more I thought about it, the more I started to change my mind. Wasn't this pretty much what I'd been thinking, just a few days ago?

I explained the idea to Hobbes. He didn't seem to think it was a terrible plan. I lay back on my bed and started figuring out what I was going to say.

I SHOWED UP at the Ashford mansion the next day. This time, instead of hiding, I walked up to the front gate and rang the bell. There was a short pause after I announced myself, then I was buzzed in.

The inside of the mansion was very quiet. Usually you can't get away from the noise of traffic in London, but the walls of the mansion must have been soundproofed or something because the carpeted halls were silent except for the ticking of a clock. An armsman in Ashford livery escorted me to an unmarked door on the first floor and sent me through.

Charles, the head of House Ashford, is a man in his sixties, trim and healthy-looking despite his age, with a neat square beard and sharp blue eyes. He wore an understated but elegant-looking suit and was sitting straight-backed in a carved chair, writing at a dark wooden desk that was bigger than my bed. He didn't look up or react as I walked in.

I was used to Charles's rudeness by now and didn't let it bother me. I looked around the study, examined the wall-mounted map, then when Charles still didn't talk, stepped over to the bookshelves.

"I seem to recall," Charles said without looking up, "that I told you not to return to this house without invitation."

"Yes," I said. The books were a mixture of old and new, with titles like *Being and Time* and *Principles of Management*. One caught my eye: *Matter Sigl Development 1918–1989*.

"At least your memory works," Charles said. "Now tell me what this urgent matter is that you felt the need to bring to my attention."

"I'd like some advice."

The scratch of Charles's pen continued. "I hope that's a joke."

"Not a joke. I'm in a weird situation with my job and I wanted to ask you about the corporate drucraft world."

"And I should do this because . . . ?"

I'd spent a while thinking about how to answer that question. I decided to start with the same line Bridget had used. "You owe me."

Charles set his pen down on the desk and finally looked up at me with his cold blue eyes. "Explain."

"I'm your grandson," I told Charles. "I know you don't like me, but you should still be helping me at least a *little* bit. As it is, the only times you've so much as lifted a finger have been right after your niece or her armsmen have committed some sort of violent crime against me, and even then all you seem to really care about is covering it up."

"What were you expecting?" Charles asked. "A display of parental love and generosity?"

"It'd be nice."

Charles studied me for a few seconds, tapping a finger on his desk. "Did your school teach you the history of the Second World War?"

"A bit."

"The three principal Allied powers in the Second World War were England, America, and Russia. The leader of Russia was Joseph Stalin. You at least recognise *his* name? Good. Stalin's eldest child was named Yakov, and he trained as an artillery officer. When war broke out, Stalin ensured that Yakov was sent to the front lines, where his regiment was overrun and surrounded. Yakov chose to surrender, which sent Stalin into a rage—he thought his son should have killed himself before letting himself be captured. So he had Yakov's wife thrown in prison."

I looked at Charles in disbelief.

"When the Germans discovered who Yakov's father was, they tried to trade him in a prisoner exchange for a German field marshal. Stalin told the Germans that his son wasn't worth a field marshal. The Germans tried to trade Yakov for a different prisoner instead, and Stalin refused that too. Yakov died in a concentration camp."

I stared at Charles.

"If you think that familial love and loyalty will protect you once you step into the realms of real power," Charles said, "then you are very definitely not ready for them. You wanted advice? There you go. Was there anything else?"

". . . Yes." Charles's story had shaken me a bit, but I'd come prepared. "Back in that raid in September, while Calhoun was busy fighting off those soldiers from Tyr, one of Lucella's armsmen tried to shoot him in the back. I stopped him."

Charles looked at me with a slight frown.

"Ask him if you don't believe me," I said.

"And you're hoping for gratitude?"

"No. Knowing you, you'd probably just make some snarky comment about how if I want gratitude I should get a dog."

A ghost of a smile flickered across Charles's face. "Then what's your point?"

"I didn't *have* to stop Calhoun from getting shot," I said. "Actually, it would have been a lot safer for me to keep my head down and let things play out on their own. So what do you think's going to happen the next time?"

"Are you expecting there to be a next time?"

"No, but I also wasn't expecting it to happen the *first* time. In case you haven't noticed, the members of your family kind of have a track record of dragging me into their problems. So it seems pretty likely to me that at some point in the future I'm going to find myself in some position where I'm going to have to choose between doing something that really helps your family, and something that really hurts it. If that happens . . . *when* that happens . . . it might be kind of in your interest for me to have a reason to like you, as opposed to hating your guts."

Charles studied me for a few seconds. The focus in his gaze was slightly unnerving, and I tried to keep my gaze steady.

"What exactly do you propose?" Charles asked.

"I want to learn about the drucraft world from an expert," I said. "I'm not asking for money or sigls. Just a couple of hours of your time every month or so."

Charles looked at me sardonically. "You think a couple of hours of my time is *less* valuable than money or sigls."

"I mean—"

"All right, all right," Charles said, waving me off. He glanced at a clock on his desk. "I have a meeting in an hour and seventeen minutes. I'll give you that long, but consider yourself on probation. Act stupid enough and I'll throw you out."

"I don't know anything about this stuff," I protested. "How am I supposed to know which questions are stupid ones?"

"Asking questions about a subject you know nothing about doesn't make you stupid, it makes you ignorant. One is tolerable, the other isn't." Charles looked at the clock. "You have one hour and sixteen minutes for me to do something about the latter. I suggest you use it."

"So, I used to work for a drucraft corporation called Linford's—"

"I know who Linford's are."

"—until they suspended me, when I got contacted by some mysterious guy who offered me locating work for lower fees but without a Well Registry account. Now I'm getting offered a bigger job for bigger pay." I summarised yesterday's email.

"Sit down and stop shifting your feet," Charles said. "Now what was your question?"

I sat. "Who are these people and what's the job?"

"You're doing shadow work for a major drucraft corporation, either Linford's or one of its affiliates," Charles said. "The job is a raid on a Well and your Mr. Smith is the handler. It may be a 'legitimate' raid where they intend to retain your services afterwards, a scam where the sole purpose is to cheat you, or anything in between."

I stared.

"Next question?" Charles asked.

"Wait, wait, wait," I said. "Did you know this was going on?"

"I'd never heard about it before you walked into this room."

"Then how—okay, first off, why do you think I'm working for Linford's?"

"You were contacted by your Mr. Smith right after you were suspended," Charles told me. "Who else would know you were a locator looking for work? Yes, it could be that some other drucraft corporation just happened to pick up your file at exactly the same time, but that's rather a coincidence, don't you think?"

"Why suspend me if they were just going to hire me again?"

"The business world is comprised of the surface economy, which is conducted openly, and the shadow economy, which is not," Charles said. "Corporations operate simultaneously in both. You would have been introduced to Linford's via one of its surface-economy members. Someone who sits in an office and wears a nice suit. Yes?"

I thought of Maria and nodded.

"For their surface-economy operations, corporations want conformists," Charles said. "Box tickers who won't rock the boat. For certain jobs, however, one does *not* want conformists. The fact that you were contacted so soon after your suspension suggests you were probably scouted in advance. Did you spend any time talking to Linford's employees who seemed unusually interested in you, or who asked if you were willing to do extra work?"

"Maria said something about some company effort to ramp up supply back in the autumn," I said slowly. "She asked if she could put my name forward." I looked at Charles. "Does she know about this?"

"Corporations typically keep a certain separation between their surface and shadow operations. If your Maria has been there for any length of time, she'll probably have a good idea of what's going on, but she'll know better than to talk about it."

"Why would they do this in this incredibly complicated way? Why go to all this trouble?"

Charles studied me for a couple of seconds. "Do you know what a raid is?"

"It's when someone takes essentia from a Well that isn't theirs."

"Specifically, they drain it in the form of unshaped aurum," Charles said. "What do you think happens to it afterwards?"

". . . I'm not sure."

"Use your brain," Charles said impatiently. "What are raiders going to do with aurum? They can't make it into sigls. They don't have the expertise and they don't have the infrastructure. So what are they going to do with it?"

"Sell it, I guess."

"Sell it to who?"

"Other criminals?"

"You think there's some nebulous, secret criminal organisation that buys up aurum and turns it into sigls?" Charles looked amused. "Even the corporations who spin that story don't actually believe it. Use your *brain*, Stephen. Who actually *uses* Well essentia?"

"Well . . . the people who make sigls. Houses and corporations."

Charles looked at me with raised eyebrows.

I looked back at him as I realised what he was saying. *Wait* . . .

"By total weight, something like twenty percent of the sigls sold in the Exchange are made from illegally acquired materials," Charles said. "Some estimates put it as high as thirty-five. Every single drucraft corporation has a back channel for acquiring aurum that 'fell off the back of a lorry,' and once it's been converted into a sigl it's almost impossible to trace it back to a specific Well."

"Maria made it sound like corps were the *targets* of raids."

"They are. They're just also the perpetrators. The trade in illegal aurum is far too profitable for any corporation to pass up, but since it's illegal, corporations can't acquire it officially. So they employ what are referred to as 'deniable assets.'" Charles paused. "That's you, in case you hadn't figured it out. Now, consider this. Do you have any evidence linking this Well job with your Mr. Smith?"

"No," I admitted.

"And do you have any evidence linking Mr. Smith to Linford's?"

I shook my head.

"So let's say the job goes wrong and you're picked up by the police," Charles said. "They offer to drop the charges in exchange for you fingering your employer. You point them at Linford's, but when they go to Linford's, the corporation will produce records showing that you were suspended months ago. Mr. Smith? Who's that? Anonymous emails? Nothing to do with us. Without any evidence, all the police will have left is you."

"So going on these things is a bad idea."

"No, getting *caught* is a bad idea. Oh, and if you turn down the job, you can expect to be blacklisted for cowardice."

I was silent.

"And now you know why they go to 'all this trouble,' as you put it," Charles said. He glanced at the clock. "Next."

I gathered my thoughts; a lot of what I'd believed about the drucraft world had just been turned upside down, but I didn't want to waste time. "Maria had me suspended from Linford's because my friends talked about drucraft too loudly. Why would they do that when they're a drucraft corporation?"

"Because success in corporations and other large organisations is typically determined by the ability to discern and follow political rules that no one ever explicitly states," Charles said. "That includes rules that appear arbitrary or pointless. Following them, particularly ones that are personally costly, signals to your superiors that you're willing to put the welfare of the organisation above your own. I doubt this came out of nowhere. If you think back over your interactions with Linford's, there were probably plenty of hints that you missed."

I remembered Maria nagging me about getting a finder's

stone. "So if I'd followed those rules, would I have been successful?"

"You'd have been kept on. You wouldn't have been promoted."

"Why not?"

"Because Britain currently produces far more university graduates than its economy actually needs. There aren't enough comfortable white-collar jobs to go around, meaning that the candidates for those jobs have to compete viciously. The successful ones spend every spare minute of their lives networking and staying late at the office and carefully grooming every aspect of their appearance and behaviour to be the very model of a good, obedient worker. You can't possibly compete."

"Even if I'm a better drucrafter than they are?"

"Actual hard skills are almost entirely irrelevant in the corporate hierarchy. Results matter at the top and at the bottom, but there isn't much accountability in the middle. So if you're hoping to get promoted for being a drucraft prodigy, I suggest you forget it."

I thought about what Charles had said. "You didn't answer my question from before."

"When?"

"When I asked you why Linford's would care about me talking about drucraft," I said. "Why do they care?"

Charles sighed. "I was hoping you wouldn't notice that. Do you *really* want to know?"

I nodded.

"Linford's suppresses public discussion of drucraft because our current ruling class suppresses public discussion of drucraft. And Linford's, like most corporations, aligns itself with the ruling class."

"Then why don't *they* want people talking about drucraft?"

"Because it doesn't fit in with the popular narrative. And while stronger and more confident regimes can afford a bit of inconsistency when it comes to popular narrative, ones that are under threat get a lot less tolerant of troublemakers kicking the tyres. Understand?"

"Um . . ."

"All right, let me break it down for you. Two central pillars of modern Western ideology are that humans should be equal and that things should get better. These principles became widely accepted during the twentieth century due to a general increase in material prosperity, which was built upon two things: the development and monetisation of scientific breakthroughs made between the seventeenth and nineteenth centuries, and a stable culture with a high level of social trust. Follow?"

"Yes . . ."

"Both of these things have now been eroding for some time. There haven't been any significant breakthroughs in drucraft, physics, or chemistry for more than a century, and in the absence of that, the most we've been able to do is exploit our natural resources more efficiently, whether by better drilling techniques for oil and ore, or better locating techniques for finding and draining Wells. However, we're now running up against natural limits—almost every country on Earth is running its Wells at capacity already, meaning there are no new areas to expand into, and at the same time, this country's social fabric has been weakening. Crime is higher, trust is lower, institutions are worse at doing their jobs. This means fewer resources to go around, which means greater unrest, which places our ruling class under pressure. And rulers under pressure are a lot quicker to crack down on dissent."

"What do you mean, under threat? All I did was talk to a friend and they're acting like I robbed a house!"

"Our ruling class couldn't care less if you rob a house. They care *very much* about you drawing public attention to the existence of drucraft."

"Why—?"

"Because one threatens their position and the other doesn't. Drucraft requires sigls, sigls require essentia, and essentia is a highly limited resource that, like all limited resources, is monopolised by the rich and powerful. The people who run this country may not be all that bright, but they're smart enough to realise that if they go to a populace who've been raised to believe things such as 'everyone should be equal' and 'things are supposed to get better,' and try to explain why the average members of said populace *aren't* receiving, say, lifesaving medical attention, while the rich and powerful *are*, then it's not going to go well for them. So instead their solution is to pretend the whole thing doesn't exist. Drucraft isn't real, and if it is real it doesn't work, and if it does work then it doesn't matter because you shouldn't be talking about it anyway. This message is developed and amplified by academia and the media to become orthodoxy." Charles glanced at the clock. "All right, that's long enough. Off with you."

I got to my feet, then paused and looked at the bookcase. "Can I borrow one of your books?"

"No. Source your own reading material."

I headed for the door.

"Oh, Stephen?"

I looked back.

Charles had taken out a folder and was skimming through the contents. "You remember what I said about corporations regarding people like you as deniable assets?"

"Yes."

"It's a very short step from 'deniable' to 'disposable.'" Charles glanced up at me from over the top of his papers, his sharp gaze resting on me for a moment. "Keep that in mind."

———

I GOT BACK home, let Hobbes inside, and lay down on my bed, staring up at the ceiling. Charles had given me a lot to think about.

Hobbes hopped up onto the bed and walked back and forth across my stomach, rubbing his face against my hand and purring. I scratched his neck, making him close his eyes contentedly, and thought about what to do. If Charles was right—and despite my dislike for the guy, he seemed to have a habit of being right—then this job could very well be a setup, really dangerous, or both.

On the other hand, it was also a way into what Charles had called shadow work. More and more I was getting the feeling that even if I could get reinstated at Linford's, I didn't have a future there. I was never going to get promoted and I was never going to make more money than I'd done already. Shadow work had a much higher risk, but with the chance of a much higher reward.

But how to make sure I actually *got* that reward?

I spent a while thinking, while Hobbes settled down on my pillow and went to sleep. Finally I took out my phone and texted Accept to the number on the email. Then I started to plan.

CHAPTER 10

THE MESSAGE ARRIVED on Christmas Eve.

I reached the meeting point just as the sun was setting. The air was cold but not freezing; ever since the snow had melted, it had been just cool enough to remind you that it was winter, without ever quite reaching the point where you saw frost on the pavements in the morning. The text had directed me to a plaza between King's Cross and St. Pancras stations, a little wedge of open space paved in stone.

I spotted my contact straightaway, a rough-looking man in a cheap suit. He was sitting on a bench underneath the bare branches of one of the plaza's forlorn-looking trees, and he was the only one there. Men and women passed by, their footsteps echoing on the grey stone, but none stopped to sit down.

I walked up to the bench and sat down.

"Name?" the man said.

"Stephen," I told him.

The man reached into his coat and took out an envelope. I tried to take it but he pulled it away. I gave him a questioning look.

The man held up the envelope to me. "Read."

I took a look. An address and some directions had been scribbled on the front. "Okay?"

"Address is where you'll meet the rest of your team," the man said. "Directions are to the Well. Once you've secured it, call the number on the back."

"Who's the rest of the team?"

"Not a clue, mate."

"Okay . . . who's going to be at the Well?"

"Don't ask me."

I frowned. "Then what *do* you know?"

"You go to the address on the envelope and meet the rest of your team," the man said. "You have any questions, call that number. But you do that after it's secured, all right?"

I gave him a dubious look.

"You taking the job or not?" the man said.

I could see from the thickness of the envelope that it was full. I took hold of it. The man didn't pull it away this time, but he didn't let go, either. "You taking the job?" the man repeated.

I nodded.

"You going to be at that address?"

"Yeah," I told him.

"Seven p.m.," the man told me. "Take the Metropolitan Line to Watford or Amersham. Station is Moor Park. Don't be late."

I nodded.

"You understand?"

"Yes," I said in annoyance.

The man finally let go of the envelope, then got up and walked away. I waited for him to disappear, then cracked open the envelope. It was filled with £20 notes that looked as though they'd just come out of a cash machine. I counted them quickly without taking them out. Fifty.

I stuffed the envelope into a pocket, then spoke over my shoulder. "You can come out now."

There was a pause, then a teenage girl in a long winter coat stepped out from behind one of the trees. Someone paying attention might have noticed that the tree shouldn't have been big enough to hide her. Someone paying *really* close attention might have noticed that she'd never stepped behind the tree in the first place.

"How'd you know I was there?" Bridget asked.

"Because it's you," I told Bridget. As soon as I'd told her the time and place I'd known she wouldn't be able to resist sticking her nose in. "Plus I felt the essentia from your sigl."

"You can actually sense that?" Bridget asked. She looked genuinely impressed. "Even Calhoun can't do that."

"You and Calhoun grew up on top of one of the strongest Wells in London. I'm surprised you can sense anything."

"So is this how people usually get hired for raids?" Bridget asked.

"Sometimes," I said, pulling out my phone. I didn't want to admit to Bridget that I knew hardly any more about this stuff than she did. "Now give me a sec."

Bridget peered over my shoulder. "What are you doing?"

"Looking up directions," I told her. Just as the guy had said, Moor Park was way out northwest on the Metropolitan Line, right on the edge of London. I didn't know the area at all. "Damn, this is going to be a long trip."

"Why not just drive?"

"Because I don't have a car."

"I do."

"You aren't even old enough to have a licence."

"That's what my driver's for," Bridget said, pointing a thumb back over her shoulder. "Do you want me to call him?"

I stared at her.

"What?" Bridget asked.

"Your family," I told her, "is *really* annoying."

"What did I do?"

I shook my head and got up. "I'll meet you there," I told her over my shoulder as I walked towards the station.

BY THE TIME I reached Moor Park it was pitch dark. I walked away from the station, taking occasional glances at my phone to make sure I was going the right way. The city was quieter out here; I could see fields and forests on the satellite map, and the roads had few cars. It made me a little uncomfortable; I've spent pretty much my whole life in or close to Central London, and to me the streets here felt unnaturally still. Lights glowed from the windows, making me think of families inside sitting down to their Christmas Eve dinners.

I met Bridget a couple of streets away from our destination; she was waiting under a streetlight, the yellow light outlining her in a harsh neon glare. She wasn't invisible this time. The thing next to her was.

"You took your time," Bridget said cheerfully as I walked up.

"Not all of us have chauffeurs," I told Bridget. She had an active Light sigl on one finger, but the invisibility field it was projecting wasn't centred on her. "Speaking of which, you didn't tell him to park here, right?"

"He's a few streets over."

"What did you tell him?"

"That I'm visiting a friend."

"Your parents?"

"I told Papa the same thing. And Mummy's in Germany."

"They don't expect you to stay in for Christmas Eve?"

"Why would they?"

I shook my head. Ever since I could remember, my dad had always been around for Christmas. Sometimes we'd visit my aunt and uncle, sometimes we'd just play cards at the dinner table, but we'd always be together. I really couldn't understand Bridget's family. "All right. Time for some ground rules."

"You'd better not be trying to send me home," Bridget said with a frown.

"I'm not, but get something clear: this is *really* dangerous. The only reason I'm letting you come is because I owe you a favour."

"Why?"

"What do you mean, 'why?'"

"Well, that doesn't stop you, does it?" Bridget said. "I know I'm not going to be heir, but I don't see why I should have to stay at home while everyone else gets to do things."

"This isn't about you getting to do things," I said in exasperation. "Look, you can come along, but only if you do exactly as you're told."

Bridget didn't answer.

"You have to *do what I tell you*. Okay?"

Bridget shrugged.

"What does that mean?"

"If I feel like it."

I stared at Bridget for a second, then shook my head. "Go home."

"What?"

"*Go home.*" I pointed eastwards. "You don't belong here."

"I'm better at drucraft than you are!" Bridget said indignantly.

"I don't need someone who's good at drucraft. I need someone I can count on to do what I tell them."

"Why are you being so mean about this?" Bridget demanded. "Everyone always wants to shut me out of everything."

I looked skywards, fighting the temptation to just activate my invisibility sigl and walk off. For all I knew, this whole raid could be some sort of trap. The last thing I needed was having to worry about some sheltered rich girl who thought this whole thing was a game.

But I didn't. Annoying as Bridget was being, I did feel some sympathy for her. I knew what it was like to be left behind and kept in the dark. "Okay," I began. "You know how when you're a kid, and your dad or some other guy takes you out to help with a job, the first thing they drill into your head is to pay attention and do exactly as you're told?"

"No."

"What?"

"Papa never took me out to help on jobs. Neither did anyone else."

"Uh," I said. "Okay, how about when you join a team? Like a security shift, or for football? You know how to begin with, they expect you to shut up and pay attention until you know everything works . . . ?"

I trailed off. Bridget was looking at me in blank incomprehension.

"You have no idea what I'm talking about, do you?" I said.

"How would I?" Bridget asked. "I've never done any of this stuff."

I paused, briefly stumped. I tried to think of some sort of experience we could have had in common. "All right. Have you ever read any books or watched any movies where the sheltered princess runs away from home?"

"Sure."

"You remember what happens in those stories?"

"The princess gets sick of everyone trying to restrict her and tell her what to do all the time," Bridget said. "So she runs away and has adventures and no one takes her seriously to begin with, but eventually they learn to respect her and she beats up all the bad guys and saves the day."

I stared at Bridget.

"What?" Bridget asked.

"Oh my God," I told her. "No wonder you're so annoying." Come to think of it, that *is* how all those Disney movies go, isn't it?

Bridget gave me an indignant look.

"Look, you want to know what *really* happens when a rich girl runs away from her family?" I asked. "She goes off and has some adventures and eventually comes home. And the guys who were *with* her get all the blame. She goes back to her nice, comfortable life, while they get fired or thrown in prison."

"That *might* not happen," Bridget said defensively.

"You just told me a few days ago that no one at your school will let you do anything because they're afraid they'll get blamed if anything goes wrong," I told her. "Did it ever occur to you that maybe they're *right*? The way they see it, they're just trying to get through the day and go home to their families without having some rich arsehole ruin their lives because his daughter got her knee scraped. Honestly, sounds to me like they're just being smart."

"Then what am I supposed to do?"

"It's *not about you*," I told her. "That's what you don't seem to get. This isn't some sort of theme park where you go on the Raider Experience. I don't know who I'm going to find once I get to the meeting point for this raid, but I'm willing to bet every last one of them is doing this for a living. And when you're doing something for a living, the last guy you want at your back is someone who's only there because he's bored."

"I'm not a guy."

"Doesn't make it any better."

We stood there on the darkened street looking at each other for a few seconds. "Last chance," I said. "Are you going to do as you're told?"

"Fine," Bridget said.

She didn't sound very enthusiastic, but it was something. "Okay," I said. "Stay out of sight. And that goes double for your bodyguard."

Bridget gave me a look of simulated innocence. "What?"

"You know 'what,'" I told her. That invisible presence next to her had stayed quiet throughout our conversation, shifting slightly from side to side. I had a pretty good idea of what it was, and there was a reason I'd been staying away from it. I hoped Bridget had it under control. "All right, let's go."

A FEW MINUTES' walk brought us to the meeting point. There was a small crescent side road, cast in shadow except for the orange glow of a streetlight.

"This is where we split up," I told Bridget, halting. "Stay unseen from now on."

"Until when?"

"Until I tell you otherwise."

Bridget didn't answer. I looked at her.

"What?" Bridget asked.

"*Now,*" I told her.

Bridget rolled her eyes and faded from sight. There wasn't a telltale warp in the air as there was when I used my invisibility sigl; she just seemed to fade away to nothing. All I could see was a very faint distortion, and even then I had to move my head from side to side to be sure. I couldn't help but feel a flicker of envy; for all the work I'd put into it, my sigl wasn't even close to a match for Bridget's.

I heard the faint sound of retreating footsteps, accompanied by the click of claws. I took a deep breath, touching the sigl rings on my fingers for reassurance, then turned and headed for the streetlight.

As I drew close a man stepped out into the neon glow. He was wearing white brand-name trainers, a tracksuit striped in various shades of blue, and several thick gold-coloured rings. His hair was cut in a mullet. "Hey, hey!" he called in a Polish accent. "You our number eight?"

"Uh," I said. "I think so?"

"Took your time about it, hey?" He beckoned.

I walked forward cautiously, giving the guy a sidelong look. He was maybe thirty or forty, bouncy and running to fat. As I drew closer, I got a whiff of aftershave that made me wrinkle my nose. Was I in the right place?

But as I got into the shadows of the crescent and my eyes adjusted, I saw the shapes of a half a dozen or so other men concealed in the trees. They were hanging back and watching.

"You in the right place, little boy?" Mr. Mullet asked. He was grinning at me in a way that wasn't entirely friendly.

"I was wondering that when I saw you," I told him.

"Just talking, just talking!"

One of the men from the shadows called out something in a language I didn't recognise. The mullet guy answered, the one in the shadows said something again, and they both laughed.

I stood there silently.

Mullet turned back with a grin. "He asked if the corps are sending kids now."

"I'm not a kid," I said shortly. I'd had a feeling this might happen. I might be twenty-one, but I look like an overly pretty teenager, and while that can work in my favour some of the time, it's really damn annoying when I'm trying to get people to take me seriously.

"Oh?" Mullet gave me a speculative look. "Maybe you show us what you can do, hey?"

"Get lost," I told him.

A mischievous look came into Mullet's eye. "So what's the story? Maybe you're the kid of one of the corp men, hey? Here to keep an eye on us for your dad?"

"No!" I said quickly, but the damage had been done. Mullet stepped back into the shadows, and now a couple of the men behind him were muttering in their native language, shooting me suspicious looks. I swore silently; now they were going to think I was here to spy on them. *Great.*

Then a voice called out to me from the other side. "Hey!"

I looked over; a couple of figures were standing in the shadows, but I couldn't make out their faces. With a shrug I walked closer. Maybe someone was willing to trust me after all . . .

Then as I drew near and my eyes adjusted to the darkness I realised there was something familiar about the two figures. Both were heavyset, with dark hair and Eastern European looks. It was hard to make out their faces in the shadows, but I had the feeling I'd seen them before.

"Told you locating was a shit job," the front man said.

"Pa—it's you!" I said with a grin, remembering at the last second not to say his name. Pavel probably wouldn't appreciate me shouting it out. From over Pavel's shoulder, Anton gave me an unsmiling nod.

Pavel and Anton were a pair of Romanian locators I'd met earlier in the year. They'd been working for Linford's, just like me, and it had been thanks to studying their finder's stones that I'd figured out how to make continuous sigls. "You still working for Linford's?" I asked.

We spent a couple of minutes catching up; apparently the answer to my question was yes, but there were some complications that Pavel wasn't keen on discussing. Anton stayed silent; he'd always been the less friendly of the two. Actually, to be honest, I wasn't really friends with either of them, but it was a step up from being surrounded by strangers.

"So who's the mullet?" I asked.

"The what?" Pavel asked.

I nodded. "Him."

"You mean Bou?" Pavel said. He pronounced it "bow," as in "bow and arrow."

"That's his name?"

Both Pavel and Anton laughed.

"Is he supposed to be in charge?" I asked. "The boss?"

Anton snorted and said something in Romanian. "Just a big mouth," Pavel translated.

"So who decides when we start?" I asked. "Is there a signal, or . . . ?"

"Eh."

I looked around. There were four others besides Pavel and Anton, and as they moved around and spoke, I began to get an impression of them. There was Bou—I was pretty sure that I shouldn't be calling him that, but it was the only name I had—and the other Pole he'd been speaking to. The next two men were ones I didn't recognise, and when I asked Pavel and Anton who they were, they just shrugged. Both looked like typical locators, tough and grizzled, with the wary look of those who are used to getting a bad deal out of life.

No one was paying me much attention, but I was still feeling uneasy. No one seemed to be in charge or giving orders; the men were divided into pairs and the pairs weren't mixing. The men didn't seem to trust each other or like each other. In fact, if the way I'd been recruited was any guide, it was a good bet that they didn't even know each other.

It didn't feel like a team that you could trust to watch your back. Actually, it didn't feel like a team at all—just a bunch of guys who were only here because someone was paying them. If something went wrong, I was pretty sure they'd cut and run.

Then a movement in the shadows caught my eye. Squinting into the darkness, I realised that there weren't six other people here; there were seven. It was just that the last one had been staying so still and quiet that I hadn't noticed them.

I glanced at Anton and Pavel, but they were talking quietly in Romanian. With a shrug, I walked over to our mysterious eighth member.

I was about halfway there when I noticed two things. First, unlike the others, this person was using a sigl; there was a weak Life effect emanating from their head. Second, it was one I'd seen before.

There was a faint sigh from the darkness and I heard a familiar voice. "I *knew* you'd come over."

"Nice to see you too," I told her.

The girl in front of me was Ivy, the only female locator I'd run into since I started the job. I wasn't sure what to make of Ivy. She was a locator, but she didn't use a finder's stone. She worked in London, but she didn't have a London accent. She looked African, but worked for a Japanese company and spoke Japanese. Apart from her name, all she'd told me about herself was her phone number, and if she hadn't had to split a payment with me, I don't think she'd even have given me that. On the other hand, she had actually *sent* that payment, and when the two of us had got into a fight with a gang of raiders, she'd stood her ground. So out of all the people here, she was the only one I more or less trusted. Given what we were here to do, that was probably more important than her unfriendliness.

"So you *are* a raider," Ivy said. She was hanging back too far out of the light for me to see her expression, but she sounded disapproving.

Okay, so the unfriendliness might get a bit annoying. "Not exactly," I said.

"What do you call this, then?"

"It's just a job."

Ivy shrugged and looked away. Something about the way she did it nettled me. "Hey," I told her. "Ever heard the saying 'people in glass houses shouldn't throw stones'?"

"And?"

"You're here too."

"It's a legal raid."

"What?"

"The Well's owned illegally," Ivy said. "The guy who owns it was supposed to sell it but he didn't."

"Which guy?"

"Some rich Russian. Anyway, the police aren't going to come."

"If the guy owns the place illegally, why don't they just send in the bailiffs?"

"What's a bailiff?"

"The guys who show up if you don't pay your rent."

"Are you talking from experience here?"

"What's that got to do with it?"

We stood in silence for a couple of seconds. Bou was saying something to the other members of the team.

"Is it just me, or is this job a bit weird?" I asked Ivy.

"Why?"

"Well, how much are you getting paid?"

"None of your business."

"Will you quit it?" I asked, exasperated. Ivy's attitude of default suspicion could get *really* annoying. "I'm being offered five K. You?"

Ivy was silent for a second. "Four," she admitted after a moment.

"Okay, so split the difference, that's eight times four and a half. Thirty-six thousand pounds." I gestured to the people around us. "Shouldn't getting the bailiffs in be cheaper than that?"

"Are you always this nervous?"

"I'm not nervous."

"I mean, last time you were talking about how you thought I might be dangerous," Ivy said. "This time you're worrying about money."

"It's not about the money," I said in irritation.

"If you say so."

I bit back a comment.

I heard raised voices; looking around, I saw the other men were starting to move. Anton caught my eye and beckoned me over. I approached and Ivy followed.

"We're going," Anton told me once we were close enough.

"Why now?" I asked.

Anton shrugged and he and Pavel walked on. Everyone else was already gone. Ivy and I were the only ones left.

I took a last look back at where Bridget was waiting in the darkness and followed the others, Ivy pacing me to one side.

THE CRESCENT LED into a narrow access road bordered by hedges and trees, and as we kept going the sounds of traffic behind us faded away. We were in that fuzzy edge of London that's neither city nor country, where if you pick a direction and start walking, you can find yourself either in residential streets or in woods and fields. This seemed to be a woods-and-fields part.

The road ended in a gate, which the men at the front climbed over without slowing down. Pavel and Anton did the same with some muffled curses. I followed more easily, then waited for Ivy.

The lights stopped at the gate; beyond was a gravel drive that led into darkness. Pavel and Anton were heading on, fading into the shadows, and the others were already out of sight.

I hesitated.

Ivy walked past, giving me a glance that said, *Are you coming or not?* I followed slowly, with frequent glances behind. I knew I was probably just reinforcing Ivy's belief that I was a coward, but I really didn't like this. My mind kept going back to the raid I'd witnessed in September. Those soldiers had arrived in a police van, they'd been equipped with guns and sigls and thick armour, and they'd been under the command of a squad leader. The whole operation had been organised and disciplined, and even when Calhoun had fought them off, they'd still withdrawn in good order.

This raid was the exact opposite in every way. We'd arrived scattered, on public transport, with only the gear we'd brought from home. There was no one in charge and no contingency plan if things went wrong. Worst of all, I still had no good idea of what we were getting into. I didn't know what I'd been expecting, but it had been something more impressive than this.

Was Linford's just incompetent? Or was there something else going on?

I picked up my pace and hurried to catch up with Ivy. We walked the rest of the way in silence.

CHAPTER 11

THE GRAVEL DRIVE came to an end, opening out into darkness. Beyond I could see the lights of a house, isolated and lonely. All around were trees and fields.

"Hey," Bou said. "What took so long? Let's go!"

"Go where?" I asked. There was nothing in sight but for the lights of the house.

Pavel gestured at the house. "Security."

"So should we scout it?" I asked.

I got a couple of blank looks.

"Look around," I explained. "Check for cameras, alarms . . ."

"Hey, hey," Bou said with a laugh. "The little company prince thinks he's a soldier."

"I'm not a prince and I already *said* I'm not from the company."

"Have to go in anyway," Pavel said.

"Don't be so scared, hey?" Bou said, throwing his arm around me; given how much bigger he was than me, it nearly knocked me over. "Listen to your *kolega*. Russians are all cowards, hey? You go in strong, they run away."

I gave Bou an annoyed look; I hadn't known any Russians growing up, but my dad had told me about the Russian guys he'd run into on his security jobs, and "all cowards" was definitely not how he'd described them. But Bou just gave me a clap on the back that made me stagger. "I've done this before, okay? You just stick close to me. I know what I'm doing." He started towards the house and the other men followed.

I looked at Ivy. "Do *you* think this is a good idea?"

Ivy made an equivocal sort of gesture. "I guess he knows what he's doing."

"He's a pain in the arse," I muttered, rubbing my shoulder.

"You're just annoyed because he called you 'little prince.'"

I glared at Ivy, but she looked away with a slight smile. We followed the others.

The house wasn't big, and as we drew closer, I became sure it didn't contain a Well. But as I focused, I started to think that I could sense something off to the right, at the very edge of my range. "Do you feel that?" I asked Ivy.

"Feel what?"

I pointed off into the darkness. "I think the Well's—"

There was a crash from up ahead. Light spilled out into the night as the front door of the house was kicked open; the shadows of men muscled their way through. Ivy and I shared a look and started to run.

We reached the door seconds after the others; from inside I could hear bumps and shouts, followed suddenly by silence. I hesitated a moment and entered, blinking in the electric light. It looked like an old groundskeeper's cottage, cramped and run-down. There was a small hallway, an open door . . .

. . . and as I walked through I saw that everything was already over. The room within was a kitchen, and it had been occupied by exactly one person. He must have been sitting in a chair scrolling on his phone, or watching the football match that was still blaring away on the TV, and right now he was backed up against the wall, surrounded by the guys who'd gone in with Bou. He was middle-aged and a bit fat, and he had his hands up with a frightened expression.

"You stay quiet, you don't get hurt," Bou was saying. "You understand?"

The man nodded quickly.

"There any more?" someone asked.

"Just him."

I blinked. *That was it?*

"Where's the Well?" Bou asked the man.

The man gave him a blank look.

"Listen, you don't want to give us any trouble, hey?" Bou said. "You better—"

"It's off in the woods," I broke in. I didn't really want to sit around and watch Bou browbeat some minimum-wage security guard.

"Ohh," Bou said, turning his grin on me. "Little prince knows more than the rest of us?"

"I don't know where it is, just the direction," I said shortly. "Look, leave this guy alone and I'll find it for you. Okay?" I turned and walked out without waiting for an answer.

"Hey," Bou called after me. "You put in a good word for me with your boss, you hear?"

THE WELL WASN'T hard to find. It was on the other side of the big field next to the groundskeeper's cottage, hidden in a small copse. Even using finder's stones, the others could have tracked it down quickly.

I circled the copse twice and found nothing. If there were any traps or cameras or alarms, I couldn't see them, but by this point I was pretty sure there was nothing to find. This wasn't some high-security area; it was just a big field with a fence.

Maybe the Well didn't rate anything better? It was a Light Well, the most common type in the UK, and studying it, I put its strength at a high C+, maybe the very lower end of B. It would have earned me a finder's fee of nearly £20,000 had it been unclaimed and had I still been registered at Linford's, neither of which was currently true. Its real value would be much more—from what I remembered, high C / low B sigls sold on the Exchange for hundreds of thousands of pounds. Shouldn't this grade of Well be a bit better protected?

A whisper of movement from behind made me snap my head around, but as I squinted into the darkness I recognised the telltale green glow of Life essentia. "What is it?" I called softly.

"Bou's called in the Well," Ivy told me.

Ivy moved up to my side and we both studied the Well for a minute. "Does this feel too easy to you?" I asked.

"Why?"

"Look how little security there is," I said, gesturing. "We practically walked in."

"It's only B-rank Wells and up that get good security."

"This is on the edge of B."

"Maybe they're just cheap?"

The worry at the back of my mind wasn't going away. I closed my eyes and reached out with my senses, searching for some sort of hint or clue.

It was only because I was concentrating that I noticed the sound. It was very soft, a low humming or buzzing off to the south. I opened my eyes and looked, searching through the darkness. "Ivy? Can you see anything?"

Ivy turned to look in the direction of my finger. "No," she said after a pause. "I don't . . . wait. There's something in the air. Over the trees, near the cottage. It's going away, behind the trees . . . It's gone."

That hum had sounded like motors. "A drone?"

"I think so," Ivy said. I could hear the frown in her voice. "I wonder what it was doing."

It was the last push that tipped me over the edge. Between Charles's warning, the way Bou was acting, and the lack of security, my unease about this job had been growing for a while, but the glimpse of that drone was what finally made it crystallise. I still didn't know what was going on or was going to happen, but all my instincts were sending me a warning. "We should get out of here," I told Ivy.

Ivy just looked at me.

"I know you think I'm just scared," I said, "but there is a *reason* I'm acting like this. I think something bad's coming."

I heard Ivy sigh. "Nothing bad's coming."

"Oh, for—" I fought to hold back my frustration. This girl was *so* freaking annoying. "How can you be so suspicious about me, but so confident about this?"

"Because I *asked* about this," Ivy said. "This raid's safe. They told me there wouldn't be heavy security or any police."

"Who told you?"

"My company."

"And you trust them?"

"More than I trust you."

We stared at each other in the darkness.

"Okay," I said when it was clear Ivy wasn't going to speak. "I'm going to go back to the entrance and keep a lookout. I need you to go scout the perimeter of this place. Find out if there are any other ways in, and more importantly, if there are any other ways *out*."

"That'll take ages," Ivy objected. "And it's freezing."

"You can go back to the cottage to warm up afterwards."

"I could go back there to warm up right now."

"Look," I said. "Think of it this way. If I'm wrong, then nothing we do in the next couple of hours is going to matter very much. Worst that can happen is that we both get cold and bored. But if I'm *right*, then the worst that can happen is something a hell of a lot more serious. And if it does, then we're both going to be very, very glad we didn't go back and sit in that cottage and wait for someone to tell us what to do." I looked at Ivy. "Wouldn't you rather be prepared, just in case?"

Ivy gave me a long, sceptical look, then sighed. "I can't believe that when I first met you I thought you were some sort of dangerous raider." She shook her head. "Fine, whatever. Let's get this over with."

Ivy disappeared into the shadows, her movements quick and confident despite the darkness. I turned and headed back towards the way we'd come in.

THE NOISE AROUND me dropped off as I moved through the night. The only lights were the fuzzy glow of the London skyline, the only sounds that of distant traffic and the whisper of the wind.

Oddly enough, now that I was alone in the dark I felt a lot more relaxed. I was on my own and potentially in danger, with very little prospect of help. But "little prospect of help" also meant that I didn't have to worry about having to help anyone else. It's not that I'm the antisocial type—I've never had trouble getting on with people and I was always quick to make friends at school. But ever since I'd stepped into the drucraft world, I'd felt as though the stakes in my life had become a lot higher. Mistakes *mattered* now, and if I was going to be doing jobs like this, I didn't want the guy watching my back to be someone like my ex-friend Gabriel.

I didn't actually think any of the other men on my raiding team were as bad as Gabriel, but they hadn't impressed me much, either. They were too sloppy and too loud, and the whole time I'd been following them I'd been on edge, wondering if they were about to blunder into an ambush. Out here in the darkness and the quiet, the only way I could get ambushed would be if I did the blundering, and that suited me just fine. I trusted my own abilities; I didn't trust theirs.

As I walked I ran through the inventory of the sigls I was carrying. Slam and flash sigls on my left hand; mending, light, and haywire on my right. Strength and lightfoot sigls on the cord around my neck, diffraction sigl at my belt. What was I forgetting? Oh, right, vision sigl. I took out the headband and fastened it around my forehead. My invisibility's the most powerful spell I have, but I *did* wish I had a way of using it that didn't make me look like a pound-shop ninja.

Different sigls have to be worn in different places. Enhancement types, like my strength and lightfoot sigls, work best on the torso, so they can spread evenly to every part of the body. The vision sigl obviously had to be next to my eyes. Weapon sigls work best on the hands, where you can extend them away from the body.

It was a lot to remember, and I was actually getting to the point with my sigls where I was having trouble keeping track of them all. Of course I knew where they *were*, but there's a difference between knowing where something is and being so familiar with it that you use it instinctively and automatically, like an extension of your own body. And that's how familiar you need to be to use something effectively in a fight. If I was going to keep adding to my loadout, I might have to start leaving some of my existing sigls at home to make room.

The orange glow of streetlights began to show through the trees, and a minute later I was back at the front gate. Up ahead was the access road. I started searching for a good lookout post, and as I did I took out my phone and called Bridget.

Bridget answered on the second ring. "Can I come and find you yet?"

"No."

"But I'm *bored*."

"If the worst thing that happens to you tonight is getting bored, you can count yourself lucky," I told Bridget curtly. "I've got a job for you. Is your invisibility sigl running?"

"Yes . . ."

"Stay near that crescent where I met the other raiders. I want you to watch for anyone going up the access road."

"Why, who's coming?"

Hiding in the hedges wasn't going to work. It was too close to the road, with no way out if things went wrong. "If I knew that, I wouldn't need you to keep a lookout."

"This sounds boring," Bridget complained.

"I'm going to be doing exactly the same thing as you, just somewhere different," I told her. "You wanted to see what a raid was like; well, this is it. If it's not exciting enough for you, feel free to have your chauffeur drive you home."

Bridget hung up in a huff. I stuck my phone in my pocket and looked around. The access road was brightly lit by the streetlights, but the hedges weren't that tall. If I could just find somewhere high enough . . .

Aha. Off to one side was what looked like an old barn. I circled it, settled on a drainpipe as the best means of roof access, then channelled essentia through my lightfoot sigl and climbed up.

The roof was covered in grey-black slates that creaked alarmingly under my hands and feet, but with my sigl I weighed no more than a medium-sized child, and I was able to make it up to the peak of the roof and take hold of the chimney.

I stopped and looked around. This was much better. I could make out the yellow bloom of the access road, the gravel drive fading into darkness, and even the dim glow of the windows of the cottage, just barely visible through the trees. I wondered if Ivy was back yet.

I took out my phone and dialled her number.

Ivy took a long time to answer, and when she did she sounded in an even worse mood than Bridget. "What?"

"How's it going?"

"I'm freezing, there's mud all over my clothes, and my feet are wet," Ivy complained. "There was a giant puddle in the corner of the field. Why is there a giant puddle in the corner of the field?"

"What did you find?"

"Oh, thanks for the sympathy. Nothing, just so you know. There's fences and hedges all around. I might as well not have bothered."

"Guess that means we don't have to worry about someone sneaking up behind us," I said. I didn't mention that no other way for people to get in also meant no other way for us to get out.

"Yeah, that was not worth getting soaked and frozen to check. I'm going back to the cottage where it's warm."

"Can you tell the others to be ready to move?"

"Move where?"

"Somewhere that's not here."

"*You* tell them."

"Fine. You come to me, climb up onto the roof and take over, and I'll give them the message instead."

"Why are you on a roof?"

"It was the only place with a view of the gate."

"You are the *weirdest* boy I have ever met," Ivy said with a sigh. "You realise there's zero chance they'll listen to me, right?"

"Why wouldn't they?"

"Because they're getting paid four K each," Ivy told me. "Five, according to you. You really think they're going to walk away from that because a girl like me tells them to?"

"Well . . ." I thought for a moment. "Yes."

"You're an idiot," Ivy said with finality.

"Just tell them, all right?"

Ivy hung up.

I put the phone away, suddenly less certain of myself. Now that I thought about it, Ivy was probably right. For the men on this raid, £4,000 was a lot of money; they weren't going to leave that on the table without a very good reason.

Besides, what did I really have to go on? Suspicions and warnings. Maybe Ivy was right and I was just being paranoid . . .

. . . *no.* Now that I was alone, out here in the darkness and the quiet, I was surer than ever that I was in danger.

I shut off the essentia flow to my sigls and settled down to wait.

Time passed. A cold wind blew across the treetops, cutting through my fleece and clothing and making me shiver. I tried to use the chimney for shelter, but it didn't really help.

My phone rang. I took it out, bracing myself for another argument with Ivy, but as I looked at the screen I saw that it was Bridget. "Hello?"

"Someone's coming," Bridget told me.

"Who?"

"I don't know. Some van."

I craned my neck, frowning. I couldn't see anything.

"Are these your guys?" Bridget asked.

"I don't know. I'll call you back." I put my phone away. After a moment, I took it out again and flicked it to silent mode.

I must have waited for less than a minute, but sitting up on that roof, it felt like more. When I finally heard the growl of the engine, I realised why it had taken so long. Through the hedge I could see the van's lights, and it was crawling up the access road at no more than ten miles an hour.

The van crept up to the gate and stopped. Its lights stayed on. Seconds ticked by.

I watched from the rooftop, my unease building. Could that van be from Linford's? After all, the whole plan had been that we would secure the Well and then men from the corporation would arrive to drain it. The men inside that van *could* be on our side.

The van doors opened and men got out.

They weren't on our side.

I don't know how I was so sure, but I was. The night was dark, and the men were distant; I could only see their heads or upper bodies, and I wasn't close enough to make out their faces or hear what they were saying. But *something* about them sent a chill through me. My dad always used to say that there was a big cutoff in the security world. You had the clock-punchers, the ones who were just in it for the payslip and who'd make themselves scarce as soon as a fight broke out. Then you had the ones who were serious. I'd asked him once how you could tell the difference, and what he'd said had stuck with me. He'd said there were two ways: you could watch their eyes, or watch how they moved. The tough ones always moved like they had a purpose.

The men around that van were moving with purpose. They slipped around the edges of the van, assembling next to the gate. Three, four, five. Several had their right hands down by their sides; I couldn't see what they were holding, but something about their stance made me think weapons. They formed a small cluster in front of the gate, one man addressing the others. Whatever he said, it was short, then he held up his left hand, clenched into a fist, and spoke in a voice loud and fierce enough for me to hear. "*Vo imya Peruna*."

There was a rumble of assent from the other men.

I felt my hair stand on end. All of a sudden the winter night had taken on a different character; the wind dropped and the trees seemed to be leaning in, holding their breath. The leader glanced briefly in my direction and I froze. Despite the darkness, I suddenly felt horribly visible, a small creature under the gaze of something vast and powerful.

Then the man looked away. Those around him were doing something that looked like pulling on gloves; as they did, I felt a flare of essentia and saw the green glow of Life drucraft spring up. I couldn't make out the details at this range, but something about the signatures looked familiar.

One of the men moved to the gate; there was the click of metal and the gate swung open. The others slipped through and began advancing up the drive. They moved quickly and confidently; maybe it was my imagination, but they seemed to be faster than before, like a video set to a slightly higher speed. I was able to track them in the darkness for a few seconds by the glow of their sigls, then they passed out of my range and the glow faded. The leader was the last to leave, sweeping the area with one last lingering glance before following his men.

I stayed very still for thirty seconds. Only when I was sure that the men weren't coming back did I take out my phone and tap Ivy's number. I crouched there on the roof, shivering with cold and adrenaline, and listened to the phone ring, willing her to pick up. *Come on*, I thought as I heard the phone ring five times, then six, then seven. *Come on come on come on* . . .

Click. "Hello?"

"Get out," I said quickly. "Get out *now*."

"What?" Ivy said. There were voices in the background and she sounded distracted. "What did you say?"

"A group of men just showed up in a van. I don't know who they are, but they're heading for the cottage, and you *do not* want to be around when they get there."

"Just a second," Ivy called to someone else, then turned her attention back to me. "What men?"

"I told you, I don't know," I said urgently. I twisted, shifting position as I looked around me. "They sounded—"

My foot slid onto a tile. I'd used it as a foothold on the way up, and it had held my weight. Unfortunately, my weight now was three times my weight then.

With a sharp crack the tile snapped, sending my leg plunging through. I grabbed for the chimney and missed, slammed against the roof, felt my fingers scrape along the tiles as I scrabbled for a hold, remembered my mass sigl at the last second, and sent a frantic surge of essentia through it as I slid all the way through and plummeted into the darkness of the barn.

I landed on my back with a slam and lay gasping, trying to get my wind back. Stars swam in front of my eyes and I coughed, breathing dust; the place smelled of dirt and old straw. My back was aching, but I wasn't badly hurt and after a few seconds I managed to struggle to my feet.

I looked at my phone, still clutched in my right hand, and saw that the system logo was flashing; the impact had knocked it into a restart. I stood up and held still, listening for the sound of footsteps approaching the barn.

Nothing.

Once I was sure no one was coming, I started searching for a way out, my emotions a mixture of chagrin and nerves and fear. By the time I'd found a window that I could crack open, my feelings had narrowed down to two: extreme relief that I'd fallen from the roof *after* those men were out of earshot, and extreme embarrassment that it had happened in the first place. So much for not making any blunders.

I scrambled out of the window and back into the night, and as I did I pulled essentia from my body and split the flows, keeping my lightfoot sigl running while sending a similar flow through the diffraction sigl at my waist and a thinner one through the weaker sigl set into my headband. My vision shimmered and turned blue as I faded from sight. I could feel a slight strain as I did, like the feeling you get when you hold up a weight that's a little too heavy. The total cost of these three sigls was very close to the maximum my body could sustain.

Those men had been gone more than long enough to make it to the cottage. I was running out of time.

I headed towards the cottage at a loping run, trying to balance stealth and speed. Between the darkness and my invisibility, I knew there was no chance I'd be seen, but the crunch of gravel beneath my shoes set my teeth on edge and I couldn't seem to muffle it no matter how carefully I placed my feet. I strained my eyes at the blackness, wishing uselessly for Ivy's ability to see in the dark. Call her again? No, too late for that, those men had to be there by now. I wondered what they were—

A flat, echoing sound came from up ahead, muffled by the trees. It made me stop dead, and a chill went through me as I realised that it had been the sound of a gunshot. It was followed by two more, along with the tinkle of breaking glass. Distant shouts drifted through the night, followed by a bang, then the noises blurred into an indecipherable murmur.

The murmur faded away to nothing. The night was silent again.

I broke into a run.

CHAPTER 12

I DON'T KNOW how long it took me to cover the distance to the cottage, but by the time the lights of the building loomed up out of the darkness, everything was still. The cottage was standing silent in the night, just as it had when we'd arrived. With one difference: the front door was ajar, light spilling through the gap. I stood behind a tree, hand resting on the bark, and strained my ears. I could hear *something* from inside the house, bumps and shifting noises, along with a low mutter that could have been voices.

I hesitated, alone and afraid. I wanted to creep forward, but the shadows around the cottage were deep and dark, and I remembered those gunshots. Was there someone there now, weapon aimed and ready?

The quiet was broken with a bang as the door flew open hard enough to bounce off the wall. Squinting in the sudden flare of light, I saw a small figure sprinting across the yard and into the fields, tearing away in the direction of the Well. It took me a moment to recognise from her shape that it was Ivy; I opened my mouth to call but she was already out of earshot and from how fast she was running I knew she wouldn't hear me.

A second later I was glad I'd kept my mouth shut. Another figure emerged from the door, this one bigger and taller. He looked in the direction that Ivy had gone and started after her, his movements swift and precise. The light from a window glinted briefly on something in his hand, then he was out of sight, his padding footsteps fading into the dark. I caught a glimpse of the green aura of Life essentia, then he was gone.

It was one of the men from the van; I recognised the aura of that sigl. Some kind of enhancement effect. I hesitated a moment longer, then followed him.

The lights of the cottage faded behind me as I was swallowed by the darkness. If I'd been quiet before, this time I was as careful as a mouse, placing each foot softly and gently. The night felt oppressive and hushed. The air was cold on my skin and the scents of grass and leaves felt as though they were carrying a whiff of something else, like gun smoke or blood.

The shapes of the trees loomed up ahead; beneath them, the Well glowed in my essentia sight. I slowed down even more, taking one careful step at a time. My lightfoot sigl was living up to its name, and it felt as though the grass barely bent at my touch. I strained my eyes at the darkness, trying to see.

I spotted the man first. I couldn't actually *see* him; it was close to pitch black and neither he nor Ivy was carrying a light. But I could make out the aura from his sigl, a green glow the size and shape of a man. Now that I got a closer look, I finally recognised where I'd seen it before: it was the same type I'd seen on Calhoun in his fight against those soldiers. Something that boosted reflexes, maybe, or reaction time? I remembered how fast Calhoun had moved; this one didn't look as strong as Calhoun's, but it was still bad news.

I spotted Ivy a second later. Again it was her sigl that gave her away, a green aura in the night. She was behind a clump of trees on the far side of the Well, silent and still. I felt a flash of gratitude for my essentia sight; without it, I might have walked right into them.

It was a shock when the man spoke, enough to make me start. I couldn't understand what he was saying, but it sounded like he was talking to Ivy. The man took another couple of steps and spoke again, his voice coaxing, with an undertone of threat. It felt like the wolf speaking through the door: *Little pig, little pig, let me in.*

Ivy didn't move.

The man took another step, coming out from under the shadow of the trees. There was just enough light for me to make out his silhouette and for me to see that whatever he was holding in his right hand, it wasn't a gun. It looked more like rope or string.

He was going to be on top of Ivy in only a few more seconds.

I stepped out of cover.

I channelled essentia as I did, cutting off the flows to my invisibility, lightfoot, and vision sigls and activating the strength sigl at my chest. Power flooded into my muscles and I felt the sense of strain go away as the majority of my essentia reserves were freed up. I crept up behind the man, then took a deep breath and snapped my fingers.

The man jumped and spun, his hand darting to his jacket. I closed my eyes and triggered my flash sigl right in his face.

Light flared, bright enough to dazzle me even through my eyelids. I opened them to see spots swimming across my vision, but the man was much worse off; he was scrubbing at his eyes and swearing, but he was still trying to pull something out and I was on him before he could manage it. Blinded, he was an easy target and I managed to land a good hook to his jaw; he staggered, something went tumbling to the grass, and I pressed in, landing good hits to his body and ribs. And that would have been the end of it, if this had been a punch-up down at the pub. I'd hit him hard enough that any normal guy would have backed off by now.

But I wasn't at the pub and this wasn't a normal guy. The man grabbed me, hampering my blows, then as I struggled to get free slammed his knee up with brutal force. I managed to twist enough that it didn't actually break my ribs, but it still sent a shock of pain through me, and he followed it up with a head butt that left me seeing stars. He measured me up for a kick that would have knocked me out cold, but I managed to send a surge of essentia through my slam sigl; compressed air hit him in the face, knocking him back just far enough that his foot went whistling past my nose. I channelled and sent a haywire beam into the guy's chest in the desperate hope that it'd do something.

It did, but not as much as I'd hoped. The guy's movements became jerky, and as he came in for a punch he stumbled and missed, but he just ended up staggering into me and we ended up in a wrestling match instead. And when I say "wrestling," I don't mean the kind with flying kicks and clotheslines, I mean the kind where the other guy's trying to sink his nails into your body parts and rip them off. He nearly tore my ear off my head; I hit him in the throat hard enough to make him choke and let go, but he kept a grip with the other arm and I was quickly realising that even with my sigl this guy was stronger than me. Pain flashed through my side as he kneed me again; I hit him in the stomach and he grunted, but he was still holding on and he drew back for another punch—

Life essentia flashed green, surging through the man's body. He jerked, spasming, and went tumbling to the grass, pulling me down with him.

I looked up to see Ivy, a dark shadow with green essentia radiating from her head and hand. She bent down; again green light jumped into the man's body, and again he jerked.

I stared up at her.

"What are you waiting for?" Ivy whispered, fear tinging her voice. "*Help!*"

"Right," I scrambled to my feet, shaking off the hits I'd taken. "How . . . ?"

"This isn't going to keep him down! Get something to stop him!"

I looked around at the darkness of the clearing, searching for ideas. Trees, night, grass . . .

The grass. The man had dropped something. "Can you see anything in the grass?" I hissed at Ivy.

"No—yes!" Ivy pointed at a slightly different spot. "There!"

I moved over and began running my hands across the ground. "Further," Ivy whispered. "No, your left. Your other left!"

My fingers touched something hard. I lifted it up, squinting to catch what little light was coming from the sky, and after a second realised that it was a bundle of plastic zip ties.

Tripping and stumbling, Ivy and I managed to drag the man over to one of the trees. He was still awake enough to put up a fight, and Ivy had to stun him with that Life sigl twice more. The last time seemed to knock him out more thoroughly, and he didn't put up any more resistance.

By the time we'd bound the guy's hands together behind the tree trunk and stepped back, we were both panting. I looked down at the man; I still hadn't seen his face. "You think that'll hold him?" I whispered to Ivy.

"How should I know?" Ivy whispered back. Her voice was high and a little panicky. "You think I've done this before?"

We were cut off by the buzz of a mobile phone. Ivy and I both looked at each other, then at the man. A faint light was flashing from the man's jacket pocket. The phone buzzed for nine or ten rings, then stopped.

"Where are the rest?" Ivy whispered once it was quiet again.

"What do you mean?"

"The *rest*!" Ivy's voice was starting to rise; she sounded on the verge of snapping. "Are they coming? Where are they? How did—?"

"Whoa, whoa, whoa." I held out both hands. "All I saw was you and him. He was the only one following you."

Ivy stared at me for a second, then abruptly turned away, covering her face with her hands. I saw her shoulders tremble. "You okay?" I asked. "Are you hurt, or—?"

I saw Ivy shake her head. "No," she said, her voice muffled.

"What happened?" I asked, trying to sound calm. I glanced down at the man; his breathing was slow and heavy and he seemed to be unconscious.

"Why didn't you say something?" Ivy said, turning on me suddenly. Her voice wasn't as high pitched anymore, but there was still a wild, uneasy tremor to it. "You knew this was going to happen! Why didn't you warn me?"

Okay, that stung. "What the hell do you think I was trying to do?"

"Is it true what that Bou guy said? Are you working for them?"

"No! Well, okay, yes, but only the same way you are. They didn't tell me anything they didn't tell you."

Ivy ran a hand through her hair and looked away; it was hard to tell, but it looked like she was shaking. "Okay, look, never mind," I said. "Start at the beginning and tell me what happened."

"Bou said there were a couple more security guards," Ivy said. There was still a slight tremor to her voice, but she seemed to be getting herself under control. "He was laughing, saying it was no big deal, we should chase them off. The others headed for the front door, but . . . something about how Bou was acting made me suspicious. He was just trying to shoo me out when the shooting started."

"Shooting at who?"

"I don't know! There was shooting and yelling and breaking glass and then Bou barged into me—knocked me down and went running out the back. And by the time I got up I was alone in the hall. I could hear people shouting and I knew they were about to come in."

"So what did you do?"

"I hid," Ivy said in a small voice.

I blinked. "Where?"

"The hallway cupboard."

It took me a second to remember the piece of furniture Ivy was talking about. It had been a tiny thing by the front door that had looked like it was for an electricity meter or something. "You actually fit in there?"

". . . Yes."

"Huh. Then what?"

"Men came through," Ivy said. "I don't know how many. Some were shouting in what I think was Russian. Then I heard one of the men we went out with. He sounded . . ." Ivy hesitated. "Like he was hurt. They all went into the kitchen. I think the Russian men were shoving them in."

"And then?"

Ivy was silent for a second. "I came out," she said. "I could hear noise from the kitchen but there was no one in the hall, so I crept up to the front door. But its hinges creaked and someone called out and I knew they'd heard me, so I threw the door open and ran as fast as I could. I was most of the way to the Well when I realised someone was chasing me, and then . . ."

"Yeah, I saw the rest," I said. "The two Romanians, Anton and Pavel, did you see them?"

Ivy shook her head.

"But you heard them?"

"I don't know."

"Were they hurt?"

"I don't know."

I looked back towards the cottage. Its lights were hidden by the trees, but I couldn't hear or see any movement.

"So what now?" Ivy asked.

"Well, I don't think we're getting that four thousand pounds, for a start."

Ivy's voice cracked slightly. "I'm *serious!*"

"Sorry," I said. "Bad joke." My mind was racing. So those Russians were . . . what, a response team? And despite my and Ivy's small victory, it was pretty clear that their side had won. Anton and Pavel were either wounded, captured, or both, and the same probably went for the others. At least the ones who hadn't run away, like Bou. *Well, guess he was telling the truth about one thing,* I thought sourly. *He really did know what he was doing.*

"What should we do?" Ivy asked.

I sighed. I didn't like it, but as far as I could see, there was only one choice. "Go back and take a look."

Ivy stood very still. It was hard to tell in the darkness, but I thought she was staring at me. "What?"

"Find out what happened to the others," I clarified.

"Did you not understand what I was telling you or something?"

"Yes . . ." I said slowly. "What's your point?"

"And you're going to go *back*?"

I thought for a second. "Yes."

"Uh-uh," Ivy said with a shake of her head. "No way."

"What do you want to do instead? Run?"

"*Yes!* Isn't that what you wanted?"

"That was when we were all together," I said in annoyance. I was tempted to make a snarky comment about the raid being "safe" but knew it wouldn't help.

"And now we're not."

"They're still our team."

Ivy stared at me.

"We don't have time to sit around arguing," I told her. "I'm going back. You going to help?"

". . . No."

I didn't say anything. I just gave Ivy a short, expressive look that very clearly communicated what I thought of her, then bent down to search the man we'd knocked out. He was starting to stir and groan but didn't put up any resistance as I went through his pockets. I found a phone, a wallet, a set of car keys. There was his sigl, mounted on a ring on his left hand, still pouring essentia into his body . . . and then something heavy and cold and metallic, stuffed into his front waistband. A gun.

Feeling the handgrip of the gun brought home to me the dangers of what I was about to do, and all of a sudden going back to the cottage didn't seem like so good an idea. If this guy had had his gun out when I'd jumped him, that fight could have gone very differently and very badly. Instead, at some point before I'd reached him, he'd put away his gun and taken out a packet of zip ties.

But there wasn't much point discussing that with Ivy. I took the gun and stood up to see Ivy looking at me. "Main gate's that way," I said, pointing back the way I'd come. "Their van's parked there but it's empty. You can walk straight past."

Ivy stared at me.

"What are you waiting for?" I said irritably. "You can make it to the gate on your own. See you around, I guess." I turned and walked off into the darkness.

I MADE IT back to the groundskeeper's cottage a couple of minutes later. Light was still spilling from the windows, but someone had closed the door. The building was silent and still.

I'd activated my invisibility and vision sigls again, and seeing the blue tinge to the scenery gave me some slight feeling of security. That guy we'd fought hadn't been able to see through my invisibility field; the other ones shouldn't be able to, either.

Probably.

I took a deep breath and started towards the cottage.

Crossing that fifty yards or so of ground was one of the hardest things I'd ever done. Part of it was the danger of the unknown. I didn't know if someone was watching from the shadows with a weapon levelled, ready to fire, and with every step some part of my mind was wondering if the next thing I'd see was the flash of a gunshot. My invisibility was good, especially in the dark, but it wasn't perfect.

But the biggest thing that was slowing my footsteps, the biggest thing making me want to stop and back away, was knowing that I didn't have to do this. Bad as things were right now, I'd been through worse, like that time I was cornered in my bedroom by Diesel and Scar. But the thing about being cornered is that it takes away any sense of responsibility. You can give up or you can fight, but you know you're not really making the decisions.

This time I *was* making the decisions. At any moment I could stop, turn around, and get the hell out of here, and that was something new for me. I was used to having to choose between bad options, but I wasn't used to being able to just *leave*. It felt like being tempted by a little whispering voice at the back of my head: *This isn't your problem, just walk away.*

I didn't walk away. I kept going forward.

The reason was very simple; it was because of my dad. My dad had told me stories when I was growing up, and something that had always been there in the background of those stories was how you were supposed to act as a man. There wasn't an instruction sheet or anything, but I knew that one of the big ones was being dependable. A real man was supposed to be someone you could count on. I hadn't made any promises to the guys on this raid, but I *had* taken on a job with them, and the way I saw it, that meant I owed it to them to at least give it a try.

But it's one thing to feel that you're supposed to do something, and another to actually do it. Right now I didn't feel like someone who could be counted on; I felt like someone who was horribly out of his league. The fight with that man at the Well had happened too fast for me to be scared, but now that I looked back on it, I had the nasty feeling that Ivy and I had won mostly by luck. What the hell was I doing heading towards four *more* guys like that?

With each step I took, the cottage seemed to loom bigger and darker and more threatening. I came very close to turning and running away.

But I didn't. With a final rush I made it to the wall and rested my fingers against the rough bricks with a sense of relief. Now no one looking through the windows could see me. I held still for a count of twenty, listening for any sign that someone had heard my approach, but there was no sound.

Ivy had said that the men had gone into the kitchen. Carefully, placing one foot at a time, I moved clockwise around the cottage until I could see the bright splash of the kitchen window, throwing light out into the darkness. A mutter of voices made me pause, and I stopped for a few seconds, listening.

Nothing.

I crept up to the window and peered through.

CHAPTER 13

THE KITCHEN WAS packed. Men were everywhere, lying on the floor and standing around the table, and in those first confused seconds it looked as though an army had moved in.

As I squinted more closely, I realised that my first rough count of about fifteen had been exaggerated. There were in fact eight: four on their feet and four lying down. One was standing by the door and using a mobile phone, two others were talking in low voices by the sink, and the fourth had a gun out and was watching the ones on the floor. It was the first time I'd been close enough to make out their faces, but from the glow of Life essentia I recognised them as the Russian speakers who'd arrived in the van. They were all in the twenty-to-forty age bracket and looked hard and tough.

The four men on the floor were harder to make out; their faces were either turned away from me or they were too close to the window. They were lying on their fronts with their arms behind them, and it took me a second to realise that they were bound. Only when I recognised his brown anorak did I realise that the one by the table had to be Pavel, which made the bigger guy next to him Anton. There was no sign of Bou.

I did a quick head count. Five had arrived in the van: these four plus the one Ivy and I had left in the woods. Bou, that security guard, and one more from our team were missing, but it was the men from the van I was worried about, and knowing that I didn't have to worry about one of them sneaking up behind me made me feel a little safer. I kept watching.

The man at the door finished his phone call and turned back to say something to the others. He was older than the other three, with greying hair and a face that looked like it had been carved from granite. There was a short exchange in what might have been Russian, then the leader hit another button on his phone.

Something at my hip buzzed loudly, and I nearly jumped out of my skin before realising that it was the phone I'd taken from the man at the Well. It sounded hideously loud and I felt a flash of terror, but no one inside seemed to hear. The phone kept buzzing as the man inside looked at his own phone, frowning. At last he stabbed another button and the buzzing at my hip stopped.

I took a long breath, trying to calm my racing heart.

The leader was arguing with one of the others; the voices through the window were too muffled for me to make out and I don't speak Russian anyway. Whatever the other guy said didn't seem to make the leader happy. He pointed; the two Russians with their hands free grabbed the man in the brown anorak and dragged him to his feet.

It *was* Pavel, and he wasn't looking good. There was a darkening bruise on his forehead; his eyes darted left and right, passing over the window without seeing me. The leader said something to Pavel, his tone short and clipped.

Pavel stammered out an answer.

The leader turned and gestured. The Russian with the gun

who'd been covering the others approached and used his foot to shove one of the men on the floor over.

I caught my breath as I saw the man's face. It was Anton, and he looked ghastly. His face was far too pale, there was blood smeared up one side of it, and the front of his clothes was covered in dark stains; there was a small, ominous red patch on the floor where he'd been lying. The gunman gave Anton's stomach a light kick and Anton curled up with a gasp of pain.

The leader asked Pavel another question, this one with a menacing tone.

Pavel looked frightened. He started talking fast in some language I didn't speak; maybe Russian, Romanian, or a mixture of the two. He kept going, words pouring out for more than a minute until the leader cut him off sharply.

The gunman asked the leader a short, two-word question. He was still standing over Anton; his gun pointed casually down at Anton's head.

The leader seemed to consider. Pavel's eyes darted frantically around the room. The two men holding him looked on indifferently. I watched, frozen.

"*Nyet*," the leader said. The gunman nodded and let the barrel of his weapon drop.

The tension in the room seemed to ease. The two men who'd been holding Pavel up shoved him down again, and the leader turned away, going back to his phone.

I let out a soft breath. No one was looking at the window. I slid aside and put my back to the wall.

My left hip pocket held a phone. My right hip pocket held something else. I reached in and took it out.

The handgun looked sleek and dark in the blue-tinted light of my vision sigl. The barrel and grip were squarish, with grooves in the sides, and the whole thing was made of metal, scuffed and nicked from use. It was surprisingly heavy. I took a hold of it—the grip was a little too big for my hand—and hefted it.

And right there and then I decided that there was no way I was using that gun. I don't know what I'd been thinking when I'd taken it off that man. Part of it was just making sure he couldn't use it on me, but I think at some level I'd had some vague idea of doing the thing in action movies where the hero takes a weapon off one of the bad guys and uses it to shoot all the others. But now, standing there in the darkness, I realised what an awful plan that was. This wasn't a movie, I wasn't the designated hero, and the men in there sure as hell weren't going to throw up their hands and fall over as soon as I pointed a weapon in their direction. They were tough, capable, and certainly a lot better with guns than I was. In fact, I wasn't even sure if I knew *how* to use this thing. There was a little lever along the side with a coloured spot; I let my invisibility drop just long enough to see that it was green. Did green mean "safe," or did it mean "ready to fire"? It wasn't like I could pull the trigger to check!

But even if I'd known the answer to that question, it wouldn't have changed anything. My dad had told me something a long time ago that had always stuck with me: don't carry a weapon unless you're willing to use it, and don't use it unless you're will-ing to kill with it. He'd been talking about knives, not guns, but the principle was the same. When I thought about what going into that cottage with gun drawn actually *meant*, I knew I wasn't willing to do it. It might have been different if they were hunting me, but going in and trying to take advantage of my invisibility sigl to shoot them down before they even knew I was there . . . no. It was too cold-blooded, too murderous.

I wasn't willing to murder those guys, and that meant I had no business trying to use this thing. I stuffed the gun back in my fleece pocket with a flash of relief.

But the relief didn't last. Okay, so doing a John Wick impression was out. What did that leave?

I couldn't fight them. I'd barely been a match for the first guy, and that had been two on one with the advantage of surprise. Sneaking wasn't going to work, either—my diffraction sigl was fine for hiding in the shadows, but indoors, in bright light, I'd be spotted instantly. Probably those guys wouldn't know *what* the weird goldfish-bowl distortion in the air was that they were looking at, but they wouldn't have to.

I couldn't call for help. The police were obviously out. Ivy was gone. All that left was Bridget, and there was no way I was calling her in. Things were bad enough without me having to worry about her getting shot as well.

If fighting was out, and sneaking was out, and calling for help was out, what did that even leave? It was hopeless.

I shook myself. *No. Focus.* If things seemed hopeless, that just meant I wasn't looking at them the right way. Start at the beginning. Why were these guys actually *here*?

They were here to defend the Well. And if that was their objective, they might not even care about Anton and Pavel and the rest, right? So long as the raid failed, then from their perspective, that was a win.

What else did they care about? Each other, presumably. Like the guy we'd left tied up in the woods . . .

An idea started to form in my mind. I sneaked a cautious look back through the window to check that nothing had changed, then carefully withdrew to a position where I was out of earshot but had a line of sight through the window. I manoeuvred until I could make out the shape of the leader, silhouetted against the bright lights of the kitchen, then reached into my pocket and took out the man's phone. The screen glowed at me; the notification at the top was in a language I couldn't read, but I recognised the format and the "(2)" next to it. Two missed calls.

All right. I thought this had a chance to work—maybe not a *good* chance, but every other plan I could come up with was worse. The key would be to keep it short. I rehearsed what I was going to say, repeating it to myself in my head, then once I was as sure as I was going to get, I tapped the phone before I could lose my nerve.

The phone buzzed quietly in the darkness. Squinting through the night, I saw the leader take out his phone. An instant later I heard the line click and a harsh voice spoke. "*Shto?*"

I swallowed, took a breath, and spoke, trying to sound tough and menacing. "You should have sent more men."

A pause, then the voice spoke again, this time in accented English. "Who is this?"

"You can keep those ones," I told the leader. "We'll take your man and the Well."

"Who is this?" the leader repeated. "What do you—?"

I hung up. After a moment the phone lit up and began to buzz. I ignored it and after eight or nine rings it went dark.

Looking through the window into the kitchen, I could see activity breaking out. The leader was talking with one of the other men, pointing in the direction of the woods. I couldn't figure out what they were saying, but I'd obviously stirred them up.

Now all I could do was wait. Calling again would just make them suspicious, and as soon as they started asking questions it wouldn't take them long to smell a rat. Staying silent, though . . . that was another story. Right now, all those guys knew was that someone had managed to take down one of their number and steal his phone. Which meant that for all they knew, they were up against some team of elite raiders, not a twenty-one-year-old with a handful of sigls and a girl who'd already run away.

Of course, if they just decided to hole up in the cottage, I was stuck. But something told me these weren't the kinds of guys who'd ignore a challenge.

There was the faint creak of hinges and light came pouring out of the front of the cottage as the front door opened. One by one, the men came out, and as I saw their stances I knew they were taking this seriously. All had their guns out, and they were advancing in pairs, one moving up while the other covered him. I counted them as they went past. Two . . . three . . . four.

The four men disappeared into the night, heading towards the Well. I stayed very still, listening for the sound of footsteps coming back. Nothing.

Not too soon.

Not too soon.

Now!

I darted across the grass. The cottage door had been left open, and I went in fast, letting my invisibility sigl drop and channelling the essentia into my lightfoot and strength sigls instead as I ran through into the kitchen.

Startled faces looked up from the floor: Pavel, the Polish guy Bou had left behind, and one of the ones whose name I didn't know; he had sharp features and a square jaw. "Eh?" Pavel said, staring at me.

"Scissors," I said quickly. From a glance I could see that Pavel and the others were bound with more of those zip ties. I needed something to cut them.

"What?"

"Scissors, knife. Something that can cut. Quick!"

"Cut—there. Drawer over there!"

I yanked the drawer open and wasted a precious few seconds scrabbling through the contents before grabbing a pair of kitchen scissors. I darted back to Pavel, running calculations in the back of my mind. The Russians would be arriving at the Well any second. How long before they came back?

The zip ties binding Pavel came apart with a snip and Pavel rolled to his feet, rubbing at his hands. "Knife," I snapped, pointing at the drawer, and turned to cut the others free as well.

The Polish guy figured out what I was doing and made things easy, twisting around so I could cut his bonds and scrambling to his feet as soon as I was done. Square-jaw was the opposite. When I came towards him with the scissors he started thrashing around and yelling in some language or other.

"Shut up!" I hissed, but the guy kept thrashing and I couldn't get close; he seemed to think I was going to cut his throat or something. I finally managed to catch his flailing hands long enough to cut the zip tie binding them, but he immediately lashed out and nearly clobbered me in the head, at which point I gave up, dropped the scissors where he could reach them, and turned to Pavel and Anton.

My heart sank as I saw them. Pavel had found a knife, cut Anton's bonds, and got the bigger man onto his feet, but Anton looked ghastly. The front of his clothes was soaked with blood, his skin had an ominous greyish tinge, and his eyes were fluttering. He was standing, but only because Pavel had the other man's arm over his shoulders and was more or less holding him up.

"Which way?" Pavel asked me. Behind him, the Polish guy was looking at me as well.

With a nervous feeling I realised they were expecting me to tell them what to do. I looked at Anton and wondered if he could even make it, but all of them were looking at me and I knew there was no help for it. "Follow me," I ordered and headed for the door.

I felt my insides knot up as we came out into the night. We were silhouetted against the light; if the Russians were waiting for us, we'd be sitting ducks. I gestured for the others to follow and headed for the drive, expecting at any minute to hear the crash of a gunshot.

But none came. We made it off the grounds and onto the drive with no sound except for the shuffling of our footsteps.

As I moved from grass onto gravel, I started to relax the tiniest bit. If the Russians were here, they would have ambushed us by now. Glancing around, I could see that Pavel was supporting Anton; Anton was struggling but he was managing to stay on his feet. If he could just keep going for a few minutes more—

The green glow of Life essentia shone from the trees ahead.

I skidded to a halt with a surge of panic and was just about to dive to the ground when I recognised what I was seeing. The green aura was too small to be a body enhancement. It was only the size of a head, like the one belonging to—

Ivy's voice floated out of the darkness. "Hello?"

"What are you doing here?" I asked.

Ivy hesitated and I realised it had been a stupid question. She'd been waiting in a position where she could watch the cottage. "Come on," I told her, and kept going along the path.

Ivy hurried to catch up with me. "Where are we going?"

"Van."

"How are we going to—?"

I shook my pocket. The keys I'd taken from the man in the woods clicked.

"Oh."

"Watch the others," I told her. "I need to make a call." I pulled out my phone and dialled Bridget's number.

Bridget answered straightaway. "Finally! I've been calling you and—"

"Yeah, I had it on silent for a reason. Come up the access road to the van, we're getting out of here *now*."

"Were those gunshots—?"

"Yes."

Bridget paused a second. "Okay. Coming."

I hung up. Someone grabbed at my sleeve and I turned.

There was a man in the darkness behind me. I couldn't make out his face but he was saying something and from the sound of his voice I realised it was the square-jawed guy who'd given me so much trouble getting him free. "What?" I asked.

The man fired off another burst of rapid-fire words.

"Whatever language you're speaking, I don't," I said. "And keep your voice down!"

"He's telling you to give him the gun," Pavel said. He was having trouble supporting Anton, but they were still moving.

"No," I told Square-jaw irritably, then turned back to Ivy. "I'm going to make sure there's no one at the van. Stay with Pavel and Anton."

Ivy hesitated, then gave a nod.

I ran ahead. We were nearly out, but the noise from Square-jaw had made me nervous. By now the Russians must have found their guy at the Well; as soon as they noticed we'd stolen his car keys it wouldn't take a genius to figure out where we were going.

The streetlights from the access road were visible through the trees and I knew we were nearly out. I darted forward, straining my essentia sight, searching for the telltale glow of Life essentia that would mean the Russians were there already. The gate appeared, then the van; the gate had been left open and I slipped through and paused in the shadows of the hedge. The access road looked bright and open and dangerous after the darkness of the woods.

Still nothing. Just a few faint currents of free essentia.

But they could have their sigls deactivated, or have another guy waiting. I moved up, circled the van, and peered through the windows. Only when I saw nothing did I finally relax.

The crunch of feet on gravel made me look around with a flash of adrenaline that turned quickly to annoyance as I saw that it was Square-jaw. He must have followed me when I made my run along the drive. He hurried up to the van and tugged at the handle. "Keys!" he told me in a thick accent.

"Yes, I've got them," I told him, looking around. I couldn't see any trace of the others. Bridget wasn't here either.

"Keys!" There was a frantic note in Square-jaw's voice. "Open!"

"Give me a second," I told him. I walked up next to Square-jaw and the van, still trying to watch in every direction at once. *Come on, Pavel.* We just needed everyone to make it so that we could get the hell out.

"Give me."

"What?" I asked, and I turned to Square-jaw to see that he was pointing at me. Following his finger, I saw that he was pointing at the outline of the handgun in my pocket.

"Give me!"

"No," I said in irritation, looking away towards the gate.

The punch caught me completely by surprise. It landed on the side of my head, causing what felt like an explosion of light and sound in my brain; my vision greyed out and I felt myself hit the ground. Someone was scrabbling at my clothes, going through my pockets; I struck out feebly. Gradually the grey stars filling my sight began to fade; I looked up with a spinning head, blinking and confused.

I was lying on the road about ten feet from the van. Square-jaw was backed up against the van door. The gun that had been in my pocket was in his hand, and it was pointed at me.

"Keys!" Square-jaw shouted.

I stared at him blankly.

Square-jaw made a beckoning motion with his free hand. "Keys! Now!"

"You don't even need them," I said in confusion. It was a stupid thing to say but my head was still spinning. "You could just walk away."

"Give me!" Square-jaw shouted. "Now!"

He doesn't understand what I said. Now that I was looking closely at Square-jaw I could see the dilated pupils, the tightened lines on his face, the way the gun was trembling in his hand. If I'd been paying more attention, I would have realised how panicked he was.

The two of us stared at each other. I knew I should say something, but my head hurt too much to think. As if in slow motion, I saw Square-jaw's hand tighten around that gun. It was pointed at the centre of my body and I had just enough time to wish that I'd bought that armour vest.

A short, high-pitched whistle sounded from my left. Bridget's voice rang out, sharp and commanding. "Leo, worry!"

Square-jaw and I both turned.

The creature rushing towards us looked something like a dog, in the same way that a lion looks something like a cat. It had a massive body, with a broad, heavy head and four widely spaced paws that pounded on the road as it rushed forward. Thick ropes of muscle bunched and flexed as it leapt at Square-jaw.

Square-jaw brought the gun around and squeezed the trigger. Nothing happened, and he had an instant for his eyes to go wide before the dog slammed into him with the force of a small car, bowling him over.

I scrambled to my feet, shaking away the cobwebs as I got my sigls ready, but as I did, I saw that the dog was wholly focused on Square-jaw. He'd locked his massive muzzle onto the man, growling, and was shaking him like a baby with a favourite toy. The joints in Square-jaw's body were making the exact same sort of hollow rattling sound too.

"Are there any more?" a voice said from behind me.

I turned to see Bridget walking up. She was keeping a casual eye on the dog but mostly seemed to be concerned about me. "I . . ." I said. "No. Is that . . ."

"Leo," Bridget said, giving the giant dog a glance as he continued to worry at Square-jaw. "If this is just a raid, you don't want him dead, right?"

"This guy was supposed to be *part* of the raid," I told her. I felt stupid. I'd been so busy watching for the guys who were supposed to be our enemy that I'd turned my back on the one who'd nearly killed me.

"Oh," Bridget said, and shrugged. "Well, I guess he's not anymore."

I walked past the scuffling mass on the floor, ignoring the gasps from Square-jaw and the growls from the dog. I suppose I should have checked that the dog wasn't actually going to kill the guy, but given that he'd been about to shoot me I was having trouble caring. I picked up the gun from where it had fallen to see that little lever on the side was still showing a green dot. "So I guess green means 'safe,'" I said to no one in particular.

"What?"

The sound of crunching footsteps made me look up to see the rest of our raiding party emerging from the darkness. Pavel was still half carrying Anton and had been joined by Ivy, who was struggling under Anton's weight but doing her best to help. The Polish guy was hovering behind, casting nervous looks back. All of them stopped to stare at us.

Ivy looked down at the huge dog on top of Square-jaw, whose gasps had tailed off into whimpers. "Um."

"He tried to shoot me," I said curtly. "What are you waiting for, an invitation? Get in the van!"

It was probably a measure of how the night had gone that no

one argued. Pavel and the Pole lifted Anton in through the side door while I kept a wary eye on the gate. I couldn't see anything past the circle of light from the streetlamp, and I swore to myself that if I got out of this, the first thing I was doing was getting some kind of night-vision sigl like Ivy's.

"Uh," Ivy said, looking down at Square-jaw and the dog. "Is he . . . ?"

"Leo won't kill him," Bridget said helpfully. "If I'd ordered him to do that, it would have been over a *lot* faster."

From the expression on Ivy's face, she wasn't sure how reassuring that was, but she climbed into the van. Pavel had managed to get Anton propped up on one of the back seats and now scrambled into the driver's seat. "Keys?" he called.

I climbed in and tossed them over. Pavel pressed a button and the engine started with a growl.

Bridget whistled. "Leo!"

Without a backward look, Leo left Square-jaw moaning on the road and came bounding up into the van, the vehicle creaking under his weight. I gave Square-jaw a last unsympathetic glance and rolled the door shut.

The van reversed, turned, and pulled away down the access road. I had one last glimpse of the gates receding behind us and then we were away, disappearing into the streets of West London.

WITH SIX PEOPLE plus one very large dog, the van was crowded. Anton stayed quiet, but he was still breathing heavily and was obviously in pain, gasping every time the van hit a bump in the road or took a corner too hard.

While we drove, I used my mending sigl to do what I could. It was designed exactly for situations like this, but I knew there was no guarantee it would be enough; mending sigls are only meant to keep someone alive long enough to get them to a hospital. Luckily for Anton, we were right next to one. Mount Vernon Hospital was only a few minutes away, and Pavel got us there in record time. We pulled into the car park and I helped Pavel lift Anton out.

"You okay to get him inside?" I asked. Lights shone from the hospital building but the car park was dark and cold; a chill wind was blowing, making me shiver.

"It's okay, it's okay," Pavel said. He turned away, Anton's arm slung over his shoulders, and hurried into the hospital.

Guess I don't get a thank-you. I climbed back into the van.

". . . just a big couch potato really," Bridget was saying to Ivy, scratching the dog's head. "He'd do nothing but eat and sleep if I let him."

"He's really pretty," Ivy said. "Can I . . . ?"

"Go ahead."

I gave Ivy a weird look as she reached hesitantly across to Leo. With smooth black-and-fawn fur and a head the size of a football, the giant dog was definitely *striking*, and you could probably stretch it to "majestic." "Pretty," though, was pushing it. Still, the creature sat complacently as Ivy scratched his head.

"Hey," a voice said from the passenger seat.

Bridget and I looked around to see the last remaining other member of our raiding team, the Polish guy. Technically the second Polish guy, I suppose, though being from the same country hadn't stopped Bou from ditching him along with the rest of us. "What is it?" I asked.

"Money."

I paused. "What?"

"Where's the rest of our money?"

"I'm not the one who hired you," I said slowly and clearly.

"Money," the Pole repeated stubbornly.

I stared at the guy for a long moment before jerking my thumb at Leo. "You have ten seconds to get out of my face before I feed you to the dog."

"What do you think, Leo?" Bridget said brightly. "Midnight snack?"

Leo lifted up his ears and gave a deep *wuff*.

I've never seen a guy make it out of a car so fast. There was a slam and the sound of running feet, and the Pole was gone.

I leant my head back against the seat with a thump, closing my eyes.

"Um," Ivy said. "Now what?"

Why are you asking me? I wanted to say, but didn't. "Find a place to dump this thing that won't lead them to this hospital," I said tiredly. I would leave the guy's phone and gun too, while I was at it.

"If we pick a spot, I can tell my chauffeur to meet us," Bridget suggested helpfully.

"Good," I said, then paused and opened my eyes. "Wait. Can anyone here drive?"

The two girls looked back at me blankly.

AN HOUR OF extremely annoying logistics later, it was done. Ivy and I stood near Moor Park station, watching the red taillights of Bridget's car carrying her and her dog away into the night. She'd been insufferably smug about saving me, but given that she *had* saved me it seemed a bit ungrateful to complain. Once her car was gone we headed into the station and down to the platform.

The London Underground at night has a lonely, desolate feel, especially the stations out on the edge. Ivy and I were alone on the platform except for a scattering of people at the far end and one old man asleep on the bench. We stood for a while in silence.

"Who was that?" Ivy asked at last.

I was too tired to come up with a clever answer. "My sister."

Ivy blinked. "Oh."

We stood a little longer in silence. A cold wind blew down the platform, and with a shiver I looked up at the dot-matrix indicator. Eleven minutes until the next train into London.

"Thanks for coming to help," Ivy said eventually.

I gave her a puzzled look. "When?"

"At the Well."

"Oh, right." With everything else that had happened, it had gone right out of my mind. "You seemed like you needed it."

"I know, but I wasn't expecting . . ."

"What?"

Ivy hesitated. "Nothing."

We stood in silence for a while, and I looked sideways at Ivy. She looked very subdued. I remembered that talk we'd had at the Well, where she'd told me that her corporation had told her that this raid was supposed to be safe, and that she trusted them more than me. I wondered if she still felt the same way.

When Ivy finally spoke, though, it was about something different. "You're really good at fighting."

"Not as good as my dad," I said absently. I wished he was here.

We fell silent again, and this time we stayed that way until the train arrived with a rumble and a whine of brakes. We boarded the train, and as the doors hissed shut and the vehicle began to pull away, leaving Moor Park behind us, I finally let myself relax.

CHAPTER 14

IT WAS CLOSE to midnight by the time I got home. I was sore and exhausted, but my mind was still going round and round and I was too wired to sleep.

Hobbes gave me an ecstatic welcome, rearing up and rubbing his head against my legs. I stroked him for a while, told him that, no, I wasn't feeding him, I'd already fed him in the afternoon and I didn't want him getting fat, and finally went out for a walk, Hobbes trotting at my side.

I wandered the streets of Plaistow, taking random turnings. The Christmas night was cold and quiet, and the streets were all but empty; even Plaistow Road was mostly clear of traffic. I watched the lit windows pass by, lost in my thoughts, while Hobbes sprang from walltop to walltop, ranging ahead before coming back to pace me again.

Now that it was all over, I felt burned out and empty. Partly it was just the inevitable crash from the high; I'd been running on adrenaline for much of the night, and now that I was finally safe, all the exhaustion that I'd been holding at bay was catching up with me. Not to mention my bruises; my sides hurt from the fight at the Well, my back ached from that fall, and I had a throbbing pain in the side of my head from Square-jaw's punch. I'd taken some paracetamol but could already tell that I was going to hurt like hell in the morning.

But getting beaten up wouldn't bother me so much if it had been worth it. The problem was, I wasn't sure it had.

I mean, just looking at my own part in things, I'd done okay. I'd saved Ivy from that guy at the Well, and rescued the rest of my team. Yeah, I'd made mistakes, but everyone had come out alive. And now that I understood just how much danger we'd been in, I was pretty sure that "getting out alive" was the best outcome we could realistically have hoped for.

So why wasn't I happier?

Because it hadn't really accomplished anything. We'd got out of danger, but the only reason I'd been *in* danger was because I'd taken the job in the first place. I'd known shadow work was dangerous, but I'd thought of it as high risk, high reward. Instead it seemed high risk, low reward. I'd earned £1,000 for the night's work, which meant that I'd have to do this about thirty times a year just to earn the same sort of salary as a high-street retail manager. And the guy selling handsets at Carphone Warehouse doesn't have to worry about getting shot by a Russian gunman every Monday morning!

But it wasn't really the money that was the problem. What really bothered me, thinking back on it, was that I felt like a disposable playing piece. A pawn.

Looked at like that, the casual way Linford's had sent us out made a lot more sense. When you're playing chess and one of your pawns gets taken, you don't get upset about it. You just move on to the next pawn.

And come to think of it . . . most of the time, when one of your pawns gets taken, it's because you deliberately *put* it in danger.

I suppose I should have expected it, really. Back when I'd been working officially for Linford's, I'd been constantly reminded of how little they cared about their locators. For some reason I'd thought shadow work would be different—that I'd be getting into a position where I'd be a bit more important and valued. Now, with hindsight, I realised how stupid that had been. Why would a corporation like Linford's treat their deniable, disposable employees *better* than their regular ones?

In fact, the more I thought about it, the more it seemed to me that from Linford's point of view, tonight's operation had gone just fine. They wouldn't have sent us on a mission like this if they thought they were really risking anything. It was the guys at the bottom who got it in the neck when things went wrong.

So what should I do?

I'd come to the barrier that blocked off the road between Corporation Street and the main road leading south to West Ham. I leant against the barrier, feeling the cold of the metal through my fleece, wincing a little at the pain in my muscles. Hobbes hopped down from a nearby roof and came strolling over; I tapped the top of the barrier and he jumped up so that he could rub the side of his head against my shoulders. I scratched him behind the ears, thinking.

Twice now I'd been involved in corporate raids. The first time I'd been forced in at gunpoint, the second time I'd been lured in with money, but both had gone badly. What was I doing wrong?

I was playing by their rules. That was the problem. I hadn't realised it at the time, but as soon as I took today's job, I'd put myself in a situation where most of the possible outcomes were bad ones.

So how could I have put myself in a *better* situation?

The obvious answer was "not go on the raid." But I decided to forget that for a second. If I'd been free to carry out that raid however I wanted, what would I have done differently?

Well, for a start, I wouldn't have brought so many people. The more I thought about it, the more it seemed to me as though most of the raiders tonight had been a liability—I could have done the whole job a hell of a lot better on my own. One or two people would have been nice, for backup and to watch the gate in case that response team showed up . . . but apart from that, between my sigls and the cover of darkness, I was pretty sure I could have made it in and out without anyone even noticing I was there.

In fact, looked at that way, why was I even involving the corporations at all? If they weren't actually doing anything useful and had odds-on chances of betraying me somewhere along the line, why not just do the whole thing myself?

Well, because they had all the money. Sneaking into a Well was fine if I only wanted to make a sigl. If I wanted to get paid, I'd have to sell it.

But from what Charles had said, corporations *did* buy from raiders. I remembered those gangs I'd fought at Stratford and in Victoria Park. They had to be selling their loot to someone.

I stayed there for a while, turning the problem over in my mind. There were some missing pieces, but the more I thought about it, the more it seemed as though it might be a better deal. At last I pushed off from the barrier and headed home, Hobbes trotting along at my feet. I got home, undressed, and went to bed, but I was still too worked up to easily relax. It took me a long time to go to sleep, and once I did, it was to uneasy dreams about driving in a van along dark country roads, followed by pursuers I couldn't see or hear.

———

THE NEXT FEW weeks were busy.

Pavel contacted me the morning after the raid; Anton was alive and looked like he was going to pull through, which was a relief. I had some things I wanted to ask them both, but right now my first priority was upgrading my abilities. The raid had done a really good job of showing me areas where I needed to improve, and the first thing on my wish list was a night-vision sigl. Being able to see in the dark had made the difference for Ivy between escaping and getting caught.

I considered asking Ivy to let me study hers, but decided against it. For one thing, I wasn't at all sure she'd say yes, and for another, I didn't have the best track record with Life sigls. According to Maria it was my second-worst branch, and given what had happened the last time I'd tried to develop an enhancement sigl from scratch, I really wasn't keen on going through the process a second time. But I did think I could adapt the designs of my light and flash sigls to create light particles that were copies of others. By using that on the light coming into my eyes, I could amplify its strength, effectively making the image brighter. It'd have to be delicate, but I thought it had the potential to work— and by taking advantage of my Light affinity, it played to my strengths, rather than my weaknesses.

Next on my to-get list was armour. I'd looked into armour vests prior to the raid but had been put off by how expensive they were—decent-quality ones generally landed in the £500 to £1,000 range, which was a substantial chunk of my bank balance. However, the experience of staring down the barrel of a gun had shifted my priorities a bit, and it had occurred to me that out of all the possible reasons to die, it was pretty hard to get stupider than "was too stingy to buy a ballistic vest." So I went ahead and ordered one.

The vest arrived a few days later, and when I tested it I was pleasantly surprised to find that even though I'd gone for one of the heavier models, it didn't weigh me down much at all, at least not over short distances. It did make me tire faster on long runs, especially when going uphill, but that was what my lightfoot sigl was for. The company that made it, Vestguard UK, claimed that it would provide protection against "9mm, .357 Magnum, and .44 Magnum," which to me was pretty much just random numbers, but when I looked it up it seemed to translate to "handguns," which was what I was worried about anyway (it wouldn't stop a rifle, but if you're getting shot at by a rifle in the UK, you're doing something seriously wrong). More importantly, the vest was also rated against knife and spike attacks, which in my part of London are a hell of a lot more common than shootings. After some experimentation about the best way to use it (turns out it goes *over* your T-shirt, not under), I started wearing it on all my locating trips. It was tempting to be lazy and only break it out when doing something dangerous, but I remembered the attack by that boy at the football pitch. If he decided to come back for another try, I didn't think he was going to warn me first.

I never heard back from the anonymous number that had offered me the raiding job, which wasn't a surprise. What *was* a surprise was that I did hear from Mr. Smith. He sent me an email the same day I ordered the vest, saying he hoped my locating was going well and asking whether I'd be interested in further work.

The message sounded very neutral and bland, but I had the feeling the question he was *really* asking was something along the lines of "Congratulations on surviving your first raid! Please now let us know whether you are: (a) willing to continue with shadow work, (b) unwilling to continue with shadow work, (c) never an-swering our emails again, (d) currently unavailable due to being injured, arrested, or dead, or (e) other (provide details below)."

I started to write an angry reply accusing the guy of trying to get me killed, and deleted it. Then I half wrote several more re-plies dripping with sarcasm, resentment, and snark, and deleted all those as well. At last, after two days, I sent him a short, cool message saying that things hadn't changed. I didn't get an answer, which suited me fine. I knew he was lying, he probably knew I was lying, and neither of us was going to say anything about it. It would have been nice to tell him what I really thought of him, but I still needed money, which meant I couldn't afford to cut things off with the guy.

But I was looking forward to the day when I'd be able to.

ALTHOUGH MY DEAL with Bridget had been that she'd tell me some more about my mother in exchange for me taking her on a raid, I hadn't really expected her to follow through—the way I saw it, she was a teenage girl from a rich family, and probably very used to making promises that she wasn't intending to keep. Now she'd got what she wanted, I figured she'd leave me alone . . . so it came as a surprise when, in the first week of January, Bridget asked me for a meeting.

"So I found out what was going on with that raid," Bridget told me, cutting into her cake with a small fork.

"Really?" I said.

We were in the café of Kenwood House, a big stately home slash art gallery on the north side of Hampstead Heath. The café had white-painted brick walls, high windows that let the winter sunlight through in brilliant shafts to fall onto the wooden tables and chairs, and, of course, ridiculously high prices. Bridget had come back from the counter with a cake covered in strawberries and a glass of pink lemonade. I'd got a glass of tap water.

"Mm-hmm," Bridget said, taking a bite of cake. "So you said it was Linford's who was behind it, right?"

"That's what your granddad seemed to think," I said. I wasn't too worried about being overheard. The high walls of the café were echoing with the chatter of two or three conversations, the noise blending into a buzz, but the place was still big enough that we'd been able to get a table away from everyone else.

"So Linford's is a drucraft company, but apparently they're also in the intelligence business," Bridget said. "Buying and selling."

"I know that part."

"Well, one of the things they sell is information about Wells. Locations, defences, response time if it gets attacked . . ."

"What would that have to do with . . ." I began, then my eyes narrowed as the penny dropped. ". . . Wait."

Bridget nodded, taking another bite of cake. "Apparently it's a thing they do. Mummy called them 'probing raids.'"

"You told your mother about this?"

"*Our* mother," Bridget corrected. "And I didn't tell her you were on it. I'm not stupid."

"Neither's she."

"You have to give a little if you want to get a little," Bridget said with a shrug. "Besides, you really think she's going to report you to the police?"

I made a face—I wasn't happy having my mother brought into this—but let it drop. "So, anyway," Bridget said, sipping at her lemonade. "The way Linford's like to do it is they hire a bunch of new guys, then plant in one or two more whose job is to watch the whole thing and take notes. They're the only ones who know what's really going on. If the Well turns out to be undefended, the whole thing's treated like a tryout. If there's a fight, the plants shove the newbies to the front and then run the other way."

Bou, I thought. So that was why he'd been so quick to point the finger at me. "Do they maybe video it as well? Say, with a camera drone?"

"That too. Once it's all over, they'll package the whole thing and sell it to BES or Tyr or someone. And if nothing happens and they get the Well without a fight, well, that's fine too."

They come out ahead either way, I thought. If the raid failed, then Linford's wouldn't have to pay most of the raiders beyond the initial advance. And if it succeeded, they'd pick up the Well for cheap.

I *really* did not like these people.

"So," Bridget said, finishing her cake and setting down her fork daintily. "Want to hear about Mummy?"

"I suppose," I said without much enthusiasm. I knew I'd been the one who had brought it up in the first place, but at this point I kind of wanted to just bury the whole thing. Talking about it felt like picking at an open wound.

"Well, she'd like to talk to you—"

"No."

"Yeah, I told her you'd say that," Bridget said. "But she says there's another part to the story you haven't heard. She was going to tell you, but you ran off before she could finish and you haven't been answering your messages."

If she was trying to make me feel guilty, it wasn't going to work. "What part of the story?"

"She wants to tell you face-to-face."

I looked away, feeling a spark of anger. My mother could just as easily have passed that part of the message on as well. The fact that she hadn't made the whole thing feel like yet another bit of manipulation.

"So are you going to talk to her?" Bridget said when I didn't answer.

I shrugged.

"You probably should."

"If I feel like it."

Bridget raised her eyebrows but didn't say anything. I watched her as she sipped at her drink. I still had trouble thinking of her as my sister—technically I knew she was, but she still felt like a stranger. I didn't feel as though I really knew what she was like, or what made her tick.

"Bridget?" I asked.

Bridget looked confused. "What?"

Oops. "Never mind. Can I ask you something?"

"Yes, but . . . did you just call me 'Bridget'?"

Oh, well, it was probably going to slip out sooner or later. "Well, you never did tell me your name."

"So you just decided on 'Bridget'?"

"I met you on a bridge," I explained. "Bridget."

Bridget gave me a bemused look, then laughed. "You could have just asked."

"Actually our mother already told me what it was," I said. "But you really don't feel like an 'Isadora.'"

Bridget, or Isadora, made a face. "Nobody calls me that except for Mummy and Grandpa. Everyone else calls me Is."

"Is?" I thought about it, then shrugged. It did suit her better. "Well, that's fine too."

"Actually, now that I think about it, stick with Bridget," my sister said, tilting her head to one side. "I kind of like that nobody else will know who you mean. Anyway, what were you going to ask?"

"Oh, right. Why do you care about this stuff?"

"What do you mean?"

"When you first met me, it was only because of Tobias," I said. "You could have just stayed hidden, but you came out and talked to me. Then when I tracked you down in the autumn, you talked to me again. You weren't *that* helpful . . ."

"Hey!"

". . . but at least you didn't blow me off. Now you're acting as a go-between."

"I mean . . . yes?" Bridget said. "Is that strange?"

"Well, for a normal family, no," I said. "But in case you haven't noticed, your family is on the other side of the planet from normal. Your brother spends his time plotting to become the new heir to the family, Lucella's the same except more vicious about it, Calhoun *is* the heir to the family and wants to stay that way, our mother's playing some game of her own, and your granddad spends all his time running the House. It seems like the only reason any of them ever do anything is because there's something in it for them. Except you."

"Oh," Bridget said. "Well, when you put it like that . . ." She thought for a moment and shrugged. "Someone has to hold the family together."

"And going on raids helps with that how?"

Bridget flashed me a grin that suddenly made her look a lot younger. "I'm allowed to have fun too."

The rest of the lunchtime with Bridget went pleasantly—turned out, she could be quite nice company when she wanted. Although she did ask when the next raid was going to be.

In the meantime, I was working on my plans for a career adjustment.

"So you're serious about this raiding thing?" Colin asked.

"Pretty serious," I told him. We were in the Admiral Nelson, the warmth and chatter of the pub holding back the winter cold from outside. Felix, Kiran, and Gabriel were on the other side of the booth, laughing and joking. I didn't make eye contact with Gabriel. He'd tried mending fences last week when we'd met up for New Year's, but I hadn't reciprocated.

"I mean, after how the last one went . . ."

"All of the times I was in serious danger back then, it was because I was there with someone *else*," I said. "If I'd been on my own, I could have just noped out any time I wanted. Anyway, I'm not planning on hitting any more B or C Wells. At least not to begin with."

"You like living dangerously, don't you?" Colin said. "Hang on, going for a piss."

With Colin gone, I was left to watch the other three. Gabriel was in the middle of telling Felix and Kiran a long, rambling story about something that had happened at his new job. Apparently his manager had wanted to talk to him for some reason, but Gabriel had been really high, and the joke was that the manager had gone through the whole conversation without figuring this out.

". . . and so then he tells me, 'You understand that this is really important to us?' and I say, 'Yeah, yeah, of course.' And then he says, 'Because it's all about improving the customer experience,' and I say, 'Yeah, yeah, I get that,' and then he says, 'I don't want you to feel like you're being criticised here, actually I was watching while you were talking with that lady and I'd just like to say that I was really impressed with that excellent display of customer service'! You know, all that time that she was going off at me and I was just nodding and saying 'Sorry to hear that'? And he still hasn't figured it out! So then he asks me if I restocked the display and I can't actually remember, so I tell him 'Yeah, I was just in the middle of doing that,' and we end up going there together and . . ."

I closed my eyes briefly. The longer Gabriel went on, the more I itched to ask him what was the *point* of all this. All that had happened was that he'd accidentally done his job for once, and he was acting like he'd struck some sort of blow against the system.

But honestly, what was I expecting? Gabriel had always been like this. I'd heard and laughed along with plenty of similar stories when we'd been teenagers. But I wasn't a teenager anymore, and I was increasingly coming to the uncomfortable realisation that I just didn't find Gabriel very interesting. And the same went for drunken conversations in general.

I remembered Felix's words from back in the autumn—*"You're going to have to cut the guy off sooner or later."* A memory flashed through my mind—Ivy telling me about Bou barging past her and out of the back door, leaving her and the others behind—and I shifted, suddenly uncomfortable.

A movement caught my eye and I looked to one side to see Felix watching me. He was giving me a knowing look, and I had the sudden unsettling feeling that he knew exactly what I was thinking.

"Okay," Colin said, sitting down next to me. He'd returned with a new pint, and I turned back to him with relief. "So basically you're going to be doing the same thing as before, you're just not going to be checking too closely who the Wells are supposed to belong to?"

"That's one half of it," I said. Gabriel and the others didn't seem to be paying attention, but I kept my voice down just in case. "Problem is the other half. I need to figure out how to drain Wells, and I need to find somewhere to sell the essentia."

"How?"

"Still working on that."

"Well, bit out of left field, but have you thought about asking Felix?"

"Really?" I asked in surprise. I looked up, but Felix and Gabriel had vanished off to the bar, leaving Kiran scrolling on his mobile. Kiran looked up, gave us a wave, then went back to his screen.

"I mean, if you want something on the cheap, he's kind of the guy."

"Yeah, for laptops and phones," I said. Throughout our childhoods Felix had often shown up with secondhand but surprisingly high-quality electronic goods of various descriptions, and it had been generally understood that one didn't ask too many questions about their point of origin. "This is kind of different."

"Yeah, but have you noticed the way he talks about it?" Colin asked. "Seems like he might know a bit more than he's saying. And, related note . . ." Colin glanced across at Kiran before dropping his voice slightly. "I'm still interested in learning this stuff."

"Colin . . ."

"I'm all caught up on my coursework. And I *have* been helping you out."

"You know dru—this stuff is *hard*, right? It takes a lot of time and a lot of work."

"Yeah, but come on," Colin said. "It's, like, a whole new field of science to study. Who wouldn't get excited about that?"

I should have learned by now that I couldn't put Colin off forever. "You have any idea how much I've got on my plate already?" I said with a sigh. "Fine. When do you want to start?"

DESPITE MY MISGIVINGS, teaching Colin didn't take too much effort, at least not at first. I'd seen a book on Charles's shelves called *A Beginner's Guide to Drucraft* and after a bit of effort managed to track down a secondhand copy. Once it arrived I passed it on to Colin with instructions to read it twice and do all the exercises. I figured that if he got through all that without running out of patience, then I'd worry about actual lessons.

In the meantime, things were going well enough. I heard from Pavel that Anton was out of hospital and should recover fully in a few weeks. I sent a message to Ivy and we actually had a decent conversation for once—she was still a long way from friendly, but it was a step up from how things usually went. I kept working on my darksight sigl research and made notes of a couple of others I'd probably need. And in the meantime I kept on scratching out a living by finding Wells for Mr. Smith.

I didn't hear anything from Calhoun. It had been three months now since he'd offered me that security job, and I hadn't heard a word from him since. It was actually kind of a relief—yeah, I could use the cash, but I had enough on my plate right now without having to deal with the Ashfords as well. For now, if they were willing to leave me alone, I was happy to do the same.

But there was one big glaring area where I wasn't happy at all, and that was my search for my father. Earning money and shaping sigls was good, but I couldn't see any way in which either of those things was going to help me find my dad.

The problem was that I still couldn't see any way forward. I was sure that Byron and the Winged had the pieces of the puzzle that I needed, and I was sure that if I could just get them to answer my questions, I'd have everything I'd need. Unfortunately, I was *also* sure that going up to them and asking for what I wanted wasn't going to work. I'd learned the hard way by now that it was a terrible idea to deal with these sorts of people from a position of weakness. I had absolutely no leverage on Byron, which meant he'd be free to promise me everything and give me nothing.

But if asking them wasn't going to work, what would?

I worked away at the problem as the days went by, turning it over and over at the back of my mind, coming up with increasingly outlandish plans and rejecting them all. As January wore on, I began to think that I might have to approach Byron after all. I didn't want to come across as desperate, but I was running out of other ideas.

But in the end, Byron was the one to contact me first.

CHAPTER 15

IT WAS A Thursday morning in the third week of January. The sun was shining, but there was frost on the rooftops. Last night had been miserable; the landlord still hadn't fixed the boiler, and when morning had come I hadn't been able to face a four-hour locating shift in zero-degree weather. Instead I was sitting on my bed with my back against the wall and my duvet wrapped around me, looking down at my headband and light amplification sigl. I'd laid them out on my mattress and was trying to figure out how to combine the two.

As a way to see in the dark, my new sigl worked fine—it was a small, pale sphere that worked exactly as intended, amplifying incoming light to make a darkened room as bright as day. The problem was mounting it. The amplification sigl absolutely had to be worn next to my eyes, the closer the better, and the problem was, my vision sigl—which let me see while invisible by turning ultraviolet light into something visible to the eye—*also* had to be worn next to my eyes. And if I set both sigls into the same headband, I ran into issues with essentia meant for one sigl leaking into the other.

I could fix the problem by spacing the sigls out, having one over the right eye and one over the left, but then they'd both be off centre, which wasn't so much of a problem for the vision sigl but which really messed up the amplification one. The easiest solution was to put them into two different headbands and only wear one at a time, but I kept remembering that ambush at the football ground, when I'd had to fumble my vision sigl out of my pocket. The extra seconds needed to change a headband could cost me my life.

Could I figure out a way to make some sort of super sigl that combined the effects of both? No, they both did completely different things—one changed light's frequency while the other amplified it. I couldn't think of any effect that'd do both . . .

I sighed. No wonder the Ashfords bought their sigls from the Exchange. Doing all this on your own was *really* hard.

My phone buzzed and I glanced over. Maybe it was Colin asking about—

Byron: Hello, Stephen. How's it going?
Byron: I haven't heard from you in a while.

I paused.

My first impulse was to send back a message that was cautiously polite—this was the opening I'd been waiting for. But . . . no. I didn't want to seem too eager.

I picked up my phone and typed Yeah, there's a reason for that and hit "Send." The message vanished off into the ether and I sat back to wait.

My phone pinged a minute later.

Byron: So suspicious. What did I ever do to you?

Stephen: You? Nothing, yet. That friend of yours is another story.

Byron: What friend?

Stephen: Boy in his early twenties, thin, wears a strength sigl?

Byron: I'm not sure who you mean.

Stephen: After we had our chat in September, he showed up in my neighbourhood and tried to put a few holes in me. Does that narrow it down?

There was no response for a few seconds, then my phone started to ring. The screen said "No Caller ID."

I let it ring. The phone kept going for fifteen or twenty rings and stopped. Then it started up again.

I settled down to wait.

The phone finally stopped ringing and almost immediately pinged with a message.

Byron: Pick up your phone.

Stephen: No.

Byron: I'm serious.

Stephen: I'm busy.

There was a pause. The typing icon appeared and disappeared several times as I watched.

Byron: I promise you that I'm neither lying nor hiding anything when I say that I had nothing to do with this.

Stephen: Well, bully for you, but your friend made it clear that if I didn't stay away he'd rip me into pieces and shove the bits down my throat. So I don't see how it matters.

Byron: It'll matter very much, quite shortly. Come meet me this weekend.

Stephen: I think I'll pass.

Byron: The attack on you did not happen with my knowledge. Show up and I'll make sure it doesn't happen again.

I looked down at my phone, thinking. I'd probably acted reluctant enough at this point to make Byron believe that I was scared. The truth was that dealing with this boy wasn't really my biggest worry. Yes, he was nasty, but I felt by this point that I had a decent handle on what he could do. It wasn't as though I *wanted* him to track me down for a round three, but if I actually thought that it would help me find my dad, I'd do it in a heartbeat. So while Byron offering to shut this guy down was nice, it wasn't what I really cared about.

But it seemed like it was all I was going to get. I typed Fine into the phone, then tossed it onto the bed, leant back against the wall, wrapped my duvet more tightly around me, and closed my eyes with a sigh. I wasn't looking forward to this. Someone ambushing me was something I knew how to deal with. Byron was a very different kind of problem, and something told me that he was a much more dangerous one.

THE LAST TIME, Byron had let me pick the time and the place, presumably because he'd been trying to make me feel safe. This time, he didn't ask me for my opinion on either. I had the feeling that this might be his real personality showing through.

The spot Byron had picked was a wine bar next to Hampstead Heath station. It was less than a hundred yards from the house where that boy had attacked me; in fact, I was pretty sure I'd run right past it during my escape. At half past noon on that Saturday, I pushed open the door and walked in.

The bar was long and narrow, with bare brick walls that had

been left unpainted. Oversized glasses sparkled from black-topped tables. I saw someone wave from the back end of the bar and walked over. "There you are," Byron told me as I approached. "You certainly took your time."

Byron was dressed in his usual expensive-looking suit and was sitting in the corner of one of the booths, leaning against the wall. He was smiling and seemed in better humour than he had been during our phone conversation.

But it was the person slouching in the chair next to him I was more concerned about. It was the boy I'd last seen at Clapton Football Ground. Whip thin, with a narrow face and short black hair, he had the build of a runner or a dancer, but it was his eyes that struck me the most. They were very dark, and as I approached they watched me with a cold, dead look that made me think of a shark.

I stopped a few steps from the table.

"Sit down, Stephen," Byron said, beckoning.

I looked at the boy. He stared back at me.

"Sit," Byron said, a trace of sharpness creeping into his voice.

"You know what?" I said, not taking my eyes off the boy. "I'm not sure that's a good idea."

"Mark?" Byron said to the boy. His voice was silk, with a threat of something else beneath. "We talked about this."

The boy stared at me for a few seconds more, then broke eye contact, looking down and away.

"There," Byron said, gesturing again to the seat opposite. "Now that that's settled . . ."

"This is *not* settled," I told him. "And I think you've got the wrong idea about how much I want to be here."

Byron let out an exasperated sigh. "You really like to make my life more difficult, don't you?" he told the boy next to him. His voice was light, but he wasn't smiling, and when he turned back to me his expression was serious. "Stephen, I give you my word you are entirely safe. Please sit down so we can discuss this in a civilised manner."

I didn't feel as though any of this was especially civilised. But there were a couple of other customers and a waitress in the bar; it was still pretty empty, but public enough that I didn't think Byron and his friend would try anything in broad daylight. I moved forward and sat, keeping a little distance from the table.

"Much better," Byron said. "Can I get you something? This place is a little pretentious, but the wines really are quite good."

If I had to rank every single person in the world on the basis of how happy I'd be to get drunk with them, these two would be at the bottom of the list. "No, thanks."

"As you like." Byron called the waitress over and they started talking about wines, using words like "body" and "tannic." I took the chance to study the boy sitting across from me.

Mark—if that was his name—didn't react to my gaze. He was dressed casually in jeans and a T-shirt, with a fine chain around his neck disappearing below his clothes. I suspected that chain held a strength sigl and possibly more, but whatever sigls he might have, they were inactive right now. Actually, "inactive right now" was a pretty good description of how he was coming across in general. He seemed completely disengaged.

But I didn't let my guard down. If he'd gone from murderous to disengaged, he could turn back again. Byron might claim that I was safe here, but I didn't believe him.

"There," Byron said once the waitress had gone. "Now, then."

I turned my attention back to Byron.

"It seems to me that there have been some serious miscommunications," Byron said. "Stephen, you seem to be under the impression that we from the Winged are your enemies."

"Yeah, I can't imagine how I could have got *that* idea."

"And Mark here has apparently been under the impression that you are a threat to his position."

I glanced at Mark. He didn't react.

"Both of these things are completely untrue," Byron said. "I really wish you'd told me earlier that you and Mark had already run into one another. We could have sorted this out right from the start."

Mark continued to stare off to one side.

"But Mark and I have had a long talk, and we've established that this isn't going to happen again. Haven't we, Mark?"

"Sure," Mark said, speaking for the first time.

Byron looked at me with a smile. "There."

I looked dubiously at Mark. He still hadn't turned to face us. "He doesn't seem all that happy to me."

"He can be a little temperamental," Byron said with a wave of his hand. "The important thing is that I can give you my personal assurance that from now on you'll be safe."

"So was he right?" I asked.

"About what?"

"About me being a threat to his position."

Byron sighed. "Don't be silly."

"Why is it silly?" I asked. I kept an eye on Mark as I spoke.

"As I told you, I'm something of a talent scout," Byron said. He gave Mark a possessive pat on the shoulder. "Mark here is one of my protégés. He's quite capable, don't you think?"

"Seems that way."

"Still," Byron said, removing his hand from the boy and resting his eyes on me. "I'm always on the lookout for new prospects."

The waitress arrived with a glass of wine, putting the conversation on pause. Byron sipped and gave some compliment to the waitress, who blushed and smiled. She asked both me and Mark if we wanted anything. I shook my head. Mark ignored her.

"So," Byron said once the waitress had gone. "Have you had any more thoughts?"

"About?"

"My offer."

"Not really."

"For heaven's sake, Stephen," Byron said with a sigh. "This hard-to-get act is getting old. You nearly got yourself perforated back in the autumn and you're looking even shabbier now than you did then. Isn't it about time you accepted that you could use some help?"

I ignored the "shabbier" part. "I nearly got perforated *because* of your friend," I told Byron. "Now you're surprised that I don't want to hang out with you?"

"If you'd cooperated from the start, all this unpleasantness could have been avoided."

"As in, back when you asked me to move in? Thanks, but having this guy as a roommate doesn't sound like my idea of fun."

I'd been watching Mark, and as I said "move in," I saw his eyes flicker. *So that's what it takes to get a rise out of you?*

"You're not going to be sharing accommodation with Mark," Byron said.

"You're damn right I'm not, because I'm not moving in with any of you. This is about as close as I care to get."

"Calm down, Stephen."

"Calm down? Really?" I turned to look at Mark. "If I moved into your house, how many days would it take before you tried to knife me in my sleep?"

Mark met my gaze, his eyes dark and expressionless. "I wouldn't use a knife."

"Mark!" Byron said sharply.

"Are you hearing this?" I demanded of Byron. "He won't even promise not to kill me!"

"Of course not," Byron said in irritation. "I haven't promised not to kill you, the waitress hasn't promised not to kill you, the woman at the fruit stand across the street hasn't promised not to kill you. Just trust me, please."

"No," I said flatly, and got to my feet.

"*Sit down*," Byron ordered.

I paused. Byron's eyes suddenly seemed very large and dark, and the rest of the world faded away. Without thinking about it, I reached for the chair.

I felt a strange sensation, like thin ice breaking. A memory flashed through my mind: my footsteps echoing on stone, the dust-and-wax smell of the old church. Then it was gone, and I was left standing in the bar, one hand still on the back of the chair, staring at Byron.

I turned and hurried away. I had a moment to register the surprise on Byron's face, then I was pushing the door open, the cold air of the London street hitting my face. Sounds rushed in from all around: the rush of traffic, the shouts of people, the rumble of a train passing by underneath the bridge.

I hurried across the road, past the fruit stand, and into the station. Once I was through the ticket gates, I ran down the stairs to the platform, then waited for a train, one eye on the tracks and one on the stairs to see if anyone was following. I kept watching for any sign of Mark or Byron right up until the train arrived, the doors hissed shut behind me, and the train pulled away from the platform.

I DIDN'T FEEL good on the journey back. I'd known that Byron wasn't going to just hand over what I wanted, but I'd thought that maybe Mark's attack on me might give me some leverage. My plan had been to pretend to walk out in the hope that Byron might tell me a bit more about my father.

It hadn't worked, and I'd come away with nothing. Worse, I

had the feeling that I was *lucky* to have come away with nothing. I'd known that Byron was dangerous, but I'd underestimated just how dangerous. My thoughts kept going back to that fleeting moment when Byron's voice and eyes had filled my mind, driving out my own will, and each time I shivered. Just for that instant, I'd felt like a small animal frozen in the gaze of a predator. I didn't understand what had happened, but something told me I'd had a narrow escape.

I got home to find a bunch of messages from Byron on my phone. I swiped away without reading any of them, then curled up on my bed and tried to figure out what to do.

I DIDN'T COME up with any answers during the rest of that day. But Hobbes came back home in the evening and curled up next to my side, and I spent a couple of hours that night stroking him and feeling his warmth against me. When I finally fell asleep, I didn't have any bad dreams.

When I woke up the next morning everything felt clearer. One feeling from yesterday had stood out in my mind: that sense of being a small animal beneath the gaze of a much bigger one. Because that *was* how things were for me. The Winged, the corporations, the Houses . . . all of them were much bigger and more powerful than I was. I was a mouse scuttling between the feet of huge, looming predators, any of which could crush me without even noticing.

If I was a mouse, I needed to think like one. Which meant I had to operate in the shadows. These groups might be big, but they were clumsy. As long as I didn't draw their notice, as long as I only showed them what they were expecting to see, they'd have no way of knowing what I was really doing. I just needed to camouflage myself and to bide my time.

So I started putting that into practice.

Top of my to-do list was a new sigl. For a while now I'd been wanting some kind of aggressive sigl that would let me fight back against the kinds of enemies I kept running into, but I was starting to realise that "fighting back" was the wrong way to think about things. I didn't need to fight back; I needed to *survive*. And the best way to do that was not to get noticed.

At the moment my only real stealth option was my invisibility, which, while effective, had some major drawbacks. The diffraction and vision sigls combined ate up more than half of my essentia capacity and required constant concentration, which meant that while they were both running it was very hard for me to do anything else. For what I had in mind, I needed something that would conceal my identity, but which I could keep running in the background while focusing on other things. And as it happened, last spring I'd run into someone with a sigl that I thought might be just what I was looking for.

Two days after my meeting with Byron, I got another job offer. Just like last time, the message was from an anonymous number and talked in vague terms about securing a Well. I read the message carefully, then sent back a reply asking for more details. I got a response stating that they weren't able to give any details due to the confidential nature of the operation and that I'd be fully briefed closer to the time.

I pressed them on it, but they refused to budge, insisting that these were the same terms they offered to everyone, that I could take it or leave it, and warning me that if I said no, that this could have negative effects on other employers' willingness to approach me afterwards.

I thought about it for a day, then thanked them politely and refused. I never heard from that number again.

I got back in touch with Byron. I didn't really want to answer his messages, but had the feeling that he—or Mark—might come looking for me if I didn't. Byron apologised again for Mark's behaviour and said he regretted how the meeting had ended. I responded neutrally, but when Byron suggested another meeting I said only that I'd have to take some time to think about it. I was learning.

January came to an end. My financial situation wasn't great; I'd been finding fewer Wells since the beginning of winter, and food and heating prices in London had gone through the roof. At the rate things were going, I'd run out of money sometime around midsummer.

But before that could happen, I finally heard back from Calhoun. I woke up one morning to find a message from him saying that Johanna Meusel would be arriving in London in two days and that I should arrange for a meeting with her and her head of security at my earliest convenience.

CHAPTER 16

THE HOTEL WAS close to Victoria station. With green plants and Union Jacks projecting out from the first floor, and a front porch that looked like a Greek temple, it looked less like a hotel and more like the mansion of a very eccentric millionaire. I had some trouble with the doorman, but Johanna's name eventually got me through.

Once inside, I didn't know where to go. Following the white-and-black-tiled hall led me into a reception area with some sofas; fancy chandeliers hung from the ceiling. A flat-screen TV was discreetly tucked away in a corner, tuned to a news channel. The banner at the bottom read "UK ENERGY PRICES REACH RECORD HIGH"; above the banner, the channel was showing an American talk show host.

". . . but a clean conscience is worth a buck or two," the talk show host was saying. His audience burst into cheers and applause and he clapped a few times himself before going on. "I'm willing to pay . . . it's important! I'm willing to pay four dollars a gallon." He smirked. "Hell, I'll pay fifteen dollars a gallon because I drive a Tesla." The audience laughed.

There was no sign of Johanna. I turned and left.

I eventually found her in the hotel's restaurant. Forest scenes were painted on the walls and the windows looked out onto leafy window boxes, giving the place an idyllic, Garden of Eden sort of look. Johanna and a man I didn't recognise were sitting at a table, and Johanna waved me over as soon as I entered. "Hello, Stephen," Johanna said with a smile as I walked over. "It's been a while."

When I'd first laid eyes on Johanna Meusel I'd thought she was the most beautiful girl I'd ever seen, and looking at her now didn't do much to change that impression. Her light brown outfit was less eye-catching than what she'd worn to that party, but with her near-white hair and sculpted features, she stood out just as sharply. There were a few other people scattered around the restaurant, all smartly dressed, and as I reached Johanna's table I saw a couple of the men glance between me and her. They didn't quite raise their eyebrows, but you could tell what they were thinking.

The man sitting at the table with Johanna was much older, maybe forty or so. He was heavily built and muscular, with dark hair and eyes, and a beard that covered a square jaw. Unlike the other men in the restaurant, his eyes stayed on me. His manner wasn't exactly threatening, but it wasn't friendly, either.

"Come and sit down," Johanna said, gesturing to a chair. "Would you like anything to eat?"

I took a glance at the menu and managed not to goggle at the prices. "I'm fine."

"So, introductions," Johanna said. "Stephen, this is Hendrik. He's my head of security and an old family retainer of House

Meusel. He and my father knew each other when they were young."

I gave Hendrik a nod; the man returned it but didn't speak. I noticed that Johanna didn't introduce me to Hendrik in return and realised she must have told him about me already. "Calhoun said you wanted to meet me?"

"Oh, we can get to that later," Johanna said. "Why don't you tell me what you've been doing?"

A waiter came and took orders while Johanna plied me with questions. Hendrik said nothing the whole time, shaking his head when the waiter looked at him. Between his silent presence and the unfamiliar environment, I felt very out of my depth, and my answers to Johanna were awkward, though she didn't seem to mind.

". . . so I'm still working as a locator for now," I said as the waiter arrived, setting down a tray with a teapot and cups.

"Is the market for that any better?" Johanna asked as Hendrik poured the tea. "Light and Matter essentia is in quite high demand with everything that's happening at the moment."

"Yeah, well, none of that seems to filter down to the bottom," I said. Hendrik lifted the teapot and glanced towards me, and I shook my head.

"Sigl providers aren't going to pay anything they don't have to," Johanna said with a nod. "It does give locators a stronger bargaining position, though."

"So, I don't want to be rude or anything," I said. "But what do you actually want? Don't get me wrong, it's nice talking to you, but from what Calhoun said you're here to attend some sort of elite university. You've got to have better things to be doing."

"It's more like an exchange term," Johanna said with a smile. She didn't seem bothered by my bluntness. "And my schedule's actually fairly free at the moment. But, yes, I didn't ask you here just for social reasons."

I looked at Johanna, waiting.

"Well, let's be direct about it," Johanna said. "Hendrik and I are wondering how much we can trust you."

"Why wouldn't you?"

"You have a bit of a conflict of interest."

"Ah," I said. *So she knows about that.*

"I looked into it after I met you," Johanna said, answering my unspoken thought. "I'd thought I knew everyone in the Ashford family tree. You were a missing link."

Johanna seemed remarkably unashamed about having me investigated. I hoped that it hadn't been as easy as she was making it sound. "Okay, so you know how I fit into House Ashford," I said. "Why would that make you not trust me?"

Johanna looked at me in surprise. "You really are new to this, aren't you?"

"I hear that a lot."

Johanna smiled but became serious almost immediately. "Everyone from your side of the Ashford family—you, your brother and sister, your mother, your stepfather—has a very strong interest in seeing Calhoun's engagement fail. So for Calhoun to engage you as security feels a little like . . . how would you say it? Setting the fox to guard the chicken house?"

"Henhouse," I said. "You know there's no way in hell Charles would ever pick me as heir, right?"

"Don't take this the wrong way," Johanna said, "but we only have your word for that."

I opened my mouth to justify myself . . . then stopped as I remembered Charles's lessons. This wasn't how you were supposed to act in this world. "What reason do *I* have to trust *you*?" I countered. "I mean, you told me right when we first met that you had your own ambitions. How do I know you're not just using Calhoun for some reason of your own?"

Johanna tilted her head, studying me. "All right," she said. "I'll tell you where I'm coming from if you do the same."

I paused, then nodded. "Deal."

"So you may not know this, but I'm the second child of House Meusel," Johanna explained. "I have one brother, Albrecht, who's five years older than me. Ever since I was a little girl I've known he was the one who was going to take over the House once he grew up. The only big question was who he'd marry, and that was settled a couple of years ago. He ended up engaged to a nice girl from House Bornschein—the ones from Saxony-Anhalt. The wedding's this summer."

"Okay."

"So as you might be able to guess," Johanna went on, "everyone in my family's very willing to help me find a husband. My mother and father, obviously. But also Grandmama, and Albrecht, and his fiancée." She smiled slightly. "For a while I was getting an invitation to a different ball or party every day of the week."

It was so weird hearing Johanna talk about her world. "Is that their way of giving you a hint?"

"Oh, they'd never actually push me out," Johanna said. "House Meusel has a lot of holdings; there's always work to be done. But Grandmama's always said I'd be wasting my talents as an estate manager, and as for Anna . . . well, she's told me I'll always be welcome in the family home, but I'm not sure she'll feel that way forever."

"All right," I said. I still didn't really understand what Johanna was getting at.

"The point is, almost everyone in my family wants my engagement with Calhoun to succeed," Johanna said. "Almost everyone in *your* family wants it to fail."

"Ah," I said. Now I got it. "So you've got an incentive to make this work, while my family's got the opposite."

"Exactly," Johanna said. "Now, I don't think any of them would go as far as outright murder. But I'm sure it's occurred to all of them at one point or another that it would be very convenient if I happened to suffer some kind of highly unpleasant accident."

You might be underestimating them when it comes to the murder thing. "I guess I can see why you'd be concerned," I admitted, and glanced over at Hendrik, who'd been watching the whole conversation patiently. "And why you'd bring him along."

Johanna looked at me expectantly.

"All right, here's the thing," I said. "I'm not from your world. All of this stuff you're telling me about families and marriage alliances? I honestly don't understand any of it. I mean, I can *follow* it, but I don't *get* it, not really. My dad taught me drucraft and discipline and how to be a man. He didn't teach me this House politics stuff, which you and everyone else from your world can apparently do in your sleep. And Charles Ashford knows that, which is why he made it really clear the first time I ever met him that there was no way in hell that he was ever going to appoint me as heir." I shrugged. "Honestly, it's a bit of a relief. The kind of people who play these games and spend their whole lives plotting to get themselves named heir . . . I've met a couple like that from House Ashford, and it doesn't seem like it's done them any favours. I'm outside the family, and I'm happy that way."

"So why'd you take the job?" Hendrik said, speaking for the first time. Despite his looks, he had a casual, easygoing sort of voice.

I shrugged. "Still need to eat."

Hendrik studied me for a second, then nodded, as if accepting the answer.

"And what if Tobias or Lucella came up to you in a month or two and offered you a good deal of money to sabotage things?" Johanna asked.

She's done her homework, hasn't she? "I'd tell them no."

"Why?"

"What do you mean, 'why'?"

"You don't see yourself as part of the family," Johanna said. "If you're only doing it for money, what happens when someone offers you more?"

"I told Calhoun I'd do the job," I said, holding back my annoyance. Hadn't I already explained this part? "That means I'll do it."

Johanna tilted her head, studying me for a few seconds longer, then smiled unexpectedly. "All right." She reached down and produced a leather folder, then took out a sheet of paper. "Here's my schedule for the next couple of weeks. Pass on any venue details to Hendrik as soon as you get them."

The meeting shifted to business while we shared contact details and information. After fifteen minutes or so Johanna mentioned that she had an appointment, at which point I took the hint and prepared to leave.

As I got to my feet something occurred to me. "Hey, Johanna?"

"*Ja?*"

"You said for a while you were getting invitations nonstop," I said. "You must have got a lot of proposals."

"A few."

"So why'd you pick Calhoun?" I asked. "Couldn't you have found a House where you *didn't* have to worry about the other members trying to assassinate you?"

Johanna smiled. "Maybe I just wanted a change."

It was only a few minutes later, once I'd said my goodbyes and was walking through the hotel's front door back out into the cold February air, that it occurred to me that Johanna might not have been completely honest with that last answer. But then, it had been a rather personal question.

AND SO BEGAN my stint as a bodyguard.

I got my first call two days later, from Calhoun's PA, Clarissa. Apparently Calhoun was taking Johanna out to some place called the Ritz. I passed the information on to Hendrik and then showed up early on Saturday afternoon.

Things didn't go to plan. It turned out that the Ritz was another upper-class hotel, but one with a much stricter dress code. The doorman took one look at my jeans, fleece, and trainers and refused to let me in, and this time Johanna's name didn't help. I was getting slightly panicky and was on the verge of trying to use my invisibility sigl to sneak in when Hendrik showed up, saw at a glance what was going on, and told me not to worry about it. His job was close protection; my job was to keep my eyes open for anyone I recognised, and I could do that just as well watching the front door. So I did as he said, standing out in the cold and feeling rather exposed and embarrassed. When Calhoun and Johanna finally got out of a taxi, I was sure Calhoun was going to say something, but he only gave me a slight nod as he walked up the steps to the hotel with Johanna on his arm. (The doorman let *them* pass without a word.)

The whole thing was kind of frustrating. Back when I'd met Calhoun in the autumn, he'd told me he'd explain things nearer to the time. He hadn't. All I had to go on was Hendrik's instruction— keep an eye open for anyone you recognise—and what did that even mean, anyway? Presumably he was talking about the Ashfords, but I didn't like being left in the dark.

Calhoun and Johanna left a couple of hours later (still without a word) and I met up with Hendrik, who told me that everything had gone fine and that I could head home. I did, at which point I had to figure out what hourly rate to charge. Calhoun had told me to send Clarissa my invoices, and my first instinct was to ask for something like £10 to £15 an hour, which was what I'd been paid back when I'd done bar work. On the other hand, I remembered Maria charging £100 an hour for a consultation and, when I'd objected, telling me that for an essentia analyst that was on the low end.

I went back and forth for a long time, and in the end sent off an invoice where I charged £30 an hour plus travel expenses. It was almost three times what I'd been paid in the Civil Service, and I waited on tenterhooks for the rest of the day, half expecting to get an angry refusal. But all I got was a notification telling me that the invoice had been paid. I didn't even get questioned about the number of hours I was claiming, which was quite a change from the Ministry of Defence, where my manager had docked my pay for the time I'd spent having lunch. Calhoun might not be willing to spare the time to talk to me, but at least he wasn't cheap.

From that point on things settled into a routine. I accompanied Calhoun and Johanna on three more dates (one restaurant dinner, two theatre trips) and managed to scrounge together an old shirt and trousers that at least meant that I didn't get stopped at the door, though I'd still get looks. I'd been worried that I'd be expected to check for bombs or assassins or something, but Hendrik explained to me that he'd handle that; my job was to keep an eye open, and, yes, that meant looking out for the Ashfords specifically. So I got into a pattern where I'd research the place online, show up a bit in advance to have a walkabout, then wander around once Calhoun and Johanna arrived. It wasn't actually too different from working security at a bar, minus the kids smoking joints and creepy guys trying to grab my arse.

That said, while it wasn't *too* far removed from bar work, the differences were still there. It wasn't the first time I'd seen the kind of world the Ashfords and Johanna lived in, but it was the first time I'd been exposed to it at length. And when you're exposed to something for a while, you start noticing things.

I suppose to some people it would have been fun. The dates that Calhoun was taking Johanna on were the kind that the girls in my old school used to dream about, and that guys in my old school used to wish they had the money for. Gleaming cars that Calhoun would exit, then walk around to take Johanna's hand and help her out of. Private boxes at the theatre with an attendant to usher them in. A special table at the restaurant with a waiter hovering nearby. They didn't go to any red-carpet events, but wherever they went the staff seemed to treat them differently. No matter the place, Calhoun only had to raise a hand and someone would be at his side in seconds. It was a window into the everyday lives of the ultrarich, and, like I said, I guessed a lot of people would have found it fun.

I didn't. At all.

It was that stupid TV show. The one I'd seen when I'd gone to meet Johanna, with the talk show host laughing about fuel prices. Because, of course, the kinds of people who stayed in those kinds of hotels could *afford* to laugh about fuel prices. Or about rents, or the cost of food, or everything else that I had to struggle with every single day. They lived in this glittering world with people rushing to solve their every problem, while I had to check my bank balance every week and divide it by my rent to see how many months I'd have before I'd be kicked out on the street. I had to go home and deal with that every single day, while they got to spend their time deciding what overpriced restaurant to visit next.

It pissed me off. It *really* pissed me off. It wasn't so much that they had so much more than me; it was the fact that for them, things like not being able to pay the heating bill were a joke. It was all just *content* for them, a background drama that they could casually tune in to and maybe strike poses about, like those arsehole politicians and celebrities you always see on TV talking about how much they care about the underprivileged. And watching Calhoun and Johanna, I started to associate them with that too.

On some level, I knew I wasn't being fair. It wasn't Calhoun's fault that he was the nephew of Charles Ashford, and it wasn't Johanna's fault that she was the second child of House Meusel. Neither had ever actually done anything bad to me, and while they never seemed to have the time to talk, they did at least treat me with a certain basic level of respect. It would have been easy for either of them to make it obvious that they looked down on how I dressed or acted, the way the doormen at those hotels did, and in my few interactions with the two heirs I found myself watching them closely for exactly that. But if they really did feel that way, I never saw any sign of it, and after a while I'd start feeling foolish, and I'd shake the whole thing off and resolve to stop being so petty.

But then I'd go home to my freezing house and my cramped little room, and I'd feel that resentment flare back up. That was my battle for most of that February, one where the enemy was within.

WITH THE MONEY I was getting from Calhoun, I didn't have to spend so much time hunting for Wells. I immediately put my new free time to use on my new sigl project, which I'd nicknamed "shadowman."

The active camouflage sigls that I'd seen Bridget and Calhoun use worked because they were asymmetrical: outgoing light was replaced by a duplicate of the incoming light from the other side, while incoming light was copied but otherwise left unchanged. The result was that anyone looking at them saw a reproduction of the scene immediately behind them. I knew I couldn't manage the copy-and-duplicate trick on that scale, but I *could* see how to make a sigl that blocked outgoing light completely. This let me bypass the whole make-people-see-through-you problem, which was the really hard part, and since it didn't affect incoming light, it'd let *me* see just fine. The resulting effect was a cloud of darkness that was a weird mixture of highly stealthy and highly obvious. Anyone would be able to know that I was there, but they wouldn't be able to see or identify *me*—which was the part I cared about.

I had all I needed to raid a Well, except for one thing—a buyer. There was always the option of going through Mr. Smith, but I really didn't want to go down that route if I could help it. So, figuring it couldn't hurt to ask, I decided to take Colin's advice and give Felix a try.

It went a lot better than I'd expected.

"Sure," Felix told me.

"Wait," I said. "You actually know guys who'll buy this stuff?"

"No, but I know a guy who knows a guy. Have to ask around a bit, you know, put out some feelers."

I blinked. "Huh."

"What are you looking so confused about?"

"I kind of thought you were going to blow me off," I admitted.

We were in the Admiral Nelson in the late afternoon; the pub was mostly empty, with a few middle-aged men nursing their drinks, staring at their phones, or both. The others were due later, but I'd asked Felix to come early.

"I kept trying to shut you up before because you kept bringing it up in front of bloody Gabriel," Felix pointed out. "I *told* you, you're not supposed to talk about this stuff."

"Then how do *you* know about it?"

"Well, the nobs don't want us talking about it, but they got to buy their shit from somewhere, don't they?" Felix said. "And they're not going to ask too many questions about where it comes from, so long as you keep your mouth *shut*."

Yeah, I'd learned my lesson about that one. "So wait," I said. "All these years I've been learning drucraft and dancing around the subject with you guys—you knew the whole time?"

"Actually, I thought you were bullshitting," Felix admitted.

"What?"

"I mean, all that meditation stuff just sounds like crap to me."

"Okay, okay, hang on," I said. "I know I was pretty vague about it, but you must have known that I was doing actual drucraft. Even if I didn't use words like 'sensing,' you should have been able to figure it out eventually."

"Sensing?"

"Sensing essentia."

Felix gave me a blank look.

"You know, the three disciplines? Sensing, channelling, shaping . . . ?"

"What are those again?"

"Wait," I said. "How can you know about drucraft but not that? Why would you learn about drucraft and *not* want to learn about that?"

"Drucraft is what they do with aurum, right?"

I tried to figure out how to answer that.

Felix shrugged. "Yeah, this isn't my thing. All I know about aurum is that it's worth money. Sorry."

I gave him a disbelieving look.

Felix sighed. "Look, Stephen, let me tell you a secret, okay? All this drucraft stuff of yours? It's just another business. You've got the guys who source it, the guys who process it, and the guys who sell it. Doesn't matter if it's gold, or booze, or SIM cards. It's all just product."

"But you can *do* things with drucraft," I said. "It's *real.*"

"Yeah, so? You give a few grand of aurum to some random kid, is he going to be able to do anything? Best he can do is sell it on and make a bit of cash before someone takes it off him."

I opened my mouth to answer, then closed it again.

Felix waved his hand. "Look, don't worry about it. You need a connect, right? I can hook you up. But you'll owe me, okay?"

"Yeah," I said, and I knew he meant it. Felix is honest in his own way, but he doesn't do anything for free. We talked a little longer, then I made my excuses and left before Kiran and Gabriel arrived.

I wandered home with my hands in my pockets. I'd got what I wanted, but Felix's words had left me uncomfortable. Because he did have a point—for the average drucrafter, even a talented one, getting access to a Well *was* pretty useless. I could make my own sigls, but I was increasingly coming to realise just how rare that was. For the vast majority of people, the best they could do was to sell it . . . and my dealings with the corporations had taught me just how lopsided those deals tended to end up being.

But even if I could understand where Felix was coming from, I still thought he was wrong. Drucraft was more than just something to be bought and sold, or a power to be used. When I was using my sensing, or practising my channelling exercises, or shaping an essentia construct, I felt as though I was touching something that went deeper than the things I saw from day to day. I might use it to earn a living, or to defend myself, but I didn't feel as though that was what it was *for*, not really. It seemed more important than that.

I sighed and put the whole thing aside. For now at least, earning my living was the best I could hope for. But maybe I ought to go take another look at those books of Father Hawke's.

IN BETWEEN WORKING for Calhoun and developing my new sigl, I was getting pressured by two separate people via text message. Both wanted to see me, and neither seemed willing to take no for an answer. One was Byron; the other was my mother.

My mother wore me down first.

"So I hear you're helping out Calhoun?" my mother asked.

"News travels fast in your family," I told her. We were sitting on a park bench near the redbrick bridge on the Heath. All around us, bare branches of trees reached up towards an overcast winter sky. The wood I was sitting on was cold enough to make me shiver.

"*Our* family," my mother corrected.

I looked off down into the woods, trying to hide a flash of anger. *Now* I was part of the family?

"So how did it happen?" my mother asked when I didn't speak.

I didn't meet her eyes. "Calhoun asked me."

My mother gave me a quizzical look. "That's all?"

"What else would there be?"

"How did you get him to trust you?"

"I didn't. He came to me."

My mother looked at me for a few seconds, then smiled. "So it's like that?" She shook her head. "Calhoun's always done that, ever since he was a little boy. He'd just decide he liked or disliked someone, and once he'd made up his mind you couldn't get him to change it."

I looked at my mother in interest. She *would* have known Calhoun from when he was young, wouldn't she? It was oddly reassuring, hearing her talk like this—it made House Ashford feel more like a real family and less like—

"But it's a good move," my mother added. "Daddy's made it obvious by now that he's serious about making Calhoun heir. Trying to sabotage him at this point would seem like you were working against the House. Helping him is a much better look."

I sighed, my mood souring. *And we're back to normal.*

My mother frowned slightly, noticing my expression. "You do have to think about these things, Stephen."

"Why do you care?" I asked. "You did everything you could to keep me away from the family for twenty years, why do you suddenly care what they think of me now?"

My mother hesitated, her mouth slightly open; she seemed off guard, and for a second she looked naked and hurt. Then she looked away, down at the cold earth. I did the same. We sat in silence for a minute or two.

"I did try to see you," my mother said.

I looked at her in surprise.

"It was a couple of years after Isadora was born," my mother said. "You would have been about seven."

"You said Charles wouldn't let you."

"He wouldn't," my mother said. "At first. But once Tobias and Isadora were born . . . well, I told him it shouldn't matter anymore. He argued, but in the end he agreed. So long as I was discreet."

I looked at her, waiting. "So?" I said when she didn't go on.

"Your father wouldn't let me."

I blinked. "What?"

"Outright forbade it. I kept asking for months. He wouldn't budge."

"But why?"

"You'd have to ask him."

I paused. "What happened next?"

"Tobias had his first essentia reading," my mother said. "That . . . changed things. Approaching you after that . . . it would have sent a different message."

"Why?"

"It doesn't matter," my mother said with a shake of her head. "Just . . . I want you to know that I did try."

We sat in silence for a little while. "Have you managed to find my dad?" I asked.

My mother hesitated for an instant. "No."

Have you really been trying? "It would be nice to get his side of the story."

"I know, and I promise that if I do learn anything, I'll tell you. But right now I honestly have no idea where he is."

I sighed inwardly. That part, at least, I'd expected. We talked a little longer, then I went home.

THE NEXT MORNING found me fencing with Byron.

I've told you already, I typed. You want to convince me that I can trust you, tell me what happened with my father.

The message from Byron came back quickly. I'd be happy to. In person.

Stephen: Yeah, that's not going to happen.

Byron: Come on, Stephen. Don't be like that.

I didn't like the way he kept on using my name. I've already told you, I typed. After how things went the last time I'm not too keen on another meetup.

Byron: I've already apologised for that.
Stephen: If you want to show you actually mean it, then give me something.
Byron: As I said in the beginning, you're going to have to make some sort of good-faith gesture for us to believe you're serious. I think meeting up in person is a very small thing to ask.

"Damn it," I said out loud, and took my hands off the keyboard. This wasn't getting anywhere.

I stared at the screen, the nasty feeling nagging at me that I was being played. Byron was making it all sound oh so reasonable— all I had to do was come meet him in person. It would be easy to give in and say yes. But then what? What was stopping him from making another demand, and then another?

I had the feeling that that was exactly what Byron wanted. Get me into the habit of doing what he asked, then strike when my guard was down. But what was I going to do about it?

There was a knock from downstairs.

I sat up on my bed, frowning. The house was quiet; Ignas and the others were out at work and Hobbes had disappeared through the window after breakfast. I was alone.

The knock came again. It was coming from the front door.

I reached for my bedside table and slipped on my sigl rings, one after another. Then, on the principle of better safe than sorry, I added the neck chain with my strength and shadowman sigls too, before going downstairs.

The front hallway was quiet. The wooden stairs creaked as I

stepped off them and onto the hall floor. Ahead of me, the front door was still. The only sound was the distant murmur of traffic.

The knock came a third time, insistent.

I opened the door.

The boy standing on the doorstep was a little shorter and a little younger than me, with dark brown hair and eyes. His features weren't much like mine, but looking at them now, with hindsight, I could see an echo in them of my mother's. It was Tobias, my half brother.

"Hey," Tobias said with an open, friendly smile. "Mind if I come in?"

CHAPTER 17

I STARED AT Tobias for two seconds, then started scanning the street.

"How's it going?" Tobias asked.

I couldn't spot any strange cars or minivans. No essentia from Tobias, either. It didn't seem as though there was anyone hiding nearby, at least not close enough to matter.

"So . . ." Tobias said. "You're looking better. Life treating you okay?"

"What are you doing here?" I asked.

"Oh, you know," Tobias said with a shrug. "Was just in the area and thought—"

I started to close the door.

"Wait, wait!" Tobias called. "I've got something for you."

"Like what, another knife for my back?"

Tobias put a hurt expression on his face. "There's no need to—"

I started to close the door again.

"Okay, okay! Look, can we at least talk inside?"

I stared at Tobias for just long enough to make it obvious that

I was thinking about slamming the door in his face, then opened it a few inches. Tobias squeezed through and I shut it behind him.

With the door closed, the hallway was dark and gloomy, lit only by the small window above the doorframe. "So, none of the other guys around?" Tobias asked, glancing down towards the kitchen. "Who was that one who let me in the last time, Matt something?"

"What do you want?"

"How about we go up to your room and—"

"You can tell me here," I said, "or I can throw you out." There was no way I was letting Tobias into my room. I preferred having him down here, within arm's reach, so that if he tried anything I could clock him around the head. In truth, I wasn't really worried about him doing anything physical—I'd dealt with my half brother a few times by now and I was pretty sure that wasn't his style. But he was very good at making trouble.

"All right, all right," Tobias said, raising his hands. "How are things going with Calhoun?"

I suppressed a sigh. "How do you know about that?"

Tobias smiled. "I've got my ways."

"Our mother told you, huh?"

The smile slipped slightly.

"You know," I said, "I get the feeling you didn't exactly impress her much the last couple of times you tried to screw Calhoun over."

"I'm not trying to screw anyone over."

"I don't believe you," I told him.

"Why not?"

"Your lips are moving."

Tobias grinned. "Want me to take up ventriloquism?"

I had to resist the urge to laugh. My half brother is actually kind of fun to hang out with when he's not being such a little shit. "Look, Tobias, whatever you're planning, just drop it, okay? These plots of yours *never* work. Just go home and do something useful with your life."

"I'm not plotting anything," Tobias said, looking very indignant. "I'm trying to help."

I sighed. "Oh, my God."

"How do you think Calhoun's doing with the Meusel girl?"

"How should I know?"

"You've been watching them."

"I've been watching just in case *someone*"—I didn't add *like you*—"tries to mess with them."

"Yeah, but you're going to listen in, right?" Tobias said. "You know, you hear things, you see things . . ."

I just looked at Tobias.

"You know," Tobias said again.

"I'm not you," I told him.

"But you must have noticed she's not looking all that impressed."

"Get to the point."

"Okay," Tobias said. "What if you took her out yourself? Show her a good time, stop her from getting too bored. I mean, Calhoun's only taking her out, what, every five days? Not exactly a whirlwind romance."

"Are you serious?"

"What?"

"Don't 'what' me. You want me to hit on our cousin's fiancée?"

"Hey, they haven't formalised the engagement yet. She's a free, consenting adult, she can do what she wants."

"And you think she's going to want to do *this*?"

"Sure, girls love this stuff. The more guys asking them out, the better."

I made an exasperated noise.

"Come on, what are you afraid of?" Tobias asked. "You get to go out with one of the most beautiful heiresses in the drucraft world."

"First, she wouldn't go out with me," I said. "Second, Calhoun would fire me."

"He doesn't have to know," Tobias said with a shrug. "And I already called her up. She's fine with it."

". . . What?"

Tobias fished around in one of his pockets and pulled out a couple of slips of paper. "Here you go."

I looked down at the tickets—they read "St. Martin's Theatre"—and then back up at Tobias.

Tobias raised his eyebrows.

"What are you getting out of this?" I asked when Tobias didn't speak.

"What, I can't even do a favour for my—?"

"Cut the bullshit."

"Okay, okay! Jeez, you're suspicious. Look, way I see it, Charles just wants *someone* from House Ashford to marry into House Meusel. He doesn't mind who. And if I can help grease the wheels, brownie points for me, right?"

I gave Tobias an extremely sceptical look.

"I'll just leave them here," Tobias said, laying the tickets down casually on the hallway radiator. He reached for the door and glanced back with a grin as he turned the handle. "Show's at seven thirty tomorrow. Don't be late!" The door closed behind him and he was gone.

I stared after Tobias, then down at the tickets.

"So Tobias did call?" I said into the phone.

"Yep," Hendrik said.

"And she said yes?"

"Dunno."

"What do you mean, you don't know?"

"Didn't ask."

I stared out of the window at the winter sky, thinking.

"You want to talk to her?" Hendrik asked.

". . . No. It's fine."

"Okay."

"Thanks." I hung up, then looked down at the tickets on my bedside table. The tickets looked back up at me.

It was more tempting than it should have been. Johanna was the most beautiful girl I'd ever met, and strolling into a theatre with her on my arm did sound good, especially since I'd just spent the past three weeks watching Calhoun do the same. I wondered if Tobias had been telling the truth about her saying yes. The funny thing was, I could actually see it. My instincts told me that Johanna was at least a little bit interested in me, though I knew that wouldn't necessarily stretch to doing anything.

I could just call her and ask, but that would be risky. So far, I hadn't done anything that I could be called out for. Once I actually took the step of phoning her up, I'd be crossing a line. Still, it was tempting . . .

I shook my head. *No.* I picked up my phone and sent a short text to Hendrik saying sorry, but I'd have to cancel. I hit "Send" and immediately felt better. Doing this behind Calhoun's back had felt scummy. Besides, I'd learned my lesson about trusting Tobias. He was definitely trying to pull something; the only question was what.

Well, time to find out.

COVENT GARDEN ON Saturday evenings is a hive of activity. Men and women crowded the streets, hurrying across the road and jostling each other on the pavements and ducking into and out of restaurants and bars. The streets were slicked wet from the afternoon's rain, reflecting back the yellow glows of the lights hanging from the wires overhead. Homeless men huddled in the shelter of doorways, begging from the passersby. The noise was constant, traffic and shouts and movement blending together in a riot of sound.

I walked down the wet cobbled street, shivering at the cold breeze blowing off the stone, until the shape of St. Martin's Theatre loomed up out of the night, lit up in red neon. Glowing orange letters on its front wall announced "*AGATHA CHRISTIE'S THE MOUSETRAP.*" I headed for a side entrance.

The girl on the door was wearing a smart waistcoat and a lanyard around her neck. She scanned my ticket and checked her tablet. "Says here your box is for two?"

"My friend's just coming," I told her.

"Just so you know, the doors are closed fifteen minutes after the performance starts."

I gave her a smile. "That won't be a problem."

The inside of the theatre was compact, with narrow curving corridors and thick carpets to muffle sound. Men and women walked by carrying plastic glasses full of beer and wine. I went up a twisting staircase and found the door saying "Box B." I couldn't sense any essentia or see anyone hanging around.

I waited for the corridor to empty, then activated my invisibility sigl and stepped inside.

The murmur of the crowd jumped up at me as I entered the box. It had been a very long time since I'd been inside a West End theatre, and the first thing that struck me was how beautiful it was. The walls were some kind of polished wood, reflecting the lights of the chandeliers, and the curtains were thick with gold braid. My box was up on the far right, giving me a view down onto the heads of all the people in the stalls moving around and taking their seats. It looked amazing, and I spent a few seconds taking it all in before turning my attention to the box itself. It was small and cosy, with a single seat and a small table. The table held two glasses and an ice bucket.

Time to get to work.

I searched the box, keeping my movements slow and careful so as not to disrupt my invisibility. The seat was padded and comfortable-looking, sized for two, and the ice bucket held a bottle of champagne. I crouched to look under the chair and table, examining it from several angles.

Nothing.

I scanned the theatre, looking for anyone who seemed to be paying my box an unusual amount of attention, then I moved on to searching the box itself. The front balcony and the right side were clear, as was the door. The left wall—

There was a camera on the left wall.

It was small, made from some darkish plastic that blended into the shadows, and it had been tucked away on a small ledge just above floor level. Very easy to miss, especially if you had someone else in the box to distract you.

I sighed. I knew it. I fucking *knew* it. I'd just been starting to wonder if this whole thing was a false alarm, and Tobias had actually been telling the truth for once in his life. But I hadn't really believed it, and this was *exactly* the kind of bullshit I'd expected from him.

Now what?

I stood there as the last people filed into the theatre, thinking. I don't know much about cameras or video surveillance—Kiran's the electronics guy—and I didn't know whether the little camera was recording to its own hard drive or broadcasting to a receiver somewhere. But I was pretty sure that whoever had placed the thing was going to want his camera back. Which meant all I had to do was wait.

I sat down to do exactly that.

The lights went down, an announcer asked everyone to turn off their mobile phones, and the curtain went up. I sat there, invisible, and watched the performance. Having to keep my invisibility sigl active was kind of a nuisance, and it was hard to sit comfortably in my armour, but I enjoyed the play all the same. I've only been to the theatre a few times in my life, and never in these kinds of seats. I didn't manage to guess the murderer, but I did pick up on the clue about people not being who they said they were, so the twist at the end didn't feel like it came out of nowhere. During the interval there was a knock at the door and a theatre attendant stuck his head in, looked around the apparently empty box in slight confusion, and withdrew. Apart from that, I was undisturbed.

The play ended and the lights came up. Chatter broke out around the auditorium as the audience got up and began to file out. Queues formed at the exits, growing first longer, then shorter. The theatre emptied until there were a dozen people left, then eight, then three, then none.

I stayed hidden. Cleaners appeared with black bin bags, picking up ice cream cartons and plastic cups. The whirr of a vacuum cleaner started up from somewhere. Eventually the cleaners left and the theatre was silent.

I waited.

It was maybe an hour after the play's end that I heard soft footsteps from the corridor. They weren't the first I'd heard, but the others had been brisk; these were slower, more cautious. I sat up, coming alert.

There was a soft knock at the door.

I rose to my feet—and paused. I could feel essentia, just out in the corridor. It was hard to tell with the wall in the way, but it felt like Matter.

The knock came again.

I backed off into the corner of the box and held still. The door cracked open.

The boy standing in the doorway was maybe a little younger than me, close to Tobias's age. He was well dressed but with a weaselly look, and as he squinted around the box, his eyes passing over without seeing me, he looked rather like a mouse trying to decide if it was safe to come out of its hole. Apparently deciding that it was, he slipped inside, closing the door behind him.

I studied the boy, checking for active sigls or essentia. Nothing. I glanced in the direction of the corridor, but that Matter signature was gone.

The boy was giving the champagne bottle and the melting ice a slightly puzzled look. After a moment he turned away and took a couple of steps, bending down to retrieve the camera.

I let my invisibility drop and walked up behind the boy just as he rose, turned, and found himself face-to-face with me. His eyes went wide and he gave a strangled yelp.

I smiled.

The boy tried to dart around me. I grabbed him and let essentia flow into my strength sigl; power flooded into my muscles as I slammed him back against the wall. "Nope," I told him.

"Oh shit, oh shit," the boy muttered.

"Yep."

"Uh," the boy stammered. "It's not what it looks like! I wasn't— I mean, I work for the theatre, we monitor the boxes for—"

I smacked him.

"Ow!" The boy clutched his ear. "What the fuck?"

"Try again," I told him.

"I wasn't spying! I don't know what you want!"

I sighed, then kept a grip on the boy with one hand and lifted up my other hand where he could see it. I channelled a thread of essentia through the light sigl on my little finger, causing a small, ominous blue-white glow to spring up. "Lie to me one more time," I told him, "and you're going over that rail."

The boy stared at the glowing sigl, fear in his eyes. "Okay, okay! It wasn't my idea! It was Tobias!"

"Of course it was Tobias," I said impatiently. "What did he say?"

"That there'd be two people coming, you and this girl, and he wanted pictures. Stills and video. That's all!"

"What kind of pictures?"

The boy hesitated. I tightened my grip.

"Ow, fuck! Okay, okay! He said he wanted it explicit."

"So did he order up the champagne? Or was that you?"

"That was him! My job was just the pictures, I swear!"

I wondered if it was just champagne in that bottle, or if Tobias had put in something extra. I wouldn't put it past him. "How much was he paying?"

The boy hesitated.

"Eh," I told him. "Come to think of it, I don't really care." I let go of the boy. "Get lost."

The boy jumped away and to the door as soon as he was free. He took hold of the handle and hesitated, his eyes darting down to the camera. He'd dropped it when I'd grabbed him.

"No, you're not getting it back," I said.

The boy grimaced and ran out into the corridor. I heard his racing footsteps fading away as the door swung slowly shut.

With a sigh, I bent down to pick up the camera, then glanced out over the darkened theatre. It was silent and empty.

It was pretty obvious now what Tobias's plan had been: get some suggestive photos featuring me and Johanna, then use them to stir shit. Charles had threatened to disinherit Tobias if he tried anything, but Tobias probably figured that if I was the one in the box, I'd have got the blame. He was probably right.

But it still didn't strike me as a particularly clever plan. Even if things had gone Tobias's way and he *had* managed to sabotage the engagement, he hadn't been nearly careful enough in covering his tracks. It seemed to be a theme with Tobias. He was good at coming up with plots, not so good at realising what was going to happen once people figured out that he was the one behind them.

Well, it wasn't my problem anymore. I stuffed the camera into my pocket, took a last glance around the box, then activated my invisibility sigls and saw the world shift back into blue as I faded from sight. Time to go home.

I slipped out through the door, closing it softly behind me as I glanced left and right. The white-walled corridor felt very bright after the gloom of the auditorium. There was no one in sight, though I could sense some Matter essentia down the hall.

I turned towards the stairs, already thinking of how I was going to get out. The doors on the ground floor would be closed, but they had fire-escape bars, and—

—wait. Matter essentia down the hall?

I started to turn and had a glimpse of a reddish glow streaking towards me before something slammed into my lower back.

I lost my breath in a gasp; the impact sent a flash of pain through me and slammed me against the wall. I brought up my hand in reflex and had a blurry glimpse of a human-shaped cloud of essentia before I triggered my flash sigl into where its face should be.

Light exploded outwards. The flash dazzled me, but I heard a curse and felt something hiss past as I jumped away. I straightened up, blinking away the spots in front of my eyes, searching for my invisible attacker.

The air in front of me shimmered and took the form of a young man holding a knife. He was wearing a set of black goggles with a high-tech look; as I watched, he pulled them off and frowned. "I thought these things were anti-glare."

I stared at the man. He was in his midtwenties, dressed in an eye-catching mix of black and red, and handsome, with a sharp nose, pale brown hair, and greyish eyes that were currently fixed on the goggles in his free hand. The sleeves of his collared shirt were rolled up, exposing forearms that were lean with muscle, and he moved with predatory grace.

My thoughts raced. Who the hell *was* this guy? Had Tobias sent him too? My eyes fixed on the gleaming dagger in the man's hand and I felt a chill as I realised it had struck right in my kidneys.

But there was no blood on the blade. My back ached, but my armour had done its job, and I said a silent prayer of thanks to whoever had designed that vest. "Who are you?" I demanded, trying to make my voice sound tougher than I felt.

The guy glanced up at me and his frown cleared. "Oh, right." He stepped back into a sweeping bow. "Knight-Apostle Vermillion, of the Brotherhood of the Winged." He looked up at me expectantly.

I stared at the man, fear flitting through me. I had the sinking, lurching feeling that you get when you suddenly realise that you've got yourself into something really, really bad.

"This is the part where you're supposed to introduce yourself," the guy added when I didn't speak.

I swallowed. "You're not here because of Tobias?"

Vermillion—if that was his name—straightened with a quizzical look. "Who?"

The faint hope that this was some sort of extremely screwed-up family initiation flickered and died. What had I stepped into here?

"Hey," Vermillion told me. "Introduce yourself."

". . . Stephen."

Vermillion cocked his head. "That's it?"

"Um," I said. I didn't have a clue what this guy's deal was, but if he was talking, he wasn't stabbing me. "I haven't got any titles, if that's what you're asking."

"You could come up with one."

"What?"

"Well, you know," Vermillion said. "Not exactly an epic battle for the ages, is it? I mean, think about it. You spend all the time setting the stage and building things up, and then the other guy walks in and it's some teenager in a fleece calling himself 'Stephen.' I mean, at least make an effort. Something like 'Stephen, Lord of Light,' or 'Stephen, Master of Fang and Claw.' 'Stephen' just makes it sound like you're not even trying."

I stared at the guy.

"At least you picked a decent place for it." Vermillion glanced around. "Nice aesthetics, lots of history. Auditorium would have been better, but you can't have everything."

"Uh," I said. "Okay, how about we take a break while I come up with something? Say a week or two?"

Vermillion grinned. "At least you've got a sense of humour."

He wasn't radiating any essentia. No visible weapons apart from that knife. I still had no idea how I was going to get out of this; all I could think of was to keep him talking. "You going to tell me why you tried to stab me?"

"Oh, that," Vermillion said. "Nothing personal. Just looking out for my little bro."

"Your *what*?"

"You know, Mark?"

My heart sank again.

"Apparently you're supposed to be his replacement?" Vermillion said. He studied me critically. "I guess I can see it."

My thoughts flashed back to that text conversation with Byron. I hadn't committed to anything, and we hadn't done anything . . .

. . . but Mark didn't know that. And if he'd caught a glimpse of my name on Byron's phone, all he'd know was that we were still in contact. "I'm not doing anything with Byron."

"You turned him down, right?" Vermillion said with a nod. "I keep telling Mark, that's how you do it. Byron likes the chase. You start acting needy, that's when he gets bored. Mark ought to be taking lessons instead of trying to kill you."

I really didn't understand what this guy was talking about, but . . . "Uh, I could give him some tips?"

Vermillion waved his knife dismissively. "Nah, too late for that. Mark's on his last chance anyway. He's just hoping that if I take you out of the picture, Byron'll pay attention to him long enough to give him one more shot."

"Yeah, you . . . really don't need to stab me to take me out of the picture," I said. "If I'd known this was going to happen, I would already have gone out of the picture. *Way* out of the picture." Holy shit, I'd had *no* idea what I was messing with by talking to Byron. These people were insane.

"Well . . ." Vermillion said. "Honestly? That's not the *real* reason I'm here. I mean, if this was just Byron looking for a new toy, I'd have told Mark to suck it up and stop being a whiny little bitch. But if you really are what he says . . . well, we're going to end up facing off sooner or later. So I want to see what you're made of."

". . . What?"

"Oh!" Vermillion snapped his fingers. "Just remembered." He looked down at the goggles in his left hand. "There's a brightness cap you can turn down." He shifted his grip on his knife and started to adjust a dial.

I didn't wait for him to finish. I held out my left hand and triggered my flash sigl at full power, sending a burst of blinding light into his unshielded face.

But as I opened my eyes, spots fading from the afterimage, I saw that Vermillion wasn't even bothering to look in my direction. "Going to have to do better than that," he told me.

I felt a chill. Vermillion had sensed me activating my sigl and closed his eyes at the same time that I had. For the first time, I was up against someone whose drucraft skills were as good as mine.

"All right," Vermillion said. He slipped the goggles onto his forehead, adjusting them slightly, and as he did his face changed, the casual, almost playful look disappearing. He pulled the goggles down, covering his eyes. "Let's do this."

Vermillion's image shimmered and vanished, and he lunged. I was already moving, jumping back, triggering my diffraction and vision sigls, and throwing out a slam in the direction of his head, all at once. As I landed I changed direction, dodging left. I knew the invisibility wouldn't hide me completely, but I hoped it might at least buy me some time.

It didn't.

The red blur curved towards me as Vermillion followed my dodge. I saw a flicker of movement and brought my arms up into a boxing guard, cringing with the knowledge of what was coming.

Pain flared as the knife bit into my forearm, coupled with the nauseating scrape of metal on bone. I couldn't see Vermillion or his blade and I threw out slams and another flash, holding up my forearms in a desperate attempt to keep the knife away from my face and body. Fiery lines of pain opened up on my arms as the blade cut into me.

I lashed out with my foot and felt a jolt as my shoe connected; Vermillion grunted and I took the chance to jump back. My arms were wet with blood, stinging and burning. I dropped my invisibility and sent essentia surging into my new sigl instead.

The world around me seemed to dim, essentia pulsing in my sight as the sigl's field turned light into darkness. My shadowman sigl was a one-way gloom effect, converting outgoing light into essentia while leaving incoming light untouched. From my perspective, it created an odd, wispy, shrouded effect, as ambient light in the area around me was reduced. It was eerie, but I could still see.

The effect on Vermillion would be very different. I'd fought a guy with a shadowman sigl before, and I knew that to Vermillion I'd seem like a human-shaped mass of darkness, bigger than me by a foot, translucent and blurry at the edges and deepening to an utter lightless black at the core. If you didn't know what it was, it looked scary as hell.

Vermillion's red blur paused, then advanced. His movements were slower, now, more cautious. I felt as much as saw a stutter, and jerked quickly back; I heard the hiss of a blade cutting air, but he didn't follow up instantly.

He can't see me, I thought with a flash of hope. Somehow Vermillion could see through my invisibility, but I knew from my reading that most anti-invisibility effects worked by finding a frequency that the invisibility sigl didn't cover. My shadowman sigl didn't work on frequencies; it just blotted out the whole spectrum, meaning that invisibility counters did nothing.

Unfortunately, while my shadowman sigl made it impossible to *see* me, it also made it very, very easy to tell where I was. All you had to do was aim for the exact centre of the darkness, and from the way Vermillion was moving, he'd already figured that out. His red aura slid closer.

I triggered my slam sigl, aiming for Vermillion's head. Now

that I looked closely I could see that his invisibility wasn't perfect; you could make out the outline of his body from where the light refracted at the edges. I didn't just fire once but kept going, blasts of compressed air slamming into Vermillion with a *whuff-whuff-whuff*.

Vermillion grunted, then came forward in a rush, and this time managed to get a grip. I felt a sharp blow and a stab of pain, and slammed an elbow into him with the strength of panic, breaking his hold and driving him back. I could feel a bruise on my stomach and knew his knife hadn't penetrated, but looking up I saw that the red shadow was already pacing forward again.

With a chill I realised I was losing. It's a feeling you sometimes get in the ring, a cold deep down in your bones telling you that you're not going to win. Half of my sigls were useless and the other half weren't doing enough.

Vermillion stutter-stepped forward; I jumped back and felt the whiff of a near miss. My arms were wet with blood and I knew I didn't have long. Desperately I tried to think, the research I'd done on invisibility sigls flashing through my mind. Transparency sigls. Matter, but often grouped with Light because they did the same thing, altered the refractive index of his body, made light pass through. Still the same problem: you can't see either. How was he bypassing that? He wasn't running any other sigls. All he had was that knife and those goggles—

The goggles. It had to be the goggles.

Vermillion moved in for another lunge, and I turned and ran.

I sent essentia flooding through my lightfoot sigl as I raced down the corridor and up the stairs. I knew I was getting further away from safety, but it was the only direction to go. I heard pattering footsteps behind me and knew that Vermillion was right on my tail, but with the Matter effect reducing my mass, I flew up the steps.

The steps ended on the theatre's second floor, with a landing and short corridor. A door to the side read "UPPER CIRCLE," with a fire alarm on the wall. Beyond was a dead end.

I skidded to a stop and turned, dropping my lightfoot effect and pouring its essentia into my strength sigl instead. Power flooded into my muscles as the barely visible blur of Vermillion mounted the steps behind me and closed in.

I sprang forward to meet him.

I felt Vermillion flinch as we crashed into each other. I'd been hoping to knock him down the steps, but he was too quick, twisting sideways so that we both thumped into the wall. I grabbed for his arm and chest, and prayed.

It half worked.

The fingers of my right hand closed on Vermillion's shirt. The fabric was slippery, but I managed to get a good grip and yanked him down into me as I smashed my forehead right into his face. Pain exploded through my skull but I felt the grinding crunch as something broke.

But while my right hand got a grip, my left hand didn't. And by the time I realised Vermillion's knife hand was free, it was too late.

Agony exploded in my leg, fire lancing through nerves and muscles. I was already pushing myself away and I staggered as I did, struggling to keep my balance. Each step sent a new flare of pain down my right leg and into my hip, and I half fell against the wall, clutching at it to keep myself upright.

The air shimmered and Vermillion's shape solidified out of nothing. He ripped the goggles off with his free hand and shook his head; his nose was bleeding and he looked dazed. He looked down at the goggles to see that their lenses were cracked. "Ow," he said.

I didn't speak. Pain was flooding through my body and I was

feeling light-headed. Vermillion's knife had gone into my upper thigh. My jeans were wet with blood and I could feel more oozing out.

Vermillion shook his head again and stared in my direction, squinting into the darkness. He looked down at his knife; the steel was red with blood. "You know," he said. "I could just wait for you to bleed out and—"

I reached around the edge of the door and smashed the fire alarm.

The bell exploded into noise above my head: an incredibly loud *DRINGDRINGDRINGDRING* that just kept on going and going. Vermillion grimaced at the noise and said something.

"Sorry," I shouted at him. "Can't hear you."

"Seriously?" Vermillion shouted.

"So?" I shouted back. "Want to keep going till the police show up?"

Vermillion hesitated and I saw his eyes flick around me, searching through what to him would be darkness. I held my breath, my heart in my mouth. Pain was pulsing through my leg and without the wall to lean on I didn't think I could even stand up. If Vermillion came in to finish me, I wouldn't last thirty seconds.

But Vermillion couldn't see how badly I was hurt. And, more importantly, he'd couldn't use that transparency sigl any more without blinding himself, meaning that if he wanted to come in, he'd be exposed to anything I could do to hurt him. I didn't *have* anything that could hurt him, but he didn't know that.

I saw Vermillion's expression shift as he made his decision. A smile tugged at the corner of his mouth. "Not bad," he called, throwing me a salute. He had to shout over the fire alarm. "I'll see you around." He turned and disappeared down the stairs.

I held myself up against the door, listening to the sound of

Vermillion's retreating footsteps until they were drowned out by the clamour. Only then did I let myself slide down the wall and crumple to the floor with a thump that sent a flare of agony through me. I let the shadow effect drop and looked down at my leg. My jeans had shifted and I couldn't see the wound, but the fabric was dark with blood and I could feel more oozing out.

I took a deep breath, placed my mending sigl against my leg, and tried to stop myself from bleeding to death.

CHAPTER 18

IT WAS A cleaner who found me first, a middle-aged black guy whose eyes went wide at the sight of the blood. He ran off to fetch an attendant who asked some questions, then a manager arrived and asked more questions, and somewhere along the line someone dialled 999 and put them on speaker and the emergency services dispatcher asked me some questions too. I had trouble following any of it. My leg was hurting with a fiery throbbing pain that was getting worse as the adrenaline from the fight wore off, and all my attention was focused on my sigl and the essentia flowing through it and into my thigh. The bleeding didn't stop— it kept oozing, soaking my jeans and the carpet underneath until I felt as though I was lying in a spreading pool of my own blood. I couldn't tell if my mending sigl was working. All I could do was keep channelling and hope that it'd be enough.

By the time the paramedics showed up I was exhausted and light-headed—it was getting harder and harder to maintain my concentration, and when they asked me to take my hand off the wound I finally let my sigl wink off. Blood was smeared all over my skin and my sigl rings, and as the paramedics called for a stretcher I found myself vaguely wondering if drenching your sigls in your own blood made them work better.

I was carried down out of the theatre and into an ambulance. I don't remember much about the trip except that it was bumpy and uncomfortable. Then there was a rush of cold air and transfer into a hospital, and white corridors and lights that hurt my eyes, and more questions, and at some point I was given an injection. The nurse doing it told me that it wouldn't knock me out, but it did.

I WOKE UP sometime later. I was in a hospital bed and a nurse was talking to me. She told me that I had visitors and asked if I'd like to see them. I said yes without really thinking about it, and she went out and shut the door. I looked around and realised I was alone in a hospital room. The walls were green, there was a switched-off TV, and cupboards and medical equipment were all around me. My leg still hurt. I was just wondering why I was in a private room when the door opened and I saw two men come in.

They were wearing police uniforms.

Oh, I thought, my heart sinking. *That's why.*

THE FOLLOWING INTERVIEW was tense.

My thoughts were fuzzy from the drugs and the pain, but there's nothing like danger to sharpen your mind, and I knew I was in danger now. When you're an average working guy in London, the police aren't exactly your enemies, but they most definitely aren't your friends. The policeman doing the questioning wanted to know who'd attacked me and why I'd been in the theatre. He was polite but persistent, and I knew he wasn't going away without answers.

My dad had always told me that the best thing to do when dealing with the police was to say as little as possible. Don't volunteer anything, don't lie if it's something that you can be caught on, and most of all, don't try to be clever.

So I didn't. Vermillion was the easy part—I gave a description of the guy and said that I'd never seen him before, which was true. I left out the details of our conversation, only saying that he'd gone for me and that I'd tried to fight him off before breaking the fire alarm. Once the policemen started asking why I'd been in the theatre after opening hours, things got harder, and I had to lie and say I'd fallen asleep in the box. Explaining the camera and my armour vest would have been harder, but luckily the hospital staff must not have told the policeman about them because he didn't mention either.

Unfortunately, when the policemen asked why I'd been in a private box, I couldn't think of any way of deflecting the question. I knew that if I tried to lie about *that*, I'd be caught out straightaway. So I told him the Ashfords had bought the ticket for me. He was suspicious—I could see it in his eyes—and he and his partner pushed me a bit, asking more questions and going back over my previous answers, but I told them that my leg was hurting and that it was hard to remember, which was true. The pain was coming back, getting sharper and more distracting, and at last the policemen left. The nurse came back in with some pills; I took them and drifted back off to sleep.

It was cold, and the earth was full of bones. Moonlight slanted down through the leaves as I hurried between the tree trunks. From far overhead, I heard the rush of wings.

"Don't look at it," Father Hawke told me. He was at my side, pacing me. "Not yet."

The thing came again, passing overhead the other way, but this time it was closer, louder. The wind screamed; I tried to shout, but my words were lost in the noise.

"Not yet," Father Hawke said again, but his voice had changed, and as I turned to look I saw that he'd changed into some creature with feathered wings and silver hair. It looked at me gravely with eyes that were both old and young. "Stephen."

"Stephen."

I woke with a jolt. I tried to sit up, tangling in my sheets and bedding before my hand closed on the top of the bed and I was able to pull myself upward. Pain stabbed from my leg as I remembered I was still hurt. I looked around wildly, my eyes settling on the other boy in the room.

"Stephen," he told me calmly. "You're dreaming."

It was Calhoun. He looked clean and well dressed and was sitting with legs crossed ankle to knee, an open book in his lap. I looked at his silver-white hair and felt a weird jolt of déja vù. "Where am I?"

"The Grafton Way Building of University College Hospital, just off Euston Road," Calhoun said. His voice was quite normal, and as I listened the fear and confusion of the dream began to fade. "You were muttering and thrashing around."

I stared at Calhoun for a second, then leant back against the headboard, wincing at the jolt that came from my leg. I looked around at the green-painted walls of the hospital room, the memories of last night filtering back. The theatre; Vermillion; the police. "What time is it?"

"Eleven thirty, Sunday morning," Calhoun told me. "I got a call from the Metropolitan Police last night." He hesitated. "The hospital staff asked for your next of kin. I . . . stretched the truth a little and told them I was the closest one available. Strictly speaking, I should probably have sent them to your mother, but . . ."

"Yeah, I'm glad you didn't." I was tired, in pain, and feeling weirdly disconnected and drained; the last thing I wanted right now was to have to deal with my mother as well. I looked down and saw there was an IV running into my arm.

"What happened?"

My thoughts were still a little fuzzy. I was probably still drugged. "Got stabbed."

"I'd like to hear the full story."

"*Now* you want to hear the story?" I said bitterly. I knew I should be keeping my mouth shut, but it slipped out before I could stop myself. "Back when you hired me, you said you'd tell me more. You haven't told me a damn thing."

Calhoun nodded. "I know, and I'm sorry. I've been meaning to take the time to talk to you, but I've been running around dealing with one emergency after another and you seemed to have things in hand. I put it off longer than I should have."

"What emergency?"

"Our House is facing some problems," Calhoun said. "Nothing you're responsible for. But I appreciate that you've been helping with Johanna."

I remembered Tobias's insinuations that I should try making a move, and how I'd been tempted, and felt a brief flash of shame. "You really want the story?" I asked Calhoun.

"Please."

I gave Calhoun a brief summary of the attack. Unlike with the police, I included Tobias's part in it. I was expecting Calhoun to zero in on that, and he did.

"This man who attacked you," Calhoun said. "Did he use Tobias's name?"

"Acted like he didn't even recognise it. I don't think he was lying, either."

"He wasn't. Once I was finished talking to the police last night, the first thing I did was go to Tobias and get the story out of him."

I looked at Calhoun with interest.

"Tobias bought those tickets and hired that boy," Calhoun said. "But he swears up and down that he doesn't know anything about the attack. He probably doesn't. Assassins aren't his style."

There was an odd reluctance to Calhoun's tone. "Why are you acting like that's a bad thing?"

Calhoun was quiet for a second. "Tobias didn't hire anyone else," he said at last. "But he did *talk* to someone else."

"Who?" I asked. But even as I said it, I knew the answer.

"Lucella."

I was silent.

"Did your attacker use her name?" Calhoun asked. "Or give any other information that could be used to prove she was involved?"

"No."

Calhoun nodded. He looked unhappy, but not surprised. "That'll make it hard to convince Charles."

"I mean . . ." I said. "You're really expecting him to care? I'm pretty sure I could walk into that guy's study with a knife in my back and the first thing he'd tell me would be not to bleed on the carpet."

"He's not *quite* that bad," Calhoun said. "But . . . you're right that the chances of him doing anything about this are slim."

"Then why even bother?" I asked. After last year, the idea of expecting Charles to side with me on something like this felt like a bad joke.

"You were injured while in my service."

I gave Calhoun a puzzled look. "Wait, you think you're responsible or something?"

"To an extent."

This guy is really weird. The thought flitted briefly through my mind that I should take advantage of this to get more money or something, then I mentally shook my head and let it go. For some odd reason, the traces of resentment that I'd been feeling towards Calhoun were gone. "Forget it," I told him. "This isn't on you."

"If I hadn't ordered you to watch—" Calhoun began.

"What happened with *Tobias* was on you. What happened with Lucella wasn't."

"What makes you so sure?"

"Because this isn't the first time she's pulled this crap," I told Calhoun. Now that I thought about it, she'd probably never even talked to Vermillion—all she would have had to do was call Mark and let him handle the rest. "Passing on information that she knows'll stir up shit. Last time it was a texted photo. This time she probably just let him know where and when I was going to be."

"Let who know?"

I shook my head. My feelings towards Calhoun might have improved, but not to the point where I was willing to bring up the Winged.

"Well," Calhoun said when I didn't speak. "If you don't want to talk about it, I won't push you. But if you're willing, I can make arrangements for you to be transferred to a private hospital with medical drucrafters. It'll be a little more uncomfortable in the short term, but your recovery will be much faster."

I thought about it. "Okay."

Calhoun nodded and rose to his feet. "Then I'll leave you to rest."

"Wait," I told him.

Calhoun paused.

"Why did you hire me?" I asked. I wouldn't normally have said anything, but I was still feeling a little fuzzy from whatever drugs they were giving me, and this was something that had been bugging me for a while.

"You asked me that back in the autumn," Calhoun said.

"Yeah, and you didn't really answer. I mean, I've been doing my best, but I'm an amateur at this stuff. That guy Johanna's got with her? He's a *real* bodyguard. I know you said you just wanted another pair of eyes, but anything I can do, someone like him could do better."

Calhoun looked at me quizzically. "Is it so surprising that I'd want to employ family?"

"No one from your family wants anything good for me," I said. It came out sounding more bitter than I'd meant it to.

Calhoun studied me for a second. "I suppose I can understand why you feel that way." He sat back down in his chair and met my eyes. "During the raid last September, you helped me. I know you were there for your own reasons, but you could still have stayed out of it. You didn't. That was why. I have plenty of people I can hire. I don't have many I can trust."

"And you trust me?"

"When Tobias came to call, you could have tried to play it to your advantage. Instead you walked into his trap to find out what it was." Calhoun shrugged. "I'd say I was right to take a chance on you."

"Yeah, thanks."

Calhoun smiled slightly. "I'm aware it didn't work out so well from your point of view. Just know that I'm grateful. If you ever need a favour, feel free to ask."

That caught me off guard, and I wasn't sure how to answer. In the end all I did was nod. Calhoun said goodbye and left.

After Calhoun was gone, I spent a while staring at the door. *Weird guy*, I thought again. I still wasn't sure how I felt about him.

With a wince, I settled back down in the bed. The pain in my leg, which I'd been able to forget while Calhoun had been distracting me, was getting worse. I started looking around for my phone.

WHEN CALHOUN HAD promised to get me transferred to a private hospital, I hadn't expected it to lead to anything soon. As it turned out, though, I was moved that very same day.

The hospital Calhoun had met me in, UCH, was already a step up from what I'm used to. For most of my life a hospital trip had meant a short bus ride to Newham University Hospital, followed by hours of boredom sitting in a cold waiting room breathing in piss- and disinfectant-laden air. UCH is nicer—less pee, shorter waits. But the new hospital was something totally different. I got a view of it as the ambulance pulled in off Euston Road, a gleaming building of glass and yellow brick, and when I was wheeled inside it was into a light and roomy reception area with a front desk that wasn't sealed away behind a thick barrier but instead was open to the air. I was taken upstairs to a private room with a view out over the London skyline.

The doctor who met me was Indian, with glasses and a friendly bedside manner. "Ah, good to meet you," he said, leaning forward to shake my hand as I lay in bed. "Stephen . . . Ashford, was it?"

"Oakwood."

"Oakwood, that's right," the doctor said, consulting a clipboard. "I'm Dr. Saini and I'll be in charge of your treatment. So we're looking at multiple incisions and one major puncture wound to the right adductors—that's the right inner thigh. Ever had sigl treatment before?"

"No . . ."

"Don't worry, it's quite comfortable," the doctor assured me. "We'll have you up and walking before you know it. Now, before we can start our tests, we'll need you to fill out some forms . . ."

———

COLIN CAME TO visit that same evening. "Okay, dude," he said as he walked in. "What the fuck?"

"Close the door," I told him.

Colin tried to slam it. The effect was rather spoiled by the auto-closing mechanism, which slowed the door's swing to a crawl. "Again," Colin said as he walked up to my bed. "*What the fuck?*"

"Could you narrow it down a bit?" I asked. "Because I've had a lot of things happen lately that you could be talking about here, and—"

"You got yourself *stabbed*?"

"Okay, so it's that part."

"You know, when you came to me last year with that crazy story about being kidnapped, I thought you were making shit up," Colin said. "Then there was that raid in Chancery Lane, and that was pretty fucking nuts, but you made it sound like it was a one-off. But now someone's going after you with a *knife*?"

I sighed. "Sit down and I'll explain."

For the third time in twenty-four hours, I told the story. Unlike with Calhoun and the police, I told the full truth. Colin took it less calmly than they had.

"Jesus Christ," Colin said once I was done. "At least that Mark guy only wanted to scare you off. This one sounds like a fucking serial killer. How many of these nutjobs are there?"

If Byron really was a recruiter for the Winged, he probably had a whole contacts list full of them. "A lot, I think."

"What are you going to do?"

"Well, it was Mark who called this guy in," I said. I had to fight back the urge to yawn. The tests had taken up most of the day, and I was *really* tired. "If I can settle things with him, Vermillion shouldn't have any reason to come after me."

"Settle how?"

"Well, he's doing all this because he thinks I'm a threat to his position. If I can convince him—"

"Whoa, whoa, whoa. *Convince* him?"

"I've got—"

"No."

"Colin . . ."

"*No*," Colin said. "Dude. Take a step back and *look* at yourself. Every time you talk to me about this, it's something worse. First it was someone trying to bundle you into a car. Then I found you half-starved to death. Then it was a guy trying to beat you up, and now it's *this*. What's it going to be next time? Am I getting a call from the hospital telling me you got shot?"

"*Colin.*"

"Don't 'Colin' me. What's this really about? It can't still be about a job. Is it finding your dad? You think if you chase after these people long enough, you're going to catch up to him?"

I hesitated.

"If it is, then drop it," Colin said. "It's not worth it."

"These people *do* know what happened to my dad," I argued. "If I can figure out the right way to come at them, then—"

"Then *what*?" Colin demanded. "You think that's going to solve anything? You ever consider that maybe there's a good fucking reason your dad told you to leave this alone? Maybe if he hadn't got involved with them, he wouldn't have had to run off in the first place! What do you think he'd say if he could see you right now? You think he'd be happy?"

That hit hard. I couldn't think of an answer.

Colin stared at me. The anger in his expression surprised me. "It's not worth it," he told me again, then shook his head, seeming to calm down a little. "Okay, okay, I shouldn't be acting like this when you're in hospital. But listen to me, all right?"

". . . All right."

"Okay," Colin said. "So what'd the doctors say?"

COLIN STAYED AND we talked for a little while longer (he promised to make sure Hobbes got fed) but I was tired and it was getting late. Eventually he left, and the hospital shut down for the night.

I tried to sleep, but despite my exhaustion, I couldn't. Colin's words—"*it's not worth it*"—kept going round and round in my head. I found myself arguing with an imaginary Colin, trying to defend myself. It wasn't like I'd gone out last night looking for trouble. Vermillion had jumped me, not the other way round.

But while part of me wanted to defend myself, another part—a more honest part—knew that Colin had a point. Yeah, it had been Vermillion who'd picked the fight, but it wasn't as though I was totally innocent. I could have told Byron no, or ghosted him, but instead I'd made the choice to meet with him and keep answering his messages afterwards, stringing things out even when I knew it was dangerous, hoping that he'd drop some clue to how I could find my dad.

My dad. I remembered Colin's question—"*you think he'd be happy?*"—and felt myself flinch. I knew the answer was no. He'd be furious that I was risking my life.

It's a lot easier to do risky stuff when you're alone. If I'd still been living with one of my parents—maybe even with my aunt—I wouldn't have been so quick to do things like this. But as Colin had reminded me, I *did* have people who cared about me. They just didn't know what I was doing.

Come to think of it, that was probably why I didn't want Calhoun to tell my mother where I was.

Was I really doing the right thing, looking for my dad? He'd told me to stay away. Yeah, he hadn't specifically named the Winged, but I was pretty bloody sure he wouldn't want me hanging out with them.

But what else could I do?

I tossed and turned, unable to sleep. My leg made it worse— Dr. Saini had prescribed me something for the nerve pain, but he'd warned me that it wouldn't completely go away for another couple of days. Say I *did* cut things off with Byron—would that even help? Mark hadn't believed me when I'd told him I wasn't interested in taking his place. Maybe he'd just come after me again.

I found myself thinking about something Vermillion had said. At the time I'd been focused on not getting stabbed, but the more I thought about his words, the more they nagged at me. *"If you really are what he says, we're going to face off sooner or later."*

"If you are what he says" . . . What a weird way to phrase it. The "he" had to be Mark or Byron. What could they possibly have told Vermillion to make him think that it was a good idea to stick a knife in me? Colin had called Vermillion a nutjob, but while the guy was scary as hell, he hadn't sounded crazy. He'd sounded like he knew exactly what he was doing.

At last I reached for my phone and dialled Colin's number. It took him a while to pick up, and when he did he sounded half-asleep and grumpy. "What's wrong?"

"There's someone I need to talk to," I told Colin. "Can you take a message to West Ham Church?"

CHAPTER 19

"Well," Father Hawke said next morning as he walked into my hospital room. "You look a lot better than the patients I'm usually called in for."

I pulled myself up in my bed. I was still drowsy from a night with little sleep, and seeing Father Hawke in the clean, well-lit hospital room was a little surreal. He looked rather out of place here.

"Is something wrong?" Father Hawke asked.

"I wasn't sure you'd come," I admitted.

"Hospital visits come with the job," Father Hawke said with a slight smile. "But I'm glad to see you're not looking for last rites. What seems to be troubling you?"

I hesitated.

Father Hawke tilted his head, looking down at me. With his height and the angles of his face, he did look like his namesake.

"I need to know more about the Winged," I said at last.

Father Hawke paused, then pulled over a chair and sat, glancing over towards the closed door before focusing on me. "Go on."

"I told you last time that a guy called Byron was trying to re-cruit me," I said. "He's got a . . . junior or underling or something, a boy called Mark. Mark's afraid I'm going to replace him, and so he called in help from some guy calling himself Vermillion. He was the one who stabbed me."

Father Hawke nodded.

"Vermillion said something about Mark being on his last chance," I said. "What does that mean?"

"For cults like the Winged, there's a sharp divide between the rank and file and the inner circle," Father Hawke said. "The vast majority are what you might call associates. The lawyer who bails out their members when they're arrested, the administrator who does them favours in return for special considerations, the mus-cle they hire on the side. Most don't really consider themselves members at all. After that you have the aspirants—the ones try-ing to rise through the ranks." Father Hawke paused. "The man you call Byron is part of the inner circle. I've never met this Ver-million, but I'd expect him to be the same. The boy you call Mark would be an aspirant. He's attempting to break in."

"How does that happen?"

"Two ways," Father Hawke said. "The first—and this is the path most aspirants dream of—is to be noticed. That simply by being true to themselves and living their chosen life, the uni-verse itself will sit up and take note of how impressive they are. Unfortunately for them, what *they* consider worthy of note and what the *universe* considers worthy of note are rarely the same thing."

I wasn't sure what that meant. "And the other way?"

"The aspirant can approach a member of the inner circle in the hope of being sponsored directly," Father Hawke said. "A mi-nority of them are willing to guide an aspirant through certain rituals designed to show the aspirant's dedication. In the case of the Winged, that most often takes the form of systematic transgressions against social taboos."

"And that works?"

"Usually not," Father Hawke said. "Quite often the sponsor has no real intention of raising the aspirant in the first place. And even if they do, the most common result is that the aspirant just ends up beating their head against the wall until something breaks. But every now and again it really does work and the aspirant gets exactly what they wished for. At a price."

"You think that's what's going on with Mark?" I asked. "He's desperate because he can't break in?"

"How long has he been with Byron?"

I'd first run into Mark last May. "Nine months at least."

Father Hawke nodded. "Among the Winged, last week's rising star can be this week's embarrassing burden. If he feels he has little time left, he's probably right."

"So what should I do?"

"I wouldn't have thought you needed me to tell you that," Father Hawke said. "You don't have to do anything. Just stay away and he'll self-destruct one way or another."

I was silent.

"But that's not the only thing you're worried about," Father Hawke said. "Is it?"

"Before he attacked, Vermillion told me something." I looked at Father Hawke, watching him closely. This was the part I really wanted an answer to. "He said that if I really was what they said I was, we were going to end up facing off sooner or later."

I paused. Father Hawke didn't react. "Go on," he said.

"That was it. What did he mean?"

Father Hawke studied me for a second. "I think you already know."

I frowned. "I don't."

"Really?" Father Hawke said. "You have all the pieces. You're bright enough to put them together. I think you're just afraid of what the answer might be." He got to his feet. "Think it over. Then come to me once you're ready."

I sat there for a while after Father Hawke had left, staring at the door.

MY NEXT FEW days were dominated by drucraft treatments either carried out or overseen by Dr. Saini. Drucraft healing turned out to be more drawn out than I'd been expecting—what Dr. Saini called the "first-pass" repair was done in a day, but after that came multiple sessions with a specialised sigl designed to speed muscle regrowth. Dr. Saini explained that doing a quick fix on a leg wound was easy—the hard part was making sure there wasn't any lasting loss of function. So the treatments took the form of sessions with the rebuilding sigl, interspersed with physiotherapy sessions that worked the leg to make sure none of the muscle groups were weakened. I'd also taken some nerve damage from that slice to the forearm, which I hadn't even noticed at the time but which had left my hand motion slightly restricted. Rebuilding that took several sessions more.

Still, even if it wasn't instant, it was blazingly fast compared to natural healing. I'd been admitted on the Sunday; by Wednesday, the nerve damage to my arm was fixed and my leg was perfect except for the occasional twinge. Dr. Saini said that they'd keep me a couple of days more for monitoring, but barring any complications I could go home at the end of the week.

I had some visits—one from Kiran, a second from Colin, and even one from Felix, which surprised me—but in between visits and sessions I was left alone, and for the most part what I did with that time was sit and think. What was I going to do?

Now that Father Hawke had pointed it out, it was kind of obvious. Mark was unstable, and it probably wouldn't be long before somebody did society a favour and got rid of him. When it came to people like that, my dad always used to say that you should do yourself a favour and let someone else be the one to do society a favour.

But would that actually solve anything? Byron would still be out there. Vermillion would still be out there. And I'd be right back where I started, no closer to finding my dad and with some extra enemies to worry about as well.

I thought of Felix, and how he saw the drucraft world as just another place to make deals. Maybe I was looking at this the wrong way. Could I turn the Mark problem to my advantage?

I kept on thinking, and gradually an idea started to form. I slept on it, and the next day, I called Calhoun.

"Stephen," Calhoun said once I got through to him. "Everything okay at the hospital?"

"Yes," I said, then braced myself. I've always had trouble asking for things. "If you don't mind, I'd like to call in that favour."

WHEN I WAS discharged that Friday, I didn't hang around. First thing I did after going home and getting an ecstatic welcome from Hobbes was to meet up with Colin and do some shopping. Saturday was spent on planning and coordination. By Sunday morning I was ready.

I took the train to Hampstead, a white envelope stuffed into my pocket with "Mark" written on the front. I got off at Hampstead, went to Byron's house, pushed the envelope through the letterbox, and rang the bell. I didn't wait around for an answer—I took off at a jog and didn't stop until I'd made it back to the station.

My phone buzzed while I was on the train, in between Gospel Oak and Kentish Town West. The message was from an unknown number and simply said: What?

The Overground line around Kentish Town runs at treetop level. Looking out the window, I could see rooftops stretching away into tower blocks, sunlight and shadow patchy on the tiles. I typed back: We need to talk.

Mark: Why?

Stephen: Because of what your friend did last week.

Mark: Don't know what you're talking about.

Stephen: Okay, then I go to Byron and tell him the whole thing happened because of you. That the way you want to play it?

There was no response. I looked down at the screen as the train juddered under my feet.

Stephen: You still there?

Mark: Fine.

Stephen: Meet me tonight.

Mark: Where?

Stephen: Same place we had our last one-on-one. Ten o'clock. Don't be late.

THE SKY DARKENED as the day went on. I watched the clouds anxiously—a wet night would make things harder—but while they stayed heavy and sullen, they didn't turn into rain. The sun went down at six, painting the underside of the clouds in fiery light.

I left my house at eight and headed north. I spent a while making calls and checking that everything was in place, then headed for Clapton Football Club.

———

THE FOOTBALL GROUND was dark and silent. The turf on the pitch was a little more torn up than the last time I'd been here, and empty crisp packets and beer cans were scattered around the edges. At the corner of the ground, the Life Well was a feeble glow. It's always a gamble, betting on a temporary Well. Often when you catch one early in its life cycle, it'll look like it's going to turn into something special, but as the weeks go by and you keep visiting, you'll see its growth taper off until it peaks and starts to shrink. This one was well into its downslope phase; in a couple of months, no one would be able to tell it had been there at all. Just because something has potential doesn't mean it'll turn into anything good.

I found a spot under a tree and checked my earpiece. It was a loaner from Kiran; I'd have to give it back after tonight. "Testing," I said into the cold night air.

"Sup," Colin said through the earpiece.

"You hearing me?"

"Loud and clear. When you want to launch this thing?"

"Half an hour before the deadline. Nine thirty."

"You think he'll show?"

"Worst case, he bricks it and we're back to square one."

"Uh, I'm pretty sure *worst* case is he brings along the guy who stabbed you to finish the job."

"Yeah, well, that's why you're on lookout," I told Colin. "Speaking of, you're definitely out of sight?"

"All the way over in the park. Don't worry about me, it's you they're after."

I grimaced, touching my leg. It hadn't hurt for a couple of days, but I still kept expecting it to. "Thanks for the reminder."

Time passed. The temperature dropped, a cold wind sweeping down from the rooftops. I shivered, running through warm-up exercises and mentally going through my sigls. My armour was a steady weight underneath my fleece and jumper; it gave me some reassurance, but not as much as I would have liked. My fight with Vermillion had taught me both the upsides and the downsides of an armour vest. It really did stop knives, just like the manufacturer promised. On the other hand, that fight had also been an extremely painful lesson in just how many parts of your body an armour vest *doesn't* cover. Standing out there in the darkness, I didn't feel very protected at all.

The clock ticked over from 9:29 to 9:30. "Liftoff," I told Colin.

"All right. Here . . . we . . . *go!*"

I looked south, towards where the passage met Upton Lane. The sky was dark, and I channelled essentia through my low-light sigl; the clouds seemed to lighten, and the glows from the windows became bright enough that I had to shield them with one hand. After a minute I saw it: a tiny dot, just barely visible against the night sky.

"Got it," I told Colin. "How's the video feed?"

"Coming through fine. Quality's not great, though."

"You're not rating it for a bloody review site. Will you see the guy or not?"

"Chill. He goes by, I'll see him."

I tried listening for the sound of the drone but couldn't hear it. As I'd hoped, the sound of traffic from the nearby roads was enough to drown it out. "So why were you so set on a drone?" Colin asked over the phone.

"Well, I got to thinking after Christmas," I said. "And it seemed to me that if you're trying to get into a place, a camera drone's pretty useful."

"We're not trying to get into a place."

"Yeah, but I'm thinking ahead a bit. Next few months, I might be trying to get into some other places. Be handy having someone to recon them with a drone and keep watch while I'm inside."

"Watch for what?"

"People showing up who maybe aren't happy about me being inside."

"Exactly *what* kind of shit are you planning to get yourself into here?"

We waited a little longer. I shifted from foot to foot, mentally running over our plans and hoping I hadn't forgotten anything.

"You remember the signal?" I asked Colin.

"Dude, this is like the third time you've asked that."

"Just tell me one more time."

Colin sighed loudly. "'There's something you need to know.'"

"'Should know.' Not 'need to know.'"

"Jesus. It doesn't matter, okay? I'm—huh."

"What?"

"Low battery."

"On what? The drone?"

"It's got five minutes left."

"Wait, what?" I felt my heart rate speed up. "It hasn't even been up twenty minutes!"

"Yeah, but the battery life on these things is shit."

"Why didn't you tell me that?"

"Didn't you read the specs?"

"You were supposed to do that part!"

"Come on, it's a cheap-arse model off eBay. Everyone knows they have crappy flight time. You go on the forums, it's like the number one thing they complain about."

"*I don't read those forums!*"

"Well, I just thought everyone knew that."

"Shit." I thought fast. "All right. Pull it back and see how fast you can charge it."

"Okay . . . wait."

"Wait? What do you mean, wait?"

"Guy just went into the passage."

My heart rate jumped. "What did he look like?"

"Thin, about our age. I'm calling the drone back before it drops out of the air."

The phone line went silent. I stood there in the darkness, my mind racing.

"What do you want to do?" Colin asked. Now that he'd seen someone, his voice was sounding tense too.

I looked towards the corner of the football pitch. I had maybe thirty seconds. "Was anyone with him?"

"Couldn't see."

I hesitated, then made a snap decision. "We go with the original plan. Listen for the signal. Make the call the second you hear it."

"All right," Colin said, and hesitated. "Don't leave it too late. Going dark now." I heard the sound cut out as he muted his microphone.

I took a deep breath, straightened up, and waited.

Mark took a little while to appear, and when he did, all he did was poke his head out into the gap in the fence. Even with my low-light sigl, I could only make out a fuzzy white dot where his face should be. He didn't move, and neither did I. Eventually Mark stepped into the grounds and began to walk forward.

Watching Mark's movements, I noticed he seemed more cautious this time. That was probably a good sign. If he had backup, he'd be acting more confident, right?

Right?

I exhaled and tried to stay calm. I'd wanted to have Colin

watching from above for this part, and with that gone I suddenly felt a lot more vulnerable. I fingered the phone in my pocket; if everything went completely to crap I could send a panic signal, but that'd take seconds I might not have. Too late to worry about it now. I forced it out of my mind and focused on the boy approaching.

Mark came to a stop about thirty feet away. His dark eyes watched me without expression.

No visor this time. Maybe this could actually work. "I think it's time you and I had a talk," I told Mark.

Mark studied me for a few seconds. "So talk."

Okay, here we go. "You want to be raised to the inner circle of the Winged," I said. "And you're hoping Byron can get you there. But now Byron's interested in me instead. Right?"

Mark didn't answer.

"Here's the thing," I told Mark. "I don't want to join."

"Then why you still talking to him?"

Telling Mark about this was a risk, but I had to try. "He knows what happened to my dad."

Mark looked at me, his expression flat. "Your dad."

"He worked for Byron five, ten years ago. They had a falling-out and my dad disappeared. I want to know where he is. Byron's holding that over me." I paused. "You get me what I need to find him, and you'll get exactly what you want. You want me out of the picture? I'll stay as far away as you like, as long as you like. Whatever your issues with Byron are, you can work them out with him. I won't get in the way." I looked at Mark. "So? We got a deal?"

Mark stared back at me for a long time before speaking. "You're actually for real, aren't you?"

". . . Yes?"

Mark paused, then broke into a weird, rising laugh. My hackles rose at the sound. Something about it made me think of a fraying rope.

The laughter cut off abruptly and Mark stared at me, his eyes boring holes into my skull. "You think you're smart, don't you?" he told me. "You've seen it all." His face twisted suddenly. "I fucking hate kids like you. You prance around on the outside and then come swanning in like you own the place. 'Make a deal'? *Fuck you.* Byron should have had one of his guys work you over the way Oscar does. Couple of weeks of that and you wouldn't be talking about *deals.* You'd be crying and promising anything just to get out. But no, Byron decides he's going to be *nice*, so you get to pussyfoot around deciding if you want to dip your toes in the water." Mark stared at me with loathing. "You talk like you've got a choice. *I* didn't get a choice."

I looked back at Mark. The older boy's body was like a stretched wire, quivering in the night. I held very still. "There's something you should know," I told him.

"Yeah?" Mark asked. "What?"

I couldn't hear anything through my earpiece. I hoped Colin had got the message. "Why did you bring in Vermillion?"

"Why the fuck does it matter?"

I kept my voice calm. "I was willing to keep this between us."

"I don't give a shit."

"Yeah, didn't expect you to. But it changes the equation a bit. See, I've gone up against you enough times now, and I know what you can do. You're tough, but not *that* tough."

I saw Mark's eyes narrow; apparently he'd taken that as an insult. "But Vermillion?" I said. "He's a straight-up psycho. You don't hang around guys like that, you stay the hell away from them."

In the darkness behind Mark, I saw movement. A shadow emerged from the gap in the fence. "Yeah?" Mark said. "So what are you going to do about it?"

"Like I said, I was willing to keep this between us," I told Mark. "But if you're going to bring your friends to the party, I don't see why I shouldn't do the same."

Mark smirked. "Going to go running to your rich family?"

"Pretty much."

"Okay," Mark said, spreading his hands invitingly. "Go ahead."

I stayed silent.

"Come on," Mark said. "Give them a call."

"I don't think you quite understand," I told Mark.

"What's the matter, lost your phone?"

"No," I said. "I *already* gave them a call. That's the only reason I'm telling you about it."

Mark's smirk faded.

"You might want to turn around," I added.

Mark turned around.

Two men stood in the darkness on the football pitch, big and hulking and wearing ski masks. To my eyes, the glow of Life essentia surrounded them, radiating outward from the same strength sigls that all House Ashford armsmen carried. They both held guns, levelled at Mark.

Mark went still.

"ALL RIGHT," CALHOUN said an hour later, swinging the minivan door shut. He walked over to me and held out a small cloth bag, along with a set of keys. "Here you go."

I untied the bag's drawstring and looked inside. The street was poorly lit, and I had to tilt the bag sideways to catch the glow from one of the working streetlights. Sigls glinted up at me, set into a neck chain and a bracelet.

"Didn't have time to identify them," Calhoun said.

I pulled the drawstring shut, then slipped the bag and the keys into my pocket. "It shouldn't matter."

Calhoun nodded but didn't get into the car. "You know, you could leave this with us."

"I don't do this myself, he's never going to take me seriously."

"He might not anyway," Calhoun pointed out. "There are . . . alternatives."

I was silent for a moment. A small part of me wanted to take Calhoun up on his implicit offer, to wash my hands of the whole thing and let the Ashfords solve it for me, but I knew that was cowardice speaking. "No," I said at last. "Thanks."

"All right." Calhoun took hold of the door handle. "I'll be taking Johanna out on Saturday." He raised an eyebrow. "Think you've had a long enough holiday now that you can get back to work?"

"I'll be there," I told him dryly. "But just so you know, I'm raising my rates."

Calhoun smiled slightly, then got into the van. I watched it disappear around the corner, then went inside.

THE BUILDING LOOKED like it had once been a shop, but the shelves were empty, as was the hall beyond. Calhoun hadn't told me how he'd got access to the place and I hadn't asked. I opened the door to the basement and went down.

The basement was dusty and smelled of mould. A single bare lightbulb hung from the ceiling. At the far end was Mark, a black bag over his head, recognisable only by his clothes. His back was against a metal support beam, his arms pulled awkwardly behind it.

I walked around Mark to check that the handcuffs holding him there were secure. From the way the bag shifted I knew he was awake, but he didn't make any sound. Once I was satisfied, I walked back, crouched down in front of the older boy, and pulled the bag off his head. "Okay," I told him. "Let's try this again."

CHAPTER 20

MARK DIDN'T LOOK in good shape. There was a darkening bruise on his cheek; when the Ashford armsmen had moved in to cuff him, he'd tried to fight back, and it hadn't ended well. But his dark eyes glittered with the same fire.

"Deal is the same," I told Mark. I didn't take my eyes off his. "You find out what Byron knows about my dad, and give me a way to contact him. I stay away from Byron, and from you."

Mark didn't answer.

"But since you already said no," I continued when Mark didn't speak, "this time I'm giving you a little extra motivation." I held up the bag. "These are your sigls. You want them back, you do as I say."

"Or you'll do what?" Mark said, his teeth showing. "Sell them?"

"No. I'll walk out to the middle of London Bridge and throw them in the Thames."

That got a reaction. "You can't do that." Mark's words came out in a hiss. "They're worth—"

"I don't care," I told him. "I don't care about money, I don't care about the Winged, I don't care about *you*. The *only* thing that matters to me is finding my dad, and if I have to fuck you over to do it, that's exactly what I'll do. You understand?"

Hate glittered in Mark's eyes, then a mask seemed to come down and his expression went blank. He took a deep breath, then let it out. "Fine."

"Fine?"

"I'll do it." Mark's voice was toneless. He rattled the cuffs. "Take these off."

I started to move towards my pocket, and paused. *That was too easy.* I looked at Mark.

He stared back at me.

I leant in suddenly until our faces were only inches apart. Mark tilted his head back but didn't look away. I stared into his eyes. Dark, blank voids. Nothing on the surface. I kept staring, looking deeper.

And then I saw it. That same glitter. Not just hate. Contempt.
He's still not taking me seriously.

I pulled away, frustration surging up inside me. I wanted to shout at Mark; what did it *take* to get through to this guy? Maybe I should tell him what Calhoun had been hinting at outside. That if he didn't get with the program, then—

No. That was just more of the same. It might make Mark back off, but it was the Ashfords he'd be scared of, not me. As soon as he thought he could get away with it, he'd come after me again.

What was I doing wrong?

I was being too civilised. Making deals, trying to be reasonable. Mark didn't give a shit about being reasonable. So long as he saw me as someone who got his way through smooth words and a pretty face, he was never going to respect me.

Unbidden, a memory flashed through my mind of that night I'd saved Hobbes. Cold fire in the stars.

I sat back on the concrete floor and looked at Mark. *Really* looked at him this time, from head to toe. *What do you see?*

Something damaged. Broken.

"You really hate me, don't you?" I said.

Mark didn't answer.

"What was that you said back there?" I asked Mark. "'You've got a choice.' That's what pisses you off, isn't it? I can walk into your world and walk out again. You have to live there." I tilted my head, studying Mark. "You know, my dad used to say that most of the killers he met, they didn't start out that way. They used to be regular guys. But then things got bad, and they had to make some changes. Get rid of some bits of themselves." I paused. "You've had to do that. I haven't. I guess you figure that makes you better than me. You think that if I had to go through what you had, I couldn't handle it. Right?"

Mark looked at me.

"Right?"

"Yeah," Mark told me.

I nodded. "Maybe you're right. Maybe if I'd had your life, I'd have just given up. I mean, *you* haven't, I'll give you that much. Might be better for everyone else if you did, but you're still fighting. So maybe you're right. Maybe I just can't handle it."

Mark watched me warily. He looked cautious now. *Good.* I kept staring at him.

"Okay," Mark said at last. "So are you going to—"

I moved fast, getting into his face. Mark jerked his head back and I stared into his eyes from inches away. I didn't put on any masks this time—I dropped all my shields and let him see into the rage burning inside me, all the anger and frustration that had been building ever since I started dealing with the Winged. All I wanted to do was find my dad, and every time, *every time*, I found these guys standing in my way. Byron, with his smug lectures and his refusal ever to give a straight answer. Mark, with his aggression. Vermillion, with his knife. I'd talked to them, and bargained with them, and fought them, and I was *sick* of it, sick of every one of these prancing, self-centred fucks. "Or maybe you're *wrong*," I said in a low snarl. "Maybe I'd be like you, but worse. Truth is? I don't really know. What I do know is I am *sick* of your shit. You have been pissing me off ever since the summer, so you know what? Let's do this." I bared my teeth. "You want to know if I can be as much of a psycho as you are? Let's *fucking* well find out together. What do you say?"

We stared into each other's eyes, seconds ticking by. I didn't blink, and neither did he.

Then something seemed to shift in Mark's face. The glitter faded from his eyes. "Byron has a letter for you," he told me.

"From who, my dad?"

Mark nodded.

"Can you get it?"

Nod.

I kept staring at Mark for a long moment, then got to my feet. I pulled the mask back on as I did; it left me with a strange feeling, like wearing a piece of clothing that didn't quite fit. I pulled a spool of thread from my pocket and started unwinding it. "I want that letter and anything else you can find," I told Mark without looking at him. "I won't say anything to Byron, but if he notices your sigls are missing and starts asking questions . . ."

"I'll need them."

"Tough shit." I finished unspooling the thread, took out the keys, tied one end to the ring. "You get them back when I get that letter. Oh, and by the way? First thing I'm doing once I get out of here is hiding this bag somewhere no one's ever going to look. So if I should happen to have some 'mysterious accident,' well, then it's going to suck to be you."

Mark didn't look happy, but I hadn't expected him to. "How do I know you'll give them back at all?"

"I keep my promises," I told him. "Even to arseholes like you." I dropped the key ring at one end of the room, trailed the free end of the thread over to Mark, and dropped it into his cuffed hands. "Get to work," I said, then turned and left.

I was out of the building long before he got free.

AND THEN THERE was nothing to do but wait.

It's a weird feeling to live with violence and danger, and then go back home and find everything just the way you left it. Hobbes was delighted to see me, and I had to spend a solid hour petting him before he'd stop pestering me for attention. Ignas and the others wanted to know where I'd been, and I had to reassure them that my hospital trip hadn't left any lasting injuries. Colin had left some messages on my phone.

And then eventually I managed to satisfy them all that I was okay, and all of that just . . . stopped. And I was back exactly where I'd started, in my little room above Foxden Road, with my sigls and my cat.

I spent most of the next day lying on my bed, staring at the ceiling. I knew I should be doing something productive, but it was hard to focus. Everything felt unreal, like the fight at the theatre and the hospital stay and the confrontation with Mark had been a very long and vivid dream. Or maybe that world was real, and *this* was the dream. I wasn't sure anymore.

My room felt smaller for some reason, and I found myself noticing the peeling paint and the cracked woodwork more than I used to. Hobbes was the one thing that felt fully real, a little bundle of warmth and fur and life. I stroked him as he slept curled up against my side, and wondered whether this feeling would fade with time.

But as it turned out, it didn't have the chance.

I WAS TYPING out a text to Colin that evening—he was claiming he'd finished all those drucraft exercises and was nagging me about when we could start real lessons—when I heard a sharp *tak* from the window.

I paused, then went to look. Foxden Road was dark, but I could make out a shape below in the shadows. I grabbed my sigls and went downstairs.

The muted roar of a football match was coming from the downstairs bedroom, comforting and familiar. I stopped in the hallway to double-check my sigls, then walked out.

Mark was standing in the shadow of a white Transit van, down the road near the big oak tree. I walked down the pavement and stopped at a safe distance. The sounds of traffic drifted over the rooftops, but other than that the street was quiet. It was a Monday night and most people were in bed.

"Well?" I asked Mark.

Mark took something white from his pocket and flicked it at me. It skittered across the paving stones and came to rest at my feet.

I glanced down. It was a postcard-sized envelope, addressed to me at the old Plaistow house where my dad and I had once lived. But it was the handwriting that made my heart leap. Even from a glance, I knew it was his.

I picked up the envelope, studying the postmark and then

flipping it over. It had been opened. No return address. "Where'd you get this?"

"Byron was sitting on it."

"How did he get it when it was addressed to me?"

"How the fuck should I know?"

"This was posted three years ago," I said. Anger was flaring up within me and I had to fight to hold it back. I remembered all those conversations with Byron, the way he'd pretended to be my friend. He'd had this the whole time, and he'd said *nothing*. "How'd you know where to find it?"

"Byron showed it to me in January," Mark said. "Soon as he found out we'd met, all of a sudden he wanted to talk to me again." Bitterness crept into his voice. "Didn't give a shit about *me*. Just wanted to grill me about how we'd met. Then he dragged me up to his study so that I could read it."

"And?"

"And it's just a bunch of fucking numbers."

". . . Numbers?"

"Byron said it was a code. You have no idea how pissed off he was when I couldn't tell him anything. He *really* wants to find your dad."

"He doesn't know where he is?"

"No, and used to be he didn't care. Last spring and summer, you know how many times he mentioned your dad? Not once." Even in the shadows, I saw Mark's face darken. "Then you show up, and all of a sudden it's the most important fucking thing in the world. All so he can get a hold on *you*."

I held back a shiver. All this time, and I hadn't known. But for the first time, I felt a sliver of hope. If Byron didn't know where my dad was, but this letter held the key . . .

"What else do you know?" I asked.

"Byron doesn't tell me shit anymore. About your dad, or anything else."

"You didn't ask him?"

"You know what's going to happen to me if he finds out I took this?" Mark demanded. "And you want me to start asking *questions*? When I'm not supposed to be getting within half a mile of you?" Mark shook his head. "That's all I know. Now give me my sigls."

"Wait here," I told him.

Once I was safe in my room, I opened the envelope and unfolded the single sheet of paper inside. I hadn't wanted to do that in sight of Mark—if he'd been planning something, that would have been the time—but the contents of the letter were exactly as he'd said. Line after line of numbers, in my father's handwriting.

I wanted to keep reading, but Mark was still out there. I went into my cubbyhole, took out the drawstring bag with Mark's sigls, and paused. I'd taken a look at them after getting home last night. One Life, three Motion. The Life one was a strength sigl and the bigger of the Motion sigls was that missile-attack one that he'd used to take a shot at me. I didn't know enough to identify the other two.

All together, they were worth a lot. Replacing these with new ones bought from the Exchange would probably cost hundreds of thousands. Sold off secondhand, they'd be worth a fraction of that. But it wasn't really their value that I was thinking about. What they meant to Mark was power.

I went back outside.

Mark was waiting in the same spot. "Well?" he demanded.

I showed him the bag.

Mark held out his hand.

I looked at Mark. He'd done as he'd said and given me what I needed, but that didn't make him my friend. He was still an aspirant for the Winged, and if he got what he wanted, he'd become like Vermillion or Lucella. Maybe the next time the Winged came after me, it would be Mark wielding the knife.

"Give them back," Mark insisted.

You do that, you make him stronger.

There was a wild light in Mark's eyes. "You gave me your word!"

I hesitated, then tossed the bag.

Mark snatched it out of the air. He tore it open and stirred the contents with a finger, watching me out of the corner of one eye, then glanced around sharply, as if checking to see if anyone was going to take it from him.

The street was empty. Mark turned to go.

"Hey," I said.

Mark looked back.

"You still want to be one of the Winged?" I asked.

"What's it to you?"

"I'm not going to tell you it's a bad idea," I told him. "You wouldn't listen anyway. But you ever change your mind . . . look me up."

Mark gave me a long look, then turned and disappeared into the night.

I watched him vanish around the corner of Foxden Road, then shook my head. *Why did I even say that?* Oh, well, it didn't really matter. If I was lucky, I'd never see the guy again.

I turned back towards the warmth and light of home.

BACK IN THE safety of my room, I smoothed out the letter and had just laid it down on the bed when I heard a meow from outside. I pulled open the window and Hobbes slid through the gap, rubbing his head against me with a purr. He'd been lurking on top of one of the walls; if Mark had been stupid enough to try anything, it would have ended badly for him.

I sat down on the bed to study the letter. It contained exactly three words. The rest, as Mark had said, was numbers.

primroses over
    Stephen
    26.3.2 24.7.3 24.2.3 18.5.1 17.4.3 20.5.5 21.26.3 21.1.9 17.3.2 21.5.4 22.14.2 21.20.2. 21.2.10 26.12.2 31.6.5 18.15.4 328.28.2 52.13.10 330.23.2 331.1.3 17.9.7 16.1.6 16.1.5 19.3.2 22.14.7 21.6.3 19.1.7 27.30.6 23.12.7. 24.3.1 24.20.7 16.25.6 24.2.3 27.1.6. 26.3.6 45.21.2 19.28.1 43.5.1 40.12.2 36.35.1 47.2.3 46.3.3 16.11.2 45.1.3 30.6.7. 24.4.2 45.1.10 18.9.2 38.21.4 17.5.5 18.9.1 17.7.2 18.26.4 33.17.2 32.3.6 21.21.7 421.26.2 46.5.5.
    117.24.10 123.4.2 117.1.7 23.5.1 117.4.4 17.3.2.
    71.3.3 71.29.5 21.31.8 71.6.11 74.18.5 313.7.2 73.1.6 73.1.5 436.10.5. 19.24.4 390.2.4 28.2.9 34.1.8 16.1.2 29.1.2 29.3.2 28.3.2 19.9.2 35.2.5 35.1.1 397.6.3 19.2.9 126.8.3 399.10.1. 77.12.11 34.2.3. 71.1.10 19.1.3 36.23.4.4 34.3.1 111.6.1 17.7.2 36.25.5 38.30.7 66.27.7. 18.5.2 17.26.8 18.3.5 20.5.6 127.5.2 21.23.5 21.3.2 19.5.3 219.34.4 21.5.4 440.3.6 87.4.1.
    34.2.1 111.3.1 34.6.2 108.29.10 22.21.3 123.37.8 197.2.4 39.29.4 287.24.3 39.2.3 35.32.4 39.1.1 286.21.7. 32.7.9 199.4.2 199.7.8 285.3.3 18.2.2 97.8.3.4 244.19.1. 39.1.8 16.27.8 22.24.5 287.1.2 286.4.6 40.21.13 31.4.1 38.3.4 33.4.9 34.10.7 34.1.4 216.9.3 16.9.8 40.1.4 19.3.11 78.2.9 68.8.3 22.5.12 24.10.5 239.5.4 30.9.3 35.1.3 16.5.2 98.12.8.4.
    24.5.8 18.15.3 34.8.8 33.13.6 20.4.12 19.21.5 23.1.13 17.13.8 20.2.1 50.7.10 56.32.10 17.17.5. 57.11.9 24.7.3 20.3.8 50.4.5 48.8.2 26.15.9 72.14.4 73.6.1 82.4.5 43.4.2 87.1.5

24.8.2. 21.3.2 51.2.7 71.3.7 71.3.6 71.3.4 17.21.9 18.7.1 39.2.1 162.4.6.4 159.12.2 159.12.1 29.7.5 57.11.3 86.3.8 21.10.9. 18.5.4 22.1.1 22.12.6 200.18.7 277.17.7 22.11.6. 26.28.7 23.3.4 26.5.1 53.1.8 76.34.4 28.4.10. 22.14.3 35.13.10 45.1.3 34.3.5 21.16.3 435.2.3.

50.4.2 169.4.1 59.3.4 19.6.7 26.11.10 26.1.6 22.24.2 23.12.4. 50.5.1 77.1.6 26.4.4 63.28.1 33.17.3 26.1.4 22.8.7 59.3.2. 24.17.7 27.2.6 64.4.4 24.2.1.

169.4.3 460.3.3

A code. I tried to think of all the codes I knew. What kind was this?

The first thing that came to mind was a substitution cipher, where each number stood for a letter. I'd written out messages like that in especially boring lessons at school, but I knew those kinds of codes were easy to break. If Byron hadn't been able to break this one, it had to be harder than that.

I went over the numbers more closely. They were all arranged in groups of three. What did that mean?

I remembered my dad telling me about book ciphers—codes where the numbers in the message would refer to words or letters within a book. They'd been used by spies who'd had to worry about their possessions being searched. Without knowing which book the code referred to, you couldn't read the message.

But without knowing the book, *I* couldn't read it, either . . .

I shook my head. I was looking at this the wrong way. My dad had written this for *me*. How would he hide a message so that I could decipher it, but a stranger couldn't?

He'd use something that only I would know. Something we *both* would know.

My eyes went back to the three words at the top. One was my

name; that was probably to catch my eye, tell me that the message was for me. That left two. *Primroses over . . .*

And then I got it. *The opening line.*

I sprang to my computer, my fingers flying across the keys. I found the ebook I wanted in seconds, but as soon as I opened the file I knew it wouldn't work. For this to work the edition had to be *exactly* the same, and back when my dad had first read the book to me he hadn't used an ebook. It had been an old paperback, with yellowing pages.

Luckily, I knew where to get my hands on one.

THE HOUSE WAS in Tottenham, semidetached and built from whitewashed brick. The street was long and straight and lined with other houses that looked almost exactly the same. In front of each was a little strip of garden and a driveway just barely big enough for a car.

I squeezed past the Audi in the driveway, walked up to the door, and rang the bell.

The door opened to reveal my aunt, a thin woman in her late forties with greying hair. "Oh, there you are," she told me. "Shouldn't you be at work?"

"I took the morning off," I said as I walked in. Coming out of the crisp spring sun, the inside of the house felt dark and cramped.

"Well, I hope you don't make a habit of it. Anyway, if you're finally going through your old clutter, isn't it about time you moved it out? We're planning to redecorate this year."

I climbed the stairs to the attic door, then opened it and stepped through into a little room with a sloping roof. A bed with a bare mattress sat in the corner, next to a bookcase; cardboard boxes were stacked against the opposite wall. A small window let through a meagre trickle of light. The air smelled dusty and unused.

This place had been my home for a little over a year, and seeing it again didn't bring back good memories. When I'd arrived here I'd had no parents, no money, and no job, and for a long time it had felt as though I'd hit rock bottom. The climb up had been slow and painful, and even after I'd started to find my feet, I'd never really been comfortable. My aunt and uncle and their two girls are very much a complete family unit, one I don't fit into. It had been a relief to leave.

"Stephen," my aunt called from downstairs, jarring me from my reverie. "I'm going out to the shops."

I shook off my memories, called back, "Okay," then walked to the bookcase. I ran my finger down the small collection of titles, stopping on a pale yellow volume, its spine heavily creased. I pulled it out; the faded cover had a picture of a brown rabbit.

To most people, "primroses over" would sound meaningless; Google it and all you'll get are gardening instructions. But I remembered my dad sitting by my bedside when I was a child, reading from my favourite book, the one I'd ask for over and over again. And I remembered the opening line: "The primroses were over."

I unfolded the letter and got to work.

I'd spent all night thinking about what to try once I got here, and my first and simplest plan was to take each group of three numbers as referring to page, line, and word count. I grabbed a piece of paper and a pen and started leafing through, scribbling down words. Page 26, line 3, word 2 . . . "left." Page 24, line 7, word 3 . . . "very." I kept working until I came to the end of the first sentence, then stopped to look at the results.

left very tall are about the can a go screamed I'll whole

All right, Plan A was a bust. That was fine, I had others. Plan B was to work on the assumption that it was a letter cipher instead of a word one—take the first two numbers as page count/line count, but have the third number refer to letters instead.

v l t a m e d d t

Okay, that was worse. I went back to the first approach. I hadn't been counting the header line at the top of the pages. What if I did?

do ought he time a where

Damn it.

I kept trying different combinations, changing the order of the line and word numbers. Then I experimented with using chapters instead. The paper filled up with gibberish.

After nearly an hour I sat back in frustration. My aunt's house was quiet. The morning light was still streaming through the narrow window; the sky beyond was blue. What was I doing wrong?

I could see now why Byron hadn't been able to break this thing. I had the damn key, and I *still* couldn't break it.

Maybe I'd been wrong about the key? It could be a different book, or not a book at all. But my instincts told me otherwise. I knew my dad, and he knew me, and this was exactly the book he would have chosen. I went back and studied the code more carefully.

The funny thing was, the more I looked at it, the more it felt as though the page/line/word idea *should* be right. The first number in those groups of three was always between 16 and 460, and my edition had 478 pages. The second number in those groups of three was always between 1 and 37, and my edition had 38 lines to a page. That was way too close to be a coincidence.

Maybe it was encoded twice . . . no, no, no. My dad would have done this by hand, and he'd have known *I* would have to do it by hand. It had to be something simple, something obvious that I was missing.

I looked at the book, flipping through the pages. Read left to right, turn right to left.

An idea started to form. I picked up my pen and paper.

26.3.2 . . . "I." *24.7.3* . . . "hope." *24.2.3* . . . "you."

Excitement flooded through me. I worked feverishly, flipping pages as fast as I could go, counting words with a trembling finger. After I'd done the first two paragraphs, I went back and added commas, made some slight adjustments ("letter" for "letters"; "included" for "include"), then sat back to look at the result.

Stephen,

I hope you get this letter, but I know you probably won't.
In case it isn't intercepted, I've included a way at the end
for you to message me. Think carefully before you do. The
men after me will watch you to get to me. If they ever
realise we have a way to speak, they'll capture you.

Here's what you need to know.

I looked up and closed my eyes. Joy and triumph rushed through me, so intense it left me light-headed. *I've done it.* My dad had vanished four years ago, in May. Three years and ten months. That was how long it had been.

I've done it.

I've found him.

Stars swam before my eyes, making me giddy. I breathed in and out, trying to slow my hammering heart, then picked up the paper with shaking hands. He'd said that he'd included a way to message him at the end. I skipped to the end and started working backwards.

I had to stop after decoding the last few lines.

I love you very much and always will. I hate not being able to see you. Take care of yourself.

Love,
Dad

I got up and walked over to the window so that I wouldn't get the paper wet, then looked out over the rooftops, blinking to clear my eyes. Once I'd recovered, I went back to work.

The next line up had what I was looking for: two words, followed by *"at the usual place."* Maybe our email provider—my dad and I had used the same one. The line above, though, was weird. *"It may be that one day the difficult will come after you as well."*

That had to be a mistake. I counted again; no, the first three numbers definitely pointed to "difficult." But this time there was another number, a 4. If the first three numbers were page/line/word, what did that 4 mean? Fourth letter, first four letters, last four letters? "F"? "Diff"?

"Cult"?

I went back to the beginning and started working through from start to finish. I found another four-number group that seemed to decode to "cult." *"A cult that follows a . . ."*

A *what*?

Distant birdcalls drifted across the rooftops, the only sound in the little room. I kept working, adding to the paper one word at a time. Slowly, a frown began to grow on my face.

GLOSSARY

affinity (branch)—A talent or skill with one of the six branches of drucraft. Almost all drucrafters discover that they have at least one branch that they find particularly easy to work with, and at least one branch that they find particularly difficult. A strong affinity allows a drucrafter to use and create sigls from that branch more easily and with greater effectiveness.

affinity (country)—A natural familiarity with the essentia found in the Wells of a particular geographical region. It's almost always much easier to shape a sigl at a Well in the country you grew up in. Country affinity doesn't matter much to drucrafters who live most of their lives in the same place but causes problems for "sigl tourists" who want to fly into a country, acquire a sigl, and fly out.

Ashford (House)—A Lesser House of the UK. Origins in Kent and Cornwall. Family crest is three blue keys on a white field with black chevron; family colours are blue and silver. A minor family of little importance until the previous Head of House, Walter Ashford (b. 1922), acquired a significant number of Wells in postwar West Germany. Upon returning to England, the family gained an A-rank Light Well in 1986 and an A-rank Matter Well in 1991, and finally rose to Lesser House status upon negotiating purchase of an A+ rank Light Well in 1998 (The Bishop's Well). Current Head of House is Charles Ashford (b. 1953).

aurum—The raw material that sigls are made of, also known as solid essentia or crystallised essentia. It has a density of 8.55 grams per cubic centimetre, slightly denser than steel and about the density of copper or brass. If left untouched, aurum will eventually sublimate back into free essentia, though in the case of solid sigls this can take thousands of years.

Blood Limit—One of the most important principles of drucraft, the Blood Limit states that sigls are locked at the moment of their creation to the personal essentia of whoever made them. This makes sigls nontransferable: to anyone but their maker, a sigl is nothing but a pretty rock.

There are two ways to get around the Blood Limit. First, in creating a sigl, a drucrafter can choose to mix their own personal essentia with someone else's. The higher the proportion of the other person's personal essentia that they use, the more effective the sigl will be for that person, but the harder the sigl is to make. This is the method used by all commercial providers.

The second way around the Blood Limit is to use a sigl shaped by a close relative. The more closely related two people are, the more likely it is that their personal essentia will be similar enough that the sigl will accept it. This method works well between parent and child or between siblings, but its effectiveness drops sharply with more distant relations, and anything more distant than grandparent to grandchild or aunt/uncle to niece/nephew almost never works. This method has been one of the ways in which Noble Houses have preserved some measure of their strength down the generations.

Due to the Blood Limit, all sigls effectively have a finite life span. No matter how powerful a sigl may be, there will eventually come a point at which every person capable of using it is dead, at which point the sigl is useless.

Board—The ruling body that governs all matters relating to drucraft in the United Kingdom. The Board has wide discretionary powers but is still subject to the authority of the Crown and functions in practice like a cross between a board of directors and the British Parliament.

Possession of a Well of strength A+ and above grants the holder a seat on the Board; as a result, the sale and purchase of these Wells in the United Kingdom is subject to special restrictions.

branch—Different types of Wells contain different kinds of essentia and produce different kinds of sigls. These are known in drucraft as the six branches, named after the sorts of things that can be done with them: Light, Matter, Motion, Life, Dimension, and Primal. Of all the branches, only Primal effects can be created without a sigl, and then only weakly.

channeller—A drucrafter capable of controlling and directing their personal essentia, allowing them to activate triggered sigls. Becoming a channeller is generally the point at which someone is considered a "real" drucrafter.

corporations—Most corporations are not involved in drucraft, but those that are have great influence in the drucraft world. Like Houses, corporations can buy, hold, and sell Wells, and are treated by governments as legal entities in their own right. The distinction between a corporation and a House can be fuzzy, though there is a noticeable difference in terms of organisational culture: Houses tend to be more traditional and are more strongly tied to their country of origin, while corporations are much more heavily focused on profit and are typically international, with relatively little connection to the countries they operate in.

drucraft—The art and skill of working with essentia. Drucraft consists of three disciplines: sensing (perceiving essentia), channelling (manipulating one's own personal essentia), and shaping (the creation of sigls).

drucrafter—A practitioner of drucraft. Typically used to refer to a channeller or shaper.

essentia—The raw energy that powers drucraft and creates sigls. Essentia is fundamental and omnipresent, flowing through the world in invisible currents. If depleted in any location, it naturally replenishes itself from the surrounding area.

Pure essentia is completely inaccessible to living creatures: they can no more tap it than draw upon the chemical energy in a lump of stone. However, over long periods of time, essentia can be shaped by the land around it, its currents converging at a location called a Well. The essentia in a Well is still mutable but will be inclined towards a certain aspect of existence, such as light or matter.

A living creature of sufficient enlightened will can shape the reserves of a Well into a small piece of crystallised essentia called a sigl. Sigls have the power to conduct essentia, transforming its raw universal energy into a spell effect. Over a long, long time, the sigl sublimates back into essentia; this essentia is absorbed again by the land, and the cycle begins anew.

essentia capacity—The rate at which a living creature can assimilate ambient essentia into personal essentia, and thus make use of sigls. It is measured on the Lorenz Scale and is loosely correlated with height and skeletal mass; average adult essentia capacity in the UK is 2.8 for men and 2.4 for women. For a combat drucrafter, an essentia capacity of 3.0 and over is considered ideal, allowing them to use three full-strength sigls at once, while an essentia capacity of below 2.0 is considered crippling.

essentia construct—A sketch or sculpture crafted out of essentia. Making an essentia construct is the first step towards creating a sigl. Manifesters typically use essentia constructs as blueprints, allowing them to practise the important early stages of creating a sigl, as well as adjust its design before attempting the costly process of shaping it for real.

Euler's Limit—Sigls can only be created from essentia: many substitutes have been tried and all have failed. This means that the supply of sigls is limited by the supply of locations that possess a sufficient concentration of essentia to shape a sigl. These locations are called Wells.

Exchange—The oldest and best-known institute of drucraft trade in London, specialising in the sale of sigls to private individuals. Situated in Belgravia, between Belgrave Square and Eaton Square Gardens, it claims to be able to supply any sigl in the world. Average sigl price is in the tens of thousands; top-end sigls are in the millions.

Faraday Point—The minimum quantity of essentia needed to consistently produce a viable sigl. Below this point, effectiveness falls off sharply: a drop of even ten percent below the Faraday Point usually produces a nonfunctional sigl. A sigl created at the Faraday Point is rated as D-class.

   The Faraday Point is used to define the Faraday Scale. A Well with a Faraday rating of 1 can sustainably produce exactly one D-class sigl per year.

Faraday Scale—The most common measuring scale for Wells, used in Europe, Japan, Russia, Australia, India, and some parts of Africa and South America. The Faraday rating of a Well is a measurement of how many D-class sigls the Well can sustainably make in a year.

   The Faraday Point is a "soft" limit and as such is not considered one of the Five Limits of drucraft (which are much closer to being absolute restrictions).

Five Limits—The five most significant limitations on drucraft. More than anything else, the Five Limits shape how the drucraft world operates. In brief, the Five Limits are:

Euler's Limit: Sigls can only be created from essentia.
Primal Limit: You can't use drucraft without a sigl.
Blood Limit: You can't use someone else's sigl.

Limit of Creation: You can't change a sigl after it's made.
Limit of Operation: A sigl won't work without a bearer.

While the Five Limits significantly restrict what drucraft is capable of, all five do have work-arounds and excep-
tions.

House—An aristocratic family of drucrafters, usually one that
holds title to one or more Wells. In the past, the Great Houses
of Europe had various special privileges under the law; while
this is rarely the case nowadays, Houses still command great
wealth and influence.

Drucraft Houses are primarily found in Europe and Asia.
In countries without Houses, different institutions fill similar
roles: in the United States, the place of Houses is filled by corporations, while in China, the main drucraft enterprises are
all state owned. In the United Kingdom, the main significance
of House status is that both Great and Lesser Houses are enti-
tled to a seat on the Board.

House Ashford—See Ashford (House).

House, Great (United Kingdom)—A House in the United Kingdom that possesses at least one Well of S-class and above. At
the time of writing, there are eight Great Houses in the United
Kingdom: Barrett-Lennard, Cawley, Chetwynd, De Haugh-
ton, Hawker, Meath, Reisinger, and Winterton.

House, Lesser (United Kingdom)—A House in the United King-
dom that possesses at least one Well with a class of A+. The
United Kingdom has between thirty and thirty-five Lesser
Houses (the exact number is subject to dispute).

Houses that own no Wells of class A+ and above have no special legal status, though they will often take the title of "House" regardless, particularly if they held Great House or Lesser House status in the past.

kernel—A sigl's core, made out of the shaper or wielder's personal essentia. The fact that it is *their* personal essentia is the reason that the sigl will work for them and not for anyone else.

limiter—A device used by shapers to assist in creating sigls. Limiters give two advantages: consistency (sigls produced by the same limiter are always exactly the same, without the variation created by free manifestation) and reliability (shaping a sigl with a limiter is much less demanding on the user's shaping skills). Limiters are expensive to create and as such are typically not cost effective unless the owner plans to produce many copies of the same sigl. The vast majority of sigls sold commercially are created with limiters.

Linford's—A drucraft corporation. Corporate headquarters in London; major regional offices in New York and Singapore. Primarily a locating company, they sell the majority of the aurum they obtain. They have a small shaping department but do not supply sigls to the Exchange.

Lorenz Ceiling—The maximum quantity of personal essentia that can be channelled through any sigl before its efficiency drops off sharply. Like the Faraday Point, this is a "soft" limit rather than a hard one. The Lorenz Ceiling is defined as a 1 on the Lorenz Scale.

The Lorenz Ceiling is not affected by a sigl's size. Larger sigls have more powerful amplification effects (allowing them to draw in more ambient essentia from the surrounding environment) but cannot make use of any more personal essentia than a smaller sigl can.

Lorenz Scale—A measurement of essentia flow, used to evaluate both a living creature's essentia capacity and also the amount of personal essentia a sigl requires to function at full output.

Most commercially created sigls are designed with Lorenz ratings as close as possible to 1. A sigl with a Lorenz rating of less than 1 will be less powerful but also less draining to use (this is more common with Light sigls, due to their generally lower power requirements). Sigls with Lorenz ratings of more than 1 are rare, since going above the Lorenz Ceiling brings greatly diminishing returns. A sigl with a Lorenz rating of 1.5 will be only marginally more powerful than one with a Lorenz rating of 1, despite being much more taxing on its bearer's essentia capacity.

manifester—A drucrafter capable of creating a sigl without assistance (i.e., without a limiter or similar tool). Becoming a manifester requires advanced shaping skills. Most drucrafters never become manifesters, although there is a growing feeling that limiters have become so widespread in the modern age that being unable to create a sigl without one is no longer a significant drawback.

personal essentia—Essentia which has been assimilated by a living creature and which has taken on the imprint of that creature's mind and body. With practice and concentration, personal essentia can be directed, controlled, and channelled into sigls to produce various effects.

Primal Limit—The second of the Five Limits, the Primal Limit states that it is impossible to produce any kind of drucraft spell without a sigl. Humans can assimilate free essentia into personal essentia, but without a sigl they can't transform that personal essentia into a spell effect. The one exception to this limit is (as the name suggests) Primal drucraft, which can be performed unassisted, although much more weakly than with a Primal sigl.

shaper—Any drucrafter capable of creating a sigl. In theory this is a neutral term, but in practice, if someone is called a "shaper," it usually means that they can't create a sigl without a limiter. Otherwise, they'll call themselves a "manifester" instead.

sigl (SIG-ul)—A small item resembling a gemstone, created out of pure essentia at a Well. Sigls convert their wielder's personal essentia into a spell effect and then pull in free essentia from the surrounding environment to amplify it. Larger sigls have a more powerful amplification effect, allowing for more sophisticated and complex spells.

Sigls, once created, can be used only by their makers, though there are some work-arounds to this (see **Blood Limit**). There is no known way to alter a sigl once it has been shaped.

Though commonly assumed to be a derivation of the Latin word for a seal ("sigil"), the word in fact derives from the Old English term for a brooch or gemstone.

sigl class / sigl grade—A sigl at exactly the Faraday Point is defined as being of D-class. The mass of the sigl doubles for each half grade above D (a D+ sigl has twice the mass of a D-class sigl, a C-class sigl has four times the mass of a D-class sigl, and so on). In ascending order, and counting half grades, the sigl classes are: D, D+, C, C+, B, B+, A, A+, S, and S+. "Class" and "grade" are used interchangeably.

sigl type—Sigls fall into two types: continuous and triggered. Triggered sigls require their bearers to consciously channel essentia into them and as such can only be used by channellers. Continuous sigls are designed in such a way as to automatically pull in personal essentia from their bearers, meaning that they require no concentration and can even be used by a bearer with no knowledge of drucraft at all.

sigl weight—In casual conversation, sigls are usually referred to by their class. However, when greater precision is needed (such as when they're offered for sale), they are measured by carat weight instead. A D-class sigl has a weight of 0.18 carats, or 0.036 grams, and has a diameter of about two millimetres.

tyro—The lowest rank of drucrafter, with no ability to control their personal essentia. The only sigls a tyro can use are continuous ones.

Well—A location at which essentia accumulates. Wells are categorised by branch: for example, a Light Well collects Light essentia and produces Light sigls.

Wells can be permanent or temporary. Permanent Wells replenish themselves over time, and if properly tended can be used year after year for decades or even centuries. Temporary Wells, on the other hand, are typically one-offs: they have only brief life spans and do not usually refill themselves when drained. The distinction between the two types is sharper at higher ranks than at lower ones: Wells of class A and above will typically have storied histories of hundreds of years, while a permanent D-class Well can appear with relatively little fan-fare and may disappear almost as fast, particularly if roughly treated.

Wells are commonly described by their class, which indicates the maximum strength of sigl the Well can produce when fully charged (e.g., a C-class Well can produce at most one C-class sigl before it must be left to replenish itself). Where more precision is needed, Wells are measured on the Faraday Scale.

Benedict Jacka is the author of the Inheritance of Magic series (2023–) and the Alex Verus novels (2012–21). He studied philosophy at Cambridge University, taught English in China, and worked as everything from civil servant to bouncer before becoming a full-time writer.

VISIT BENEDICT JACKA ONLINE

BenedictJacka.co.uk
🐦 BenedictJacka

Ready to find
your next great read?

Let us help.

Visit prh.com/nextread

Penguin
Random
House